ESSENTIAL SCIENCE

The genre of SF is so large, to have absorbed absolutely c_ _ _ _ _ _ _ _ _ _ _ _ _ _.
Essential Science Fiction provides a core guide to the genre. The criteria for inclusion in the guide are based on what the many (and *not* the compilers) consider best: 'the many' includes those numerous SF enthusiasts who vote for the Hugo Award-winning novels and films, or *Locus* Awards, or who responded to the Blackwood film poll, who attended the Festival of Fantastic Films, or the countless authors whose works are three quarters of a century or more old and still in print… And there are others still! These are 'the many'. It may include you, or it may not. Either way this guide is a systematic distillation of a mass of primarily Anglophone literature, cinematic production, TV series and graphic SF.

By definition more has been left out than included. Nonetheless anyone collecting just the works herein would find that their library had amassed video/DVDs of over 50 TV series and more than 200 feature films, while shelf space would be required for in excess of 500 books.

Essential SF is introduced by the veteran SF fan, and Fan Guest of Honour of the 1996 World SF Convention, Vin¢ Clarke. Its introductory principal section consists of a short treatise on science fiction as a genre so placing *Essential SF's* contents in some sort of context. Another section explains how to use the guide. Then there is an alphabetical, cross-referenced section of entries which include a few on the SF community as well as definitions of some specialist terms. Finally there are collectors' checklists of the key works covered in the guide.

The guide represents just one aspect of a team of people, within the SF community, who engage on a variety of projects but of whom one common thread has been contributing to the Science Fact and Fiction Concatenation.

www.concatenation.org.

ESSENTIAL
Science Fiction

- A Concise Guide -

Jonathan Cowie and Tony Chester

Porcupine Books

PUBLISHED BY PORCUPINE BOOKS OF LONDON
37 Coventry Road, Ilford, Essex IG1 4QR, Great Britain.

sales@porcupine.demon.co.uk

© Jonathan Cowie and Tony Chester, 2005

This book is copyright. Subject to statutory exception and to the
provisions of relevant collective licensing agreements, no reproductions
of any part may take place without written permission of the copyright holders.

First published 2005.

Typeset by The Contact (media SF London newsletter)
http://uk.geocities.com/thecontact_2000

Printed by The Marsten Press
Bexleyheath, Kent DA7 4BJ

Marketing by Porcupine Books, specialists in SF: the interesting,
the unusual and the obscure. www.porcupine.demon.co.uk

Cataloguing Publication Data

Essential Science Fiction: A Concise Guide
compiled and written by
Jonathan Cowie and Tony Chester

ISBN 0-9549149-0-2

I. Science fiction – key works and history.
I. Title: Essential Science Fiction: A Concise Guide
II. Cowie, Jonathan   III. Chester, Tony

Dewey Decimal Classification (21st edition – 1996) 809.387 62

The publisher and authors have used their best endeavours to ensure that
URLs for websites referred to in this work were correct at the time of going
to press. However neither the publisher nor the authors have any
responsibility for the websites and can make no guarantee that a site will
remain live or that the content will remain appropriate. The publisher and
authors urge readers to check the statements made in this work for
themselves and neither the publisher nor the authors accept responsibility for
any consequential loss arising out of the use of this work.

CONTENTS

Introduction by Vin¢ Clarke	7
Acknowledgements	8
About the guide and its use	9
A brief perspective on SF	13
A – Z of essential Science Fiction	17
Appendix – The collector's core checklist	249
Books	249
Films	262
TV series	267
The compilers	269

INTRODUCTION

by Vince (Vin¢) Clarke

It's a light year or two in cultural terms from the Science Fiction of early times – when you were lucky to see half a dozen new books and possibly two films each year – and today. Now a thousand books and a score of films are produced annually. So how do you pick your way through this mass? And more. You face the accumulated treasures of all of the past! This contains the works of good authors: the late, great Theodore Sturgeon, Eric Frank Russell, Henry Kuttner, *etc.*, *etc.*, who in my opinion are still highly entertaining.

You have to read very fast indeed if you are a comparative newcomer to the genre. What you need is a short guide, skimming the field and highlighting some of the best offerings past and present. Of course encyclopaedias weighing several kilograms, scholarly works and coffee table books are fine in their respective places – shelves and coffee tables – but a smaller guide would be a tremendous help. This book is it. It is intended to serve you. For you to carry around bookshops, libraries and SF conventions. To scan the TV listings for films. It offers remarkably concise and lucid reviews and notes of the best Science Fiction.

As an old-timer in the genre I heartily commend it.

Vince Clarke (1998)
(Written on completion of the first of three biennial drafts)

ACKNOWLEDGEMENTS

We are most grateful to all those who helped in the compilation of this guide including those authors who assisted especially with publication and biographic details, the UK Festival of Fantastic Films for giving us the viewing figures for their films over the years, those who took part in the *Concatenation* polls, and our copy readers who provided much valued comment. Many did a little for which we are most grateful. Of those who helped we are especially grateful to the following: Roger Robinson (a former BECCON SF convention colleague of one of us) whose own SF book checklist was published by BECCON Publications a year into our researching this guide and which itself was a great help in filling in gaps; Tony Bailey of London's LOTNA Group; Brian Ameringen (another former BECCON colleague) of Porcupine Books; Graham Connor (the other founding *Concatenation* co-editor with both of us); Les Chester (proofing and comments); and finally Vince Clarke who commented on our original entry list and gave invaluable advice as to the (then proposed) guide's user-friendly format. Vin¢, as SF fan cognoscenti will know, was a much loved fan of long-standing culminating in him being Fan Guest of Honour at the 1995 Scottish **World SF Convention (Worldcon)** and **Eurocon**, but to us he was better known as a member of our local NW Kent SF Society. His help commenting at the outset on the guide's groundwork was the last SF venture he participated in shortly before his death in 1998. We are grateful that he was able to pen a short introduction while this project was in its embryonic stage and comment on how it might be shaped. Assuming we have realised much of the project's original aims, we hope that he would have approved of the final result. We are therefore delighted to be able to launch this work the year of the 10th anniversary of his being Fan Guest of the World SF Convention, coincidentally a year which once more sees a Scottish Eurocon/Worldcon.

Finally, despite our efforts it is almost inevitable that a guide of this size, covering many of the genre's aspects both literary and visual, will have some errors. Rest assured that these are solely of our making and not the above good folk.

Jonathan Cowie & Tony Chester (November 2004)

ABOUT THIS GUIDE AND ITS USE

Given that SF as a genre is so large, it is impossible for any person to have read absolutely everything, let alone seen all the SF offerings on TV or at the cinema. So if an SF buff is truly to be a buff but without an all-encompassing collection or knowledge, what are the essentials that s/he should have read and seen? The answer surely is 'the very best that the genre has to offer'. In other words, the material that defines its shape and has influenced SF's evolution. This then is an attempt to provide a core guide to such material. What this guide certainly is not, is a complete listing of *all* SF, or even all of its most notable works: there are other, much larger reference texts for that. (Such as the **Clute** & Nicholls' excellent *Encyclopedia of Science Fiction* (1993).) The work here is more a concise guide to a select listing of what is in essence the 'best' of science fiction; hence may be regarded as 'essential SF'.

Of course one then comes to the next question: how to define 'best' to include in our guide to essential SF? We could have cited all those works that have received critical acclaim, but that would have resulted in too voluminous a tome (Clute's job). Indeed, the same would happen if we confined ourselves to 'award winning' works; SF prizes are simply so numerous. However we have used some awards among our indicators of 'best'. But this guide is for the many, so the criteria for inclusion do not take into account those awards decided upon by a small panel or committee. Even the Nebula Award, which is decided upon by the SF Writers of America was not used by us – you are, after all, SF readers and viewers, not writers. (Though, for information purposes, we sometimes refer to the Nebula and other awards once a work has been included for other reasons.) The criteria for inclusion centred on a number of mass-vote awards, polls and surveys of SF fans. In other words the criteria of 'the many'. Important among these is the **Hugo Award**, voted on by those thousands registered with the **World SF Convention**, and the annual *Locus* poll. It also includes: multiple Eagle Award winners; top films as revealed by UK **Festival of Fantastic Films** viewing figures over the years; the Bob Blackwood, Jon Flynn and Diane Blackwood's top ten film poll of fans from Worldcons (World SF Society membership) between 2000 and 2003 (including then registrants for the 2005 Worldcon); and we have listed the works cited in the ***Concatenation*** all-time poll (based on respondents from those attending the 1987 UK ***Eastercon*** and a follow-up survey in eastern Europe).

Not surprisingly, as it turned out, the majority of works listed in this guide scored on more than one of the core criteria. This consistency at the very least confirmed to us, as compilers, the value of our methodology. We appeared to be getting something right.

Then we have the secondary criteria. If an author has two or more works included, then such authors themselves have an entry, which in turn cites their more celebrated and/or landmark works. These other works are listed in the appendix in a non-bold font.

Finally, we have in addition included TV series that either had record-breaking viewing figures for their time or which have connections with writers and films that have entries in their own right determined by the afore primary criteria.

This is how *we* have defined 'best'. Of course *you* may disagree, and are free to do so. However our definition had to be pragmatic and no definition can be all encompassing. This then was our starting point. If you disagree with it then feel free to produce your own guide: anyone doing so will earn our respect for we have not found this task easy.

With regard to the entries relating to the SF community in various countries and local SF groups, here we have included typical examples of groups that we know of and which have further details on the web you can follow up on. As for conventions, we have included those that have either stood the test of time or are the main events for their respective countries. Such entries are included as an introduction to some of the community's principal facets or are illustrative; this SF fan dimension to the guide is not meant to be encyclopaedic but illustrative. The web page addresses in these entries were checked for accessibility just prior to publication to reduce net rot problems.

It is important to note that this is a core guide to essential 'Science Fiction' and not the associated genres of fantasy or horror. Nonetheless, some SF has fantastical or horror elements. Therefore ***Alien***, which is as much a horror film as it is SF, is included. Likewise, so is ***Frankenstein***, but *Dracula* (whose concept's basis is arguably supernatural and not SF) is not. Having said this, some fantasy is included if the work concerned fell within our core criteria of SF fan accolade: consequently the Hugo-winning ***The Princess Bride*** is included, even though it contains no discerning element of pure SF. Fortunately such anomalies are few. (And we hope that someone else will produce a guide to the best fantasy.)

In addition to the material identified by the above core criteria, we have included some works that narrowly missed receiving more than one of the core-criteria awards. But these instances are barely a handful. In the main we found that while some entries missed some of our core criteria by a whisker, they made it in by meeting another of the core criteria. Consequently *The Matrix* – which narrowly missed getting a Hugo even though it accrued the most first place votes for the Hugo for Best Dramatic Presentation in 2000 as a voting system was used at that Worldcon that allowed for second and third choice considerations to be taken into account – made it into this guide due to coming into the Blackwood/Flynn 2003 survey of WSFS members top ten SF films.

We have added further material by including some works of historic note: after all SF was being written, and films made, before the Hugo or the Festival of Fantastic Films *etc.*, existed. Here we have included works that have endured and that are still in print. This last because part of the reason for producing this guide was to provide those comparatively new to the genre's broader aspects with a collector's check list: we felt it important that book collectors had a reasonable chance of finding the titles cited.

We hope that readers and viewers will not need reminding that the classic works of yester-year are not directly comparable to contemporary offerings. SF has developed with time, as has science and society. For instance, the human genome was not sequenced in rough until the year 2000, the internet did not exist in its current form before the 1990s, home computers were not common before the 1980s, ditto satellite communication before the 1970s: one could go on. Consequently when reading or viewing SF, one needs to bear in mind the state of the world at the time of its creation, and not with the benefit of today's cultural hindsight. Comparisons of decades-old SF with today's are fairly meaningless unless, of course, one is looking at the genre's development. In short, we offer no apologies just because some of the works cited are dated: this is because indeed they are!

We had to decide what to do about short stories and novellas. We have only included a few Hugo Award-winning shorts and novellas, in the main due to problems in ascertaining whether they were still in print and in which tome, as well as because all these potential entries would again have made this core guide far too large (and expensive). However we have included some, particularly if the stories are representative of the authors' work or are landmarks in some way or, indeed, were subsequently expanded into novels, or we know have been reprinted in a number of paperback collections.

We are sure that despite our attempt to systemise the compiling of the core of the best SF has to offer, that many seasoned SF readers and fantastic film buffs will have firm opinions as to our selection and its omissions. Perhaps those with large collections will not find this guide as useful as a check list compared to those who have more recently discovered the genre's joys, or those who do not want to spend much time and effort, preferring instead to cut to the chase. Even so we hope that seasoned fans will find this guide a handy quick-reference work; indeed we hope they actively enjoy the critical process of finding out whether or not they agree with our assessments.

Finally, how to use this guide?

Entries are in alphabetical order, as are the listing appendices. *Within* each entry there are occasional references in bold, such as '***Alien***' above. This means that there is an entry with that title in the main body of the guide. The titles of these entries are grouped under author, film and TV series in the appendices, again in bold. However these main body entries do also cite other authors, films and TV series in a normal typeface. This indicates that these are only cited *within* entries as opposed to having entries themselves.

There are a few differences between the main entries and the appended collectors' check lists. The main one is that the appended books' listing is alphabetical by author and not book title. Though, as *per* above, if a book entry is in bold type then it has its own entry in the main body of the guide; if in normal type then it is cited *within* a main body entry. This same rule applies for the film and TV list appendices. This means that collectors can tick off either a smaller core list of works, or a more expanded catalogue. In addition, some of the works appended are cited within parentheses. This means that the work should not be considered as 'essential SF', rather the opposite and that it is included for completeness' sake in the appendices because it was mentioned in passing within an entry. Finally, some of the works listed in the appendices have exclamation marks by them. This is a warning for you to check the appropriate entry within the main body of the guide for an anomaly.

Hopefully, if we have done our job properly, once you have started using this guide, much of the above will be self-evident. If we have not, we are sure that many of you will not be slow in telling us.

A BRIEF PERSPECTIVE ON SF

This core guide is a guide to Science Fiction works, and while we believe that that in itself is of some utility, we feel it equally useful to provide some sort of contextual setting for the genre as a whole. Hence this brief summary perspective.

Strangely, for a genre that is shunned by many mainstream aficionados, SF has played a part in fictional works for many years, indeed back to the very birth of written communication if not, one might reasonably suppose, to the earlier point where stories were told by prehistoric people over camp fires. However, these last were not SF, but of the related genre, fantasy. Records of tales of monsters, magic and strange lands go back thousands of years and appear in virtually every culture whose writings survive today. Fantasy, though, is not SF. In fantasy, monsters have no *raison d'être*, they simply exist or were created by the gods. In fantasy, magic just happens to exist and work. Conversely, in SF there is a rationale based on some sort of quasi scientific explanation: for science fiction is fiction that has a basis, albeit a tenuous one, in science. SF monsters' existences have a rationale. For instance, they may be mutants, or alien creatures, or prehistoric creatures that have survived in a remote ecosystem, or technologically resurrected, or some such. There is no magic in SF, though high technology frequently substitutes for this. Indeed **Arthur C. Clarke** once said that any sufficiently advanced technology was indistinguishable from magic. (In fact today existing technology seems like magic to the uninitiated and so is misunderstood and misused: the huge over-the-counter sale of antibiotics in some countries to cure colds and flu are a testimony to that, and it contributes to the rise of antibiotic resistance.) Of course others have separated fantasy from SF differently. The comedy fantasy writer Terry Pratchett once commented that fantasy contained scantily clad women in tight fitting black leather, while in SF they were scantily dressed in white or metallic garb.

Though SF does not have as long a history as fantasy, its own roots can be traced back thousands of years. Anaximander of the sixth century BC concluded that the Earth was not flat and was enveloped in a spherical sky (though his Earth was cylindrical and not spherical). This was only a short step away from realising that there were other worlds and, possibly, other intelligent beings. The Greek notion of *aperoi kosmoi* (an 'infinity of worlds') began in the fifth century BC. Archelaus, preceptor of Socrates, and his disciple

Xenophanes believed that the Moon might be inhabited. By the time of the Roman Empire and the first century BC, the idea that there were 'other Earths and various tribes of men and beasts' had become common place. They were popularised by well-known philosophers of the time such as Epicurus. Such concepts of other worlds and alien beings are today fundamental SF tropes.

Among the first stories that could arguably be called SF were some of those by Lucian of Samosata (Samosa) in the second century, and certainly they were the first known examples of fiction featuring aliens and a battle between the Moon's inhabitants and those from the Sun over the colonization of Venus. Ironically entitled *True History*, this was arguably the first **space opera**.

By the 17th century, a number of key figures involved with the renaissance openly discussed SF concepts of aliens and other worlds. Indeed the first Secretary of the Royal Society, Reverend John Wilkins, set out 14 such propositions in *The Discovery of the World in the Moone* (1638). In this sense these were comparatively enlightened times for, despite a purported interest in the public understanding of science, no officer of the Royal Society (UK) has sought this past century to use the popularity of SF as a vehicle to promote an interest in science.

The critic **John Clute** refers to many of the early works of SF as 'Proto SF'. His argument (which has a certain, albeit debatable, logic to it) is that using geese or horses to pull you to the planets was known by the author to be an impossibility and so therefore cannot be a true SF concept. For Clute, and others such as **Brian Aldiss**, proper SF began with the publication of Mary Shelley's ***Frankenstein*** in 1818. Certainly *Frankenstein* was a landmark publication, one that resonates with the ethical dilemmas posed by modern-day molecular and genetic biology. Indeed today we take for granted the saving of life through organ transplantation and 'test tube babies', while the ethical debate over issues such as cloning continues. This brings us on to the relevance of SF to society as a whole.

SF should not be ignored, and certainly is not by those with an eye to making a buck or two. Whatever your views, series like ***Star Trek*** and the ***X Files*** each attract on the order of 100 million viewers worldwide, while the block-busting ***Indiana Jones and the Last Crusade*** has grossed nearly half a billion dollars! As alluded to above, many involved with mainstream writing dismiss SF as lacking any true literary merit. This is arguably in no small part due to C. P. Snow's hypothesis of the immiscibility of the twin cultures of science and art. Few non-scientists could quote more than one of Newton's laws of motion. Even fewer could quote any of the laws of thermodynamics.* Consequently it is not surprising that for many, without any scientific or technical training, SF appears meaningless. Equally it is not surprising that various trade polls on both sides of the Atlantic (and which is corroborated by a *Concatenation* poll of the 1987 UK Eastercon) state that broadly half of those who read SF also buy science fact books. Another half (not all necessarily the same) have either a job or a degree that relates to science and/or technology. Some three quarters of SF readers regularly watch science fact documentaries. In short there is a connection between living in a technology dependent society and SF. That science and technology are continually advancing means that these links are growing and that SF writers have more raw material to draw upon. But are these links of any value? We would like to think so, and there is hard evidence that SF does fulfil at least one function – to stimulate an interest in science! A mid-1990s UK Government agency survey of some 10% of UK physics graduates, one of the most comprehensive surveys of its kind into physics graduates' attitudes, revealed that some 26% felt inspired to study physics due to an interest in SF. Yet is this really surprising? Perhaps not, for SF is the genre of the future...

---

* Though strangely the reverse is not true: scientists have a better understanding of the arts. Most scientists (and SF readers) can, for example, quote a line or two from half a dozen of Shakespeare's plays, and know the titles of a dozen or so of that author's works.

A – Z OF ESSENTIAL SCIENCE FICTION

==
b = born   *col.* = collection   *crtd* = (created) first published
dir. = director   *fb* = first broadcast
==

Abominable Dr Phibes, The – film, UK (1971), *dir.* Robert (*The Final Programme*) Fuest (see **Michael Moorcock**). Somewhat in the vein of *The Phantom of the Opera*, a disfigured composer devotes himself to exacting revenge on the doctors whom he blames for his wife's death. Set in Victorian times, Phibes uses the science of the day to execute his macabre plans. Vincent Price is aptly cast in this comedy horror that is a Fantastic Film Festival favourite. Principal cast also includes: Joseph Cotten and Virginia North. A fair sequel, *Dr Phibes Rises Again* (1972, *dir.* Robert Fuest), followed in which Phibes arises from suspended animation to seek an ancient Egyptian elixir of life for him and his wife.

Ackerman, Forrest J. – collector, editor, agent, US (*b*1916). Ackerman is arguably the most famous of SF collectors. Associate editor of the **fanzine** *The Time Traveller* (1932), Ackerman has spent a lifetime in SF and has even appeared in around 100 films. His extremely large collection of books, fanzines, and film memorabilia was housed in his Hollywood home, the Ackermansion in Glendower Avenue, which was open to visitors most weekends up to 2003. His contribution to SF is renowned (he is even attributed with coining the term '**sci-fi**') and he has been a Guest of Honour at many conventions including the **World SF Convention** and the **Festival of Fantastic Films**. Notably he received a Hugo in 1953, its year of inception, for #1 Fan Personality.

Aldiss, Brian – author, UK (*b*1925). A long established author who first received major recognition from the SF community in 1959 when, despite it being decided that there would be no Hugo Award category that year for 'Best New Author', he nonetheless received a special runner's up plaque. Equally at home in the mainstream with works such as *The Hand Reared Boy* (adolescent comes to terms with his sexuality), he has even written a travel guide to the former Yugoslavia. That he is recognised beyond the science fiction literary community is demonstrated by his having been nominated for a term as Chairman of the Society of Authors. He has, of course, been honoured many times by the SF community itself and has been a Guest of Honour at the 1965 and 1979 **World SF Conventions**. His contribution to SF is not just restricted to fiction but also includes critical and encyclopaedic works, such as *Billion Year Spree* in 1973 (which won him the Pilgrim Award of 1974) and ***Trillion Year Spree*** (1986, which also won him a Hugo (Non-Fiction category) Award with David Wingrove), as well as a self-starred drama presentation in the late 1980s (with Ken Campbell), *The SF Blues*, about the way he views his own activities as a writer. His first SF novel was *Non-Stop* (1958, revised 2000), concerning the unwitting descendants of what soon transpires to be a multi-generation starship crew; except that onboard they are no longer alone. His major SF works include ***Hothouse*** (1962) and the *Helliconia* series about a planet whose seasons arise from an elliptical orbit 2,000 Earth years long about its sun during which civilizations rise and fall. He has also edited several collections of other writers' short stories including an annual series of *The Year's Best Science Fiction* with **Harry Harrison** from 1968 through to 1976 – which interestingly occasionally included non-fiction contributions (such as a collection of reviews of ***2001: A Space Odyssey***). (See also **Chris Foss**.) More recently he co-authored *White Mars* (1999) in collaboration with the renowned physicist Sir Roger Penrose which concerns a society left on Mars by an oppressive, and resource mismanaging, regime on Earth. He has written two autobiographical books, *When the Feast is Finished* (1999) with a focus on his late wife, and *Twinkling of an Eye* (1998). He is known in critical circles for being a champion of the **new wave** and by SF professionals for furthering **World SF**. His short story *Super-Toys Last All Summer Long* was made into the Kubrick/Spielberg movie *A.I.* while Roger Corman filmed Aldiss' *Frankenstein Unbound* (1973) (see ***Frankenstein* – films**).

Alien – film, US/GB (1979), *dir.* Ridley (***Blade Runner***) Scott, H R Giger Chief Designer (*cf.* ***Heavy Metal***), screenplay by Dan (***Dark Star***) O'Bannon. Contrary to *Time Out*'s billing as an, "empty bag of tricks whose production values and expensive trickery cannot disguise imaginative poverty", this film actually broke new ground for both horror and SF. The alien monster was a clear biological creature with a defined life cycle. The imagery was up to the best provided by one of the leading SF art-house comics, *Heavy Metal*, of the time; which is not surprising given Giger's work in the field. And of course Ridley Scott went on to direct other notable films including the SF classic ***Bladerunner***. The plot revolves around a space craft *en route* for Earth, its crew in suspended animation. They awake to find that the ship has automatically responded to an emergency beacon. Landing, one of the crew is infected by an alien which it turns out is in its nymph stage, whereas the adult is a ferocious creature that begins killing the crew. Not only did the film win a Hugo in 1980 in the Best Dramatic Presentation category it was also voted 4th favourite film in the *Concatenation* SF poll and it, and *Aliens*, are on the list of all-time best attended movies shown at the Festival of Fantastic Films. *Alien* also came 5th in the Blackwood/Flynn WSFS top ten poll. Each alone are eligibility criteria for inclusion in this guide. Not surprisingly three highly commercial sequels were made to *Alien*, but of these only the second, ***Aliens***, came close to capturing the original spirit and sense of wonder. The 'alien' has also appeared in a number of independent shorts, both live action and animation. Graphic novel spin-offs have included encounters with **Batman** and **Judge Dredd** not to mention the **Predators** who also featured in a cross-over film in 2004. Principal cast: Tom Skerritt, Sigourney (***Galaxy Quest***, ***Ghostbusters***) Weaver, John (***Contact*** and ***Frankenstein*** – films) Hurt, Veronica (*Lost in Space*) Cartwright, Harry Dean Stanton, Ian (***Time Bandits***) Holm, Yaphet Kotto. However it is worth noting that, contrary to common belief, it is alleged that the stunt man was not that billed in the credits as playing the alien but was the veteran UK stunt master Eddie Powell (as discussed at the 1998 and 1999 Festivals of Fantastic Films). Apparently not only did he play the role of the alien but he modified, for purely pragmatic purposes, the alien costume. (Also see **van Vogt, A. E.**)

Aliens – film, US/GB (1986), *dir.* James (***The Terminator***) Cameron. The sequel to ***Alien*** won the Best Dramatic Presentation Hugo Award in 1987 and also came 10th in the Blackwood/Flynn WSFS members' top ten film poll. Having come up with one of the most ferocious creations on celluloid, the sequel strengthened the human side with a hard-bitten space-marine squad, and further raised the stakes by pitting them against a whole colony of aliens. The imagery of *Aliens* was almost, but not quite, up to that of the original. It made up for this with more action (inevitable through numbers), special effects and an element of black humour. Ripley (played by Weaver again) is rescued from deep space and hibernation to be sent on a mission back to the world where her original crew mates first encountered the alien, but this time with a platoon of the aforementioned marines. In the years that Ripley had been in suspended animation the planet had begun to be terraformed but all contact had suddenly been lost with the terraforming team. Ripley and marines land to find a nest of aliens in the heart of the terraforming complex. *Aliens* was also voted 7th in the *Concatenation* top 30 all time film poll. *Aliens* was followed by *Alien^3* (1992) and *Alien Resurrection* (1997) which, for some fans, did not seem as true to the original concept even if they did have their respective moments.

Amazing Stories – magazine, US (*crtd*1926). Though not the first pulp magazine to publish SF, it is generally agreed that science fiction came of age as a genre when **Hugo Gernsback** published the first issue in April 1926. Founded on the work of **Wells, Verne** and Poe, *Amazing* was briefly ascendant before facing the competition from others such as *Astounding Science Fiction* (see *Analog*). Gernsback lost control of the title in 1929 and founded, in direct competition, *Science Wonder Stories*, through which he is effectively credited with creating **fandom** by the inclusion of letter columns which published correspondents' addresses. *Amazing* in over 70 years has, as one can imagine, had its fair share of ups and downs. *Amazing* has had several editors including Raymond Arthur Palmer (a.k.a. RAP) – see **Fandom** – who reputedly boosted its circulation from 27,000 to over 100,000. However it was soon to face competition from other 'pulps' such as *Astounding Stories* (see *Analog*). By the late 1950s and early 1960s *Amazing* had a US circulation of about 50,000. However by the year 2000 its circulation had slumped to around 10,000 when the magazine folded. (Note: *Amazing Stories Quarterly* was a sister publication (1928–34).)

American Flagg! – comic, US (*crtd*1983). Created by Howard Chaykin for First Comics (one of the first creator owned publishing companies to arise in the early 80's), *American Flagg!* is set in the mid-21st century when the Plexus Corp (on Mars) is selling off a USA that is little better than a Third World country. Reuben Flagg, an ex-porn star, joins the Plexus Rangers and is repeatedly caught up in intrigues, both political and financial, as markets are fought over by competing media cartels. While highly irreverent and wickedly funny, this is still very good SF and, while it would take some diligence to collect all the issues, there are three graphic novels reprinting the first 9 issues of the comic in hardcover in 2004: *Hard Times* (1985), *Southern Comfort* (1987), and *State of the Union* (1989).

American Gods – novel (2001) by Neil Gaiman. Convicted for a crime his wife committed, Shadow learns of his spouse's road death just prior to his release. On returning to the world he is given another blow when the job he is counting on falls through. Totally dispirited he sets off for home and encounters a Mr Wednesday and becomes his errand person. However it transpires that Mr Wednesday is no mere mortal and that there really are Gods walking the Earth. These are the old European Gods that have followed the migration to America, but there are also the new 20th century Gods. *American Gods* won the 2002 Hugo and also the 2002 Bram Stoker Award (Horror Writers of America) for 'Best Novel'.

Analog – magazine, US (*crtd* 1930). This magazine started life humbly in January 1930 as *Astounding Stories of Super-Science*, though at this time the contents were oriented more towards 'adventure' fiction than SF *per se*. **Hugo Gernsback** had started *Amazing Stories* in 1926, establishing the US market for SF 'pulp' magazines and proselytising science therein (for non-US early market see **Stella**), but *Astounding* leaned more toward '**Space Opera**' in its early incarnation. It did, however, attract such authors as Leinster and Williamson through its first editor, Harry Bates. The title was abbreviated to *Astounding Stories* in 1931 but the full title was reinstated in January 1933.. A few hiccups and a change of publisher later, F. Orlin Tremaine became the new editor in 1933, slightly changing the direction of the magazine, and publishing stories by (among others) **E.E. "Doc" Smith**, Don A. Stuart (**John W. Campbell jnr.**), Stanley G. Weinbaum, and even H.P. Lovecraft. Tremaine became an editorial director of the magazine's publisher, Street & Smith, in 1937 and appointed Campbell as his successor. In 1938 the title became *Astounding Science Fiction*, and just over a year later it was publishing stories by **van Vogt**, **Asimov**, **Heinlein**, and **Sturgeon**. This period from the Summer of 1939 is accepted by many as the beginning of the so-called '**Golden Age**' of science fiction and marked the first publication of many classics of the field including: van Vogt's *Slan* (1940), Asimov's *Nightfall* (1941), and Heinlein's *Fifth Column* (1941 – a.k.a. *The Day After Tomorrow*). Through a combination of quality, luck and good distribution *Astounding* led the market, and Campbell's leadership (and the higher rates of pay) ensured 'author loyalty', and the readership was hooked by the serials of those authors. These included the first publication of Asimov's Robot and ***Foundation*** tales, van Vogt's ***Weapon Shops*** and ***Null-A*** stories, and E.E. Smith's ***Lensman*** series. The 1950's saw more credible competition arise, but *Astounding* arguably still led the field with the use of artists such as Chesley Bonestell and **Frank Kelly Freas**, and by attracting authors such as **Poul Anderson**, **Robert Silverberg**, and **James Blish**. *Astounding* won the first ever Hugo for Best Magazine in 1953, and also took the honours in 1955-57. It was in 1960 that *Analog* first appeared in the title (science fact is 'analogous' to SF), and the magazine changed publishers again in 1962, while continuing to win Hugos (1961, '62, '64 and '65). It continued its policy of publishing imaginative serials, such as **Frank Herbert's *Dune*** (*Dune World* 1963-4 and *The Prophet of Dune* 1965), and also continued to attract frequent contributions from authors like **Harry Harrison**. With Campbell's death in 1971, Ben Bova became the new editor, which provided another shot in the arm as he introduced stories by **Joe Haldeman** and **Roger Zelazny**, as well as tales by **Frederick Pohl** and the artwork of **Rick Sternbach**, while himself winning Hugos as Best Editor (which category had replaced Best Magazine) in 1973-77 and 1979. The 1980's saw a decline in magazine publishing, and *Analog* gained a new editor (Stanley Schmidt 1978) and once more changed publishers' hands, moving to Davis Publications in 1980 to join 'sister' publication *Isaac Asimov's Science Fiction Magazine*. However, it still continued to publish award-winning fiction from the likes of **Greg Bear**, Spider Robinson, **David Brin**, and **Lois McMaster Bujold**. Though the 1990's have seen magazine publishing fade ever more into the background, *Analog* has continued to provide a home for the short story and still had sufficient sales to ensure a 70th Anniversary issue. Its circulation in the year 2000 was some 47,000.

And Call Me Conrad – novel (1965) by **Roger Zelazny**. Alternate title of 1966 Hugo award winning novel, ***This Immortal*** – see separate entry.

Anderson, Gerry – TV producer, UK (*b*1929). Anderson made his name with several children's "**sci-fi**" series and primarily those with puppets. In order of production: *Supercar* (a cross between an air craft and submarine); *Fireball XL5* (a patrol spacecraft safe-keeping the Earth from a variety of bad guys); *Stingray* (a submarine fighting an undersea race led by Titan – Anderson's first colour production); the legendary ***Thunderbirds*** (a billionaire's family who run a rescue operation using fantastic machines); *Captain Scarlet* (an indestructible man who spearheads the world's fight against robotic Martians); *Joe 90* (a boy who can have the brain patterns of experts implanted); and *The Secret Service* (a spy team using a vicarage as cover and a device that makes one of them small). His live action series (in addition to *The Secret Service* which was mixed live and puppet action) included: ***UFO*** (an undercover organization protects the world from alien organ-leggers); *Space 1999* (a nuclear accident tears the moon and its base from Earth orbit to roam the galaxy); and *Space Precinct* (the alien and human staffed police station). In the main (*Space 1999's* first series excepted (Anderson was over-controlled by US producers)) each series marked an improvement in use of puppets and/or models as well as story line. Consequently a generation grew up in the 1960s and 1970s on sequential Anderson series. *Thunderbirds*, in the late 60s and early 70s, probably marked the peak of Anderson's commerciability with numerous spin-off merchandise and a 630,000 circulation comic *TV21* (with its own spin-offs *Joe 90* and *Penelope*) that drew together a number of the series into one fictional 21st century world. Graphic artists working on *TV21* included Keith (**Dan Dare**) Watson and **Don Lawrence**. *TV21* (or *TV Century 21* to give it its full but little-used title) was created by Alan Fennell (1936-2001) who was also the script writer for a number of episodes of *Fireball XL5*, *Stingray* and *Thunderbirds*. When after a quarter of a century, in the mid-1990s, *Thunderbirds* was re-broadcast (for the first time in the video recorder age) UK viewing figures reached 6.83 million. In 1995, when the World SF Convention made one of its rare manifestations in the UK, Gerry Anderson was warmly welcomed as one of the two professional guests (the other being the more usual SF author of international standing), and in 1998 he was one of the four principal guests at the UK Festival of Fantastic Films. In 1999 a new 26 episode (10 minutes each) science fantasy series, *Lavender Castle*, was broadcast in the UK. It was the first time a series was shot direct to hard disk and combined stop-motion animation with computer graphics. In terms of Anderson's historic placement overall within the genre, little remembered is that the TV series **Star Trek** was first serialised in the UK in comic strip form in *TV21* before it was broadcast in the UK by the BBC, nor that *TV21* ran an above average series of children's *Project S.W.O.R.D* short stories about an organization trying to hold civilization together in a resource-depleted world. For details of the Gerry Anderson fan club and their conventions surf *www.fanderson.co.uk* Or send an SAE to Fanderson, 10 Sen Close, Warefield, Bracknell, Berkshire, RG42 2QB, UK.

Anderson, Poul – author, US (1926-2001). Anderson is one of America's more prolific authors with well over three score novels to his name and a couple of score collections of short stories. A workmanlike author, Anderson invariably provides the proverbial good read. A number of his books contribute to a 'Technic History' universe which spans from the post World War II years through to the end of the twenty first century, by which time mankind has spread throughout the solar system (*cf. The Boat of a Million Years* below). Aside from space colonisation Anderson has invariably explored virtually all of SF's common tropes including anti-robot riots and explorations of the oft portrayed schism between technology and humanism: he has even written a number of fantasies including sword and sorcery. Aside from his Technic History series, Anderson has looked at mankind and the world outside of time. In the Hugo-nominated *There Will Be Time* (1972) Anderson's protagonist, one Jack Havig, happens to be a natural time traveller who moves up and down the centuries as easily as walking around the block. Again, the Hugo-nominated *The Boat of a Million Years* (1989) uses the perspective of immortals to examine mankind's development and progress. Ultimately disillusioned the immortals leave for the stars. However, while Anderson has had considerable recognition, he has never had a full-blown novel receive the popular acclaim bestowed by a Hugo win or come top of the annual *Locus* readers survey. Short stories and novellas have, though, brought Anderson such success. His *The Longest Voyage*

(1960) won the Best Short Story Hugo. *No Truce with Kings* won the Hugo for Best Short Fiction in 1964, *The Sharing of the Flesh* (1968) won the Best Novelette Hugo, *The Queen of Air and Darkness* won it for Best Novella in 1972 (the title story of a 1973 collection), *The Goat Song* (1972) won the Best Novelette Hugo, *No Hunters' Moon* got the Hugo for Best Novelette in 1979, while *The Saturn Game* was acclaimed the Best Novella in 1982 (a stand alone version was published in 1989).

Android – film, US (1982), *dir.* Aaron Lipstadt. Lone inventor Dr Daniel (Klaus Kinski) on a space station has built an android artificial intelligence played by Don Opper (who also co-wrote the script). On the look out for stimulation, the 'Android', Max 404, is only too happy to grant landing permission to a passing ship in distress. However on board are escaped convicts, so setting the scene for innocence to battle evil. The film is not long at 80 minutes, nor does it have a huge budget. Its strength comes from the exploration of emotion and ethics that the real world may well one day have to face if computer technology continues to leap forward. The film was voted 13th in the *Concatenation* all-time film poll.

Andromeda Strain, The – novel (1969) by **Michael Crichton**. This, his first novel under his own name, was sold for an amazing $250,000. The book tells the story of a returning space probe carrying a deadly organism which threatens to become a plague of global proportions. Secured in a super-secret, ultra-advanced lab below the desert, code-named 'Wildfire', a dedicated team of scientists race to understand the microbe and develop a defence against it before it can escape. Crichton presents his fiction in factual, almost documentary, terms and frequently includes graphs, charts and illustrations with his text—a trick often utilised by those who adapt his work for the big screen—and writes an unfussy story of scientific deduction. The characters are ordinary people who have to undertake an extraordinary job in a methodical way, despite a 'race against time' element being added by the organism's ability to mutate without warning. The drama comes not from conflict, but the all-pervading tense atmosphere and, as such, the book did not immediately suggest that it could be made into a successful movie. However, this was achieved in 1971 by director Robert (***The Day the Earth Stood Still***, *Star Trek: The Motion Picture*) Wise. Principal cast: Arthur Hill, James Olson, Kate Reid, and David Wayne.

Ansible – fanzine (UK). *Ansible* is a monthly news sheet by the Hugo Award-winning David Langford (see also **Fan Funds**). Due to its size, news consists of word bites covering, primarily UK, SF author, book, and written-based SF conventions. Much of the news focuses on Langford's circle of friends and core contacts, many of whom are authors and editors. Consequently *Ansible* is a source of much of the science fiction community's day-to-day news of who is publishing for whom, antics at conventions and launch parties, and other such gossip. The con listing consists of UK SF conventions of all types (but primarily focusing on writing and TV SF) as forthcoming conventions from other countries are listed in the *Fans Across the World* newsletter, with which *Ansible* has a distribution arrangement. The Random Fandom regular column deals with news of SF buffs within the SF book convention-going community as well as the trials and tribulations of such convention organisers (conrunners). One key role *Ansible* plays is being the principal regular vehicle communicating to UK fans news of the independently run fan funds established to send and receive fans from the US and Australia to leading conventions—the fans chosen are voted for with the eligibility for voting part including the requirement to make a contribution to the appropriate fund. Dave Langford was nominated for the Hugo for Best Fan Writer many times before winning it in 1987. He has won a Hugo several times since including in: 1989, 1990, 1991, 1992, 1993, 1994, 1998, 2000, 2001, 2003, 2004 and twice in 1999 and 2002. It should be mentioned that Dave Langford is an author and SF columnist in his own right (hence the second Hugo in 1999 which was for his fiction writing). Up to 2001, *Ansible* used to be distributed regularly at the London SF Circle, and occasionally at the UK Eastercon (where Langford has been known to produce the daily convention newsletter) but these days most find it in cyberspace on *www.ansible.demon.co.uk* or *www.dcs.gla.ac.uk/SF-Archives/Ansible/amsilink.html*

Apollo XI, News Coverage of... – TV broadcasts (1969). Nothing should surprise anyone in the world of science fiction. Indeed, it is sometimes said that today's science fiction is tomorrow's science fact. While this last may be glib, it is a sound bite that resonates with many. Therefore when in 1969 people around the world watched Man land on the Moon, on TV in their living rooms, it was as if an element of SF had come true. SF fans were especially caught up in the wave of sense of wonder that swept the world and so in the following year at the World SF Convention they voted the Apollo 11 news coverage to win the Hugo Award's 'Best Dramatic Presentation' category. In 1969 the (St Louis venued) Worldcon gave a 'special award', that is cited with the Hugos, for 'The Best Moon Landing Ever'. This *Essential SF* entry is included as a reminder that arguably to get the best out of SF you need to be aware of, if not have an interest in, popular science.   Science Fiction is, after all, fiction underpinned with a little science.

Asimov, Isaac – author, US (1920-1992). Along with **Clarke** and **Heinlein**, Asimov is frequently cited as one of the three 'founding fathers' of modern SF. Though born in Russia, he was brought to the US in 1923 and gained citizenship there in 1928. A member of the *Futurians* SF group (*cf.* **Frederick Pohl**), he attended Columbia University, gaining a BSc. in Chemistry (1939) in the year he made his first SF short story sale, *Marooned Off Vesta* (1939), to ***Amazing Stories***. He subsequently obtained an MA in 1941 and a PhD in 1948, by which time he had written his most famous works. He became associate professor of biochemistry at the Boston University School of Medicine from 1949-58, then embarked on a career of writing popular science books and articles (gaining a 'special' Hugo for "adding science to science fiction" in 1963), abandoning SF from 1958-1972. Perhaps his most famous SF short was *Nightfall* (1941) — indeed, in many polls this is cited as the most famous US science fiction story of all time — which he sold to mentor **John W. Campbell jnr.** at *Astounding Science Fiction* magazine (see ***Analog***).   In this intriguing tale, the inhabitants of a planet, with a complex orbit involving six stars, are approaching a time when all six 'suns' set. Night occurs just once every 2000 years disrupting society. This story was expanded into a novel-length version in 1990 by **Robert Silverberg**, which was very poor and added nothing to the original, but could hardly be worse than the 1988 film by Paul Mayersberg, which should be avoided at all costs. *Nightfall* was also the title story in a worthy Asimov collection of shorts, *Nightfall and Other Stories* (1969). However, it is Asimov's 'Robot' and '***Foundation***' stories with which he is most associated and which, ultimately, became the focus of his post-1972 career. Asimov, with Campbell, created the now-famous Three Laws of Robotics which helped transform the robot from

SF monster to Humanity's servant. They are: (i) A robot may not injure a human being or, through inaction, allow a human being to come to harm; (ii) A robot must obey the orders of human beings, except where such orders conflict with the First Law; and (iii) A robot must protect its own existence, except where this conflicts with the First and Second Laws. Though these laws did not appear until the third of Asimov's robot stories, *Liar!* (1941), they were the bedrock of all that followed, most of which can be found in the collection *I, Robot* (1950) and *The Rest of the Robots* (1964). This last appeared in two forms, the first is a paperback collections of shorts, but the giant hardback version is a definitive collection that includes the two classic Elijah Baley detective novels, *The Caves of Steel* (1953) and *The Naked Sun* (1956). These novels were set early on in the Trantor timeline (before the Empire was properly forged) when the bulk of humanity lived underground (in 'caves of steel') while a lucky minority had established themselves on other worlds. Elijah Baley was a police detective who with his robot partner, Daneel Olivaw, solved murder mysteries. Asimov's most ambitious works were the tales comprising the **Foundation** sequence, set in the declining years of the Trantor empire run from the planet Trantor, and featuring the work of 'psychohistorian' Hari Seldon. Psychohistory is a sort of sociological statistical analysis that attempts to anticipate future events through the study of large groups of people. The original trilogy of books, *Foundation* (1951), *Foundation and Empire* (1952), and *Second Foundation* (1953), are collections of the magazine stories that appeared in *Astounding* from 1942-1950, and won a 'special category' Hugo in 1965 for Best All-Time Series. His first true novel (*i.e.* not a collection culled from magazines) was *The End of Eternity* (1955), a time-travel book cited by some as Asimov's best work, though perhaps a better candidate can be found in his Hugo award-winning **The Gods Themselves** (1972), which marked his return to the field after his hiatus. The 1970's saw at least two notable short story collections, *Buy Jupiter!* (1975) and *The Bicentennial Man* (1976), and in 1977 Asimov helped found the first new SF magazine for two decades, *Isaac Asimov's Science Fiction Magazine*. However the serious Asimov reader will note that much of his works, including the afore-mention 'Robot' and '*Foundation*' stories, were set in his 'Trantor' universe: Trantor being the administrative planet at the heart of a giant interstellar empire of humanity so old that it is forgotten that Earth was mankind's original home – the theme of his first novel, *Pebble in the Sky* (1950). Among Asimov's non-fiction books there is one that looks specifically at SF, *Isaac Asimov: The Foundations of Science Fiction* (1982), and this won the 1983 Hugo for Best Non-Fiction Book. During the 1980's, Asimov began the ambitious task of melding together his 'Robot' and '*Foundation*' series with mixed results, though ***Foundation's Edge*** (1982) did win a Hugo and topped the *Locus* annual readers poll. The other books in the series include: *The Robots of Dawn* (1983), *Robots and Empire* (1985), *Foundation and Earth* (1986), *Prelude to Foundation* (1988), and the posthumously published *Forward the Foundation* (1992). Just prior to his death, Asimov won a Hugo for Best Novelette, for *Gold* (1991). Asimov died on April 6th, 1992, reportedly due to heart and liver failure, with around 500 books to his name. He received numerous obituaries including in the premiere science journal *Nature*, but his legacy lives on. Roger MacBride Allen wrote a popular robot trilogy prior to Asimov's death, and the *Foundation* stories were continued by **Gregory Benford**, **David Brin** and **Greg Bear**. Though many were dissatisfied with the later stages of Asimov's career (as with Clarke and Heinlein), the fact remains that he was absolutely integral to the development of the genre, contributed his fair share of classics to it, and is firmly recognised as being one of the top 20th century writers of the genre. In 2002 an autobiographical collection of essays compiled by his second wife, Janet Jeppson, was published, *It's Been A Good Life* (2002). This collection revealed that the great man had been brought down by AIDS due to an HIV-tainted blood transfusion he received in 1983 during a by-pass operation.

Astounding Stories – magazine, US (*crtd* 1930). See *Analog*.

Aurora, The – see **Prix Aurora**.

Australasia – Outside of the US and Europe, Australasia is the next most active part of the world for SF. (See also **Clubs, Conventions**) Australia has itself hosted three **World SF Conventions** (**Worldcons**) but regional and national conventions are regularly held in both that country and New Zealand. Its pincipal SF award since 1969 is the Ditmar. It recognises excellence by Australians in Science Fiction, Fantasy and Horror. They are named after Dr Martin James Ditmar (Dick) Jenssen, a founding member of the Melbourne Science Fiction Club. One of its longest running Australasian SF news zines is *Thyme*, founded in 1981 (see **fandom**) but news can also be found on the web pages of the Australian SF Bullsheet: *http://members.optushome.com.au/aussfbull*. One way into Australian 'sci-fi' fandom is through the commercial SF club 'Friends of SF', see their website: *http://www.fsf.com.au/* and a listing of conventions can be found on *www.vicnet.au/~sfoz*. Meanwhile many of the New Zealand's SF community's key activities are promoted on *www.sf.org.nz* and its national convention (natcon) is held over Easter weekend.

Awards, SF – see **Australia** (for the Ditmar), **Campbell** (**John W. jnr.**), **Eagle Award**, **European SF Convention** (for European SF Awards), **Hugo Award**, **Premio Italia**, **Nebula Award**, **Prix Apollo**, **Prix Aurora**, and **Seiun Award**. There are far many more SF Awards than these, but this concise guide to SF is not meant to be encyclopædic. However you will find passing mention to the A. C. Clarke Award, British SF Association Award, and World Fantasy Award, among others, within this guide.

Babylon 5 – TV series, US (*fb*1993). Arguably *Babylon 5* broke new ground in being the first true **space opera** TV epic. *Babylon 5* was the first in which there was an over-all story, of the detail and proportions of ***Dune***, that spanned not only a number of episodes but five seasons up to 1997 with continuation in a new series (*Babylon 5 – Crusade*). The overall visionary behind *Babylon 5* was Michael Straczynski with the helping hand of the acclaimed SF writer **Harlan Ellison** as the series consultant. Ellison not only helped shape the overall story but his hand can also be seen in the not-too-infrequent throw-away SF concepts that pepper the series; not to mention the number of genre tropes the series uses from telepaths to time travel. *Babylon 5* itself is an O'Neill colony in orbit about an alien world in a system bordering a number of interstellar domains. Its function is to provide a diplomatic station for the fractious powers of this part of the Galaxy, so placing it at the heart of whatever political intrigue is going on. The first series contained just a few episodes that directly related to the over-all story, and most episodes were self-contained. This meant that at first there was little to signal viewers that *Babylon 5* was more than just another series (albeit one a cut above the average) and that a larger yarn was being spun into a very rich tapestry. Critical attention to the series therefore took a while to develop (something that was never afforded *Crusade*). As for the series' overall premise: there are two elder species each of whom seem to want something different out of the Galaxy's lower technology races (including Mankind as the youngest of these). These elder species cultivated traits in the cultures and biologies of the spiral arm (including introducing humans to telepathy) and so discretely involve themselves in the business on the interstellar diplomatic station *Babylon 5*. Despite the early hesitation, the first arc storyline nonetheless soon warmed and featured at least three major interstellar battles involving roughly a dozen alien cultures, and the destruction of a similar number of planets. All this was portrayed with state-of-the-art special effects. Such a high body count did not prevent a score of characters developing though some, like the telepath played by Walter Koenig (formerly Chekov in *Star Trek*), only appeared once or twice a season early on (though more regularly later). The relationship between individuals of different cultures also grew. Then there were the references to other SF works. For instance, the name of Koenig's character, Alfred Bester, is itself testimony to *Babylon 5's* creators' appreciation of the genre's roots (**Alfred Bester** being the real-life author of ***The Demolished Man***), but there were other references such as to ***The Prisoner*** and ***Blake's 7***. *Babylon 5* has won a number of awards including the Hugo for Best Dramatic Presentation in 1996 for the episode '*The Coming of the Shadows*' and in 1997 for '*Severed Dreams*'. The final episode, *Sleeping in Light*, only just missed out on the 1999 Hugo for Best Dramatic Presentation by a few votes. There have also been a number of novelizations, including one by **Robert Sheckley**. Principal cast: Michael O'Hare (Cmndr Jeffery Sinclair), Bruce Boxleitner (Captain John Sheridan), Claudia Christian (Lt Cmndr Susan Ivanova), Jerry Doyle (Michael Garibaldi), Mira Furlan (Delenn), Richard Biggs (Dr Stephan Franklin), Bill (*Lost in Space*) Mumy (Lennier), Tracy Scoggins (Elizabeth Lochley), Stephen Furst (Vir Cotto), Walter Koenig (Alfred Bester), Jason Carter (Marcus Cole), Jeff Conaway (Zack Allan), Peter Jurasik (Londo Mollari), Andreas Katsulas (G'Kar), Andrea Thompson (Talia Winters), and Patricia Tallman (Lyta Alexander).

Back to the Future – film, US (1985), *dir.* Robert (***Contact***, ***Who Framed Roger Rabbit?***) Zemeckis. Eccentric Professor Doc Emmett Brown (Christopher (***Who Framed Roger Rabbit?***) Lloyd) steals nuclear fuel from Middle Eastern terrorists to power his time machine car, a De Lorean. The terrorists turn up but Doc Brown's teenage sidekick, Marty McFly (Michael J Fox), escapes using the time machine into the 1950s past where he alters his own family's history. In order to put things right and to return 'back to the future' he solicits the help of the 1950s Doc Brown. *Back to the Future* is a hugely enjoyable comedy adventure but not just that, it also manages to explore some of the classic skiffy time travel paradoxes one would expect when jaunting around the space-time continuum. The film tantalisingly ends in the present with Doc Brown returning from the future (our future) saying that there are problems with Marty's (yet-to-be-born) kids. We had to wait until 1989 for the sequel, which itself was made back-to-back with *Back to the Future III* (the release of which was held over until 1990). The SF really got going in *Back to the Future II* with Marty and Doc Emmett Brown going both into the future as well as returning to the 1950s but having to miss bumping into themselves as the previous *Back to the Future I* was played out in the wings. The last film in the trilogy took them further back in time to the wild west with Marty adopting the pseudonym 'Clint Eastwood' (who is nearly branded a coward but who takes a tip from an Eastwood western to survive a gun fight). The trilogy of films are together a set piece and make for one of the best time travel romps on the big screen. *Back to the Future* won the Hugo Award for Best Dramatic Presentation in 1986. The trilogy was also voted into the *Concatenation* top 30 all-time best SF films.

Ballard J.G. – author, UK (*b*1930). Born in Shanghai, China, Ballard and his father were placed in a civilian prison camp after the attack on Pearl Harbour. Returning to England in 1946, he read medicine for two years at Cambridge, worked as a copywriter, and went to Canada with the RAF. His first published short story was in *New Worlds* magazine in 1956. This periodical, under the editorship of **Michael Moorcock** among others, was in the vanguard of the British **New Wave** literary SF movement, primarily in the 1960s. Ballard wrote SF full of surrealistic imagery and iconoclastic themes, which eventually paved his way into the literary mainstream. ***The Crystal World*** (1966) is typical of a 'disaster' novel where Ballard's protagonists, far from running to the hills, seem instead to thrive on the phenomena. In this case, a matter/anti-matter explosion at the galactic core has far reaching effects on Earth, crystallising the environment and its inhabitants as their store of time is used up. *Hello America* (1981) similarly takes his characters into a familiar, yet twisted landscape. In 2030 the SS Apollo takes the descendants of Americans back to the land their ancestors deserted when the economy collapsed a century earlier. The cities abandoned have been retaken by the environment, and the effects produced seem to gibe with the mythology that has grown up about the country. Some of Ballard's later non-SF work has been adapted into successful movies, including Spielberg's *The Empire of the Sun* (1985), containing semi-autobiographical material, and David (***The Fly*** and ***Scanners***) Cronenberg's controversial *Crash* (1996), which was banned in cinemas in Westminster, London.

Banks, Iain – author, UK (*b*1954).   In terms of books sold in the 1990s (according to the UK *Bookseller* trade magazine data), Iain Banks became one of Britain's top five contemporary **hard SF** authors. He is arguably Scotland's top SF author, or at least up there with the very best. It may therefore seem surprising that he has not (yet) won a Hugo but there are several reasons for this. The Hugo, though the most prestigious award the SF community can bestow, is dominated by the United States where for over two decades three quarters of the annual **World SF Conventions** (the Hugo-voting Worldcons) have been held.   Secondly, Iain Banks is, by his own words, 'a slacker'. He has not been overly prolific and only writes enough to make for a comfortable living.   Yet such is his talent that he only needs to write one (at the most, and rarely, two) book(s) a year. Furthermore he alternates his output between the mainstream and SF, so though he has been professionally writing since the mid-1980s he has written barely a dozen SF works. Under the name 'Iain Banks' his mainstream works have also been highly acclaimed. These include *The Wasp Factory* (his first book in 1984) and *Walking on Glass*, while *The Crow Road* was turned into a BBC TV series.   His SF titles are published under the name Iain M Banks, with the insertion of the 'M' as the publisher's way of signalling to readers which genre he is writing—Iain himself is not entirely comfortable with this marketing device. Much of his SF is set in a universe in which one humanoid dominated federation, known as The Culture, has technologically advanced so much that poverty and virtually all social ills are unknown — though neighbouring non-Culture societies do not necessarily fare so well. As to who runs everything, it could be the humans or it could be artificial intelligences and AI drones, or both humans and AIs? Everything is mega-large. The Culture ships can be kilometres long. The space stations are the size of planetoids. This is SF writ BIG! **Space opera** with a truly operatic budget and all done with a nod to good science, intelligent plots, and clear descriptive passages. In *Consider Phlebas* (1987) a fugitive AI mind hides out following an interstellar war, but many factions are after it including a humanoid shape-changing agent recruited by the Culture: the Culture does not always like to get its hands dirty. Conversely in *The Player of Games* (1988) the Culture's own top games player is sent to challenge the ruler of a distant non-Culture empire. While the *Use of Weapons* (1990) explores the motivation of a Culture-employed mercenary in a tale written from two perspectives in alternate chapters: one moving forwards in time to a conclusion and the other moving backwards to the same point. Meanwhile the AI's perspective is largely presented in *Excession* (1996) when a 'probe' (from another space-time continuum/dimension?) materialises to perplex many of the Galaxy's advanced societies, including the Culture. Iain Banks has written non-Culture SF. *Feersum Endjinn* (1994) is set on a far future Earth in which humanity lives in huge rooms many kilometres long but who have lost much of their former technological understanding. Unfortunately the Earth faces a threat that requires the harnessing of its people's former abilities, this is paralleled through the narrative of a retarded (or un-educated) youngster and part of the book is written in a childish phonetic English. Whereas *Inversions* (1998) appears on the surface to be a work of fantasy, a swords and politics story, but is in reality SF. As a body of work, Banks's SF is hard, intelligent, literary and spiced with a dash of wry Scottish humour; the literary equivalent of a good Speyside malt whisky, and just as welcome (indeed he has written a non-fiction book about that too).

Barbarella – film, Fr (1967), *dir.* Roger Vadim. Based on the cult erotic comic strip by Jean-Claude Forest, Roger Vadim created a skiffy, surreal, quasi-erotic comedy musical. Barbarella (Jane Fonda, then Vadim's real-life wife), wearing little other than the scantiest of 40th century apparel, is sent on a mission to find and return missing scientist Duran Duran (after whom the 1980s pop group was named) played by Milo O'Shea. The imagery, bearing in mind that this is a 60s film, was impressive. Crash landing, Barbarella has to find her way to the planet's capital city; a depraved metropolis. *En route* she meets the eccentric genius Professor Ping and a blind angel, as well as an incredibly inept revolutionary (David Hemmings). It is with him that Jane Fonda performs one of SF movies' most humorous sex scenes (surpassing that in the film *Space Truckers*). The film's weak point (other than that it had eight screen writers) is also one of its strengths in that, though it is very dated, it captures the psychedelic mood of the late 60s: arguably much to do with Jean-Claude Forest who was the film's artistic advisor. *Barbarella* was voted one of the top 30 in the *Concatenation* all-time film poll.

Barrayar – novel (1991) by **Lois McMaster Bujold**. Cordelia Naismith, brilliant space strategist has just beaten a Barrayian Force and so marries her former adversary's commander, one Vorkosigan. It transpires that her husband is a very important Vor Lord. When the Barrayian Emperor dies her husband becomes Regent, but the planet teeters on civil war. Cordelia's pregnancy only complicates matters. A planet and politics tale spiced with wit, *Barrayar* is part of Bujold's Vorkosigan universe which won the 'Best Novel' Hugo in 1992.

Batman – comic and characters, US (*crtd*1939). Crime fighting character generated by Bob Kane, DC Comics. Multi-millionaire playboy Bruce Wayne has a secret identity as a crime fighter (having seen his parents murdered as a child) using a bat costume to strike terror into villains as well as hiding his true identity. Batman hardly ever used a gun, rather athletic prowess together with an arsenal of gadgets instead. It is this last SF trope of using exotic technology to combat crime that makes Batman science fiction. Batman's villains (Joker, Penguin, Mr Freeze, the Riddler, and Catwoman) were equally colourful. The Batman comics have been going strong since the 'caped crusader' first appeared in *Detective Comics* in 1939, and have seen several spin-offs into other media, including: a series of short b&w serial films, a camp 1960s TV series, and more recently in a series of successful feature films. *Batman* (1989) grossed over $400m (US) by 2000. Like many of the US DC and Marvel comic heroes, Batman's image has been re-invented a number of times; notably in the 1950s under the editorship of Julius (see **Fanzines**)

Schwartz (when the crusader's chest emblem began appearing on a yellow, rather than grey, background), and in 1985 as a more tortured 'Dark Knight' character (*The Dark Knight Returns* (1986)) by Frank Miller, and it is this side that shines through particularly in the first (1989) of the recent *Batman* films. (Note: there have been a number of *Batman* graphic novels teaming him up with SF characters including: **Aliens**, **Judge Dredd** and the **Predator**). The animated feature *Batman of the Future: Return of the Joker* (2000) accompanied a TV cartoon series set later in the twenty first century. Batman/Bruce Wayne retires but takes on a new young protégé called Terry McGinnis to take his place. Batman's SF credentials have never been in doubt; aside from his use of exotic technology, he was using computers while the police (in the real world) were still using card files. Perhaps the character's appeal comes from the fact that, in the end, he is just a man and so one does not need to acquire a 'super-power' to aspire to be him (though several million dollars might help...).

Baxter, Stephen – author, UK (*b*1957). Emerging in the 1990s as one of Europe's writers of **hard SF**, Stephen Baxter soon established that not only was he writing stand-alone novels and short stories, many of his works were part of a greater scheme, one that came to be known as the Xeelee universe. The Xeelee stories (not always featuring the alien Xeelee themselves) are set in time literally from the Big Bang through to the end of the Universe. An introduction to the Xeelee series is provided by his *Vacuum Diagrams* (1998) collection of shorts. Though a mathematician by qualification a number of his stories concern aliens and exotic biology. Equally a number include alternate histories or even parallel universes. Here not many could hope to begin to match **H G Wells**, but Baxter did with his homage marking the centenary of *The Time Machine* with *The Time Ships* (1995) authorized by Wells' estate; it was nominated for a Hugo and appeared as a runner-up in the annual *Locus* readers poll, won the British Science Fiction Association Award, the John W. Campbell Memorial Award and the Philip K. Dick Award, and in 1999 co-won the Seiun Award from the Japanese national convention for best translated novel (**Stanley Robinson's** *Red Mars* was the other co-winner). In it Wells' time traveller returns to the future to rescue his Eloi friend Weena from the Morlocks, but his previous visit resulted in perturbations to the time continuum and things are very different. At the end of his first decade as a published novelist, Baxter remains an author to watch. (See also *Interzone* and *Timelike Infinity*.)

Bear, Greg – author, US (*b*1951). Though he published his first SF short story as a teenager, *Destroyers* (1967), and though he became a full-time writer in 1975, it was not really until the mid-eighties that Bear truly made his mark on SF. The son-in-law of **Poul Anderson**, Bear is a **hard SF** author who combines fascinating scientific speculation with convincing characters and a compelling sense of wonder. Perhaps the first indication that he was more than just another SF writer came with his Nebula and Hugo Award-winning novelette ***Blood Music*** (1983), which was expanded into a novel in 1985. In this an over-zealous researcher infects himself with micro-organisms that achieve sentience and then threaten (and largely succeed) in becoming a reality-warping, worldwide pandemic. 1985 also saw the release of *Eon*, in which a hollow asteroid, containing several chambers, one of which appears to be infinite in length, enters the solar system seemingly from an alternate reality. Bear layers idea upon idea, somewhat like **Greg Egan**, and it is not surprising that many of his books spawn sequels. For instance, in *The Forge of God* (1987) Jupiter's moon Europa disappears, shortly after which aliens are found in the Australian desert, promising all kinds of co-operation with Humanity. However, these are renegade Von Neumann probes who are fighting an interstellar war with organic life forms. The tale is continued in *Anvil of Stars* (1992), when humans have joined a force attacking the race that originally released the probes. Similarly *Queen of Angels* (1990), set in a complex future dominated by the use of nanotechnology, eventually gave rise to a sequel, *Slant* (1997). This exuberance of ideas may mean that Bear finds the short story form somewhat restrictive, yet his only other Hugo Award (for Best Short Story in 1987) was given to his SF short, *Tangents* (1986). Bear won a Nebula for his 1993 novel, *Moving Mars*, but this was just one of many 'Mars' books published in the early nineties. Greg Bear has even written a ***Star Trek*** novel. In addition to his career as a writer, Bear has been praised as an editor for the anthology *New Legends* (1995). (See also ***Lost World, The***.)

Beast from 20,000 Fathoms, The – film, US (1953). Based on **Ray Bradbury's** short story, *The Fog Horn* (1951), directed by Eugène Lourié (who was Renoir's principal designer in the thirties), and with Ray Harryhausen's first outing on special effects (along with Willis Cook), this film set the style for all the giant re-awakened dinosaur movies that were to follow, including Lourié's *Gorgo* (1961). The plot is by now familiar to all: A nuclear test thaws out a preserved dinosaur which heads back to its old breeding grounds, now, unfortunately, covered by New York city; this particular creature also carries plague bacteria in its blood, quite apart from its natural aggressiveness. Heroes Paul Christian, Paula Raymond and Lee Van Cleef (in his first film outing) lure the monster to an amusement park amid ferris wheels and roller coasters in order to kill it. Though the script (by Lou Morheim and Fred Freiberger) is somewhat stilted, the film is saved by Lourié's atmospheric direction, and it grossed 25 times what it cost, making $5 million at the box office. Though severely dated now, *The Beast from 20,000 Fathoms* still ranks among the all-time best attended screenings at the annual Festival of Fantastic Films.

Beggars in Spain – novel (1993) by Nancy Kress. In the near future the genetic understanding of molecular biologists enables a new breed of human to be created without the need for sleep. However as the first children grow their true potential becomes apparent. These members of *Homo superior* have to be raised secretly for fear of the prejudice of normal humans, nonetheless they have the ability to rule the world. Kress' tale of discrimination and equality had a sequel *Beggars and Choosers* (1994). *Beggars in Spain* won the Hugo in 1992 for Best Novella. *Beggars and Choosers*, though not a winner, was nominated for the 1995 Hugo for Best Novel

Benford, Gregory – author, US (*b*1941). If you ever want to know anything about plasma turbulence then Benford's your man. A professor of physics at the University of California (Irvine) and a visiting lecturer at Cambridge University, Benford has written over a hundred academic papers. Not surprisingly Greg Benford is a **hard SF** writer. His largest body of writing consists of those novels in his 'Galactic Centre Cycle'. The series starts with *In the Ocean of Night* (1977) on Earth as astronaut Nigel Walmsley encounters an alien automated probe. The probe itself is part of a 'race' with designs on humanity. And so Benford traces the history of this epic conflict to its end by the Galaxy's core where the reason for it all becomes clear, and the solution is revealed in

Sailing Bright Eternity (1995). But Benford's most critically acclaimed work is ***Timescape*** (1980). Not a time travel novel but a hard SF story about communication across time. Cambridge physicists from an ecologically damaged Earth in the future (1998) attempt to warn the past, while physicists in the past (1962) struggle to analyse what they believe is an interstellar message. While Benford in *Timescape* explores some of the philosophical questions physics raises, in *Cosm* (1998) he looks at the way science, as a profession, in the West works when a black, female physicist fights for her right to study a new phenomenon created in a particle accelerator and on the way we get a quick side tour of cosmology. *Eater* (2000), the 2001 *Locus* poll runner-up for Best SF novel, is a first-contact story. Set in the near-future, an interstellar artefact powered by a black hole approaches the Earth, however the intelligence it harbours is not strictly biological and is fascinated by carbon-life forms and aspects of Earth culture. Hopefully without spoiling the novel, let us say that *Eater* explores some of the concepts he included in his Galactic Centre Cycle series and with which he has playfully toyed arising out of his knowledge of astrophysics. Aside from novels, Benford has also turned out some fairly solid, hard SF, short stories. Some of his best have been collected in a volume entitled *Matter's End* (1994). In it one of the stories, *Shakers of the Earth*, concerned the recreation of dinosaurs from fossil-trapped DNA (but was written before **Crichton's *Jurassic Park***), while the title story, *Matter's End* is itself an interesting re-working of **Arthur Clarke's** (2004 retro-Hugo winning short) *The Nine Billion Names of God*. Of note Benford wrote the companion novella *Beyond the Fall of Night* (1991) that was a sequel to Clarke's *Against the Fall of Night* that in turn served as the basis for ***City and the Stars***. Benford found the novella format of *Beyond the Fall of Night* too constraining and decided to evolve the theme of far-future humanity in a full-blown novel *Beyond Infinity* (2004). So if you like, *Beyond Infinity* is a cousin, albeit a distant one, to *City and the Stars*. Benford is required reading for scientists who enjoy SF. *Timescape*, *Matter's End*, *In the Ocean of Night* and *Sailing Bright Eternity* were all runners-up in the *Locus* annual readers poll. Benford also was one of those who added to **Asimov's *Foundation*** series.

Bester, Alfred – author, US (1913-1987). Bester was born in New York and graduated from the University of Pennsylvania, having studied humanities and sciences (including psychology), before publishing his first SF short story, *The Broken Axiom* (1939), in *Thrilling Wonder Stories* (*TWS*), and so winning $50 in a competition. After a dozen or so stories, Bester moved into comics writing (along with *TWS* editor Mort (**Fanzines**) Weisinger, Otto Binder, and other SF luminaries), scripting tales for characters such as **Superman**, Green Lantern, and **Batman**, learning his craft from the late Bill Finger. He also scripted for radio dramas, such as *Charlie Chan* and *The Shadow*, before being lured back to the SF fold by Horace Gold, editor of *Galaxy* magazine. Then Bester wrote his first novel, ***The Demolished Man*** (1953), which won the first ever Hugo Award for Best Novel. He was at this time scripting the TV series *Tom Corbett: Space Cadet*, and novelised his experiences, ultimately selling to the movies. This gave him the money to travel in Europe where, in England and Italy, he wrote ***Tiger! Tiger!*** (1955) . Though continuing to publish SF intermittently over the next 25 years (mainly re-edited collections of his short fiction), Bester mainly worked for *Holiday* magazine until his 'return' to SF in 1974 with the short story *The Four-Hour Fugue*, which (much expanded) became the novel *Golem 100* (1980). Though Bester considered this his best novel, it has never gathered the critical acclaim of his earlier work. Certainly the eighties should have held more promise for Bester as both *The Demolished Man* and *Tiger! Tiger!* are cited as the forerunners to the '**cyberpunk**' movement of the mid-eighties, but it was not to be. *The Deceivers* (1981) was his last SF novel before his death in 1987. However, Bester had already been awarded 'Grandmaster' status by the SF Writers of America, and he was a Guest of Honour at the 1987 British Worldcon in Brighton, UK. His influence on the field cannot be underestimated, despite his limited output, and one of the nicest commemorations was surely the naming of Walter Koenig's psi-cop character, Alfred Bester, in the TV series ***Babylon 5***.

Big Time, The – novelette (1958), novel (1961) by **Fritz Leiber**. An intricate time travelling tale exploring some of this sub-genre's inherent paradoxes. It concerns a time war that rages throughout history. In essence it addresses the way both sides in the conflict attempt to alter the future through changing the past. "It is happening right now: the war through time. The battleground is the eternal present. The objective is to alter the past. And the goal is to seize control of the future. The warriors are ordinary people... like yourself." Set in a rest and recuperation zone outside the possibilities of 'the Change War', 'hostesses' and warriors from various Earth eras mix with aliens in a small drama which itself reflects the grander conflict taking place. In 1958 it won the Hugo for 'Best Novel or Novelette' for the *Galaxy* magazine version. In 1983 a collection of related short stories (again previously published in magazines in the late 1950s and early '60s) were brought together in the single volume *Changewar*.

Big Front Yard, The – novelette (1958) by **Clifford D Simak.** A house in a US desert proves to be a doorway to another house with, in turn, doorways to other worlds. And so a local, self-reliant man forges links with alien civilizations and ultimately makes good with Government forces *etc.*, *etc*. The big front yard (garden) of the title is the US desert and refers to the even bigger back yards houses have, which in this case is the Universe. This guide does not include all Hugo or poll-wining short stories but we have included this one because it so typifies **Simak's** work and the themes he works with, namely: non-urban setting; alien contact; human with supernormal powers (in this case a form of telepathy); and the, initial at least, misunderstanding of traditional authority figures. *The Big Front Yard* won the 1959 Hugo for Best Novelette. It first appeared in ***Astounding Science Fiction*** (October 58) but has appeared in several collections including *The Worlds of Clifford Simak* (1960) and **Asimov's** *The Hugo Winners* (1962).

Blade Runner – film, US (1982), *dir.* Ridley (***Alien***) Scott. Winning a Hugo in 1983 for Best Dramatic Presentation, this loose dramatization of the **P K Dick** novel, ***Do Androids Dream of Electric Sheep***, also came top of the *Concatenation* all-time film poll purely in terms of number of mentions (and not by the fans' ranking), as well as second in the Blackwood/Flynn WSFS poll of top ten SF films. Not surprisingly *Blade Runner* is also on the list of all-time best-attended movies at the Festival of Fantastic Films. Indeed the novel ***Do Androids Dream of Electric Sheep*** (some editions of which were re-titled after the film as *Blade Runner*) in its own right has been hugely popular among SF book fans. Deckard (Ford) is a future 'policeman' who hunts replicants (super-powerful and intelligent androids) that have escaped servitude. In Philip Marlowe style (less so in the subsequent director's cut without the Marlowe type voice over) the film follows Deckard tracking a group of the latest model androids who have returned to Earth and have already killed to keep their freedom. Their purpose on Earth is to override their own fail-safe mechanism—a pre-determined short life span. The future cosmopolitan and part run down world portrayed is pure **Philip Dick** (one frequently used in his novels), but the film's storyline leaves out much of two of the book's three principal strands: especially neglected are the android pets humans keep. The special effects were by Douglas (*Silent Running*) Trumbull, and the haunting soundtrack by Vangelis. Principal cast: Harrison (*Star Wars*, *Raiders of the Lost Ark* and *Indiana Jones& the Last Crusade*) Ford, Rutger Hauer, Sean (*Dune*) Young, Edward James Olmos, and Daryl Hannah.

Blake's 7 – TV Series, UK (*fb*1978). Created by Terry (*Dr Who*) Nation, *Blake's 7* was the BBC's **space opera** offering of the late 1970s; if you like it was the UK version of *Star Trek*. Though aimed primarily at a teenage audience, *Blake's 7* had a wider appeal (possibly due to a generation who earlier grew up with the BBC's *Dr Who* which also drew heavily on scripts provided by Terry Nation). In the future the Earth is the centre of a dictatorial Federation.   Renegades, Blake and his comrades manage to board a deserted hyper-advanced alien craft. With this ship, the Liberator, and its onboard computer intelligence Zen, they set about on hit and run missions against the Federation.   The Federation had the numbers, and a supporting interstellar infrastructure with access to supplies and such, while Blake *et al* had their advanced ship with alien technology such as a *Star Trek* type transporter. However unlike the first *Star Trek* series there was more of an on-going story (though not nearly as elaborate or as co-ordinated as the later *Babylon 5*) with our heroes regularly confronting one of the Federation's leaders, Servalan, and with one of the Federation's toughest soldiers, Travis, hot in pursuit. After the second season Blake (played by the Shakespearean actor Gareth Thomas) left the show, though did return at the end of the third season for an episode, as well as the last episode of the final season (and subsequently in a *Blake's 7* BBC Radio 4 play broadcast in 1998).   The actor playing Travis was also replaced half way through the run, but unfortunately the replacement Travis simply did not convey the menace of the original. Overall most of the episodes were well thought out with a number of standard SF tropes reasonably presented: indeed a couple closely paralleled well-known *Star Trek* episodes. A number of characters in *Blake's 7* changed between series which helped keep the show fresh, but Avon (an intelligent, calculating computer genius) and Vila (an excellent thief and picker of locks, but cowardly) provided constant reference points throughout and their differing characters successfully offset each other. In addition to a reasonable exploration of a number of SF tropes, the series was spiced with a little humour and did not (fortunately) take itself entirely seriously. Established UK actors appearing as guest stars also helped elevate this series above mere sci-fi, though the low budget (by today's standards), and a number of weak stories (such as the episode dealing with the origins of the Liberator) held the series back. This, and the Englishness of the whole series prevented it from penetrating the American market, though it had tremendous appeal in many non-Russian Eastern European countries: no doubt due to the analogous situation those countries then faced. Principal cast: Gareth Thomas (Blake), Paul Darrow (Avon), Michael Keating (Vila), Sally Knyvette (Jenna), Jan Chappell (Cally), Jacqueline Pearce (Servalan), Stephan Greif (Travis) who was later replaced by Brian Croucher, and the voice of Peter Tuddenham (Zen and Orac).

Blish, James – author, US (1921-1975). Blish studied microbiology at Rutgers, graduating in 1942, was drafted for two years, then went on to do postgraduate work at Columbia University. His first short story, *Emergency Refuelling* had been published in 1940, and Blish was part of the celebrated SF fan group, *The Futurians*, which included such as **Asimov, Pohl**, and others. He wrote the 1959 Hugo Award winning novel ***A Case of Conscience***, but is also known well for the '*Cities in Flight*' series (*They shall have stars* (1956), *A life for the stars* (1962), *Earthman, come home* (1956), and *A clash of cymbals* (1959)), in which interstellar civilisation is on the brink of economic collapse and the universe is eventually destroyed; and also for the *After Such Knowledge* trilogy (*Doctor Mirabilis* (1964), *Black Easter* (1968), and *The day after judgement* (1971)), in which Hell is set loose on Earth, and the might of the USAF is trained on the city of Dis in Death Valley. Blish is also well known to the fans of **Star Trek** for his 12-volume novelizations of the original series' episodes, and one of the first original *Star Trek* novels, *Spock Must Die* (1970), in which Spock is duplicated in a transporter accident (*cf.* William Riker in ***Star Trek: The Next Generation***). Blish was also one of the founders of the Milford Science Fiction Writers' Workshop, which still exists today. He lived near Oxford, England from 1968 until his death in 1975.

Blood Music – novel (1985) by **Greg Bear**. A scientist, Vergil Ulam, generates a micro-organism using mammalian DNA. The result is a cell capable of biochemical learning. Swiftly realising the possible implications – such as cheap biocomputers – Vergil sees that his 'biologic' discovery could result in considerable rewards. His results continue to prove promising and soon he has lymphocytes learning routes through micro-mazes. Not wishing for his employing company (who are already nervous of the work) to reap the rewards, he smuggles the organisms out by injecting himself with them. This should not give him any ill effects, but since the organisms can learn they adapt. Before long the organisms co-operate with each other, biochemical learning gives way to communal sentience, and they even start to communicate with their host, Vergil... Then comes the time when one host is not enough, nor are the hosts satisfactory in their normal form so they are changed. In effect the organisms become a highly infective, figure transforming disease. However the ensuing pandemic has its oddities. For instance why is it that some countries remain unaffected? How come conventional, even extreme measures, of control do not work? As with much of Bear's work, wonder leads to wonder, ultimately with the future, and nature, of our species at stake. Greg Bear originally wrote *Blood Music* as a short story (1983) in ***Analog*** which won the Hugo Award in 1984 for Best Novelette.

Blue Mars – novel (1996) by **Kim Stanley Robinson**. This is the third book of Robinson's massive 'Mars' trilogy, following on from *Red Mars* (1992) and ***Green Mars*** (1993). Like the second volume, *Blue Mars* won the Hugo for Best Novel in 1997 and topped the annual *Locus* readers poll. The whole trilogy tells the story of the creation of a utopia on the terraformed planet Mars. By the events of this novel it is possible to walk unprotected upon the planetary surface, and the colonists are entirely independent from control from Earth. Indeed, it is the Earth itself which is in trouble, due to flooding induced by the collapse of Antarctic ice sheets, and they must call upon the terraforming expertise of the colonists to avert greater disaster. Unfortunately the action, such as it is, is slowed by Robinson's digressions into the finer points of the creation of the Martian constitution, but the trilogy as a whole is certainly the best of the many 'Mars' books published in the early nineties.

Boy and his dog, A – film, US (1975), *dir.* L Q Jones based on the novella by **Harlan Ellison**. Set in a post-nuclear war wasteland, Vic (Don Johnson) and his (mutant) telepathic dog scavenge to survive. He encounters Quilla (Susanne Benton) who is sent from a fallout bunker to entice him down. The underground bunker consists of a whole town, complete with parks, whose occupants (descendants of those who originally took shelter) are in the need of fresh genetic material to prevent in-breeding. However they have no intention of letting Vic survive... Its post-apocalyptic portrayal of the future pre-dates, but is reminiscent of, *Mad Max II* and *III* while the film itself does not take itself too seriously, having its tongue firmly in cheek, especially with the closing scene. *A Boy and his Dog* won the Hugo in 1976 for Best Dramatic Presentation, and the novella won a Nebula (the SF award voted for by the SF writers' of America).

Book of the New Sun, The – novel(s) (1980-1983) by **Gene Wolfe**. This multi-awarding story was originally published in four volumes. Set in a far future when the Sun is dying, science and technology have become indistinguishable from magic, and aliens are regarded as mythological creatures, this collection can be read as fantasy. It concerns the torturer and executioner, Severian, who is exiled from the Citadel of the City Imperishable to Thrax, the City of Windowless Rooms, on the other side of the world. He carries only his sword, *Terminus Est*, and an extraterrestrial gem of indescribable power and discovers the truth of his time over four intriguing volumes, *The Shadow of the Torturer* (1980), *The Claw of the Conciliator* (1981) which came top of the annual *Locus* readers poll as well as winning a Nebula, *The Sword of the Lictor* (1982) which also topped the *Locus* poll in the 'best fantasy novel' category, and *The Citadel of the Autarch* (1983) which won the John W. Campbell Award. Collectively the tetralogy came joint 4th in the *Concatenation* readers' poll for all-time best novel. As with many similarly themed far futures, the pleasure is in discovering with the protagonist, Severian, the scientific underpinnings of his apparently fantastical world. While on the surface the world seems to have undergone a regression to an earlier age, and hence there is little obvious technology and society appears feudal, beneath appearances there are many devices under control of the Autarch and his staff. Throughout *The Book of the New Sun*, Wolfe uses an obscure but genuine vocabulary which makes the prose dense and difficult, which may be off-putting for some readers, but perseverance is rewarded by this fascinating and richly detailed story.

Bova, Ben – author and editor, US (*b*1932). As editor of ***Analog*** from 1971 to 1978, Bova transformed the magazine's fortunes, then declining, and won the Hugo for Best Editor in 1973-77, and again in 1979, by which time he had become editor of *Omni*, until 1982. Each title saw the publication of anthologies sporting their names. Bova as author is less memorable, but notable titles include *Millennium* (1976), *Colony* (1978), *Voyagers* (1981), and *Mars* (1992); his short stories can be entertaining and the collection *Maxwell's Demons* (1979) is a rewarding and typical example.

Boys from Brazil, The – film, US/GB (1978), *dir.* Franklin Schaffner. Gregory Peck plays an aged Nazi in modern times who has succeeded in developing cloned embryos of Hitler. In an attempt to recreate the characteristics that made Hitler 'great', the Nazi's have placed the child clones with a number of couples whose background and circumstances are similar to those of Hitler's original parents. However Nazi hunters have got wind of what is going on and the net begins to close. On one level the film explores a question that has dogged modern biologists: that of how much of a person's character is determined genetically, and how much by personal experience (environmental determinism)? In the film the Nazis murder the clones' various fathers so as to replicate one aspect of such determinism. Principal cast: Gregory Peck, Laurence Olivier, Steve Guttenberg, James Mason and Lilli Palmer.

Bradbury, Ray – author, US (*b*1920). If Asimov, Clarke and Heinlein are the fathers of modern SF, then Bradbury must surely be counted as one of the fathers of modern speculative fiction. He is equally at home in both science fiction and fantasy or horror and his output is divided between the written and visual forms. He has written numerous short stories, several screen (***The Beast***

From 20,000 Fathoms and *It Came From Outer Space*) and TV scripts including 42 tele-plays for his TV series *The Ray Bradbury Theatre*. Though an established name, Bradbury has not won any Hugos for his novels largely, we suspect, because his SF tends to be diluted with elements of fantasy and because most of his written output is in short-story form. (However it is surprising that the man has not won a Hugo for a short.) ***The Martian Chronicles*** exemplifies the way he moves between the genres: indeed this work itself is more of a science fantasy with its focus not so much on hardware or on Mars but on the planet's effect on the human mind. It is also illustrative of Bradbury's preference for short stories as the volume itself is in effect a themed collection of shorts. His focus on the human dimension has meant that some of his work is more accessible to non-SF enthusiasts and so he has on occasion won mainstream literary recognition, such as for ***Fahrenheit 451*** (written in 1953 and filmed in 1966 by François (***Close Encounters of the Third Kind***) Truffaut). Ray Bradbury was born in Waukegan, Illinois, he married in 1947 and has four children. During World War II he had a number of short stories published in *Best American Short Stories* and *O. Henry Prize Stories*. In 1953 he won the Benjamin Franklin Award for Best American magazine story. There are over a dozen collections of his short stories and these are well worth looking out for. *The Ray Bradbury Theatre* TV series saw him write 42 teleplays, and throughout the early fifties he came to be associated with EC Comics' ***Weird Science*** title following several unauthorised adaptations of his work. While Hugos seem to have passed him by Bradbury was nonetheless a Guest of Honour at the 1986 **World SF Convention (Worldcon)**. Much of his SF short fiction can be found in the two-volume omnibus *The Stories of Ray Bradbury* (1981).

Brave New World – novel by Aldous Huxley (1932). This work is arguably 'second only to ***Nineteen Eighty-Four*** as the most famous SF novel ever' (**Clute**, 1995). Though published well before the Hugos, it has stood the test of time and is still in print today. The story is set a few hundred years into the future. Technology (as opposed to science) is revered. Henry Ford is worshipped. Society itself is high tech and plastic. Those 'born' are genetically engineered into a caste system: the alphas, betas *etc*. The population is entertained by 'feelies' (a vision of what would become virtual reality) and drugged (especially the lower castes) by 'soma'. When a mother-to-be gets left behind, following an accident during a sight-seeing trip to the uncivilised savage reservation, the resultant son, John Savage, grows up outside the high tech society. Rediscovered years later, he is introduced to his parents' civilization. But, versed in Shakespeare and poetry, he fails to integrate. Though he finds true love, in this loveless world, tragedy follows. Huxley reportedly wrote the novel in part 'to have a little fun pulling the leg of **HG Wells'**. A reasonably faithful, two part (95 minutes each), TV movie was made in 1980 *dir*. Burt Brinckerhoff. Principal cast: Kristoffer Tabori (John Savage), Julie Cobb (Linda Lysenko), Bud Cort (Bernard Marx), Kier Dullea (Thomas Grambell), Ron O'Neal (Mustapha Mond), and Dick Anthony Williams (Helmholtz Watson). (This version is not to be confused with the far less faithful 1998 TV remake which incidentally featured Leonard (*Star Trek*) Nimoy.)

Brazil – film, GB (1985), *dir*. Terry (*Time Bandits*) Gilliam. Gilliam brings his usual sense of vision with carefully crafted sets and stunning photography to a middle class Orwellian dystopia. Again, as is typical, the director balances the terror within the film with a dash of comedy. One 'oppressed' individual, Sam Lowry (Jonathan Pryce), who fantasises about flying over a better world, comes up against the system when he allows a freelance (literally free) cowboy repairman to mend his apartment's air-conditioning. That and an accidental encounter with a 'terrorist' brings him to the attention of the state. *Brazil* came 10th in the *Concatenation* all-time film poll. Also stars: Robert De Niro, Michael (***Time Bandits***) Palin, Bob (***Who Framed Roger Rabbit?***) Hoskins, and Kim Greist.

Brin, David – author, US (*b*1950). Glen David Brin has a doctorate in astrophysics, and works as an advisor to NASA and is, quite possibly, the best regarded author of **hard SF** to emerge from the eighties. His novel *Sundiver* (1980) introduces his complex 'Uplift' universe in which most intelligent life has been uplifted to sentience by one of five Patron races, themselves being the product of a now-vanished race known as the Progenitors. Humans, however, seem to have arisen solely through evolution (though there is some speculation in later volumes that Humanity is also a Progenitor-created race), and have themselves uplifted Terran dolphins and chimpanzees. ***Startide Rising*** (1983) and

The Uplift War (1987), the second and third books set in this universe, each won the Hugo for Best Novel and topped the annual *Locus* readers poll, and the former also won the Nebula. In these novels, Humans (and their uplifted companions) discover information about the Progenitors and threaten to disrupt the stability of their home galaxy, whose Patron race has become corrupt. The resultant war spills over into three further books, *Brightness Reef* (1995), *Infinity's Shore* (1996) and *Heaven's Reach* (1998). Brin's 1985 *Locus* poll-topping novel ***The Postman*** was recently turned into an expensive flop of a movie starring Kevin Costner, but he also won a Hugo for Best Short Story that year for *The Crystal Spheres* (1984), which can be found in his 1987 collection *The River of Time*. A second collection, *Otherness* (1994), topped the *Locus* readers poll in 1995. In 2002 Brin's *Kil'n People* was published, which Brin himself says was one of the more challenging works he has written. Set in a not too distant future it addresses the possibility of routinely creating short-lived (typically a day) robotic copies of one's self. The novel is absolutely packed with one-off observations as to the possible implications of such technology and so contains much of the material that an academic might need for a treatise on the topic. It was nominated for a Hugo in 2003. With **Gregory Benford** and **Greg Bear**, Brin has contributed a volume to a contemporary trilogy continuing **Isaac Asimov's *Foundation*** series.

Brunner, John – author, UK (1934-1995). John wrote his first book *Galactic Storm* in 1951 (as Gill Hunt) and between two and half a dozen of his books were published most years throughout the '60s to the early '70s. Though many of these are now somewhat dated, John's work always contained an edge that not only reflected how well read and travelled the author was, but also the fact that he was, at heart, a political creature. Other than a few examples of environmental fiction (*e.g.* **Harry Harrison's *Make Room! Make Room!*)** Brunner's green ecological perceptions were very much ahead of his time. In the 1960s it was said that the entire population of the world could stand on the Isle of Wight, John's ***Stand on Zanzibar*** (1968) was set in the future when the world's population could fit on Zanzibar. This eco-disaster story earned him the Hugo for Best Novel in 1969. Its sequel, *The Sheep Look Up* (1972), and other novels such as *The Jagged Orbit* (1969) and ***The Shockwave Rider*** (1974) won him the reputation for being a literary writer as well as a spinner of thumping good yarns. Unfortunately these works arguably represented his career's peak despite subsequent striving. Yet among his other books there were some great skiffy milestones. ***Telepathist*** (1964) reflected that having a paranormal gift was not necessarily as great a deal as one might fantasise, especially if the genes conferring this gift also made you a twisted cripple. *The Stone That Never Came Down* (1973) is set against a near-future world where civilization is poised on the brink of collapse, the irony is that what could well save it is a new kind of viral drug that can powerfully alter the human mind permanently and even the very nature of mankind. In pure skiffy predictive terms, as with all great SF writers, John Brunner had his moments, one of his finest was with ***The Shockwave Rider*** (1974). One has to remember that it was published in the first half of a decade in which home computers were totally unknown, and indeed many mainframes (then only found in very large institutions and big business) still relied on punch-cards or reel-to-reel magnetic tape for their programming. Yet John predicted something very close to the World Wide Web, and the book featured computer viruses, although he called them 'phages' (which itself is a biological term for bacteria-infecting viruses). John Brunner was a fannish person, he regularly made an annual pilgrimage to the **European SF Convention** and in 1984 was a leading light for the organization (surprisingly late in the European SF Convention's history) of Britain's first Eurocon. He died, as he might have wished, among many of his friends at the 1996 Scottish World SF Convention, which itself was also billed as that year's Eurocon. ***Stand on Zanzibar*** (1968) won the Hugo Award in 1969 for Best Novel as well as the British Science Fiction Award and the Prix Apollo in France. *The Telepathist* (1964) was nominated for the Hugo in 1965 and was a runner up, as was *Squares of the City* (1965) in 1966. Both *The Sheep Look Up* and *The Shockwave Rider* came in the top six of the *Locus* annual readers poll in the year following their publication.

Buck Rogers – character (*crtd*1928). Buck Rogers was created by Philip Nowlan in his August 1928 novella, *Armageddon 2419AD*, in ***Amazing Stories***, but first appeared as a comic strip – and subsequently shot to fame – on July 1st 1929. Probably the first illustrated **space opera**, *Buck Rogers* appeared in both daily and Sunday newspapers and, like ***Flash Gordon*** after, the character quickly spread to radio, film and TV serials and has also had several comics incarnations, notably the Gold Key title launched July 1964 (Gold Key was the first company to produce a regular ***Star Trek*** comic, a little later). Transported 500 years into the future, Lt. (Anthony) Buck Rogers USAF and sidekick Wilma Deering fought Killer Kane and his Mongols, along with other bad guys, incidentally giving the world the word "Zap!" Probably the best remembered artist, illustrating Buck for 25 years, was Rick Yager, and collected album versions are sporadically available. The best remembered actor to play the part from the serial was Buster Crabbe (who also played ***Flash Gordon***), and he guest-starred in the 1979 US TV *Buck Rogers in the 25th Century* series once or twice, having great fun at the expense of his successor in the role, Gil Gerard.

Bug Jack Barron – novel (1969) by **Norman Spinrad**. Millionaire Benedict Howards can buy and sell presidents, so it should be no problem for him to force through the Federal Freezer Bill, which will give him complete control of the cryogenics industry, but he has reckoned without talk show star Jack Barron, who can smell when something fishy is going on. But perhaps even Barron can be bought if the price is immortality... Condemned in Parliament as "depraved" and "obscene", the original serialisation in *New Worlds* caused the UK newsagent chain W.H. Smiths to ban the magazine: a laughable response these days. Nominated for Hugo and Nebula, *Bug Jack Barron* could be seen as a prophetic novel, given that the relationship between politics and the media has become ever more intimate.

Bujold, Lois McMaster – author, US (*b*1949) Though with barely a half dozen novels under her belt, Bujold has nonetheless managed to pick up three Hugos, which is an extremely good hit rate by any standard. She only began writing novels in the mid-1980s so we can expect more from her yet. To date most of her books are in the planets-and-politics vein. They are written intelligently and seriously but contain a wry element; a trace of wit which increases her works' entertainment value. Many of her stories concern a brilliant, but disabled warrior-politician called Vorkosigan. These include her ***The Vor Game*** (1990) which won the Hugo in 1991 for Best Novel, as did ***Barrayar*** (1991) which won the 1992 Hugo Best Novel and came top of that year's *Locus* readers poll. Again ***Mirror Dance*** (1994) won the Hugo in 1995 and the *Locus* Award. In 2004 she won the Hugo for ***Paladin of Souls*** (2003). Her novel *Falling Free* (1988), which was set in her Vorkosigan universe, but before the era of her other books, won the Nebula (a non-reader award voted for by US writers), while *The Borders of Infinity* (1989) consists of three episodes of Vorkosigan's adventures and was a runner up in the *Locus* annual readers poll. Her latest Miles Vorkosigan title is *A Civil Campaign* (2000).

Burns, Jim – artist, UK (*b*1948). A professional artist whose works adorn the covers of many Sphere, Bantam and Ace SF books. Unlike some artists whose cover illustrations do not seem to quite match the book's contents, one does feel that Burns reads the works he illustrates. In the 1970s he worked mainly for UK publishers, especially Sphere, but from 1980 also US publishing houses including Bantam and Ace. He has won the 1987 Hugo for Best Professional Artist. His work can be seen in *Transluminal: The Paintings of Jim Burns* (1999). He also regularly exhibits at major SF conventions and frequently at the UK Eastercon (the annual gathering of the UK SF clans) where often a number of prints can be bought and where his originals are frequently auctioned.

Cadigan, Pat – author, US (*b*1953). Cadigan was born in Schenectady, New York, and graduated from the University of Kansas, worked in a design studio, and wrote greeting card messages for ten years. She became a full time writer in 1987, achieving prominence as part of the cyberpunk movement, though she sold her first short story in 1980. In 1988 she won a World Fantasy Award and the *Locus* readers poll for best short story, *Angel*, which was included in the collection ***Patterns*** (1989), which itself won the *Locus* readers poll for best collection in 1990. She has twice won the Arthur C. Clarke Award, for *Synners* (1991) and *Fools* (1992). In 1996 she moved to London, and was Visiting Scholar at the University of Warwick, attached to the Cybernetic Culture Research Unit.

Calculating God – novel (2000) by Robert J. Sawyer (***Hominids***). When an alien craft lands in Ontario, the being that steps out does not say, 'Take me to your leader.' Instead he asks for a palaeontologist. The extraterrestrial is interested in Earth's past. It seems that mass extinctions (like the asteroid one that wiped out the dinosaurs) are not only common to all nearby civilization-bearing worlds, but that they happened at about the same time. Is this evidence of God, and a God manipulating evolution? From this start *Calculating God* becomes on one hand a detective story and on the other an exploration of what science calls the anthropic cosmological principle set against a **hard SF** framework. Up to 2000 Sawyer had not won the Hugo, though a number of his books have been short-listed for that award, and indeed he has won a number of regional SF prizes. Indeed *Calculating God* itself did not win the Hugo for best novel (which would have automatically earned it an entry in this guide) but came second in terms of votes cast at the 2001 **World SF Convention (Worldcon)**. So why then have we included it? ***Harry Potter and the Goblet of Fire*** won the best novel Hugo in 2001 due to a clause in the Worldcon constitution that allows fantasy titles (and so ensures the eligibility of science fantasy works). However *Goblet of Fire* is pure fantasy without any science fiction. Though we have included *Goblet of Fire* so as to be true to the letter of this guide's definition of 'best' (see 'About this guide and its use'), we felt the SF work with the most votes of Hugo nominations that year kept to the spirit defining inclusion.

Campbell, John W. jnr. – author and editor, US (1910-1971). The greater part of the John W. Campbell jnr. story is inextricably bound up in his editorship of *Astounding Science Fiction* (see also **Analog**) and, during his tenure as editor there (1937 until his death in 1971), Campbell won 8 Hugo Awards as Best Editor and *Astounding* won 7 Hugos for Best Magazine. Hardly surprising when Campbell is credited with the 'discovery' of such as **Asimov** and **Heinlein**, and also the publishing of stories by **Van Vogt, Herbert** and others. Indeed, the so-called **Golden Age** of Science Fiction, usually dated from the Summer of 1939, would never have happened were it not for Campbell. However, what is commonly overlooked is Campbell's career as a writer, both under his own name and a variety of pseudonyms, the most famous of which is Don A. Stuart. In the early thirties, Campbell's space operas were considered a serious rival to those of **E.E. "Doc" Smith**, especially his 'Arcot, Morey and Wade' series (1930-32) which were eventually published in novel form as *The Black Star Passes* (1953), *Islands of Space* (1957) and *Invaders from the Infinite* (1961). However, it was in 1934 with the first of his Don A. Stuart stories (mostly published in

Astounding while it was still under the editorship of Orlin F. Tremaine) that Campbell's fiction really started to shine. Stuart's stories were more like the SF that Campbell would encourage as an editor than the foregoing space operas. Stories such as *Twilight* (1934) and the 'Machine' series, *The Machine, The Invaders* and *Rebellion* (all 1935) quickly gained Stuart a reputation as a writer of imaginative and considered SF. But it was in 1938 that Campbell, as Stuart, wrote his single most famous tale, *Who Goes There?* This story of a shape-shifting alien life form has been twice creditably filmed; firstly as ***The Thing from Another World*** (1951), directed by Christian Nyby with a lot of help from producer Howard Hawks, and secondly as ***The Thing*** (1982), directed by John Carpenter. However, shortly after the publication of *Who Goes There?*, Campbell's writing career ended and he gave his attention full time to the editing of *Astounding* until his death in 1971. More than any other *individual*, it is Campbell who can most be credited with the creation of modern SF. His passing spawned two awards in his name, the 'John W. Campbell' Award (for best new writer voted on at the **World SF Convention (Worldcon)**) and the 'John W. Campbell memorial' award (determined by a committee of writers and critics, it is for the best novel published in English the previous year).

Canticle for Leibowitz, A – novel (1959) by Walter M Miller jr. Not only was it recognised as a significant SF work shortly after its publication but it has stood the test of time and is as readable and relevant today. As with so many classics this novel was inspired in part by the author's own experiences. Having enlisted after Pearl Harbour, Miller spent most of World War II as a radio operator and gunner in the Army Air Corp. He participated in some 55 combat sorties over Italy and the Balkans. Among these was the controversial assault on the Benedictine abbey at Monte Casino, the oldest monastery in the Western world. It was this raid that later led him to write *A Canticle for Leibowitz*. The novel concerns itself with religion, human behaviour, and of course war and a monastery. The novel is divided into three parts, each telling the story of an episode of the monastery's history six centuries apart. In the first Brother Francis Gerard of Utah discovers some Holy relics, indecipherable writings of the great Saint Leibowitz '*Pound pastrami, can kraut, six bagels— bring home for Emma*'. These are added to the monastery's collection of artefacts from before the 'Flame Deluge'. In the second, monks manage to recreate some of the technology from their crude understanding of their order's collected heritage. In the final part, an advanced technological civilization has again evolved on Earth, but war threatens... *A Canticle for Leibowitz* did many things, including capture the senselessness of the then (1960s) Cold War and the futility of the arms race. It was an inspired work, and the author successfully conveys that he was writing from the heart. But it is not dour, with the seriousness of the subject matter at its heart counter-balanced by some wry humour (*e.g.* the much revered message from the past being merely a shopping list). *A Canticle for Leibowitz* won the Hugo Award in 1961 for Best Novel. It also came into the top twenty all-time best SF works in the *Concatenation* poll. Nearly 40 years after its publication, its sequel *Saint Leibowitz and the Wild Horse Woman* was published in 1997, the year following Miller's death. There had been rumours that Miller had written a sequel but these never amounted to anything while he was alive. It may have been that Miller himself was not entirely satisfied with his sequel, but in the end could not disappoint his fans? *Saint Leibowitz and the Wild Horse Woman* focuses on the relationship of the new Catholic church with the struggling-to-survive tribes during the depth of the post Flame Deluge dark age. Though not quite as poignant as *A Canticle*, *Wild Horse Woman* nonetheless retains the humour. Though Miller is essentially a one novel author, he was a consummate short story writer (indeed *A Canticle* can be considered to be three novelettes strung together). Many of his shorts have been published and two collections *Conditionally Human* (1962) and *A View From the Stars* (1965) are recommended by Miller fans.

Card, Orson Scott – author, US (*b*1951). Card writes both science fiction and fantasy and is **new wave** in his approach. Unlike a goodly proportion of other authors whose SF focus is on hardware and a sense of wonder, or whose fantasy centres on the magical and the spectacle of ancient/alternate realms, Card is concerned with human motivations. This is not to say that his SF ignores science and technology, for it certainly does not, but that the science and technology serves as a fulcrum for the events about which motivations and human reactions are explored. For instance one recurring theme is his exploration of rites of passage to adulthood in *Songmaster* (1980), *Wyrms* (1987) or ***Ender's***

Game (1985). However he is best known, in SF terms for his Ender series, the original trilogy being: ***Ender's Game*** (1985), ***Speaker for the Dead*** (1986), and ***Xenocide*** (1991). Overall the trilogy concerns environmental ethics. In the first, a young Ender is honed into Earth's top strategist who 'unwittingly' wipes out an entire civilization that is threatening Earth, and so is hailed a hero. In the second Ender has roamed the stars to escape his guilt, and the scorn of his fellows as his reputation as hero has transformed to one almost of war criminal. Because of relativistic time dilation at near light speed, many years have passed, though faster-than-light (ansible) communication keeps mankind's Starways Congress up to date with the latest events. Ender lands anonymously on a world as a speaker for the dead—someone who gives testimony on behalf of those who cannot speak for themselves—at a time when a member (or members) of the only other currently known intelligent race in the galaxy has been accused of murder. In the final volume, *Xenocide* (1991), Ender's new-found home world is threatened by a war fleet from Earth sent to destroy it as the planet contains a virus which, if spread to other worlds, could wipe out human life. Ender has to save this world yet, at the same time, has the opportunity to bring back something of the civilization he previously destroyed. Following the original trilogy Card wrote two other Ender books of which *Ender's Shadow* (1999) is of particular note. It parallels *Ender's Game*, in telling the story of one of Ender's fellow cadets, Bean. But Bean had his own origins and abilities so enabling a completely different take on the Bugger war. Nonetheless, apart from literally a paragraph or two, it meshes perfectly with *Ender's Game*. A powerful series, the Ender books are only rivalled as a literary accomplishment by his fantasy (non-SF) 'Alvin maker' trilogy concerning an alternate 18th century America. Card has won many SF awards. His democratic recognition includes Best Novel Hugos for ***Ender's Game*** in 1986 and ***Speaker for the Dead*** in 1987. This last also come top of the annual *Locus* readers poll. Card has also twice won Hugos for Best Novella in 1988 and 1989 for *Eye for Eye* and *The Last of the Winnebagoes* respectively. He has also won the Hugo for Best Non-Fiction in 1991 for his book *How to Write Science Fiction and Fantasy*.

Carrie – film, US (1976), *dir.* Brian de Palma. Principal cast: Sissy Spacek; Piper Laurie; Amy Irving; William Katt; Nancy Allen and John Travolta. Based on a 1976 story by Stephen King (which made him famous), an adolescent girl, Carrie, daughter of an obsessive and fanatically religious single mother, begins to exhibit extraordinary powers. Continually the butt of her class, she struggles to come to terms with who she is, but not without wreaking spectacular tribulations and vengeance on her tormentors. Presented in a modern Gothic style the film works its way towards a violent climax and a final shock just when you think it is all over. The story is at first sight pure horror fantasy, but the self-searching scenes in the library hint that telekinetic powers may be a natural mutation and this makes it accessible to harder SF fans.

Case of Conscience, A – novel (1958) by James Blish. A Jesuit member of an interstellar UN exploratory team is convinced that the alien way of life on a newly discovered idyllic planet proves that that world is a genuinely diabolic trap. The aliens (Lilithians) are a gentle and highly intelligent reptile-like species; perfect creatures who know no sin. The explorer takes one of the alien's seeds to Earth which grows into a terrifying creature that leads a crusade on morals. The explorer comes to see the Lilithians as never having 'fallen from God's grace' and concludes that humanity could not have been created by God. *A Case of Conscience* won the Hugo in 1959 for Best Novel and a retro-Hugo in 2004 (50 years on from the 1954 Worldcon that did not award Hugos for 1953 SF). It was able to win both awards as while the novel was published in 1958, the story was also serialised in *IF* magazine in 1953.

Charly – film, US (1968), *dir.* Ralph Nelson. Based on the classic award-winning short story ***Flowers for Algernon*** by Daniel Keyes, this faithful adaptation has not received the recognition it deserves by the general public, though for the buff it remains an absolute delight. Cliff Robertson plays the retarded factory floor cleaner artificially turned genius by Claire Broom and colleagues administering a mind-developing treatment. However Charly's genius begins to evaporate as his over-stimulated brain burns out. A powerful movie and a rare example of cinematic new-wave SF. Robertson started his own production company to bring this story to the screen. This must have seemed more than worthwhile when he won the Oscar for Best Actor.

Cherryh C J – author, US (*b*1942). Setting hard SF against a detailed and complex socio-political background, Carolyn Cherryh has created a rich universe in which to set her stories. This Alliance-Union universe is so rich that some of her novels form sub-series (such as the Chanur novels) within the Alliance-Union embrace. The Alliance-Union stories are set in time from the near future to about three thousand years into the future. In space they are mainly set within a 50 light-year radius of Earth. (Indeed one of Cherryh's hobbies was to make a 3-dimensional map of this region.) The basic premise of the Alliance-Union is that humanity has reached out to the stars. However soon three power bases form. The first is old Earth which has high technology but is politically volatile. The second is the Alliance which is effectively a co-operative of interstellar merchant traders. The third is the Union which is almost a federation of colony worlds. Of course there are players outside of these three principal ones. Many of these are alien cultures whose contact with humanity is limited due to a (*Star Trek* prime directive type) protocol that protects both the indigenous culture and our own species. Consequently, a number of her novels (such as *Serpent's Reach*, 1980) are set on these worlds and can be read without any detailed knowledge of the Alliance-Union universe. Others, such as *Rimrunners* (1989), focus on the conflicts between humans. Since 1976 Cherryh has written typically two or three novels a year and so now has over 50 to her name. They are all brim full with exotic ideas made to seem mundane, and convincing detail. Her works are complex and intelligent, and while not as grand in scope as her **hard SF** contemporaries', say, **Iain Banks** Culture series, or as hard an SF as **Greg Egan** or **William Gibson**, it is easy for the reader to become absorbed in her universe and the conflicts therein. Cherryh has won two Hugos for novels: ***Downbelow Station*** got its in 1982, and ***Cyteen*** in 1981.

Chrysalids, The – novel (1955) by **John Wyndham**. David lives in a post-apocalyptic world. No one can quite remember what the apocalypse was; now they must deal with its aftermath, Tribulation. Mutant births—human, animal and vegetable—occur with disturbing regularity in the agrarian community on Labrador. But David himself is a mutant, though not of form, but of the mind. He and at least eight other children seem to possess telepathic powers. Driven out and hunted, a few of the children must travel ever deeper into the Badlands for a possible rendezvous with hope, from the other side of the world. Wyndham's post-WWII career was markedly different from his pre-war pulp contributions. Supposedly the writer of 'cosy catastrophes', Wyndham's work was often disturbing within its middle class framework, and was for many years among the only SF regularly found in school libraries (along with **Wells** and **Verne**). *The Chrysalids* is reminiscent – in its treatment of the child mutants, as sympathetic characters in adversity usually brought about by the adult world – of **Theodore Sturgeon's** *The Dreaming Jewels* (1950) and ***More Than Human*** (1953). Wyndham examined the other side of the mutant coin in 1957, in a style more reminiscent of **Van Vogt** than Sturgeon, with the publication of *The Midwich Cuckoos* (filmed as ***Village of the Damned*** (1960)), in which the children were anything but sympathetic.

City and the Stars, The – novel (1956). **Arthur C Clarke's** re-worked novel of his 1953 book *Against the Fall of Night*, which itself was based on a 1948 short story. It concerns the far future of humankind and its evolution: a theme that he continually returned to throughout his career, such as in his novel *Childhood's End* or the film ***2001: A Space Odyssey***. The city in question, Diaspar, is an ultra technological metropolis, a last bastion for modern man. Its citizens have become divorced from their natural environment to the extent that their contact with the outside world is limited both practically by security devices and psychologically by social taboo. Indeed its citizens have even divorced themselves from 'natural' biology since they spend much of their time dormant, embedded in the city's memory banks (which form the very fabric of the city itself) to be given flesh only periodically. The book's protagonist, Alvin, is a Unique: that is, he is an artificial creation, a permutation possibly of a number of individuals, but one created by the memory banks (not 'natural' DNA). Alvin becomes curious of the world beyond the city, so tries to determine why everyone is so afraid of the outside and escape. The novel contains many SF tropes that have only become commonplace within the genre in recent years. Diaspar's citizens regularly hold what we now call cyberspace conferences and use what is now termed cyberspace. Arthur Clarke himself has noted that the book has been continuously in print for over 30 years since its original publication and has been included in, he says, "all the lists of best science fiction novels.

(Examples to the contrary will not be welcome)." Who are we to disagree? *City and the Stars* was voted into the top 20 in the *Concatenation* book poll. *Against the Fall of Night* was reprinted in 1991 in a single volume along with a sequel novella by **Gregory Benford** called *Beyond the Fall of Night*. Benford then expanded the themes in his own novel of human far-future, *Beyond Infinity*, in 2004. (*City and the Stars* continuity note: prologue no mountains; chapter 10, mountains.)

Clarke, Arthur C. – author, UK (*b*1917). Clarke was born in Minehead, Somerset, and is a graduate of King's College, London, where he obtained a 1st class honours degree in Physics and Mathematics. Although credited with the invention of the communications satellite in 1945, it is perhaps more accurate to say that it was he who first *conceived* the system, as there seems little evidence that he actually *invented* anything. He sold his first short story, *Rescue Mission*, in 1946 to *Astounding* (see *Analog*) magazine, which was about an intergalactic fleet of aliens aiding a fleet of humans escaping their dying sun, only to have their achievements surpassed by the refugees. After World War II Clarke became an active member of the London SF Circle and its monthly meetings in the White Hart pub. This was the inspiration of his much loved (by fans) collection of shorts *Tales From the White Hart* (1957). Although seen, with **Asimov** and **Heinlein**, as one of the 'Big Three' SF authors, Clarke didn't really come to prominence until the release of the film ***2001: A Space Odyssey***, directed by Stanley (see **Brian Aldiss**, *A Clockwork Orange* and *Dr Strangelove*) Kubrick, in 1968, which won the Hugo for Best Dramatic Presentation in 1969, and came 2nd in the *Concatenation* poll for Best SF Film. It is perhaps unsurprising that Clarke joined Walter Cronkite during CBS' coverage of the Apollo moon landing that year. Perhaps Clarke's best early novel was *Childhood's End* (1953), in which powerful aliens conquer the Earth in order to 'nursemaid' us through the next stage in our evolution. Evolution was revisited in ***The City and the Stars*** (1956), though this was itself a reworking of the earlier *Against the Fall of Night* (1942), and was placed joint 9th in the *Concatenation* readers' poll for Best SF novel (also see **Gregory Benford**). In the same poll, Clarke was the fourth most cited author, reflecting his popularity over several decades. ***Rendezvous with Rama*** (1973) won a plethora of awards, as did ***The Fountains of Paradise*** (1979), but Clarke's work since then, while still selling well, is considered to be below the standards set by his earlier work. Part of this is due to his poor sequels to ***2001***: *2010* (1982) (the film of which won a Hugo for Best Dramatic Presentation in 1985), *2061* (1988), and *3001* (1997); and is partly due to his unimaginative collaborative sequels, with Gentry Lee, to ***Rendezvous with Rama***, including *Rama II* (1989), *The Garden of Rama* (1991), and *Rama Revealed* (1993). Clarke made a 13-part series for Yorkshire Television, *Arthur C. Clarke's Mysterious World*, made with a Fortean sensibility, but this also dented Clarke's reputation somewhat, as he was (erroneously) seen as a scientist 'selling out' to superstition. Whatever the reason for the perceived fall in the quality of Clarke's output, he has remained one of the best-selling SF authors, and is still cited as a founding father of modern SF as well as a populariser of science fact, both with the greatest respect. He is currently a resident of Sri Lanka, where he continues to write and, up to the 1990s, to indulge his passion for scuba diving.

Clement, Hal – author, US (1920-2003). Few writers in the first few decades after World War II produced SF stories as hard as did Hal Clement (real name Harry Clement Stubbs), but then he did study chemistry and astronomy at college. His best stories were those where the science springs from his tales' settings: unlike much other **hard SF** where it arises from technology. **Mission of Gravity** (1954) is typical of this, where a high gravity world (or is it a dead proto-star?) has near normal gravity around the equator due to the centrifugal reaction from the planet's high rotation rate. *Ocean on Top* (1973) takes place in the high pressure depths of the sea, *Close to Critical* (1964) in the midst of high pressure atmosphere, and *Iceworld* (1953) on Earth... but the Earth as viewed from a high-temperature alien visitor to the Solar system who prefers the more hospitable warmth of Mercury for its base camp. Indeed *Iceworld* exhibits the second theme that runs through much of Clement's work, that of viewing life from an alien perspective while taking us along for the ride. In *Needle* (1950), and its sequel *Through the Eye of a Needle* (1978), this literally happens to the young protagonist who is half of a symbiotic relationship with a sentient and beneficent alien parasite who is in fact a cop after a fugitive. ***Mission of Gravity's*** sequel is *Star Light* (1971), and the novel also incorporates characters from *Close to Critical* (1964). Hal Clement was one of the Guests of Honour at the 1991 World SF Convention (Chicago).

Clockwork Orange, A – film, GB/US (1971), *dir*. Stanley (see **Brian Aldiss**, *2001 A Space Odyssey* and *Dr Strangelove*) Kubrick. Based on the US edition of the 1962 book of the same name by Anthony Burgess. Set in the near future, a sadistic young thug, Alex (Malcolm McDowell), is caught following a burglary and the murder of an upper-middle class woman. Alex is then brainwashed by the authorities in a Pavlovian way to feel nauseous at the thought of violence. Unfortunately he also (accidentally(?)) becomes allergic to the 'incidental' background classical music (Beethoven's 9th he used to love) being played while receiving his Pavlovian conditioning. This aversion was just one symptom of the protagonist being unable to cope with life's trials immediately after his 'therapy'. Filmed in SE London, soon after its release real young London thugs began to imitate the characters in the film who had their own identifiable dress code. This reaction combined with a 'tabloid' media outcry resulted in Kubrick withdrawing his film from UK distribution. Burgess himself was unhappy with the film, though not with Kubrick who faithfully followed the US edition's plot. However the original UK edition had an extra chapter which (according to Burgess in a 1998 BBC Radio 4 broadcast (*Kaleidoscope* 28th March)) Kubrick had never read. As to why the US edition was shorter, this was the American publisher's idea: a demand Burgess acquiesced to at the time because he 'needed the money', and which he has regretted ever since. Nonetheless *A Clockwork Orange*, typical of Kubrick films (and indeed other of Burgess' work), is a powerful offering with considerable social poignancy. It won the Hugo Award in 1972 for Best Dramatic Presentation.

Close Encounters of the Third Kind – film, US (1977), *dir.* Steven (see also **Brian Aldiss**, *Jurassic Park*, *The Twilight Zone*, *Raiders of the Lost Ark*, and *Indiana Jones and the Last Crusade*) Spielberg. Investigating UFO sightings, scientists (François Truffaut (director of *Fahrenheit 451*) and Bob Balaban) intercept an alien message giving the co-ordinates for a rendezvous. Meanwhile an electrical worker, (Richard Dreyfuss), and mother and artist (Melinda Dillon) are compelled to make representations of a mountain in Wyoming following sightings of their own. His obsession loses him his wife (Terri Garr) and family, and her son is abducted by aliens. Together they make for the rendezvous site, cordoned off with tight security, and a close encounter they will never forget. 1977 gave us both *CE3K* and

Star Wars, among others, and both were extremely popular for quite different reasons. *CE3K* won two Oscars; one for cinematography by Vilmos Zsigmund, and a Special Achievement Award for Frank Warner for sound effects editing. It was nominated for seven more, including Spielberg as director, Dillon for Best Supporting Actress, and the special effects team, including Douglas Trumbull and both Richard and Matthew Yuricich. However, *Star Wars* took seven Oscars, ironically including John Williams for musical score, who could have won for either film! Principal cast: Melinda Dillon, Richard Dreyfuss, Terri Garr, Cary Guffey and François Truffaut. Note: A 'director's cut' was later released. It was slightly longer and included shots inside the mother ship, however a scene of the electrical worker constructing a model of the mountain landing site in his living room was lost.

Clubs, SF. (see also **Conventions, Fandom, Fan Funds**). There are numerous SF clubs across Europe and in the States. Some are traditional 'fan' clubs for SF authors and TV shows with a postal membership. Of these arguably those devoted to the various TV shows such as *Star Trek* are the most numerous. Others consist of local groups and there are those 'devoted' to an interest in SF books and films. However it has to be said that local book and film clubs in the West tend to be as much informal gatherings of like-minded individuals in a public house (mainly in the UK) or cafe (mainly in the US) with meetings that often barely touch on the subject matter that brings its members together. In Eastern Europe the clubs are more formal and (especially prior to the collapse of communism) more focused around its members' amateur writing and art productions. A number of clubs are also associated with universities: for instance in the US at MIT and in the UK at Hertfordshire and Cambridge to mention just a couple out of numerous examples that have been around longer than a couple of decades. It has to be said that the membership of SF clubs varies and some may not be to your taste. Clubs also vary in their activities and size: for instance in the UK the large Birmingham SF group (*www.bsfg.freeserve.com*) regularly organises the major *Novacon* convention (in November) and produces a newsletter (or 'clubzine') *Brum Group News*. Each SF club has its own characteristics, interests and range of activities. So if your region sports a number of groups it is worth checking each of them out —the one you end up preferring may not be your closest. One of the best ways to find out about which clubs exist is to ask at your local SF specialist bookshop (if you have one) or attend your country's national SF (book and film) convention or to search out the club home pages on the InterNet (see **Fandom**). Failing this in the US you could take out a classified advert in *Locus* and/or *SF Chronicle* and in the UK in *Interzone* and/or *SFX* magazine. A number of UK clubs are hot-linked with the *Ansible* home page on the web, which itself regularly lists forthcoming UK conventions (of all types) and world conventions as well as news of where the historic London SF Circle (mainly a book and UK Eastercon related gathering but also of broader goings-on) currently meets on the first Thursday of the month.

Clute, John – encyclopædist and critic, Ca/UK (*b*1940). Canadian born, but living in the UK since 1969, John Clute is currently the foremost SF critic in Britain. His SF book reviews have appeared in a number of broadsheet newspapers and magazines both in the UK and US, but he has always been involved with the UK SF community and was one of *Interzone's* founders in 1982 as well as being *Foundation's* reviews editor (*cf*. **SF Foundation**) between 1980 and 1990. For a period in the 1980s he was a tutor for London's City Lit SF course (past alumni thereof – the City Illiterates – still gather early Friday evenings in central London to swap news); half of its students were themselves highly active within the British SF community (many intitially with the BECCON (and its **Eastercon**) conventions). John Clute is most respected by SF enthusiasts for his work as an SF encylopædist and, in 1994, with **Peter Nicholls**, he won a 'Non-Fiction' category Hugo for *The Encyclopedia of Science Fiction* (2nd revised edition) which still remains the genre's most complete reference work. (The first edition of which also won a non-fiction Hugo in 1980 which went to Nicholls as its principal editor.) In 1995 his own *Science Fiction: The Illustrated Encyclopedia* was published. Both these encyclopaedias are highly recommended and representative of Anglophone SF especially in its written form (as opposed to this guide which is a genre distillation). In 1998 he again shared a Hugo, this time with John Grant, for the *Encyclopedia of Fantasy*.

Colossus: The Forbin Project – film, US (1969) *dir.* Joseph Sargent. Colossus is the brainchild of Dr. Charles Forbin (Eric

Braeden), a supercomputer that will take over the free world's nuclear defences. Immediately upon activation Colossus informs its creators that there is another system, Guardian, and it controls the Soviet stockpiles. The two systems merge and, through nuclear blackmail and terror tactics, take over the planet. Forbin is given the task of stopping them. Based on D.F. Jones' *Colossus* (1966), this is a faithful and slickly-scripted film, courtesy of James Bridges' screenplay. Colossus could easily be seen as an ancestor to ***The Terminator***'s genocidal computer, Skynet, and even at the time, release of the film was delayed in the wake of the success of ***2001***, with the murderous HAL9000. *Colossus* also starred Susan Clark as Forbin's girlfriend and contact to the joint chiefs of staff, Gordon Pinsent, William Schallert, Leonid Rostoff, and George Stanford Brown. Jones wrote two further novels, *The Fall of Colossus* (1974) and *Colossus and the Crab* (1977), which were much weaker than the first, but are still quite readable.

Comic-con International – The major comics **convention** in the US since 1970. Tens of thousands attend. It is usually held in California and regularly has SF and film guests as well as those from the world of comics and graphic novels. Web site: *www.comic-con.org*. See also **Eisner, Will**.

Concatenation, The Science Fact & Fiction – formerly semi-prozine **fanzine** (*crtd*1987). First published as part of the BECCON 50th anniversary of the world's first SF convention **Eastercon**, its annual reviews sought to encourage science within SF and to build bridges between the then two UK Easter conventions. However by the mid-1990s desktop publishing had raised normal production standards so high – notwithstanding that UK national conventions increasingly had a science programme stream – that the editors sought new ways of being innovative. By 1999 it went electronic at *www.concatenation.org* and currently its team regularly engages in special SF projects (such as this guide). The *SF & F Concatenation* has twice won the MacIntyre Award at the UK national **Eastercon** with artist Jim Porter (the award is given both to the artist for his art and the magazine for its production standards in reproducing the said artwork). It has also thrice won the European Award at **Eurocons** in 1994 and 1997 for multi-lingual editions, as well as 2004 for its services to the European SF community. However these alone would not quite warrant its entry's inclusion in this guide, and there are many other more worthy **fanzines**, but as this guide occasionally refers to the *Concatenation* polls we thought you would appreciate some background. (See also **Fan Funds**.)

Contact – novel (1985) by Carl Sagan. It is comparatively rare to find scientists writing good SF (which is not surprising really, as their primary skills and focus is science and not the art of literary communication). However it is possible to find those with both areas of expertise. Carl Sagan was one such person. His academic credentials were many. He was a professor of Astronomy and Space Sciences at Cornell University where he served as the Director of the Laboratory for Planetary Studies at the Centre for Radiophysics and Space Research. He was a communicator and his 1970s popular science TV series *Cosmos* won an Emmy Award. Many scientists have an interest in SF (roughly a quarter, if the polls are truly representative, were inspired by SF to study science). With *Contact* Carl Sagan explored that common question between many SF buffs and space scientists of the existence of extra terrestrial intelligence. Plot premise: An astronomer overcomes sexist prejudice and ridicule in her belief in alien intelligence to carve out a career as a SETI (search for extra-terrestrial intelligence) scientist. Then one day she detects a signal from space which says 'build a device'... and so she and the governments of the world do... and it works... However the book is not just about contacting extra terrestrial intelligence, but also about the relationship between science and religion (specifically, faith). *Contact* came top of the annual *Locus* readers top ten poll in the 'first novel' category. It was also made into a film (1997) *dir.* Robert (***Back to the Future***, ***Who Framed Roger Rabbit?***) Zemeckis, starring Jodie Foster, and Matthew McConaughey, with John (***Alien***, ***Frankenstein*** - films) Hurt, Tom Skerritt and Angela Bassett. Since Carl Sagan co-wrote the original story line and co-produced the film it is fairly faithful to the novel. However there is only so much that one can pack into a two hour production and much of the philosophy of science from the novel was lost. Nonetheless the film won the Hugo in 1998 for Best Dramatic Presentation. Regrettably Sagan died before the film was completed but it was dedicated to him.

Conventions (see also **Australasia, Clubs, European SF Convention, Eastercon, UK, US,** and **World SF Convention**). As **Brian Aldiss** once commented, in days of old kings would hold feasts for their most loyal subjects; today SF conventions are grand celebrations organised by volunteer fans for the genre's writers. The first SF convention publicly held (as opposed to being in a private home) was in Leeds, Britain, on the 3rd of January 1937. Today SF conventions are held in many countries and while they may vary considerably, in the main they have in common a meeting of fans with professional authors and film directors (or, in the case of TV show conventions, actors). In the US, UK and Western Europe, conventions tend to have a party atmosphere. They are a celebration of SF where a couple of hundred to a few thousand fans gather in a hotel to listen to talks and such on a set programme amid a sea of conversation in bars and coffee rooms. The largest convention is the **World SF Convention** (**Worldcon**).

> Australia – Details can be obtained through the Friends of SF (a general interest club) P O Box 797, Farfred, NSW 1860, Australia. *www.fsf.com.au* and *www.vicnet.au/~sfoz* and Australia's SF 'Bullsheet' on *http://members.optushome.com.au/aussfbull*.
>
> France – Has held a national convention (natcon) each year since 1974 though on occasions they have been held in neighbouring Switzerland and Belgium. An international SF festival 'Utopiales' has also been held in some recent years. *http://sf.emse.fr*
>
> Germany – Has had a natcon, the SFCD cons run under the auspices of the German Science Fiction Club (SFCD) which itself began in 1955 and among whose founding members is the author Raymond Z. Gallun. *www.dsfp.de*
>
> Italy – Has held an annual national convention, the Italcon, since the 1972 Trieste **Eurocon**, details of which can be found on *www.fantascienza.com/italcon/*.
>
> Japan – A convention listing can be found on *www.mmjp.org.jp/sfmra/db/events*
>
> Norway – Has held a Norcon, its national convention (natcon) each year since 1975 and is Northern Europe's longest running series of conventions. See *www.norcon.fandom.no/english.html*. 'Scancons' have occasionally been held in each of the Scandanavian countries.

United Kingdom and Ireland – A listing is maintained on *www.smof.com/conlist.htm* as well as published in ***Ansible*** on *www.dcs.gla.ac.uk/SF-Archives/Ansible/amsilink.html* or *www.ansible.demon.co.uk*

United States – The semi-prozine *SF Chronicle* features a regular listing. SF Chronicle, PO Box 022730, Brooklyn NY 11202 0056, United States, as does ***Locus*** magazine. *www.locusmag.com*

Other countries – A convention listing is given in the *Fans Across the World* newsletter on *www.dcs.gla.ac.uk/SF-Archives/Fatw*. Alternatively ***Concatenation*** maintains a diary of national and regional/specialist SF conventions with an international dimension on *www.concatenation.org*

Convention reviews can be found in many places (and many conventions have their own promotional web sites) but check out *www.ansible.demon.co.uk* and *www.concatenation.org* as well as in ***Locus*** magazine. See **Fandom** for web-based convention calendars and sources of news. Those wishing to organise conventions can find useful advice on *www.smof.com/conrunner/* the archive of Ian Sorensen's late 1980s fanzine.

Convergent Series – *col.* (1979) by **Larry Niven**. There are two essential collections of Larry Niven short stories, *Tales from Known Space* (1975) and *Convergent Series* (1979). *Convergent Series* contains a range of stories with only one or two connected to his 'Known Space' universe. However all are either hard SF, or have a scientific logic underpinning them. The title story itself is one of the latter; a fantasy when a demon sets out to entrap the protagonist, but in turn gets caught in a mathematical series. The collection also contains one of Niven's noted tales, *Bordered in Black*, in which a space craft reaches a world low on food and high on people. In addition the collection features five stories centred around Draco's Tavern—Larry Niven's equivalent of **Clarke's** *Tales From The White Hart,* but instead of being a contemporary Earth bar whose patrons are sort of SF fans and boffins, Niven's bar is located in a spaceport and whose patrons include aliens. *Convergent Series* was voted top of the *Locus* readers annual poll in the 'single author collection' category.

Creature from the Black Lagoon – film, US (1954), *dir.* Jack (***The Incredible Shrinking Man***, ***It Came From Outer Space***) Arnold. An expedition up the Amazon gets trapped in a small backwater (not a lagoon in the true geographical sense). It turns out that the barricade has been put in place by a member (last survivor(?)) of a pre-human species who is attracted to the expedition's sole female member. The film does generate a certain tension and did spawn a sequel (which briefly features a very young Clint Eastwood) as well as a 3-D version and this (surprisingly—but we suspect because of the 3-D) has been the most popular film of all, in terms of number of viewers *and* repeat requests, at the Festival of Fantastic Films.

Crichton, Michael – author and film director, US (*b*1942). Born in Chicago, Crichton graduated from Harvard College and Harvard Medical School. He paid for his medical training by writing thrillers under pseudonyms (*eg.* John Lange and Jeffrey Hudson), but turned to full time writing after the publication of his first SF novel under his own name, ***The Andromeda Strain*** (1969). Sold for an amazing $250,000, the book became the first of many bestsellers, and was filmed in 1971 by Robert (***The Day the Earth Stood Still, Star Trek: The Motion Picture***) Wise, starring Arthur Hill, James Olson, Kate Reid, and David Wayne. A space probe returns to Earth carrying a deadly organism, which threatens to become a plague of biblical proportions. Secured in a lab below the desert, a specially created team of scientists race to understand the microbe before it can escape. Crichton presents his fiction in factual, almost documentary, terms and frequently includes graphs, charts and illustrations with his text—a trick often utilised by those who adapt his work for the big screen. He continued in this style for his next book, *The Terminal Man* (1971), which became a film in 1974, written, produced and directed by Mike Hodges, starring George Segal and Joan Hackett. In this, a man prone to violent behaviour during brain seizures caused by a car crash has a device implanted in his brain to control his outbreaks. Unfortunately the brain becomes addicted to the implant's stimulus, and he quickly loses control. In 1973, Crichton made his debut as director with ***Westworld***, for which he wrote the screenplay. In a futuristic theme park populated by robots, things start to go wrong, with the gunslinger (Yul Brynner) hunting the tourist (Richard Benjamin). Crichton has often been criticised for writing "Frankenstein" fiction, where the scientists and technologists are misguided, if not completely evil. However, Crichton himself states that his fiction is merely 'cautionary', and that he is not against science *per se*, but against the misapplication of science by political, military and corporate interests. In *Congo* (1980), a gorilla who uses sign language accompanies a corporate team looking for gems in Africa, who discover instead a lost tribe of killer apes. The corporate greed angle is nicely played up in the film version. In 1985 Crichton returned to the theme of technology run amok, directing Tom Selleck and Kirstie (***Star Trek II***) Alley in *Runaway*, where a branch of the police force has been founded purely to deal with mechanical devices that have slipped their programming. Usually this happens accidentally, but in this case the runaways are being controlled by a blackmailing villain, played totally tongue-in-cheek by Gene Simmons of the band Kiss. Crichton's only book dealing with an overtly extraterrestrial intelligence was *Sphere* (1987), later filmed (1998) starring Dustin Hoffman, Sharon Stone, Samuel L. Jackson and Peter Coyote, *dir*. Barry Levinson. A crashed alien craft is found under the sea, and a scientific and military team is sent down to investigate. As will by now be apparent, things quickly go wrong as humans, not yet ready for it, accidentally misuse the alien technology of the sphere—a device for making thoughts into reality. As though Crichton's career had not been successful enough, in 1990 he wrote ***Jurassic Park***, filmed in 1993 by Steven (see also **Brian Aldiss**, ***Close Encounters of the Third Kind***, ***Jurassic Park***, ***The Twilight Zone***, ***Raiders of the Lost Ark***, and ***Indiana Jones and the Last Crusade***) Spielberg. Both book and film were phenomenal successes. Once again the story is set in a theme park made possible by science, in this case by cloning dinosaurs from DNA fragments recovered from insects in amber. However, gaps in the DNA sequence are filled using genes from species that can change gender under particular environmental pressures while, at the same time, a corporate spy is trying to steal the sequences of several dinosaur species from his employer. The film, starring Richard Attenborough, Jeff (***The Fly***) Goldblum, and Sam Neill, won a Hugo in 1994 for Best Dramatic Presentation, and was followed by a sequel based on Crichton's novel *The Lost World* (1995), also starring Jeff Goldblum and Julianna Moore, and *Jurassic Park III* (2003) starring Sam Neil.

Crouching Tiger, Hidden Dragon – film, China/ Hong Kong/US (2000), *dir*. Ang Lee. The theft of a prized sword is all the excuse needed for a spectacular martial arts romp as a nobleman's daughter sets out to prove she is as good a fighter as any other. With characters skimming roof tops, defying gravity and running along walls the film is one visual feast of gymnastics. Science fiction? No. Fantasy? Yes. Which, due to the World Science Fiction Society's constitution (the spirit of which is to allow works of science fantasy), enabled this film to be nominated for the Hugo Award which it won in 2001 for 'Best Dramatic Presentation': and as Hugo winning is one of the criterion for listing films in this guide, here you have it.

Cryptonomicon, The – novel (1999) by Neil Stephenson. Cryptology underpins a plot that alternates back and forth between World War II and the present day and focuses on a number of characters. These include: Lawrence Pritchard Waterhouse, a mild-mannered midwesterner who hangs out at Princeton with Alan Turing and whose mathematical genius is discovered by the military; Bobby Shaftoe, the unkillable, pain-killer ridden China Marine who sent on top secret missions; and Randall Lawrence Waterhouse (Lawrence's grandson) a computer nerd who helps found the Epiphyte Corporation in the present day. *The Cryptonomicon* came top of the *Locus* poll for best novel in 2000.

Crystal World, **The** – novel (1966) by **J G Ballard**. Of all Ballard's novels this one, arguably, contains the most startling imagery. The collision of matter and anti-matter at the galactic core has begun to use up the galaxy's time store. As a result, all matter in an area of West Africa has turned into crystal. Sanders, a doctor in a hospital for victims of leprosy, journeys into the heart of the crystal realm. As he moves deeper and deeper into this world, he encounters more bizarre expressions of the phenomena. Humans become enshrouded in a kind of crystal armour. At one point he encounters a completely crystallised crocodile with jewelled eyes. All around him Sanders finds people who are quite literally becoming part of the environment. As always with Ballard this isn't simply a journey across the geographical landscape. He examines the way in which people are actually drawn towards this strange phenomena, and how some of them even see this disaster as their salvation.

Cyberpunk – a specialist sub-genre in which computer technology and cyberspace are employed by streetwise (anti- or not-of-the establishment) protagonists.

Cyteen – novel (1988) by **C J Cherryh**. *Cyteen* is set in her Alliance-Union universe (as is ***Downbelow Station***) and is the name of the central Union planet (the Union being the collective of Earth colonies). In a drive to build the most powerful industrial base off of Earth (and so secure greater independence) the Union give considerable political power to Cyteen's research community and their bio-engineering labs. With the aid of artificially generated humans, which require programming with 'tape', the growth of industry progresses rapidly, despite the uneasy relationship between the artificial and the natural humans. Controlling the scientific community is the brilliant, and ruthless, 120 year old Ariane Emory. But when she is murdered a genetic double is brought into being, and with the ability to transfer experience being developed, it looked like she would rise from the dead to inherit a scientific and political empire... *Cyteen* is many things and is both a detailed description of a techno-colony as well as an exploration of nature *vs* nurture. *Cyteen* won the Hugo for Best Novel in 1989 and came top of the *Locus* annual readers top ten poll.

Dan Dare – comic character, UK (*crtd*1950). Though in print in one form or another every decade since its creation, Dan Dare is primarily associated with the comic ***Eagle*** in the 1950s and 60s. He was an astronaut game for any adventure in true 'British' style. He was colourfully brought to life by Frank Hampson (1918-1985) in an optimistic world of mid-twentieth century standards set in the 21st. He was not a super hero. He had no super powers. He was simply 'Dan Dare – Pilot of the future' who was often found with his side-kick Digby battling an evil Venusian, The Mekon. His weekly adventures were the mainstay of the original *Eagle* through to 1969. Keith Watson took over drawing the strip from Frank Hampson in 1962; but fortunately his style was very similar to Hampson's and the magic continued until the *Eagle's* 1969 demise (also see **Gerry Anderson**). Dare briefly reappeared and re-vamped – having spent years in suspended animation – in ***2000AD*** in 1977 (again to battle the longer life-spanned Mekon). He also returned as his great great grandson (again drawn by Keith Watson) along with a descendent of Digby in a re-launched *Eagle* in March 1983. Then in 1989 the 'original' Dan Dare returned to the *Eagle* drawn by Watson and survived until 1994. Juvenile SF certainly, but picturesque, fun and pure SF nostalgia. (See also ***Jeff Hawke***.) A version of Dare appeared in a political satire, *Dare*, by Grant Morrison, published in *2000AD*'s sister-mag *Revolver* for a more adult readership. A children's TV computer animation series entitled *Dan Dare* (*fb* 2002) was created by Colin Frewin and conveyed an image vaguely reminiscent of the original graphic strip though noticeably Digby did not have his Yorkshire accent.

Dark Star – film, US (1974), *dir*. John (***The Thing***) Carpenter. In addition to directing, Carpenter also co-wrote this little gem with Dan (***Alien***) O'Bannon. Made on an absolute shoestring with its origins as a student film, the Dark Star is a four-man starship whose mission is to clear the Galaxy of planets in unstable orbits. Unfortunately in the course of their three year mission the crew become unhinged. The ship has had an accident in which the captain became injured and had to be placed in quasi-suspended animation, while much of the ship became uninhabitable (so providing the rationale for using bits of corridor and the occasional closet as sets). This hilarious black comedy, that sends up much sci-fi, provides a gritty counter to the polished portrayals of gleaming future technology found in many genre productions. Carpenter went on to make other SF box office hits such as *Escape From New York* (1981), and *They Live* (1988). *Dark Star's* alien hunt scene—despite the extraterrestrial being a beach ball with glove hands—is rumoured to have inspired the 1979 ***Alien*** classic, though Dan O'Bannon may well have been in turn inspired by a story from **A.E. van Vogt**. *Dark Star* came 3rd in the *Concatenation* all-time film poll.

Day the Earth Stood Still, The – film, US (1951), *dir*. Robert (*Star Trek The Motion Picture*, ***The Andromeda Strain***) Wise. Based on Harry Bates' classic *Farewell to the Master* (1940), this is the film that brought the memorable phrase, "Klaatu barada nikto" to the world. A flying saucer sets down in Washington and an alien and a huge robot emerge and are promptly shot at by the US army. Klaatu (Michael Rennie) therefore decides that a more cautious approach is advised, and poses as an Earthman at a boarding-house, where he meets Earthwoman Patricia Neal, who helps him to contact society's intellectuals. For these people he has a message; cease your destructive ways or face annihilation by the Galactic Federation! Considering the climate in the post-war McCarthy era for Hollywood, and the blatant use of a Christ-like 'resurrection' figure, it is a wonder that this film ever saw the light of day. But it did make it. It went on to box office success and is justly hailed as a classic of the SF genre. *The Day the Earth Stood Still*, though certainly a product of its time is, nonetheless, timeless in the sense that it is still culturally relevant today. It is a popular choice at the Festival of Fantastic Films, and also made it into the top 20 of the *Concatenation* all-time top SF films readers' poll and third in the Blackwood/Flynn poll of WSFS members for the top ten SF films.

Day of the Triffids, The – novel (1951). *The Day of the Triffids* is perhaps **John Wyndham's** most famous book. Set in the near future, a man wakes up in a hospital after eye treatment and takes off his bandages to find the rest of humanity blinded (by lights from the previous night's meteor storm). However, stalking the sightless population are strange, moving, man-eating plants—the Triffids. The few who can see can rule the world if, that is, they can win in their fight against the Triffids to survive. Wyndham's story explores the fate of society with its supporting infra-structure undermined and mankind's thin veneer of civilization removed. As for the Triffids themselves, Wyndham's writing successfully conveys real menace, unlike the 1963 film by writer/producer Philip Yordan; though the 1981 BBC TV drama series was more faithful. As for the original 1950s novel, it has stood the test of time in that, apart from a few anachronisms, it could have been written today. *The Day of the Triffids* is one of the few SF books to have been accepted by mainstream literary critics.

Deepness in the Sky, A – novel (1999) by **Vernor Vinge**. Although billed as a 'prequel' to the 1994 Hugo Award-winning *A Fire Upon the Deep* (1993), this is in fact merely set in the same 'universe'. The Qeng Ho trading fleet pick up radio transmissions from a planet thought uninhabited (since its On/Off sun is dim for 235 years and 'alight' for only 15 years at a time), and decide to go there to trade with whomever they find. However, the Emergents (an independent 'hard' technology alliance) have the same idea. Both expeditions arrive together and initially agree to co-operate to exploit the planet which appears deserted, although it has many traces of civilization. The inhabitants, known as Spiders, hibernate in underground 'deepnesses' during their sun's dim phase and are only now awakening, but are in the midst of a war of their own... *A Deepness in the Sky* won the Best Novel Hugo in 2000.

Demolished Man, The – novel (1953) by **Alfred Bester**. Alfred (working class) Bester, as he liked to be known at the 1987 World SF convention at which he was a Guest of Honour, has an established reputation within the SF community. His 1953 Hugo Novel winner *The Demolished Man* is his most acknowledged work (but see also ***Tiger! Tiger!***). It concerns one Ben Reich, head of Monarch Utilities and Resources. Having risked everything in a last-ditch take-over bid of the massive D'Courtney Cartel, only murder, bribery and blackmail are left. However, the 24th century police have peepers on their side, trained telepaths with a sense of family and a strict ethical code (see also ***Babylon 5***). What Ben Reich needs is a corrupt peeper on his side, but then he has his own nature to contend with, and his own fears of a faceless man. As if this were not enough there was always the risk of telepathic demolition...

Desolation Road – novel (1988) by Ian McDonald. McDonald's rich style and ability to string together a series of well-crafted vignettes was ideally married, in this instance, to this tale of a Martian settlement's history from its founding to its end. Along the way we meet such characters as Adam Black's Wonderful Travelling Chautaqua and Educational Extravaganza, The Greatest Snooker Player the Universe has Ever Seen, and The Amazing Scorn Master of Scintillating Sarcasm and Rapid Repartee. The work is powerful and great fun. It does not take itself too seriously but is nonetheless an ingeniously woven tapestry. *Desolation Road* came top of the *Locus* annual readers poll in the 'first novel' category.

Destination Moon – film, US (1950), *dir*. Irving Pichel. Based on the juvenile novel by **Robert Heinlein**. Arguably the cinema's first attempt to portray space travel in, what was then thought, a realistic way. During the journey to the Moon the astronauts experience zero G: one even floats off and has to be rescued. And there was the, now clichéd, tension towards the end when it is discovered that there may not be enough fuel to get them home.

Destination Moon is more notable for its historic place in SF cinema than for any inherent SF content. Indeed it was a sign of the times that the *raison d'être* for going to the Moon was to prevent the Nazis from taking it over as a missile base. Things, though, could have been much worse. Heinlein fought for control of the script and successfully thwarted a version that had hillbilly songs on the Moon. This, and the contributions of rocket expert Hermann Oberth, enabled *Destination Moon* to take the cinema away from the **Flash Gordon** and **Buck Rogers** type of early space opera towards a harder kind of SF. The Hugos began in 1953, however at the 2001 Worldcon there was also a vote for the '1951 Retro Hugos'. As part of this nostalgic exercise *Destination Moon* was voted for Best Dramatic presentation.

Diamond Age, The – novel (1995) by Neal Stephenson. Late in the 21st century nations have been superseded by enclaves of common cultures (claves). A nanoengineer is commissioned by one of the world's most powerful men to create (an illegal) interactive primer to teach the wealthy man's daughter to think for herself. Alas, before the primer can be delivered, it is stolen and falls into the hands of a working-class girl. She now has knowledge to affect the future of world events. *The Diamond Age* won the Hugo for Best Novel in 1996.

Diaspora – novel (1997). Ultra **hard SF** writer **Greg Egan** charts the far future of 'mankind'. It is the story of Yatima, an electronic intelligence 'born' in the year 2975 within a polis (a glorified computer bank) in which reside down-loaded humans and other 'artificial' human intelligences (AIs). Occupying the real world there are a range of humans from what we would call normal to the heavily genetically modified. And then there are the gleisner android robots. After Yatima has had a chance to briefly explore this future Earth, a gamma ray burst wreaks eco-catastrophe on the planet. And so the polis clones itself to go exploring among the stars where its citizens encounter even stranger life forms. At the time of writing, *Diaspora* was both Greg Egan's best and worst work . It was stunning in its breadth of vision, much of which Egan released from the earlier short story *Wangs Carpets* (also published in **Greg Bear's** (editor) *New Legends* (1995) anthology). Its weaknesses are that it is so incredibly rich in concepts that one's sense-of-wonder palate is almost dulled, and all the more so due to the lack of its protagonists' characterization; which itself is ironic given the diversity of human life portrayed. Nonetheless, despite *Diaspora's* flaws, the tapestry Egan presents is grand and he does take the AI SF trope that little bit further than his contemporaries.

Dick, Philip K – author, US (1928-1982). It is sometimes said that true genius is tinged with a touch of insanity. Philip K Dick may or may not have been insane but he was in the end a tortured soul, convinced, as he was in his final years, that he reportedly was receiving messages from higher beings. Much of his work walks the dividing line between reality and illusion but furthermore transposes, blurring, them so that reality is illusion and *vice-versa*. Such elements even survive to show themselves in the inevitably poorer, but nonetheless highly entertaining, film adaptations of his works. In ***Blade Runner*** (based on ***Do Androids Dream of Electric Sheep?*** (1968), a work of excellence in itself) the blurring is between who are replicants (androids) and who are true humans, while in ***Total Recall*** (1990) the question the protagonist repeatedly faces is which life of his is real, which a recreational program dream and which a maliciously placed memory implant? Or his novels, for example, *Time Out of Joint* (1959) in which the central character continually swaps between a life in 1959 and one in 1999. While Jason Taverner in *Flow My Tears the Policeman Said* (1974) wakes up to find himself not a TV personality with a regular 30 million audience, but that no one remembers him and his ID and credit cards have gone! Often Dick sees the humorous side of such uncertainty, albeit with a dark tinge. In *The Man Who Japed* (1956), his third novel, the protagonist is a law-abiding citizen content within a benign kind of right-wing state, when he discovers that while asleep he has been committing acts of vandalism against symbols of the said state; acts he would not normally 'dream' of doing. Such themes aside, Dick's career was a mix of producing classic masterpiece SF, such as ***Do Androids Dream of Electric Sheep*** and ***The Man in the High Castle*** (1962) with more workman-like, but very good-read, novels like *Vulcan's Hammer* (1960), concerning a supreme computer with a mind of its own, as well as ideas for the human race) and *The Game Players of Titan* (1963, about a gambler who plays against aggressive aliens with the Earth as the stake). ***Blade Runner*** in 1983 won the Hugo for Best Dramatic Presentation, while ***The Man in the High Castle*** won the Hugo for Best Novel in 1963. The novel ***Do Androids Dream of***

Electric Sheep came joint 8th in the *Concatenation* all-time poll, while Philip K Dick himself was the second most nominated author (across many titles) in the same poll. He died in 1982. Collectors' note: The Dick short story collection *Second Variety* has been reprinted and retitled as *We Can Remember It For You Wholesale*, while the collection *The Little Black Box* has also been reprinted and retitled *We Can Remember It For You Wholesale*. The title story of *Second Variety* provided the basis for the film *Screamers* (1995) *dir*. Christian Duguay, starring Peter (***RoboCop***) Weller and concerning a robotic arms race on a far off planet by the mechanical screamers against the warring humans. Dick's 1956 short story *Minority Report* was turned into the 2002 film starring Tom Cruise: it was nominated for a Hugo in 2003. His 1953 short story *Paycheck* served as the basis of the 2004 film of the same name about a man who having done a service for the establishment awakes without memory to find his payment is a collection of clues. Our amnesiac has to piece together his own history through a mire of corporate paranoia and future prediction. *dir.* John Woo, starring Ben Affleck, Uma Thurman and Aaron Echart. Another 1953 short story was turned into the film *Impostor* (2001), *dir*. Gary Fleder, in which a weapons expert central to Earth's defence against the Alpha Centaurans, is himself suspected of being an alien.

Dispossessed, The – novel (1974) by **Ursula K Le Guin**. As with many of her novels *The Dispossessed* is an exploration of an alien society, or in this case two, with seven other worlds in the wings. Set in her 'Hainish' universe, superficially the story concerns the conjecture by the physicist Shevek of 'the Principle of Simultaneity' out of which there are the distinct possibilities of instantaneous interstellar communication (ansible devices) and the implications that that will have for the nine Known Worlds. In actuality the book is an exploration of the social concept of ownership. Much of the plot takes place on two worlds. On one the society is based on a sort of socialist/beneficial capitalism while the other is an anarchy in the correct dictionary sense (order out of chaos).   On the first, ownership (acquiring capital) is fundamental. On the other, nobody actually owns anything but can borrow material goods from a social pool as they are needed for the moment. The protagonist finds that both are extremes of a spectrum and that on both worlds many are after his 'Simultaneity' idea.   *The Dispossessed* both illustrates why Le

Guin was such a mainstay of SF from the mid-1960s to the late 1980s, and why SF as a genre is a most powerful literary tool for examining our own society and what it is to be a human social creature. *The Dispossessed* won the Hugo in 1975 for 'Best Novel'. It was also voted into the top 20 of the *Concatenation* all-time book poll and came top of the *Locus* annual readers poll for the year.

Ditmar Award, The – see **Australia**.

Do Androids Dream of Electric Sheep – novel (1968) by **P K Dick** subsequently re-titled ***Blade Runner*** following the film of the same name. World War Terminus had left Earth devastated, many of the population had gone to the stars. Cities, some well-preserved though run down, are under populated: a couple in an entire apartment building represents a fairly high population density away from the city centre. In this high tech, part desolated, part run down future, people crave for the comfort of robotic animals and something to remind them of the natural world they have despoiled: only the very rich can afford real animals. Then there are those who seek solace in the new religion, Mercerism. But there are also humanoid robots, some almost (superficially) indistinguishable from real people. When these go renegade they call in special bounty hunters to 'kill' them. One such bounty hunter, Rick Deckard, gets a contract to go after six rogue Nexus-6 androids. This is his story... *Do Androids Dream* is one of Dick's most famous novels, even before the Hugo Award-winning film *Blade Runner*, and gave fans the term 'kipple' (household junk that accumulates of its own volition). *Do Androids Dream of Electric Sheep* was nominated one of the top 20 novels in the all-time favourite *Concatenation* poll.

Doctor Jekyll and Mr Hyde – See ***Strange Case of Dr Jekyll and Mr Hyde, The***.

Doctor Strangelove or How I Learned to Stop Worrying and Love the Bomb – film, GB (1964), *dir.* Stanley (see also **Brian Aldiss,** ***A Clockwork Orange*** and ***2001: A Space Odyssey***) Kubrick. This is a blackly humorous look at nuclear destruction during the Cold War period, reflecting a change in society's concerns regarding nuclear weapons. Peter Sellers stars in three roles: as a British Officer trying to get destruct codes from, while simultaneously humouring, the US general who has launched an attack on the USSR; as the US President trying to prevent the outbreak of World War III; and as Dr. Strangelove, Presidential advisor and ex-Nazi scientist. Also starring George C. Scott as an enthusiastic Military Presidential advisor, and Slim Pickens as the pilot of the fateful bomber, determined to fulfil his mission, this film is cathartic while remaining critical of the so-called MAD (mutually assured destruction) policy of the US during the Cold War. *Doctor Strangelove* won the 1965 Hugo for Best Dramatic Presentation, and placed 9th in the *Concatenation* all-time best SF film poll. Darkly funny, the film is still relevant today, but may not play well in Pakistan or India. Principal cast: Peter Sellers, George C Scott, Peter Bull, Sterling Hayden, Keenan Wynn, Slim Pickens, James Earl Jones, and Tracy Reed.

Doctor Who – TV series, UK (*fb*1963). Though the various *Star Trek* series together amount to the longest TV run of a body of SF work, the record for a single SF series with nominally the same protagonist (though played by different actors) easily goes to *Dr Who*. A juvenile offering, *Dr Who* nonetheless inspired a couple of generations (if not a goodly proportion of their parents as well) over some twenty six seasons to 1989 and in May 1996 there was a reprise in the form of a made-for-TV film. Consequently it is hardly surprising that in a 2001 Channel 4 poll of the UK general viewing public Dr Who was nominated 7th out of the top 100 all-time TV characters. *Dr Who's* overall premise is that the Universe's time flow is regulated by an ancient alien race, the Time Lords. A maverick Time Lord, called the Doctor, spends his time sight-seeing throughout the space time continuum using his Time and Relative Dimensions in Space (TARDIS) machine. The TARDIS itself is an old model whose camouflage capability is stuck in the shape of an early to mid-20th century British police box. One peculiarity about this space-time machine is that it is not entirely contained in normal 3-D space, a fortunate by-product of which means that it is larger on the inside than it is on the outside. However the Doctor's solo escapades often end with him in trouble. With a soft spot for Earth, the Doctor usually travels with a couple of human companions. They encounter weird aliens, some good, some bad. The show's regulars included the Daleks: in-effect alien cyborgs, mutants from a war, encased in machines that glide about like dodgem cars at a fairground, but equipped with a vicious death ray. There were also the Cybermen: robots out to conquer the Galaxy. Also a host of purely biological foes. Of these last the Master, another (but evil) renegade Time Lord continually harassed the Doctor. As a Time Lord the Doctor regenerated periodically becoming a new person (a suitable ploy to allow a fresh actor to take over for a few years). Each of his regenerated personalities represent a different aspect of the Time Lord brought forward to dominate the character during each aforesaid regeneration. One aspect of being a Time Traveller is that (though against the laws of time) the Doctor could encounter his 'earlier' regenerates from time to time (there were three separate such encounters). Much of the afore was referred to in the 1996 TV film, the first half of which was inspired but badly let down by an insipid second half (not to mention the loss of the TARDIS's usual ultra-modern control room and some ghastly liberties taken with the Doctor's supposed origins). In order the actors playing the Doctor during the TV series were: William Hartnell, Patrick Troughton, Jon Pertwee, Tom Baker, Peter Davison, Colin Baker, and Sylvester McCoy. Peter Cushing played the Doctor in two 1960s *Dr Who* Dalek films while Paul McGann took the title role in the 1996 TV film. The Master was played by Roger Delgado and Anthony Ainley in the TV series, and Eric Roberts in the 1996 TV film. As for the future, there is always hope. The 1996 TV film attracted a nine million audience in the UK so the market is there: all it needs is the combination of a good SF writer and a *Dr Who* buff behind the scripts and the BBC would be half way there. The BBC realised this and announced in 2004 plans for a new series with Christopher Eccleston as the Doctor.

Doomsday Book – novel (1992) by **Connie Willis**. Time travel researchers face an ethical dilemma when they return to plague-ridden Medieval Oxford, given that their knowledge of modern medicine can combat the disease. This poignant novel came top of the *Locus* poll in 1993.

Doomwatch – TV series, UK (*fb*1970). A fictional Government Department set up to watch and control advances in technology headed by Dr Spencer Quist and assisted by Dr John Ridge and Tobias 'Toby' Wren. The series was devised by Dr Kit Pedler and Gerry Davis. Episodes covered issues such as: emergent species of rats; chemical and atomic pollution; noise; defoliation and genetic experiments. The series soon established a substantial following: a then record of some 12 million! However after the first two seasons the success resulted in greater production control. Unfortunately this was for the worse and by the third series Pedler and Davis left disassociating themselves from the programme. By the third series the programme had lost its way and that was that. The programme, though dated by today's standards, did catch the growing public concern for environmental issues. But looking back, now that we have algal blooms, an awareness of pollution issues, genetic modification *etc.*, episodes do seem to have simplistic nuances. Nonetheless, for its time it was groundbreaking TV SF. Principal cast: John Paul (Dr Spencer Twist); Simon Oates (Dr John Ridge); Robert Powell (Toby Wren); Joby Blanchard (Colin Bradley); and Vivien Sherrard (Barbara Mason).

Double Star – novel (1956) by **Robert Heinlein**. Part inspired by the Prisoner of Zenda this amiable tale sees a down and out actor whisked off to play the role of his—indeed another's—life. Lorenzo Smythes, sinking his umpteenth drink, gets shanghaied to Mars. There he is cajoled into impersonating an important (look-a-like) politician who himself has been kidnapped. Peace with Mars is at stake so Lorenzo agrees, but this means that he too becomes a political, and possibly an assassin's, target. If the real politician is not found alive, Lorenzo may have to play his new role indefinitely... *Double Star* won the Hugo for 'Best Novel' in 1956.

Downbelow Station – novel (1981) by **C. J. Cherryh**.   Set in Cherryh's rich and complex Alliance-Union universe (*cf. Cyteen*). Pell is a space station strategically positioned between Earth and the influences of the Alliance and the Union. Following the withdrawal of Earth's enfeebled fleet, Pell is left alone and defenceless. It is determined to remain neutral, but is inevitably the focus of much attention. Then things suddenly get worse with the arrival of thousands of refugees from another station. The fate of the station and its thousands of inhabitants now hangs in the balance... *Downbelow Station* won the Hugo in 1982 for Best Novel and was a runner-up in the annual *Locus* readers poll.

Dragon's Egg – novel (1980) by Robert L. Forward. The Dragon's Egg is a neutron star with a surface gravity of 67 billion g's, and is inhabited by the fast-lived cheela, whose generational lifetime is about 37 minutes from the point of view of human observers. The development of the cheela is inadvertently influenced by the human scientists studying the Egg, who are soon out-evolved and, in a sequel, *Starquake!* (1985), the cheela explore the galaxy before dealing with the title's threat. Forward, a physicist formerly at Hughes Research Labs, writes dazzling hard-SF with intriguing worlds and aliens, though his plotting and characterisation is only average. *Dragon's Egg* topped the annual *Locus* readers poll in the 'first novel' category.

Dreamsnake – novel (1978) by Vonda N. McIntyre. Linked to her healer snake through genetic imprinting, the female protagonist struggles through a destructively superstitious post-holocaust world. When her snake is lost amid the primitive desolation, she must search for a replacement through the dangerous environment. McIntyre, a geneticist, began *Dreamsnake* as a short story in 1973, *Of Mist, and Grass, and Sand*, which won a Nebula, and the city in the latter stages of the novel featured in her first book, *The Exile Waiting* (1975). In 1979 *Dreamsnake* won McIntyre another Nebula, as well as a Hugo for Best Novel, and came top of the annual *Locus* readers poll.

Dune – novel (1965) by **Frank Herbert**. Co-Winner of the 1966 Hugo for Best Novel (sharing the honours with ***This Immortal*** by **Roger Zelazny**), *Dune* was first published as two serials in *Analog* magazine: *Dune World* (Dec 63 - Feb 64) and *The Prophet of Dune* (Jan-May 1965). The galaxy is under control of the Emperor, and the Houses of Duke Leto Atreides and Baron Vladimir Harkonnen are at war. The governorship of the planet Arrakis, Dune, is transferred from the Baron to the Duke by the Emperor as part of a plot to wipe out House Atreides. But Arrakis is also the sole producer of the spice melange, which both allows the navigators of the Spacing Guild to fold space, and also grants special powers to the Bene Gesserit Sisterhood, both vital players in the political game. But the galaxy may not be ready for the natives of Dune, who believe a messiah will come to wrest control from the wicked. Following the assassination of Leto, his father, Paul Atreides joins the native Fremen in a battle to bring about their prophecy... This is just the tip of the iceberg of a complex, many-stranded, and unfailingly rich plot that spawned an entire series, beginning with *Dune Messiah* (1969), then *Children of Dune* (1976), *God-Emperor of Dune* (1981), *Heretics* *of Dune* (1984), and *Chapter House Dune* (1985). There are those who believe that in general the quality of these novels declined as the series progressed, but Brian Herbert – following his father's death – is continuing the saga with Kevin Anderson in *House Atreides*: *Prelude to Dune* (1999) and other spin-off novels. The original was made into a film *Dune* (1984), directed by David Lynch, and starring Kyle MacLachlan (as Paul), Francesca Annis (as his mother and Bene Gesserit Jessica), Jurgen Prochnow (Leto), Dean Stockwell (Yueh), and others including Max Von Sydow and Sting. The cinema release was lengthened for Japanese TV, but Lynch (who had filmed all dialogue from the book and needed money to edit together a 5-8 hour version) was not consulted and had his name removed from the credits. There was also a *Dune* TV mini-series (*fb* 2000) starring William Hurt (Leto), Alec Newman (Paul) and Saskia Reeves (Jessica), and Children of Dune mini-series (*fb* 2002). The film came 16th in the *Concatenation* all-time best SF film poll, and the book (which also won a Nebula Award for Best Novel) came second in the all-time best SF book section of the same poll, while **Frank Herbert** was the sixth most cited author across all categories. *Dune* is justly acknowledged as a classic of the field for its depth of characterisation, its richly detailed universe, its environmental awareness and its almost-medieval labyrinthine intrigues, all of which helped change the face of **space opera**.

Eagle – comic, (*crtd* 1950) The original *Eagle* comic was one of two school-approved comics of the 1960s, but featured a number of SF strips including ***Dan Dare***. The original *Eagle* did not survive the end of the 1960s. A new *Eagle* comic appeared in March 1983 and survived into the 1990s.

Eagle Award – the principal comics award in the UK between 1976 and 2000 (see ***2000AD***). It has been succeeded by the UK National Comics Award.

Eastercon – The first annual UK convention, or at least the closest thing to it, took place in 1937, in Leeds, and was held each year up to the outbreak of World War II. However the present day series of national Eastercons began after the war, in London in 1948 with *Whitcon*, and they have been held over the four days of every Easter holiday weekend since. Typically, today the

Eastercon has at its focus one or two authors as Guests of Honour, together with a fan Guest of Honour. Having said this, most Eastercons usually attract a dozen or so authors as well as a sprinkling of editors, critics and other SF professionals among the attendees. Eastercons invariably have two or three simultaneous programme streams of talks, panels and frequently (but not always) reel-to-reel screenings of films. Side attractions include a book dealers room, fancy dress parade, and frequently fan and games rooms. However it has to be said that, as with many conventions, Eastercons vary in character and degree of organization from year-to-year. In a poor year it is introverted, introspective, clique-ridden and poorly run; in a good year it is friendly, open, well-prepared with a good programme and truly is the gathering of the UK SF clans providing a show case for UK SF, books, film, media and gaming.

Edward Scissorhands – film, US (1991), *dir.* Tim Burton. This is a contemporary fairy tale about an artificial child (Johnny Depp) who has scissors for hands, and his rise to fame as a hairdresser and ice sculptor following his rescue by Avon lady Dianne Wiest, after the death of his creator (a cameo and the final film role of Vincent Price prior to his own death). But dark jealousy soon brands the automaton a monster and he is forced to withdraw from society. This was a surprising winner of the 1991 Hugo for Best Dramatic Presentation, perhaps a protest at the previous year's crop of sequels, though also eligible were cult favourite *Darkman* (Sam Raimi, 1990), *Frankenstein Unbound* (Roger Corman, 1990, based on the book by **Aldiss**), independent production *Hardware* (Richard Stanley, 1990, set in ***2000AD*** territory but poorly done), the block-buster ***Total Recall*** (Paul Verhoeven, 1990, based on **Philip K. Dick's** *We Can Remember It For You Wholesale*), and the Japanese industrial-manga-SF offering *Tetsuo* (Tsukamoto Shinya, 1990). Considering the competition it overcame, *Edward Scissorhands* should treasure its Hugo. Principal cast: Johnny Depp, Dianne Weist, Winona Ryder, Vincent Price.

Egan, Greg – author, Australia (*b*1961) Greg Egan is a young writer, one of the new generation of SF authors, and like **Iain Banks** one who has both received considerable critical acclaim and who has markedly extended one of SF's dimensions. Though Egan has barely been around long enough, or yet to write enough books, to acquire sufficient profile to win many Hugos, he has already been repeatedly nominated for them: further-more he has won the **John W Campbell** Memorial Award (for 'Best New Writer' which is voted for by those attending the annual Worldcon). However he did win a Hugo in 1999 for his novella *Oceanic* (originally published by *Asimov's*). His short fiction has also twice won the Best Story of the Year in ***Interzone*** magazine. With such acclaim any aspiring SF buff should be aware of the man and his works, hence his inclusion in this guide. Egan is a writer of ultra hard SF (see ***Diaspora*** (1997) and ***Quarantine*** (1992)) and as such he is a must for the scientist who enjoys SF as well as the SF fan with an interest in science. Egan's writing is particularly rich in the physical as well as the information sciences; the latter is not surprising since Egan alternates his SF writing with computer program drafting contracts. Indeed, so specialised is his fiction it is difficult to see how anyone with little knowledge of science can grasp what is going on and the concepts being explored. ***Quarantine*** is a typical example which in essence attempts to explore the nature of reality with the 'what if?' concept of someone being able to control the collapse of alternate realities *à la* Schrödinger's Cat into actual space-time, while ***Diaspora*** provides a whimsical answer to the Fermi paradox together with a fantasy exploration of the possible nature of the Multiverse (with a fascinating detour into the manifestation of sentience). For non-science-type readers, perhaps one of his more accessible works, given the present widespread use of home computers and the InterNet, is *Permutation City* (1994) which on one level addresses the question of whether a cyberspace program can be so detailed that it becomes indistinguishable from real-space, in which case there are ethical questions to answer let alone insights into the possible nature of the universe. Egan also writes short fiction, which again is ultra-hard SF, and a number of these early works have been collected together in a volume entitled *Axiomatic* (1995). Yet given that Egan likes to dance with fiction on the edge of science fact, a boundary which itself is progressing with time, one question springs to mind: as a broad rule of thumb the better the Science Fiction the more robust it is to the tests of time (Wells' and Dick's works are virtually as readable today as when first published). So in the future will Egan's work seem as scientifically poignant as it does now? Only time will tell (or perhaps future SF fans).

Eggleton, Bob – artist, US (*b*1960). Bob [Robert Anthony] Eggleton studied art at Rhode Island College. At his first Worldcon in 1980 he exhibited several drawings and was voted the convention's best monochromatic artist. His first SF book covers appeared in 1984 and since then most leading US, and some UK SF imprints, have had covers featuring his work: currently he is producing well over a score a year. As of 2003 he has won seven Hugos for Best Professional Artist starting in 1994. Published portfolios of his work include: *Alien Horizons: The Fantastic Art of Bob Eggleton* (1995); *The Book of Sea Monsters* (1998); and *Greetings From Earth: The Art of Bob Eggleton* (2000). See also *www.bobeggleton.com*

Eisner, Will – artist, US (1917-2005) Beginning with the unique format of *The Spirit* (1940), he went on to virtually define the graphic novel with *A Contract With God.* His name is given to the Eisner Awards. This award is decided on by a small panel of professionals and have been given for achievement in comics at the US, **Comic-con International** convention since 1988 with the exception of 1990.

Ellison, Harlan – author, US (*b*1934). Ellison was born and raised in Ohio and attended, though did not graduate, Ohio State University. His first professional published SF short story was *Glowworm* (1956) and, indeed, short stories comprise the bulk of Ellison's written work. It may or may not be true that **Asimov** once called Ellison, "the best damned writer in the world", but his output has certainly been prolific and much honoured, winning innumerable awards, including eight Hugos. However, while rightly praised as an SF writer, Ellison makes extensive use of all genres. In order to encounter the majority of the SF work, the following volumes are recommended: *I Have No Mouth, and I Must Scream* (1967), which contains the 1968 Hugo Award-winning short story of the same name; *From the Land of Fear* (1967); *The Beast That Shouted Love at the Heart of the World* (1969), the title story of which won the short story Hugo in 1969; *Alone Against Tomorrow* (1971), better known in England as two volumes (*All the Sounds of Fear* (1973), and *The Time of the Eye* (1974)), and which contains the 1966 Hugo Award-winning short story, ***"Repent, Harlequin!" Said The Ticktockman*** (1965); *Deathbird stories* (1975), containing the Best Novelette 1974 Hugo winner *The Deathbird*; *Strange Wine* (1978); *Shatterday* (1980) which contains the 1978 short story Hugo winner, *Jeffty is Five*; *Stalking the Nightmare* (1982); and *Angry Candy* (1988), which has the Best Novelette 1986 Hugo-winner *Paladin of the Lost Hour*. His story *Adrift Just Off the Islets of Langerhans* won the Hugo for Best Novelette in 1975. Ellison has also won awards for editing anthologies, most notably for the follow-up to *Dangerous Visions* (1967), *Again, Dangerous Visions* (1972), which won both the *Locus* poll ('original anthology' category) and a "non-Hugo" special award. Ellison also topped the *Locus* poll in 1985 as editor for *Medea: Harlan's World* (1984), wherein scientists, artists and science fiction writers collaborate to create a world, in which the writers then set short stories. Ellison is quite well-known in the comics field, having written for several characters, including **Batman**, and many of his SF short stories have been adapted to this form. Chief among these are *Night and the Enemy* (1987), beautifully illustrated by Ken Steacy, which collects most of Ellison's Earth-Kyben stories, set in the midst of a 200-year war, the most famous of which, an October 1964 episode of ***The Outer Limits**, Demon with a Glass Hand*, was adapted in 1986 by Marshall Rogers for a short-lived line of SF graphic novels. Ellison's 1969 Nebula winning novelette, ***A Boy and his Dog***, along with other fragments from the as-yet-unpublished longer work, *Blood's a rover*, was adapted by Richard Corben in 1987 for the graphic novel *Vic and Blood*. The film ***A Boy and his Dog*** (1975) was awarded the Best Dramatic Presentation Hugo in 1976, though the award was for the film and not specifically Ellison. Visually Ellison is better known as a television writer, having written for and been creative consultant to, ***The Outer Limits*** (original series), ***The Twilight Zone*** (old and new), ***Star Trek***, for which he penned the award-winning *City on the Edge of Forever*, the ill-fated *Star Lost*, which ran for one season only, and most recently for ***Babylon 5***. Harlan Ellison's contribution to SF across the media has been greatly influential and should not be underestimated, though frequently controversial and contentious it is of a consistently high quality and integral to the field.

Empire Strikes Back, The – film, US (1980), *dir.* Irvin Kershner. This second offering from the original ***Star Wars*** trilogy was probably the weakest of the 3 films and, despite trying to flesh out the main characters, was largely saved by the revelations about Darth Vader. The film begins and ends with extended set-pieces, firstly of the assault on the ice planet Hoth, and the subsequent getaway through the asteroid belt, and finally in the cloud city on Bespin, detailing Luke's encounter with his father, Vader. In the middle is the uneasy sequence where Yoda (with the voice of Frank ***Little Shop of Horrors*** Oz) tries to train Mark Hamill in the ways of the Jedi, and Han (Harrison ***Indiana Jones*** Ford) and Leia (Carrie Fisher) begin their romance. The regulars are joined by Billy Dee Williams as Lando Calrissian, contributing to a poor cliff-hanger ending as Han is taken away by a bounty hunter. Nevertheless, *Empire* won the 1981 Hugo for Best Dramatic Presentation, came in the top 20 of the *Concatenation* all-time best SF film poll, and was nominated for 5 Oscars, winning two, for 'Sound' (beating *Altered States*(1980) *dir*. Ken Russell); and Special achievement for visual effects. The whole trilogy was digitally remastered and re-released in 1997 and 2004 (the latter on DVD only).

Ender's Game – novel (1985) by **Orson Scott Card**. The first title in the original 'Ender' trilogy (two more books were written a decade later). Ender Wiggin goes through a selection process training him to become the world's top military strategist. By the age of ten he had entered a special selection school, engaging in practical exercises with his classmates. Meanwhile Ender is separated from his loving sister Valentine who begins to develop her philosophical interests, and his politically ambitious brother Peter. The reason for the selection of children is because Earth is at war with an alien hive type species called the 'Buggers'. The human-alien struggle is closely matched, hence Mankind's desperate need for an edge – any edge, even that of a sharp young mind. Ender's training *cum* rites of passage is followed through various trials, including an electronic simulation of commanding a space fleet in confrontation with the aliens. Ender's fleet triumphs which in turn heralds the fate of the real aliens. Ultimately Ender, at the age of 11, is responsible for the death of an entire civilization. Recoiling from what he has done, he and Valentine anonymously begin a religion whereby those that have died can have someone speak on their behalf to the living with utter candour. This religion is respected by many as a kind of absolution for humanity's inhuman crime against the 'Buggers'. Of the three Ender books, *Ender's Game*, being so wrapped up with its young protagonist, almost reads like juvenile SF. Whereas the following two in the trilogy (***Speaker for the Dead***, and *Xenocide*) appear more solid works. Notwithstanding all of this *Ender's Game* did win the Hugo Award for Best Novel in 1986. Of the two subsequent post-trilogy titles, *Ender's Shadow* (1999) is of particular note which tells the story from the perspective of Ender's classmate Bean: it transpires that Bean played as nearly as key a part as Ender in stopping the Buggers, and arguably (from the readers' perspective) Ender could not have done it without him.

Enemy Mine – novella (1979) by Barry B Longyear. Two soldiers – one human, the other alien – from opposing sides of an interstellar war are stranded on an inhospitable planet. To survive they must cross the cultural divide separating them, recognise their respective biological needs and overcome their differences. An old theme to which Longyear brings fresh life. It won the Hugo in 1980 for Best Novella. In 1985 a somewhat twee, tear-jerking film version was released, directed by Wolfgang Petersen.

European SF Convention (Eurocon). The Eurocons began in 1972 so as to provide Europe with an international series of SF conventions, since up to that time 9 out of 10 **Worldcons** were held in North America (even today the ratio is 7 out of 8). (Though there was a convention in Zurich in 1959 that had a European dimension to it.) Each Eurocon still has its own feel to it and quality of organisation. Some are truly European with about a third of those attending originating from outside of the host country, others are little more than a version of the hosting country's own national event. Either way the Eurocons are, for SF buffs, a great way to visit foreign lands combining a holiday with a convention in its middle. (Indeed, by far the best way to attend such conventions in those nations where English is hardly spoken, is to stay with local SF fans: this is just one benefit from striking up friendships at international conventions. Though even with the most eastern of Eurocons, where at the very least half a dozen Anglophones attend, translators are usually provided for groups of four or five visitors. However in the main English, if not the first, is usually the second Eurocon language.) The first Eurocons were held just once every two years, but from 1982, such has been the growth in the genre's popularity, they have been held almost every year. The Eurocons also run the Eurocon Awards voted on by all who attend the mid-convention Eurocon business meeting. The Eurocon Awards are less formal than the Hugos and the categories can vary considerably from year to year. However typically there are Eurocon 'Hall of Fame' Awards for

Best: Author, Artist, Publisher, and (European) Promoter. There is also a second category of 'Encouragement' Awards given to help nurture embryonic talent. An attempt is made to alternate Eurocons between eastern and western Europe, but this depends on which countries bid to host the event two years hence. The Eurocons to date of publication have been (or are due to be) held in:

1972	Trieste, Italy
1974	Grenoble, France
1976	Poznan, Poland
1978	Brussels, Belgium
1980	Stresa, Italy
1982	Munchengladbach, (then) W. Germany
1983	Ljubljana, (then) Yugoslavia
1984	Brighton, Britain
1985	Riga, (then) USSR
1986	Zagreb, (then) Yugoslavia
1987	Montpellier, France
1988	Budapest, Hungary
1989	San Marino, Italy
1990	Fayence, France
1991	Krakow, Poland
1992	Freudenstadt, Germany
1993	Jersey, Britain
1994	Timisoara, Romania
1995	Glasgow, Britain (also a **Worldcon**)
1996	Vilnius, Lithuania
1997	Dublin, Ireland
1999	Dortmund, Germany
2000	Gdansk, Poland
2001	Capidava, Romania
2002	Chotebor, Czech Republic
2003	Turku, Finland
2004	Plovdiv, Bulgaria
2005	Glasgow, Britain (also a **Worldcon**)
2006	Kiev, Ukraine

As with the many countries' national SF conventions (such as the UK **Eastercon**), the Eurocons are highly variable affairs. This in part is due to the voluntary organisers' abilities: each year has different organisers. However of interest to participants, variability is also due to the nature of the host country. Former Soviet bloc countries understandably have fewer resources compared to those of western Europe. However a foreign visitor to the Eurocon has one advantage in that visiting fans and SF buffs are greatly welcomed. For visitors the experience of each Eurocon is invariably new, so makes for an interesting time. (Just go with the flow.) Finally, because of the extra effort it takes to travel, one meets other foreign-visiting fans and buffs who are similarly prepared to make this investment for a little adventure and so are generally more exciting souls. Indeed the Eurocon is frequently the haunt of a number of those who are (but probably would not consider it themselves) the quiet movers and shakers from various countries of the European SF community. This in itself adds some spice to Eurocons not found in national events.

Fahrenheit 451 – novel (1953) by **Ray Bradbury**. The near future sees a TV dominated society where scholars are criminals and books banned, frequently being burned ritualistically. (451 degrees Fahrenheit is the temperature at which paper burns.) Perversely, here firemen and fire engines do not go out to put out fires but to burn books. Montag is one such fireman rooting out illegal caches of books for incineration. One day he meets a rebellious woman and slowly his own beliefs change. *Fahrenheit 451* is in effect another treatment of *1984* but fortunately is sufficiently individual to stand alone. Equally the book has often been viewed favourably by mainstream critics and so has been considered as one of SF's more literary offerings of the 1950s. It won a retro-Hugo (a 50 years on Hugo) in 2004 for 1953. A stylish film version was made in 1966, *dir.* François (*Close Encounters of the Third Kind*) Truffaut. Principal cast: Oscar Werner, Julie Christie, and Cyril Cusack.

Fairyland – novel (1995) Like a lot of **Paul McAuley's** work, *Fairyland* is richly plotted. Set in the 21st century during a period of change (or more rapid change than usual) the world is reeling from continual technological revolutions be it nano- or bio-. Europe is divided between the rich First World and the Fourth World of refugees and homeless, having been displaced by war and economic change. In London, one designer of psychoactive viruses is trying to ply his trade while keeping out of the way of both the Triads and the police. The 'Fairies' of the book's title refer to slave bio dolls: to one of whom our protagonist and an ally bestow intelligence, so making it the first fairy. Ultimately *Fairyland* is an exploration of the ethics of the new technologies, and who better to engage in such a topic than a former research biologist. While *Fairyland* has not had the popular acclaim of Hugo or *Locus* poll, it did win both the **Arthur C Clarke** and the **John W Campbell** Memorial Awards. McAuley is an author to watch.

Fall of Hyperion, The – novel (1990) by **Dan Simmons**. The sequel to the Hugo-winning ***Hyperion*** and the novel that came top of the 1991 *Locus* poll. The Galactic scene that served as the background in *Hyperion*, which was on the cusp of interstellar war, comes to the fore. Humanity's dominant place is upturned as time travel and AI war usurps the *status quo*... *Fall of Hyperion* came top of annual *Locus* readers poll for best novel. The third book in the 'Hyperion' cantos, *Endymion* (1996) sees Raul Endymion accompany the person destined to be the 'One Who Teaches' into the future.

Fandom – the collective name given to the SF community of enthusiasts who regularly attend SF conventions, meet in clubs and/or engage in publishing and contributing to fanzines. (See also **Clubs, Conventions,** and **Fan Funds**.) The identity of the first ever fan group is lost in the mists of time but among the first to make a mark was in the US in the 1930s, called the Science Correspondence Club one of whose founding members was Raymond Arthur (***Amazing Stories***) Palmer. Principal sources of information on past and current fandom and fan activities ('fanac') worldwide can be found on the Fans Across the World website at *www.dcs.gla.ac.uk/SF-Archives/Fatw*. Others currently include:

- Australia – *Thyme* news fanzine, P O Box 222, World Trade Centre, Melbourne, Victoria, 8005, Australia. News of SF events can be found on *http://members.optushome.com.au/aussfbull/* and the 'bullsheet'. See also The media site of Friends of SF (*www.fsf.com.au/*). One of Australia's more active SF Societies is the Sydney Southern SF Group whose details can be found on *http://members.optushome.com.au/aussff/Southern_SF&F.html* and there is also the Futurian Society of Sydney *http://linus.socs.uts.edu.au/~iwoolf/futurians.html*
- Canada – Canadian SF professionals *www.sfcanada.ca* and the Montreal SF Association on *www.monsffa.com*.

- Denmark – *http://www.fantastik.dk/english.htm.*
- France – *http://SF.emse.fr.*
- Germany – the Science Fiction Club Germany *http://www.dsfp.de/index.html* (this site is only partly in English).
- India – *www.indianscifi.com* (media orientated, in English but not comprehensive nor enthusiastic about responding to queries).
- Ireland – *www.slovbooks.com/irishsfnews/index.php* which has a useful free e-newsletter for which you can register, and (with overshadows of Robert Rankin tributes) *www.lostcarpark.com/sfclub.*
- Italy – The Eurocon award-winning *Delos* e-magazine *http://www.delos.fantascienza.com/home/* of which a few pages are in English.
- New Zealand – Phoenixine, P O Box 11-559, Manners St, Wellington, New Zealand or alternatively on *www.sf.org.nz.*
- Russia – an English language description of what's on the Russian SF web site can be found on *http://fiction.ru/English.*
- Spain – *www.bemmag.com* or *www.bemonline.com* which these days is in Spanish only.
- **UK** – *Ansible* is on the web at *www.dcs.gla.ac.uk/SF-Archives/Ansible/* and has a reasonable (only slightly dated) launch pad into UK clubs and conventions. The British SF Association provides book and film news and reviews *www.bsfa.co.uk* as does the quarterly *Science Fact & Fiction **Concatenation*** on *www.concatenation.org.* One of the more active and long-lasting British SF groups is in Birmingham and its details can be found on *www.bsfg.freeservers.com*
- US – see ***SF Chronicle*** and ***Locus***. One of the more active west coast groups is the San Francisco Bay Area SF Association *www.basfa.org* and on the east coast the New England SF Association *www.nesfa.org* which runs the annual Boskone convention, as well as the Philadelphia SF Society (established 1935) *www.psfs.org* which supports the Philcon convention.

Importantly include an A4 stamped self addressed envelope to any of the above snail-mail addresses if you want a reply.

Fan Funds – In order to facilitate fan relations between countries there are a number of fan funds. These enable fan representatives from one country to visit another and attend a major convention. TAFF (The Transatlantic Fan Fund) was founded in 1953 by Walt Willis, Chuck Harris, Don Ford and others to send Walt Willis that year to the second Chicago Worldcon. Since then there have been over a score of races in which fans vote, making a donation for that right, for candidates from either Europe or North America. GUFF (The Going Under Fan Fund) sprang from an idea floated by Chris Priest and David (***Ansible***) Langford in 1977 to exchange delegates between Australasia and Europe. The first winner was John Foyster who attended Seacon, the 1979 UK **World SF Convention (Worldcon)**. SEFF (The Scandinavian European Fan Fund) was set up in 1983 to facilitate communication between Scandinavian fandom and fandom in the rest of Europe. DUFF (the Down Under Fan Fund) was established to fund Australasians to US based Worldcons and *vice-versa*. Finally there is the Anglo-Romanian Science Fact and Fiction Cultural Exchange which was established in 1995 by the NW Kent SF Society and the *Science & SF **Concatenation*** following pen-fan correspondence with Eastern Europe since 1992. The Exchange's original aim was to build links between UK and Romanian fandom but more recently includes contact with other Eastern European (including Russian) SF fans and the sponsorship of international events in Eastern Europe with Romanians and Hungarians.

Fantastic Voyage – film, US (1966), *dir.* Richard (***Soylent Green***, ***20,000 Leagues Under The Sea***) Fleischer. In order to save the life of a defector, a team of US scientists undergo an experimental miniaturisation process. They and their submarine are reduced to the size of a microbe and are injected into the man's body. They must make their way through the defector's blood system to the brain, where they hope to dissolve a blood clot that threatens his life. However, one of the team is a traitor and will even risk his own life to ensure the team's failure. The film is a tense thriller, with people racing against time, and antibodies, to succeed. The effects were pretty good for their day, and the film makers have at least attempted to get the biology vaguely right, even if the physics had holes: where did the team's mass, and that of the submarine, go during the miniaturization process? A novelization by **Isaac Asimov** was published in the same year which did paper over some of the cracks. (Incidentally the submarine was designed by Harper Goff who also designed the *Nautilus* in Disney's ***20,000 Leagues Under the Sea***.) Principal cast: Stephen Boyd, Donald Pleasence, and Raquel Welch.

Fanthorpe, Lionel – author, England (*b*1935). Lionel Fanthorpe has never won a Hugo, or featured in any *Concatenation* or *Locus* poll, nor is he ever likely to. However Lionel Fanthorpe, if not distinguished in the quality of his SF, certainly must vie for the title of one of the most prolific of SF authors in terms of books written *per* year and has over 200 titles under his belt. His output was mainly confined to the 1950s and '60s, and mainly to the publishing house Badger Books: reputation has it that 'Fanthorpe was their SF author', not that they owned Fanthorpe but that he was their one and only SF writer. Indeed if you ever stumble across an SF novel from Badger Books then the chances are that it is a Fanthorpe novel even if written under a pseudonym. Fanthorpe wrote under numerous pen names, including: Adam Chase, Erle Barton, Lee Barton, Thornton Bell, Leo Brett, Bron Fane, Mel Jay, Marston Johns, Robert Lionel, Lionel Roberts, Neil Thanet, Trebor Thorpe, and Pel Torro (however it is worth noting that some of these pseudonyms have also been used by other authors). At the peak of his output Lionel reputedly had five books on the go at any one time. He would dictate these onto tape for a typist to copy up. These days Lionel Fanthorpe is more widely known as the British TV presenter Reverend Fanthorpe with an interest in Fortean phenomena. None of Fanthorpe's works meet any of the criteria set for inclusion in this guide to 'essential' SF, but he is mentioned for completeness as the avid collector may want a title or two of his.

Fanzines are amateur magazines published by SF fans. The coining of the term, and that of 'prozine' (a magazine professionally produced for money), has been attributed to the US fan Louis Russell ('Russ') Chauvenet (1920-2003) in the 1940s. Fanzines come in all shapes and sizes. One of the earliest was *The Comet* (1930) produced by Raymond Arthur Palmer (see **Fandom**, ***Amazing Stories***). Some regard the first true fanzine, certainly one that might be considered major, as *The Time Traveller* (1932) edited by Julius (**Batman**) Schwartz (1915-2004) and Mort (see **Bester**) Weisinger (1915-1978) with the involvement of others including **Forrest Ackerman**. (*The Time Traveller* was retitled

Science Fiction Digest in 1933 and *Fantasy Magazine* in 1934.) Traditionally fanzines were ways of communication for fans between SF conventions and as often as not do not directly relate to SF. However, in recent decades fanzines branched out into a variety of specialist forms: personalzines (a variation of the between SF convention communicating type which focuses primarily on the editor's views and his/her readers' comments), newszines (primarily focusing on SF news – *cf.* **Ansible** – and reviews), clubzines (the magazines of SF societies (see **Clubs**)), e-zines (broadcasts on the internet such as *The Science Fact & Fiction* **Concatenation** on *www.concatenation.org*), and APAs (amateur press association publications). One of the best places to see current fanzines are at the **Worldcons** and most **Eurocons**. Recently (after 1990) the fanzine that has won the most **Hugo Awards** is *Mimosa* edited by Dick and Nicky Lynch. 'Semiprozines' are halfway between fanzines and professional magazines, usually with both commercial and fan elements to them. Arguably one of the first semiprozines was the *Fantasy Advertiser* launched in 1946 by Gus Wilmorth which within two years was 40 pages and paying authors for submissions and in 1949 had a circulation of 1,500.

Faraday's Orphans – novel (1996) by Lee Wood. The Earth's biosphere has been undermined, not by a human-induced eco-disaster, but by a geomagnetic reversal (the magnetic north becomes the magnetic south). This disrupts the ozone layer and causes tremendous climatic warming and aridity over most of the temperate zones, including the US. Mankind barely survives; civilisation is almost wiped out and teeters on extinction. There are, though, a few scattered, domed cities. Some 'civilised' survivors live in tunnel shelters, but there are violent barbarians in the old cities and roaming the land. Berk Neilson is a helicopter pilot from the domed city of Pittsburgh whose task it is to monitor the outside, deal with the few remaining civilized settlements and scout for resources. However on landing for the night in a distant, apparently deserted, city, his craft is destroyed by feral children and he finds himself in a nightmare world with one long, seemingly impossible trek home. *Faraday's Orphans* is not just any run-of-the-mill, post-apocalyptic story, nor is it just well written with good characterisation. The story has been thoroughly researched and, despite it having the liberation of being science fiction (the effects of such a magnetic reversal are over-blown to make the tale work), there is much science fact to underpin it: the reproductive biology of the various groups is particularly innovative.

Farmer, Philip José – author, US (*b*1918)   Back in 1953 Farmer was awarded the Hugo for Best New Writer the year that the prize began.   Author of *To Your Scattered Bodies Go* which won the Hugo Best Novel 1972, and *Riders of the Purple Wage* which won the Best Novella Hugo in 1968, Philip José Farmer is better known in some circles for his SF treatments of sex.   *The Lovers* (1961) explores a human-alien insectoid relationship. Fortunately, for the human protagonist (who originally was sent to exterminate the alien race), the insectoids can mimic human form.   While the *Strange Relations* (1960) collection of shorts looks at a variety of familial relationships.   Inevitably his subject matter led Farmer to touch upon eroticism and for their time these works were considered by some as risqué.   Examples include *Dare* (1965), concerning alien amazons, and *Flesh* (1960) where the aliens are decidedly perverse.   In 1969 he began a loosely connected series of books satirising a 'family' of heroic characters, including Tarzan, Doc Savage, Sherlock Holmes, James Bond and Kilgore Trout (see **Kurt Vonnegut**).   Their rivalries and sexual peccadilloes make for hilarious reading and include *A Feast Unknown* (1969), *Tarzan Alive* (1972), *Doc Savage: His Apocalyptic Life* (1973) and *The Other Log of Phileas Fogg* (1973).   Farmer is also known for his 'Riverworld' series which began with the afore mentioned Hugo-winning *To Your Scattered Bodies Go*.   In this series all of humanity is resurrected by godlike aliens, and is housed along the banks of a multi-million-mile long river.   Protagonists such as Mark Twain and Jack London delight in metaphysical musings, while now-immortal humans overindulge in various pleasures.   Farmer added seven more volumes between 1971 and 1983, before embarking on the Dayworld series (1985-90), in which the Earth is so overpopulated that each citizen is only awake for one day in every seven).

Festival of Fantastic Films – In the main, SF **conventions** are one-off affairs and even series of conventions, such as the **World SF Convention** (**Worldcon**) or the European SF Convention (Eurocon), are organised by completely different teams of volunteers each year with their respective contact points.   The Festival of Fantastic Films, however, is one of the very few conventions that have been run by the same team – led (for its first dozen years until his death) by Harry Nadler – for well over a decade and has an international dimension. That the Fest team and its associates includes former Worldcon and UK **Eastercon** runners of the 1960s and 70s is a testimony to the organisers' experience. The Festival is held each autumn in the Manchester region of the UK. The Fest began as a regional event in 1988 (which itself would not qualify its inclusion in this guide), though only a few hundred strong, in recent years its attending base has become increasingly international, and the films entered into both its amateur and independent film competition are today as likely as not to come from outside of the UK as within it. Though the Festival in the main focuses on older movies, including 'B' movies, it covers the whole SF/fantasy genre spectrum and represents one of the rare opportunities to see both old movies, and recent independent films from many countries, on the big screen. Data from the first decade of the Fest was one factor helping inform this guide's compilers as to which old films to include. Three or four guests (in the main producers, directors and actors), the film competitions, film premieres, and an extremely friendly and open atmosphere all contribute to the event making it one of the most enjoyable events of the UK SF calendar. Surf *www.fantastic-films.com*

Filk – 'Filk' music is science fiction music primarily, but not exclusively, of the 'folk' style and performed by science fiction and fantasy fans. There are even conventions devoted to filk. The first all-filk convention was in 1979 in the US. Britain had its first in 1989 and Germany's was in 1997. Surf *www.filk.com*

Fire Upon the Deep, A – novel (1992) by **Vernor Vinge**. Set in a well-populated galaxy of the far future, two human children, Johanna and Jefri, become the key to defeating The Blight, a powerful force imprisoned by the older races who have gone to the Transcend. Using the intelligent races' own galactic-scale 'InterNet' against them, The Blight is enslaving whole civilisations and seems utterly unstoppable. An alliance of species attempt to combat this ancient menace, but the galaxy seems doomed to enter a new Dark Age... *A Fire Upon the Deep* won the 1993 Hugo for Best Novel, and Vinge has since released ***A Deepness in the Sky*** (1999) set in the same universe, but taking place 300,000 years before the coming of The Blight.

First Men in the Moon, The – novel (1901) by **H G Wells**. Edwardian inventor, Mr Cavor, and his friend, Bedford, travel to the Moon by utilising Cavor's invention: Cavorite. This substance acts as a barrier to gravity. Wells reasoned that since three of the four forces of physics can be blocked by something material, then there was no reason to think the same would not be true for gravity; it was merely a matter of finding the right material! Once on the Moon, Cavor and Bedford discover the Selenites, the inhabitants of the Moon. Strange creatures, they are more akin to insects than mammalian humans. Every member of Selenite society is perfectly adapted to their task in life. With *The First Men in the Moon* Wells continues his explorations of biology, society and class. To Wells all of these things seem inter-related (*cf*. ***The Time Machine***). In 1964 *The First Men in the Moon* was turned into a movie starring Lionel Jefferies, *dir*. Nathan (***20 Million Miles to Earth***) Juran. The movie tried to stay true to the book; but as with so many of Wells' novels, there are layers of social criticisms and speculation that did not get transferred to the screen.

Five Million Years to Earth – see ***Quatermass and the Pit*** one of the all time most viewed movies screened at the Festival of Fantastic Films.

Flash Gordon – comic and character, US (*crtd*1934). Flash sprang to life as a Sunday newspaper strip on July 1st 1934 and was soon fighting Ming the Merciless, Emperor of the planet Mongo, with only his human decency and sidekicks Dale Arden and Dr. Zarkov to help him. Since then he has starred in numerous film and TV serials, films, comics, radio shows and parodies (including the soft porn *Flesh Gordon* (1974), with special effects by Jim Danforth of ***Star Wars*** fame). The original, beautifully drawn by Alex Raymond, inspired and still inspires many a **space opera**, and had a distinctive look that combined the super-advanced technology with antique design; ***Buck Rogers*** looked shoddy by contrast. The most recent film incarnation, *Flash Gordon* (1980), pretty much follows the plot of the early newspaper serial, but on the whole seems poor, despite an engaging *Queen* soundtrack. Some of the Raymond strips have been collected in album format and are occasionally available in reprint editions. (See also **Harry Harrison**.)

Flowers For Algernon – short story (1959) and novel (1966) by Daniel Keyes. Over a decade before 'biotechnology' and 'gene therapy' became popular terms among the scientifically literate section of the public, Daniel Keyes wrote an elegant, moving, charming, and human short story of an experiment to boost human intelligence. Without a rocket or ray gun in sight, Keyes' offering is an early, and classic example of **new wave** SF. Charlie is a somewhat mentally retarded floor sweeper at Donner's Bakery and the gentle butt of everyone's humour. However when he becomes the first human subject (the lab rat 'Algernon' preceded him) to have his intelligence boosted, the humour turns sour as his workmates fear his intellectual transformation. He continues to develop and soon leaves even the scientific academics that transformed him behind. But another (non-social) price for this intelligence boost begins to manifest itself and the race is on to stabilise the experiment. Part of *Flowers for Algernon's* charm is the way it is written, the story conveyed through the eyes of the protagonist and written in varying styles according to the level of intelligence Charlie possessed at that point in the story. Unfortunately for us Keyes was not a prolific writer, and never came close to the heights of *Flowers for Algernon* again: however, if you have to be remembered for one story then hope that it is of the calibre of this work. As a short story it won the Hugo in 1960 for 'Best Short Fiction', and was expanded into novel length in 1966. A faithful Oscar-winning film, ***Charly***, was made in 1968 (*dir.* Ralph Nelson).

Fly, The – film, US (1958), *dir.* Kurt Neumann. An early SF box office hit based on a short story (1957) by the French-born writer George Langelaan. The film is largely one flashback after the wife, Helene, is arrested for crushing her husband's head in a giant industrial press. He was a scientist investigating the possibility of teleportation using a matter-transmitting machine. She becomes concerned when her husband isolates himself in the basement laboratory and who always covers his head. It turns out that in one experiment he accidentally transports a fly with him. The teleportation device effectively swapped heads. The killing, it turns out, was born of mercy. Principal cast: Al' Hedison, Patricia Owens and Vincent Price.

Fly, The – film, US (1986), *dir.* David (***Scanners***) Cronenberg. The re-make of the 1958 film sets the story against a modern, high-tech backdrop. As in the original a scientist, Seth Brundle, is investigating matter transmission and, when testing the device on himself, accidentally merges with a fly. Scientifically superior (given that the premise on a molecular biology basis is inherently flawed even within the film's own premise), the portrayal of the merger is not at first apparent as the fly's genes have effectively been bio-engineered into Seth. However as the genes begin to produce proteins, so Seth slowly becomes an insect. This understandably scares his girlfriend, Veronica, all the more so since she has had sex with him... Cronenberg's up-dating is effective, though he did not make a nod to the original. A cameo appearance by Vincent Price (who played the scientist's brother in the original 1958 version) would have been welcome; though Cronenberg himself has a cameo as the gynaecologist. *The Fly* was nominated for a Hugo in 1990 but did not win. Principal cast: Jeff (***Jurassic Park***) Goldblum, Geena Davis, John Getz, Joy Boushel, Les Carlson, George Churalo and David Cronenberg. Goldblum was nominated for an Oscar, but did not win, though make up man Chris Walas (director of the inferior sequel *The Fly II* (1989)) did pick one up [*The Fly II* – film, US (1989) *dir.* Chris Walas. Veronica, girlfriend of scientist Blundle in the 1986 *The Fly*, gives birth to a son. He has some fly-like powers and lives, and is studied, in a scientific research station. However those running the station have their own agenda... A so-so action sequel. Principal cast: Eric Stoltz, Daphine Zuniga, Lee Richardson, Harley Gross, Gary Chalk, Ann Marie Lee, Frank C Turner and John Getz.]

The Forbin Project – film, US (1969), *dir.* Joseph Sargent. See ***Colossus: The Forbin Project.***

Forbidden Planet – film, US (1956), *dir.* Fred McLeod Wilcox. Who would have thought that the director of *Lassie Come Home* (1943) could have made one of the most enduring science fiction classics of all time? Loosely based on Shakespeare's *The Tempest* (and a possible forerunner of ***Star Trek***), *Forbidden Planet* is a masterpiece. Commander Adams (Leslie Nielson) leads an Earth Federation flying saucer to the planet Altair 4 whose colonists have not been in radio contact for some time. Adams, his first officer and the doctor, discover the two remaining survivors of the colony, Professor Morbeus (Walter Pidgeon as Prospero) and his daughter Alta (Anne Francis as Miranda), and Morbeus' fantastic creation, Robby the Robot (Ariel). But great secrets await beneath the planet's surface – the legacy of a long-dead race, the Krel – as well as the answers to what killed the other colonists, and what is currently killing Adams' crew... With wonderful (for 1956) special effects, which were nominated for, but did not win, an Oscar, and the first ever electronic soundtrack, *Forbidden Planet* was easily superior to most films of its time (although ***This Island Earth*** (1955) is another greatly admired contemporary). Robby the Robot was popular from the first and, indeed, made another film the following year, *The Invisible Boy* (1957), before continuing to turn up in programmes, most notably a version in the long-running TV serial *Lost in Space*, and including a guest slot on Peter (***The Lost World*** and ***The Princess Bride***) Falk's TV detective series *Columbo*! Of such things are stars made... Aside from its general popularity, this film also placed fifth in the *Concatenation* all-time best SF film poll.

Forever Machine, The – see ***They'd Rather Be Right***.

Forever Peace – novel (1997) by **Joe Haldeman** which won the 1998 Hugo for Best Novel. *Forever Peace* was the long awaited 'sequel' to the Hugo-winning ***The Forever War*** (1975): at least, a kind of a sequel, from the author's point of view, in that it uses SF to explore the theme of war – it is not in anyway set in the same continuum as *The Forever War*. Set in the mid-21st century and America is wallowing in unprecedented material wealth derived largely from nano-technology that allows goods to be created from raw materials by miniature robots. South America does not have this technology and is held in an economic strangle-hold by the US. Military unrest among the less developed nations leads to the Ngumi War, but the US does not need to send in soldiers to do the really difficult work. Instead they have 'soldierboys'. These are powerful robots controlled remotely (hundreds of miles away) by those cybernetically mind-linked to the machines. Yet those controlling the robots face as real dangers. Such mind-links to one's soldierboy and, indeed, to the rest of one's platoon comes at a price. There are also spin-off benefits. *Forever Peace* follows one soldierboy controller, Julien, as he realises these pros and cons and the implication of mind-link technology for the rest of the world.

Forever War, The – novel (1974) by **Joe Haldeman**. Private Mandella was conscripted to fight in the Forever War, defending humanity against the Tauran menace. He is to do this on some lonely outpost in the Galaxy. The only way he can get home alive is after a combat tour. However, though he will only age a few months, the journey itself will last a century or two. He knows that when he gets back everyone he knew will be dead and even society will be unfamiliar, and so he will probably re-enlist. Indeed, after a number of tours of duty, when he retires, as a veteran it is unlikely that anybody at home will even speak his language... *The Forever War* won the Hugo for Best Novel in 1976. Also it made it to the top 20 *Concatenation* all-time book poll and came top of the annual *Locus* readers poll. Its sequel, *Forever Free* (1999), sees Mandella, his lover and former comrades in arms uneasy in the future and so hijack a ship to relativistically travel further ahead in time.

Fortean – a broad class of phenomena sometimes featured in SF including: UFOs (in the strict sense of unidentified objects (not necessarily spacecraft)); cryptozoological animals; weird weather; and synchronous phenomena. Fortean specifically relates to the types of phenomena that would interest Charles Fort (1874-1932) who would use them to challenge the scientific view, more as an intellectual exercise than a dogmatic anti-science belief. Fort coined the term 'teleportation' and suggested that lights in the sky might be spacecraft.

Foss, Chris – artist, UK (*b*1946). Most noted for his spaceship covers of **Asimov** and **Doc Smith** novels for Panther Books (which rarely had any connection with the books' stories), Foss has drawn cartoons for non-SF magazines such as *Penthouse* and *Autocar* as well as for SF publications such as ***2000AD*** on a ***Judge Dredd*** strip and a multi-cover poster (progs 953-955). He even worked on the film ***Alien*** as a concept artist and did all the artwork and most of the model work for the non-SF German comedy *The Dive Bomber* (1993). Of his own works, a favourite is the cover of **Philip K Dick's** *We Can Build You* featuring a portrait of Adolf Hitler with a background character in the likeness of the author. *Science Fiction Art* (1976) is a portfolio of his early work (and has an introduction by **Brian Aldiss**).

Foundation – series of novels by **Isaac Asimov**; the original sequence of stories appeared in *Astounding Science Fiction* magazine (see ***Analog***) from 1942-1950. Set in the declining years of a galactic empire run from the planet Trantor, and featuring the 'psychohistorian' Hari Seldon, the original *Foundation* trilogy – *Foundation* (1951), *Foundation and Empire* (1952), and *Second Foundation* (1953) – charts the attempts of a group to limit the 'dark ages' that will follow the collapse of galactic civilisation using the science of 'psychohistory' – a sort of sociological statistical analysis that attempts to anticipate future events through the study of large groups of people. These Foundations (the second group is initially unknown by the first) follow the Seldon Plan, and frequently come into conflict with local planetary neighbours, not to mention the waning Empire itself. Loosely based on Gibbons' *Decline and Fall of the Roman Empire*, Asimov was encouraged to develop this universe by mentor and *Astounding* editor **John W. Campbell jnr.** The trilogy won a 'special category' Hugo in 1965 for Best All-Time Series. During the 1980's, Asimov began the ambitious task of melding together his Robot and *Foundation* series with mixed results, though ***Foundation's Edge*** (1982) did win a Hugo and topped the *Locus* annual readers poll. The other books in the series include: *The Robots of Dawn* (1983), *Robots and Empire* (1985), *Foundation and Earth* (1986), *Prelude to Foundation* (1988), and the posthumously published *Forward the Foundation* (1992). Despite some criticism these novels all sold well and, following Asimov's death, the *Foundation* stories were continued by **Gregory Benford**, **David Brin** and **Greg Bear**. However, while a good exercise in nostalgia or a tribute to Asimov these may be, they do not significantly add to the original series.

Foundation (journal) – review journal, UK. *Foundation* is science fiction's literary journal (and as such is arts focused rather than science). It is produced by the SF Foundation (see **Foundation, SF**). *Foundation* won the Eurocon Award for Best Magazine in 1992.

Foundation's Edge – novel (1982) by **Isaac Asimov**. Nearly 20 years after the original trilogy (see ***Foundation*** – series of novels), Asimov began the ambitious task of tying together much of his work with this Hugo-winning, and 1983 *Locus* poll-topping, novel. It is the first *Foundation* book to mention robots, and also ties in the Eternals from *The End of Eternity* (1955).

Foundation, SF – academic resource (UK). The SF Foundation is the UK equivalent of the US **SF Research Collection** and the Canadian **Merril Collection** not to mention a counterpart to the **Maison d'Ailleurs**. The SFF is called a foundation, according to George Hay who came up with the idea in 1970, because it was "to fulfil the same function as Isaac Asimov's ***Foundation***: to be what's now called a database for anyone wanting to research what's going to happen." The Foundation's first home was in the Department of Applied Philosophy at North East London Polytechnic, but later moved to its current home in the University of Liverpool. The Foundation has had a number of SF notables associated with it, either as administrators, researchers and writers in residence, such as: David (***Interzone***) Pringle, Malcolm Edwards (who left to become SF editor at Gollancz), and **Colin Greenland**. Today the SFF collection is curated by Andy Sawyer, and there is also a support group of SF notables called the Friends of Foundation. For details of its *Foundation* journal, a list of SFF events and services send a stamped self-addressed envelope (which is important due to the number of enquiries) to: The SF Foundation, c/o Special Collections, Sydney Jones Library, Liverpool University, P O Box 123, Liverpool L69 3DA, United Kingdom. *www.sf-foundation.com*

Fountains of Paradise, The – novel (1979) by **Arthur C. Clarke**. Winner of the 1980 Hugo and Nebula for Best Novel, this is one of Clarke's finest. Vannevar Morgan, a twenty-second century engineer, is faced with his greatest challenge—to build a space elevator, a 36,000km long cable, connected to a satellite in geosynchronous orbit. But on Earth, the cable is to be anchored on a mountain on the equatorial island of Taprobane, holy to an order of monks. And that's just the start of Morgan's troubles. When a group of students get stuck halfway up the cable, only Morgan has the experience to save them... Within months of its publication, Charles Sheffield's *The Web Between the Worlds* (1979) saw print. So similar were some aspects of the novels, including the use of a large mechanical 'Spider', that Clarke wrote an open letter to the Science Fiction Writers of America absolving Sheffield of all potential charges of plagiarism. Sheffield, President of the American Astronautical Society, arguably wrote the better novel, though Clarke's was technically superior with its use of crystalline carbon for the construction material, rather than Sheffield's crystalline silicon. One can only wonder if 'buckytubes' might provide a solution to the engineering problem...

Frankenstein – novel (1818) by Mary Shelley. Sub-title: *The Modern Prometheus*. This is probably one of the most quoted, but least read or understood, of books in the English language — many even confuse the monster with its creator. The story is well known. A young scientist – Victor Frankenstein – uses the parts of dead humans to create a living person. The creation becomes aware that he is not of his creator's society, and can never be a part of it or one of his own, so turns on his master. Indeed the story of the novel's writing, by the young Mary Shelley, itself is almost as famous as the book and is even the subject of a movie (*Gothic* by Ken Russell). In essence *Frankenstein* is the retelling of the Prometheus legend (Man defies God and is punished for it), hence the book's sub-title. So famous is *Frankenstein* that the concept has become something of a plot standby for lazy authors. (Although in more recent times frequently God has been replaced by some mystic 'nature' force and to many in the 20th century it has become an allegory for the perils of science: but can we really trust a novel, or anything else, that says being ignorant is better?) The novel has inspired a score of films. Yet unlike most of the movie versions, the monster of the novel was a sophisticated and cultured individual. Far from being a mindless monster solely bent on destroying his creator, the monster was a sensitive being. His hatred of Victor comes from Victor's abandonment of his own creation: he leaves this new being alone and without love. The monster, seeing how others are treated and how he was mistreated, comes to hate his creator. Perhaps, rather than being considered an anti-science novel, *Frankenstein* should be considered a novel about neglect and child abuse?

Frankenstein – films, various. The *Frankenstein* movies themselves are of varying quality. Few of them have stuck close to the novel. Most of them are copies or variations of the first James Whale version, US (1930). Principal cast: Boris Karloff, Colin Clive, Mae Clark, John Boles, Edward Van Sloan, Frederick Kerr, and Dwight Frye. The film introduced the world to Boris Karloff whose portrayal of the monster has gone down in cinematic history. It transferred the action to a small town in Germany. The locals, fearing Baron Victor Frankenstein, eventually destroyed him and his creation having stormed his castle burning it to the ground. Karloff's monster was an unthinking creature, filled with rage and hatred for everything. It became the model for almost every Frankenstein film for the next forty years (including a number with Karloff reprising his role). The movie spawned a complete series of films in which Frankenstein's monster was brought back again and again into increasingly silly plots. Direct sequels from the original film by the same studio (Universal) include: *The Bride of Frankenstein*, **Son of Frankenstein**, *Ghost of Frankenstein*, **Frankenstein Meets the Wolf Man,** *House of Frankenstein*, *House of Dracula*, and *Abbott and Costello Meet Frankenstein*. Subsequently the UK Hammer studio re-vamped the films in a series which included: *The Curse of Frankenstein*, *The Revenge of Frankenstein*, *The Evil of Frankenstein*, *Frankenstein Created Woman*, *Frankenstein Must Be Destroyed*, *Horror of Frankenstein*, and *Frankenstein and the Monster From Hell*. Other films were independently made (*cf.* **Young Frankenstein**). However some say that it is perhaps a shame that the great *Frankenstein* novel is mostly known to people through a series of comparatively poor (though possibly entertaining) movies and second hand accounts. Arguably an exception is **Brian Aldiss'** *Frankenstein Unbound*, filmed in 1990 by Roger (***Little Shop of Horrors***) Corman, it stars John (***Alien***, ***Contact***) Hurt as a time traveller, encountering both the creature and Mary Shelley at Deodato. Altogether there are over fifty Frankenstein movies, including Mexican, Italian, Spanish and Swedish versions, straight, parody, exploitation and sexual versions. All are surely a testament to the fascination the character has had for audiences since Shelley first set pen to paper.

Frankenstein Meets the Wolf Man – film, US (1943), *dir*. Roy William Neill. This is a spin-off movie from the Universal studio series, which itself is loosely based on the novel ***Frankenstein*** by Mary Shelley. Lon Chaney reprises his role as the Wolf Man (*The Wolf Man* (1940)) who is in search for a cure to prevent him from turning into a werewolf every time there is a full Moon shining between the clouds. He stumbles across the monster being revived after supposedly having been killed in the previous movie. Apart from having two monsters in one film, the movie does successfully build up a Universal monster universe which ultimately also contained Dracula. The film is let down in places by the script, poor editing and Bela Lugosi. Lugosi, ill and addicted to drugs, performed badly and was doubled for by veteran stuntman Eddie Parker in many scenes. Obviously the film over half a century on is dated but it, and ***Son of Frankenstein,*** remain the better of many of the other spin-offs. Principal cast: Bela Lugosi (the monster), Lon Chaney Jnr (the Wolf Man), Ilona Massey, Patrick Knowles, and Maria Ouspenskaya.

Freas, Frank Kelly – artist/illustrator, US (1922-2005). Before cinematic effects came into their own, all SF buffs had was their imaginations and the imagery of artists' imaginations. Of these, Frank Kelly Freas is one of the most respected. Arguably he did much to shape the popular image of pulp SF in the early post WWII years. After the war he studied at the Art Institute of Pittsburgh when, at a fellow student's suggestion, he sent one of his class assignments to *Weird Tales*. It was published in the November 1950 issue and the rest, as they say, is history. From 1953 he started drawing for *Astounding*, and continued when it became ***Analog***. His non-SF credits include work for *Mad* magazine and NASA (the Skylab 1 badge) as well as other astronomical work. He has won the Hugo Award for Best Professional Artist in: 1956, 1959, 1970, 1972, 1973, 1974, 1975, and 1976 in addition to being nominated a score of times. He was a Guest of Honour at the 1982 and 2003 **World SF Convention** but alas could not attend the latter due to poor health. Check out many of the *Astounding* and *Fantasy and Science Fiction* magazine covers of the '50s-70's as well as a number of paperbacks from publishers Ace, DAW and Laser Books. Much of his early work of note is contained in the volume *Frank Kelly Freas: The Art of Science Fiction* (1977). There is also *Frank Kelly Freas: A Separate Star* (1984) and *Frank Kelly Freas: As He Sees It* (2000)... AND PUBLISHERS please always credit a novel's cover artist on the copyright page!

Freejack – film, US (1992), *dir*. Geoff Murphy (director of the New Zealand art-house type movie *The Quiet Earth*). Principal cast: Emilio Estevez, Mick Jagger, Rene Russo and Anthony Hopkins. Based on the **Robert Sheckley** novel *Immortality Inc* (1957). Racing driver Alex Furlong dies on the track in an explosive crash. He wakes up in an environmentally degraded future where the population is largely sick through pollution. Time travel is a rare phenomenon as only those who will not be missed, and have no further contribution to make to their original time, can be transported forwards to the future. Being from a time when humans were healthier, Alex's body has a high medical value, so providing the motive as to why he has been 'freejacked'. Anthony Hopkins plays, with conviction, the rich businessman after Alex's body. The same cannot be said of Mick Jagger (the security chief) who initially seems out of place and who takes a while to settle into his role. However the film is logical within its own SF framework, reasonably fast-paced and with fair effects. It is a typical example of how 1990s film science fiction still owes much to, and relies heavily on, Golden Age written SF. (A version of Sheckley's *Immortality Inc* was also adapted for TV and appeared in the anthology series ***Out of the Unknown***.)

Galaxy Quest – film, US (2000) *dir*. Dean Parisot. *Galaxy Quest* is an SF fan's movie. Its plot concerns the stars of an old, no-longer run but cult, TV series called 'Galaxy Quest' (a thinly disguised *Star Trek*) who make their living through appearances at conventions and endorsing products. However their lives change when real aliens turn up having received the TV broadcasts and misinterpreted them as historical documents. They beam the actors aboard a duplicate 'Protector' – the ship from the 'Galaxy Quest' series – and ask the actors to save them from an evil interstellar warlord. Overtaken by events the actors make the best of their situation and ultimately save the day. The parallels with *Star Trek* are many and the Jason Nesmith character is, to all intents and purposes, William Shatner. The geeky side of fandom is also portrayed with the beginning and end of the film being set in a 'Galaxy Quest' convention. The film's makers went to some lengths to detail the fictional 'Galaxy Quest' series and even placed an episode guide on the web. *Galaxy Quest* was the winner of the 2000 Festival of Fantastic Films best film of the year poll and awarded the 2000 Hugo for Best Dramatic Presentation. However it should be noted that the Hugo that year was conducted under Australian rules whereby second and third choices count: by first choice alone ***The Matrix*** would have been the winner). Principal Cast: Tim Allen (Jason Nesmith (Cmndr Peter Quincy Taggert)); Alan Rickman (Alexander Dane (Dr Lazarus of Tev'Meck)); Sigourney (***Alien***, ***Galaxy Quest***, ***Ghostbusters***) Weaver (Gwen De Marco (Lt Tawny Madison)); Sam Rockwell, Tony Shalhour, Daryl Mitchell, Enrico Colantoni, Robin Sachs, and Patrick Breen.

Gateway – novel (1977) by **Frederick Pohl**. Robinette Broadhead boards the long deserted Heechee space station, Gateway, ready to gamble his life. Gateway is part of a galactic travel network abandoned by a vastly superior Heechee race and used by humans as their potential highway to the stars. However, the risk is great; the network does not always return its passengers alive, sometimes it does not return them at all. But for those who do return, and bring back usable Heechee technology, the rewards are equally vast, and so Broadhead becomes very rich, but at the same time is plagued by lost love and memories. *Gateway* deservedly won most of 1978's awards for Best Novel, including the Hugo, Nebula, and John W Campbell, and also topping the *Locus* readers poll. *Gateway* spawned three sequels: *Beyond the Blue Event Horizon* (1980), in which the backdrop is expanded upon and we learn where the Heechee went; *Heechee Rendezvous* (1984), in which the Heechee are encountered and it is discovered what they are hiding from; and *The Annals of the Heechee* (1987), which concludes the tale as Broadhead, now stored as a computer intelligence, faces the Assassins, foe of the Heechee. A collection of related stories, *The Gateway Trip,* was released in 1990.

Gateway Trip, The – col. (1990). See ***Gateway*** and **Pohl, Frederick**.

Gaughan, Jack – artist, US (1930-1985). When attending the World SF Convention make a point of checking out the fan art on display. Some of it is excellent and, presumably free of commercial time constraints and such, can be better than that of professionals. It is worth briefly citing Jack Gaughan as not only has he won the Hugo for his work on a number of occasions, namely 1967, '68 and '69, but his first was actually a fan-pro double win, unique in Hugo history – one being for professional and the other fan. He is one of the few acknowledged fan artists to become an internationally recognised professional and was Art Editor for *Galaxy SF* 1969-72.

Gernsback, Hugo – author, editor, US/Belgian (1884–1967). Though the author of a couple of novels in his own right, Hugo Gernsback is principally known as a magazine editor. His first was *Modern Electrics*, but his best known SF publication was ***Amazing Stories*** which began its run in 1926. Other of his pulps included *Amazing Stories Quarterly*, and *Science Wonder Stories*.

Gernsback's fiction and non-fiction articles featured inventions and devices that he thought we would see in the future. Indeed, an article of his in *Modern Electrics* (December 1909) was the first to use the term 'television'. He also foresaw 'canned' music (Musak), radar, floodlit nocturnal sports, liquid fertiliser as a crop accelerant, and complete blood transfusion. Whether we will see other of his concepts, such as orbiting cities, will depend on time. The Science Fiction Achievement Award, the **Hugo** given at the **World SF Convention**, is named after Gernsback.

Ghostbusters – film (1984), *dir*. Ivan Reitman. This comedy Science-Fantasy concerns itself with three parapsychologist researchers who, having had their research funding withdrawn, set up an independent ghost-busting business, trapping and removing spirits from haunted houses. However an evil deity seeks to enter this world, so who you gonna call? 'Ghostbusters!'. A romp of a farce laced with special effects. Principal cast: Bill Murray, Dan Ackroyd, Harold Ramis, Sigourney (***Alien, Galaxy Quest***) Weaver, Rick Moranis, Annie Potts, William Atherton.

Gibson, William – author, US (*b*1948). Reluctant father of **cyberpunk**, Gibson moved to Canada when he was twenty and began publishing SF nine years later with *Fragments of a Hologram Rose* (1977), a short story in *Unearth* (a short-lived US magazine). This and others – like *Johnny Mnemonic* (1981), made into a dull movie in the late nineties starring Keanu Reeves, with a script by Gibson – paved the way for his first novel, ***Neuromancer*** (1984). This book was one of the first novels to be published by Ace as part of their then 'new' Ace SF Specials series and it won the Hugo, Nebula and Philip K. Dick awards for Best Novel in 1985, as well as coming joint 9th in the *Concatenation* All-Time Best SF Novel poll. *Count Zero* (1986), *Mona Lisa Overdrive* (1988), and the collection *Burning Chrome* (1986), all expand upon the *Neuromancer* universe, though are only loosely connected with each other. Gibson then collaborated with **Bruce Sterling** on *The Difference Engine* (1990), a so-called steampunk novel, set in an alternate past where Charles Babbage perfects his mechanical computer, and Lord Byron leads an English technocracy in changing the world. *Virtual Light* (1993) and *Idoru* (1996) seem to have lost the fizz of Gibson's earlier work, and he has spent some time working on movies and on scripts for TV series, such as ***The X-Files'*** episode *Kill Switch*.

While Gibson's career is far from over, 20 years of living with the real internet has robbed cyberspace of any fascination, and his contemporaries—**Robinson, Brin,** *et al* – seem to have outdistanced him.

Gods Themselves, The – novel (1972) by **Isaac Asimov**. Arguably Asimov had already made his major contributions to SF by the late 1950s – the original ***Foundation*** series, his robot stories, short classics like *Nightfall*, and his early Galactic Empire books had all been written prior to the start of the 60s. For nearly fifteen years Asimov effectively left the SF field, ostensibly to work on popularising science through columns and fact books on a variety of non-genre topics; meanwhile SF was redefining itself throughout the 60s, largely due to the works of literary movements in both England and the US. Then Asimov made his return to the field with only his second ever genuine novel (the first having been *The End of Eternity* (1955)) with *The Gods Themselves*. In this, aliens from a parallel universe initiate an exchange of materials which, due to differing physical laws between the two universes, yield 'free' energy for both themselves and humankind. Few suspect that along with the material exchanged, the universes are also exchanging their laws with possibly catastrophic consequences for the human race, and all attempts to bring this to light are met by the stupidity of those who would ignore the risk for the sake of the free energy. The second of the three sections of the book is set entirely in the para-universe, with the aliens who initiated the transfer, and examines their complex life cycle, during the course of which we discover that not all of them are happy about the situation either. However, they have stupidity of their own to contend with... *The Gods Themselves* won Hugo and Nebula Awards in 1973, as well as coming top of the *Locus* poll, for Best Novel. Nearly three decades later, there are many who still cite *The Gods Themselves* as Asimov's best novel, despite all the later novels tying together the *Foundation* and Robot material.

Gojira a.k.a. ***Godzilla, King of the Monsters*** – film, Japan (1954), *dir.* Inoshiro Honda. Toho studios original man-in-a-suit monster (in this case the film's producer, Tomoyuki Tanaka) stomps Tokyo flat after being awoken from deep-sea slumber by an atomic bomb – similar to ***The Beast from Twenty Thousand Fathoms*** (1953) – before going on to star in at least 16 sequels. The West encountered Godzilla when Joseph Levine bought the overseas rights and added new footage with American actors, such as Raymond Burr. In some incarnations the giant lizard is evil personified, while in others he is more like a superhero, keeping the world safe from other monsters. His most recent incarnation was in the 1998 blockbuster *Godzilla*, (from *Independence Day* creators Dean Devlin and Roland Emmerich) which brought the beast a whole new generation of viewers. Gojira-movies have a cult following and many of them are appreciated by Festival of Fantastic Films' audiences.

Golden Age SF – generally attributed to stories from the late 1930s through to the mid-1940s when *Astounding* (See *Analog*) and a number of US pulps were publishing shorts, and serialised novellas and novels from many principal writers of the time.

Golem: And How He Came Into The World, The – film, Germany (1920) *dir*. Paul Wegner and Carl Boese. Principal cast: Paul Wegner, Albert Steinruck and Ernst Deutsch. In 16th century Prague, a Rabbi builds a man of clay and infuses life, or at least turns it into an automaton, so as to defend the community against the threat of massacre. Misused by its creator's assistant, it rebels and becomes violent. It is calmed by a girl offering it an apple before removing its life-giving amulet and reducing it to clay again. There are several versions of this film which in turn influenced the 1931 film version of *Frankenstein*. *Golem* is one of the all-time most attended of movies screened at the Festival of Fantastic Films.

Gonna Roll The Bones – short story (1967) by **Fritz Leiber**. Joe Slattermill, an addicted gambler in a rural setting, lives in an age of spaceships, but is dirt poor. Then one night he gets the chance to go up against the Big Gambler and bet his soul. This tale won the 1968 Hugo for Best Novelette; though there is no overt SF in the tale, much of the imagery, and some specifics of the backdrop, are very firmly of the genre.

Greenland, Colin – author, UK (*b*1954). If SF has an academic writer, then Colin Greenland could well be he, with his doctorate in English from Oxford University for a thesis on SF's **new wave**. A former writer in residence at the SF Foundation (see **Foundation, SF**), and an original member of the *Interzone* collective, Colin's work tends to be on the edge and very rich. This, while liberating for some, for others it makes his books less accessible. Of note his works include *Take Back Plenty* (1990) – a space opera with a care-free, down-to-Earth heroine Tabitha Jute – and its sequels, and *Harm's Way* (1993) – another space opera, but more a science fantasy, written as if the Victorian British Empire ruled the planets, with clippers sailing the solar winds. It has been described as a work Charles Dickens might have written if he were to do SF.

Green Mars – novel (1993) by **Kim Stanley Robinson**. The 'Mars' trilogy, consisting of *Red Mars*, *Green Mars* and ***Blue Mars***, is a long and complex story detailing humanity's arrival on, and eventual colonisation of, the red planet. Other writers have attempted this, but no-one has come close to Kim Stanley Robinson's scope and imagination. He tries to cover every aspect of the colonisation from the technical to the sociological. How will people cope with such a harsh environment? How will they cope with themselves? *Green Mars* picks up the story half way through when humans are already established on Mars and are starting to alter it to be more suitable for human life. But how far should they go? The 'Reds' want to halt all progress, the 'Greens' want to continue and make Mars a second Earth. Clashes are inevitable. If there is any fault with this book it is simply that Robinson tries to do too much. He wants to examine every aspect of the colonisation, but at the same time put forward his views on a better world. He wants a greener future and more democracy. As the 'Martians' grope towards this new world we can see his hopes for our own future. It is a utopian one. But sometimes things become lost in the shuffle or he spends too long on one item at the expense of others. Nonetheless this is a masterpiece. It won the Hugo Award for Best Novel in 1994 and came top of the annual *Locus* readers' top ten poll.

GUFF – See **Fan Funds**.

Haldeman, Joe – author, US (*b*1943). After studying physics and astronomy at college, Haldeman served as a combat engineer in Vietnam from 1967 to '69. He was severely wounded and earned a Purple Heart. This whole experience greatly informs the majority of his writing, not least his first (non-SF) novel, *War Year* (1972). However, it was with his much-acclaimed 1974 novel, ***The Forever War***, that Haldeman made his mark. It would be years before the majority of the American public, *via* the Hollywood establishment, could face the legacy of Vietnam, but in the SF genre this book was greatly treasured as an oblique comment on the pointless aspects of war. The story tells of Private William Mandella and the price he pays in alienation from his society, due to the time-dilation effects of interstellar travel (which paralleled the way soldiers returning from Vietnam found America and its people's attitude to that war changed). *The Forever War* won a Nebula in 1975, and a Hugo in 1976, also topping the *Locus* poll that year, and was voted joint seventh in the *Concatenation* readers' poll for all-time Best SF Novel. Strangely, however, this multi-award winning novel was actually an "edited" version of the novel, and it was not until 1991 that the missing section, *You can never go back* (published separately in *Amazing* magazine, 1975), was restored. *Mindbridge* (1976) was quite fascinating in its own way, but Haldeman's next unqualified successes were the trilogy *Worlds* (1981), *Worlds Apart* (1983), and the later published conclusion *Worlds Enough and Time* (1992). In this near future, the human race lives in space colonies following a nuclear conflagration. Probably the outstanding facets of this work are those of coping with the consequences of war, and moving forward from it, and this is consistent with much of Haldeman's output. ***The Hemmingway Hoax*** (1990) won the Best Novella Hugo in 1991, and the 1996 collection *None so Blind* topped the *Locus* poll that year. Haldeman has recently won the 1998 Hugo for Best Novel for ***Forever Peace*** (1997), which is not as some might think a sequel to ***The Forever War***: the sequel is *Forever Free* (1999). However *Forever Peace*, like *The Forever War,* is a comment on war and its psychological and social impacts. Set in the near future it concerns soldiers ('mechanics') who mentally-linked ('jacked'), both to themselves and their charges, remotely control battle robots. Haldeman is also known to ***Star Trek*** for his two novels *Planet of Judgement* (1977) and *World Without End* (1979), two of the better of such offerings at the time. Haldeman now lives in Gainesville, Florida, with his wife, Gay, and teaches writing at MIT as an adjunct professor.

Hard SF – SF that has either machinery/technology or scientific fact (or at least scientific plausibility) very much at its focus.

Harrison, Harry – author, US [UK resident] (*b*1925). Harry Harrison is at home both with serious writing and comedy. With regard to the latter he is perhaps most famous for his ***Stainless Steel Rat*** series, about a super crook turned interstellar law agent who takes delight in putting down bureaucrats with one hand while he takes on the forces of evil with the other. Meanwhile going over the top, almost literally, is the *Bill, The Galactic Hero* series: a cardboard cut-out pastiche of an interstellar warrior hero. Harrison has even used comedy as a vehicle for exploring an SF trope. His *Technicolor Time Machine* (1967), in which an ailing film studio uses time travel to film historic epics, is a superb blend of comedy, SF and action. Turning away from humour, ***Make Room! Make Room!*** (1966) placed him firmly on the SF map as an author with something serious to say, and in this instance it is a warning of the Malthusian trap we may well be heading towards with an over-populated Earth. *Make Room! Make Room!* is an important work, not only because it is one of the earliest eco-SF stories concerning the population bomb but, because it is so well researched. It even has an appendixed background reading list of over a score of texts and two demographic periodicals: as such it is one of an extremely small band of SF works. *Make Room! Make Room!* was the inspiration of the film ***Soylent Green***. Of note, his other serious SF stories include the *Deathworld* series, the first of which (1960) also has an ecological theme with colonists having their new homes' entire ecosystem turn against them. Harry Harrison is a consistent author and, if you've sampled the range of his writing styles, for once you will know what you are going to get by reading the back cover blurb. This reliability has helped endear him to his readers for over four decades. He has also edited several collections of other writers' short stories including an annual series of *The Year's Best Science Fiction* with **Brian Aldiss** from 1968 through to 1976 – which interestingly occasionally included non-fiction contributions (such as a collection of reviews of ***2001: A Space Odyssey***). He wrote some **Jeff Hawke** scripts for Syd Jordon in 1957 and also some **Flash Gordon** scripts. (See also ***Weird Science***.) Harry Harrison was also the first President of **World SF**.

Harry Potter and the Goblet of Fire – novel (1999) by J. K. Rowling. Harry Potter, complete with glasses and school uniform, is nonetheless an unusual kid. It is not the lightning shaped mark on his brow, nor that he has a pet owl that makes him strange, but that he has magical powers. So that he can harness them properly he goes to Hogwarts School for wizards and witches. There, with his friends Ron and Hermione, he escapes his horrible non-magical (muggle) foster family, the Dursleys. But the Lord Voldemort, who killed Harry's parents, is not far away... This children's book was not only a huge hit with SF fans but a roaring commercial success among children and their parents alike, as were all the others in the Harry Potter series and its cinematic spin offs. However it is hardly SF, other than that the school implicitly presents magic as a formulaic discipline; though there is nothing new in that, nor by itself does that make the work one of SF. The reason for its inclusion in this guide (as with the film *The Princess Bride*) is that it won a Hugo. As such it demonstrates that a public attraction, if sufficiently great, can influence science fiction's most prestigious award. In winning the Hugo for Best Novel in 2001 it became both the first outright fantasy book, and first young adult, novel to be so honoured. It should be remembered that the Hugo is not just the "Science Fiction Achievement Award" but that one of the administering body's (the World Science Fiction Society's) constitution articles allows for nominations for works of fantasy. [This last enables borderline works to be nominated that are not technically SF in the purest sense (such as for example **Superman** – for there is no hypothetical technical reason why a humanoid alien might have the innate ability to fly). The spirit of the Hugos up to 2001 had been kept with regard to the Best Novel category with no pure fantasy being nominated.] However the Hugo, and its strength, is purely and simply an expression of opinion of the thousands registering with the **World SF Convention (Worldcon)**. In 2001 Rowling's book won. Even so there were justifiable rumblings. Given that winning the Hugo for Best Novel is one of the criteria for entry into this guide, we include Rowling's work.

Heavy Metal – comic, US (*crtd*1976). *Heavy Metal* is in effect the US spin off of the French *Metal Hurlant* (1975-87) and indeed shares a number of the artists and stories (such as *The Airtight Garage of Jerry Cornelius* by Jean Giraud (Moebius). (See also **Michael Moorcock**.) Concentrating on quality, and sometimes experimental, artwork *Heavy Metal* caters for a decidedly adult audience covering both SF and fantasy. However because of the wide range of ground covered (both in terms of genre and style) its readers tend to be those whose main interest include comic artwork. However it is worth looking out for some of the graphic novel spin-offs such as Angus McKie's *So Beautiful and So Dangerous* and Richard Corben's *Den*.

Hello America – novel, UK (1981). By **J. G Ballard** it concerns two journeys, one a trip across America, the other a journey through the American dream. Following the exhaustion of its oil supply, North America falls into decline. Furthermore, the construction of a dam across the Bering Strait has turned the whole continent into a burning desert. After a century, a group of explorers return. Among them Wayne, a stowaway with dreams of the old America. Eventually, they reach Las Vegas where a mad man has set himself up as the new President and gained full access to the old super power's nuclear arsenal. Ballard's account of the journey, through the eyes of young Wayne, takes on an almost imaginary quality. From the sea, the explorers see sunlight glinting off sand and believe that New York is covered in gold. They are so obsessed with America's greatness that even everyday things, like clothing, are evidence of some past utopia.

Heinlein, Robert A. – author, US (1907-1988). He was born in Butler, Missouri, and graduated from the US Naval Academy in 1929. He served as a naval officer until 1934 when he retired due to ill-health, then studied maths and physics at the University of California. After a number of jobs, Heinlein had his first SF story, *Lifeline*, published in 1939. Older and more worldly-wise than his contemporaries selling to SF magazines, Heinlein was to transform the face of science fiction, set the pace for the so-called **Golden Age**, and profoundly influence the field for decades. In 1941 Heinlein introduced us to the recurring character of Lazarus Long, in *Methuselah's Children*, the 'father' of an extended family of immortals; extended, that is, across time and alternate worlds. *The Day After Tomorrow* (1951), originally published in 1941 as *Sixth Column* by Anson MacDonald, was part of a complex future history which attempted to cover six centuries. In this case America is over-run by an Asian enemy and the 'resistance', in the guise of a religion, use super-technology to fight back. ***Double Star*** (1956), similar to Fraser's *Royal Flash* in that the protagonist is forced to impersonate a famous figure to whom he has an accidental resemblance, won the Hugo for Best Novel in 1957. In all it is probably Heinlein's work during the

1940's and 50's that is most fondly remembered and respected, from the future histories and juveniles to delightful little time travel novels like *The Door Into Summer* (1957). Then in 1959 he wrote **Starship Troopers**. Though a fine book, it upset many who felt that it portrayed the militaristic side of Heinlein's right-wing anarchist libertarianism a little too fascistically. Equally, much of his output during the sixties was lionised by the younger, often 'hippie' generation, for its espousal of free love and mysticism, as well as its iconoclasm. Certainly this was true of **Stranger in a Strange Land** (1961) and, to a lesser extent (but only because of the change to 'sword and sorcery', making it harder to see the book in contemporary terms), of *Glory Road* (1963). *Stranger* did win a Hugo in 1961, and was reprinted in an expanded version in 1990, which is somewhat ironic as it had been, in its time, the longest SF novel ever written. The novel most unscathed by criticism from the 1960's was the 1967 Hugo award-winning ***The Moon is a Harsh Mistress*** (1966), a tale of rebellion on the Moon which turns into a sort of War of Independence. In 1969 Heinlein was a guest commentator in the US television coverage of the first moon landing. It was in 1973 that Lazarus Long resurfaced in *Time Enough for Love*, and the family and their attendant 'universes' dominated much of Heinlein's later output, in one way or another. The late 1970's and the 80's, most critics agree, marked a continued decline in Heinlein's work largely due, it would seem, to the fact that the SF genre had, to some extent, outgrown one of its parents. ***Job: A Comedy of Justice*** (1984) topped the *Locus* poll in the 1985 'fantasy novel' category, showing that Heinlein certainly still had admirers, who clearly enjoyed this story of random reality changes. Notwithstanding the decline in Heinlein's popularity, he was greatly honoured in his time, winning Nebulas along with the Hugos, being Guest of Honour three times (1941, 1961, and 1976) at the **World SF Convention**, and topping Best Author polls. ***The Moon is a Harsh Mistress*** came joint 4th in the *Concatenation* poll for Best All-Time SF Novel, and Heinlein was the most frequently cited author in the poll, taking into account his votes for other titles. Along with **Asimov** and **Clarke**, Heinlein was absolutely integral to the way SF developed, his easy-going prose substituting characters and substance for the technological invention of his peers, and introducing real-world concerns into a previously 'ghetto-ised' genre. Indeed, it was largely, some would say solely, due to

Heinlein's successful efforts to sell to non-genre publications that SF became better accepted in the literary world, and paved the way for the **new wave** of sixties US science fiction writers, such as **Harlan Ellison**, who continued to redefine the genre in literary terms. Heinlein died in 1988 in Carmel, California. (See also ***Destination Moon***.)

Hemmingway Hoax, The – short story (1990) by **Joe Haldeman**. On the face of it, this story is a sort of 'alternate worlds' tale wherein the protagonist is forced into a series of moral dilemmas, but where it is not always possible to make the desired choice, or even to retain a sense of identity. However, this work is about influences also, and deals with certain identifications of Haldeman's work with that of Hemmingway, whether such links be real or imagined. This short won both a Hugo and a Nebula for Best Novella in 1991.

Herbert, Frank – author, US (1920-1986). ***Dune*** (1965), and its sequels, are probably the titles most associated with Herbert, and won the first ever Nebula Award for Best Novel, and shared the 1966 Hugo. Born in Tacoma, Washington, and educated at the University of Washington, Seattle, he worked extensively as a journalist and published his first SF story in 1952, *Looking for Something?* Throughout the fifties, Herbert published competent but unregarded short science fiction before finally breaking through with his most enduring creation, the desert planet, Dune. Ecology, evolution and interstellar intrigue mark the entire series of novels, and their depth and intelligence was a breath of fresh air to some, and impenetrably dense to others. The sequence was first continued in 1969 with *Dune Messiah*, then came *Children of Dune* (1976), *God-Emperor of Dune* (1981), *Heretics of Dune* (1984), and finally *Chapterhouse Dune* (1985). These novels of varying quality enrich the Dune universe with detail, but add little to the original ideas contained in the first novel. The 1984 film of *Dune*, directed by David Lynch, and starring Kyle MacLachlan and Jurgen Prochnow among others, was a heroic attempt to bring the book to the big screen, but ultimately failed due to lack of commitment from the studio. Despite the book not making it into *Concatenation's* All-Time book poll, Herbert himself was the sixth most-mentioned author. This was in part due to the number of votes gathered by his non-*Dune* titles, many of which are warmly and often recommended. These include: *The Green*

Brain and *The Eyes of Heisenberg*, both from 1966, the former a tale of mutated social insects, and the latter about genetic engineering and immortality; *Whipping Star* (1970) and its 1977 sequel *The Dosadi Experiment* both look closely at aliens; and *Hellstrom's Hive* (1973), which examines an underground colony of humans bred to act like social insects, that is a utopia when viewed from within, but looks like Hell from the outside. Less popular are the books he wrote with Bill Ransom which comprise the three sequels to *Destination: Void* (1966), and are collectively known as the Pandora sequence, and the book he wrote with his son Brian, *Man of Two Worlds* (1986). It was in 1986 that Frank Herbert died, leaving behind a lasting legacy of intelligent science fiction.

Hercules Text, The – novel (1986) by Jack McDevitt. From the depths of the Galaxy the beats of a pulsar become erratic, odd, artificial....! Suddenly astronomers realise that they are receiving a highly complex message. A message that holds out the promise of new technology and a different perspective of life in the universe. But what of the cultural and even the political implications? The radio astronomers and scientists were to have tackled questions and overcome obstacles they never dreamed they would have to surmount... Similarities will inevitably be drawn with **Sagan's** book ***Contact***. However though McDevitt's book was published the following year, the script was submitted before ***Contact*** was published. The ***Hercules Text*** is one of the most believable of the first contact books of the late 20th century, and clearly McDevitt did his astronomical and SETI homework. It came top of the annual *Locus* readers poll, 'first novel' category. It also won the Philip K Dick Special Award.

Hitch-hiker's Guide to the Galaxy – radio series (also record, books & TV) (*fb*1978) by Douglas Adams. Decidedly British in humour, with its roots at least partially in the *Goons* and *Monty Python*, the BBC unwittingly let loose a show that was to captivate a nation. Broadcast at first on UK national Radio 4, *The Hitch-hiker's Guide to the Galaxy* was so successful that soon record albums of (slightly-reworked) versions of the episodes were on sale. A year later and the first of the *Hitch-hiker* books was published; these contained significant plot thread differences to the original series, but which added to, rather than detracted from, the radio broadcast's story. However the humour, many purists would say, shone through best from the broadcasts. In the early 1980s the BBC broadcast a TV version: unfortunately the limited effects and scenery was a major handicap. But if overall *Hitch-hiker's* was a great success with the British public at large, how well did it go down with SF fans? In 1979 the World SF Convention came to the UK. Now, all those registered for the **World SF Convention (Worldcon)** are eligible to vote for the Hugo Award but attendance itself is not a criterion. Consequently while nearly all UK fans who registered for the convention attended, the same was not true of overseas fans. The Hugo that year for Best Dramatic Presentation went to ***Superman***, yet just before the announcement when all those nominated were read out, by far the biggest cheer went to *Hitch-hikers*. Christopher Reeve (the star of *Superman*) acknowledged this when accepting the Award... So what was all the fuss about? The plot for the series in essence begins with an intergalactic book researcher, Ford Prefect, who has been accidentally stuck on Earth for a number of years having arrived to update Earth's entry in *The Hitch-hiker's Guide to the Galaxy*. In the current edition Earth's entry reads 'harmless' (well there are a hundred billion stars in the Galaxy and only limited space in the book's microprocessors) but Ford has spent his time wisely and plans to update it to 'mostly harmless'. Ford escaped from the Earth with his Earthman friend, Arthur, just as the planet was being blown up by the Vogons (who are known for the worst poetry in the Universe) to make way for a hyper-space by-pass. Indeed there was no point in humanity 'acting all surprised'. All the planning charts and demolition orders had been on display locally in Alpha Centauri for 50 years, so there was plenty of time to lodge any formal complaint... And so our protagonists begin to thumb their way around the galaxy with the help of a book, *The Hitch-hikers Guide to the Galaxy*, that was: "more popular than the *Celestial Home Care Omnibus*; better selling than *Fifty-three More Things to do in Zero Gravity*; more controversial than Oolon Colluphid's trilogy of philosophical blockbusters *Where God Went Wrong*, *Some More of God's Greatest Mistakes* and *Who is This God Person Anyway?*; and cheaper than the *Encyclopaedia Galactica*." Finally, *Hitch-hikers* was voted into the *Concat* all-time greatest book poll chart, but our firm advice is get the tapes of the original broadcast (especially the first season and the Christmas episode) from the BBC's merchandising arm and find out why the answer to the greatest question of them all, life the universe and everything, 'is... is... is... forty-two!' A third series was broadcast in 2004 (21st September to 26th October) with the principal characters played by the original cast with the exception of Peter Jones (The Book) who had earlier died. However this new series did incorporate the voice of the late Douglas Adams (taken from his recorded readings of his books) so as to play one of the characters. A feature film is to be released in 2005. Principal (radio) cast: Simon Jones, Geoffrey McGivern, Peter Jones, Mark Wing-Davey, and Susan Sheridan.

Hominids – novel by Robert J. Sawyer (***Calculating God***). Set in the present day, there is a parallel Earth in which Mankind never made it but instead the dominant species is Neanderthal. They have developed a different (in some respects more developed) technology than our own (though we have explored some areas they have not). All well and good. Then a Neanderthal scientist, researching quantum computing, opens a temporary gateway into our universe and falls through. Unable to speak English, he causes much puzzlement and, of course, is confused himself at this unexpected turn of events... *Hominids* is the first part of the 'Neanderthal Parallax' trilogy. It won the Hugo for 'Best Novel' in 2003.

Hothouse – series (1962), and subsequently a novel, by **Brian Aldiss**. A series of short stories originally published in *Fantasy & Science Fiction*. In the far future much of the Earth consists of a hot tropical rain forest. But it *is* in the far future and the ecologies of today have evolved and, it is hinted, possibly in part were further developed by genetic engineering. Not only do some plants have giant armoured leaves (making forest edges difficult to pass through) but in other instances human-types are directly tethered by a nerve type umbilical to special trees. Our protagonist, a youth, journeys through this exotic world and, seen through his eyes, a rich biological tapestry unfolds. The *Hothouse* stories were collected together in 1962, the year the series won the Hugo for Best Short Fiction.

Hugo Award (see also **Conventions**). The Hugo Award is the most prestigious SF award since they were first presented back in 1953. Formally known as the 'Science Fiction Achievement Award', it is named after **Hugo Gernsback**, the writer and editor. It is awarded for new works first published, screened or broadcast during the previous calendar year to the **World SF Convention** (**Worldcon**) being held. Unlike many awards, which are decided upon by a small panel of judges, the Hugo is voted for by those SF fans who have registered to attend the Worldcon (even if they are not actually at the convention itself). Consequently it has the potential of representing the views of several thousand SF enthusiasts, though in reality not every Worldcon-attendee votes, nor do all those who do vote vote in every category. When it was first presented there were seven categories, and today there are thirteen (or fourteen since any particular year's Worldcon committee can create a special category for that year). The most coveted of all the Award categories is that of Best Novel and here publishers have not been slow to recognise the fact by trumpeting the Award on winners' covers. Regrettably for the average public a number of large book chains (in several countries) who centrally approve titles to go on their shops' shelves have been slow to recognise the Hugo's significance, so it may take a few years after it has been published before an average member of the book-reading public sees a Hugo winner on the shelves. (This is just one reason why many SF buffs frequent specialist shops.) Nonetheless every novel that has won the Hugo has gone on to have a number of printings. Indeed almost every film (or the series of a TV episode) that has won the Hugo for Best Dramatic Presentation has been commercially successful, or at least achieved cult status (and frequently both). On the other hand, probably due to the Award's timing (over a year after first screening), film distributors have not recognised the Awards, which is understandable as their marketing pitch peaks in the week before and after initial release. However, what is regrettable is that TV station film selectors seem unaware of the Hugo and this is particularly noticeable when many stations compile a special season of SF films. Notwithstanding the dramatic dimension, the Hugo remains by far the most significant, and useful, SF award as far as Anglophone SF is concerned.

Hyperion – novel (1989) by **Dan Simmons**. With just three novels under his belt Dan Simmons gave us the SF equivalent of Chaucer's *Canterbury Tales*. It is the 29th century. Seven pilgrims on their way to the planet Hyperion tell their tales. Each carries their own secret. Meanwhile the Galaxy is on the brink of war. The pilgrims' ultimate destiny is Hyperion's Time Tombs. These move backwards through time and are guarded by a vicious multi-bladed creature, the Shrike. However it is the background tapestry of the Galaxy itself, emerging through the book, that is as compelling as the individual tales, and indeed the mysteries of the Time Tombs and the Shrike. *Hyperion* won the Hugo in 1990 for Best Novel. It also came top of the annual *Locus* readers poll. The book spawned the award-winning sequels **The Fall of Hyperion** and *Endymion*.

Ilium – novel (2003) by **Dan Simmons**. The kick off point for this tale is the *Iliad*, the story of the 10-year siege of Troy following Helen's abduction. This event is being witnessed by a 20th century academic brought to life by the Greek gods, though only he and Zeus know the course of the *Iliad*, this knowledge having been forbidden to the others in the pantheon. These gods live on Olympus Mons on Mars in the far future and may (or may not) be post-humans from Earth. The few thousand humans left on Earth watch the drama unfold *via* Turin-cloths as an entertainment, unaware of the existence of the gods except as players in the drama. Meanwhile the moravecs (a bio-mechanical race engineered by earlier humans) of the outer solar system are becoming worried by the amount of quantum tunnelling going on in the inner system and send agents to investigate. The humans lead lives of luxury and ease, but are restricted to just 100 years of existence, but a small group discover a 1,400 year old woman and attempt to reach the habitation rings above the planet where the post-humans are said to dwell, and where a heavenly life awaits those who reach their 100th birthday. But not all is as it seems and the multiple uses of quantum tunnelling appears to have ripped a hole in the fabric of reality letting *something* in from outside... *Ilium* came top of the 2004 *Locus* poll.

I Married a Monster From Outer Space – film, US (1958), *dir*. Gene Fowler jr. This low budget movie has it all (well in pre-60s terms at least). However though stereotypes abound, they are not the usual Hollywood stereotypes, but those of US 1950s society in general. Bill (played by the novelist Tom Tyron) is late for his wedding, as one is having been captured and replaced by an alien. He gets married to Marge (Gloria Talbot) who after a year has not gussed what is going on, though does confide to her mother in a letter that Bill is not the man she fell in love with... It transpires that Bill is not the only one in town to have been replaced by aliens. They are here trying to mate with Earth women as their own females have died, but there is a chromosomal problem (surprise). One day a suspicious Marge follows alien Bill to his space ship; after some soul-searching she goes to the doctor with this news. He believes her and sets about getting a posse to go after the aliens. Despite this bare bones synopsis, this really is a little gem of a film and a window on American society's 1950s ideals. Arguably it owes much to the subconscious exploration of psychological problems associated with virgin marriages (common during the 50s). More consciously it was in all likelihood inspired by an earlier production, *I Married a Communist* (which itself is built on the post virgin wedding night problems). (Gals, if your man turns out to be a horrible sex fiend on your wedding night, do not panic, he is probably a communist or an alien.) *I Married a Monster* contains some lovely clichés for SF fans; the aliens consider humans ugly but wish to breed with them, and they find alcohol toxic. It is also a comparatively rare example of where the low budget adds to the fun through forcing one's attention on the ridiculous nature of the situation which is taken with such dead-pan seriousness. *I Married a Monster from Outer Space* is one of the all time most viewed movies of those screened at the Festival of Fantastic Films, and is best seen with one's partner... The 1998 re-make, *I Married A Monster* (*dir*. Nancy Malone) successfully transformed the film to colour.

Incredible Shrinking Man, The – film, US (1957), *dir*. Jack (***The Creature from the Black Lagoon***, ***It Came From Outer Space***) Arnold, with a screenplay by the writer **Richard Matheson**. While out at sea fishing, Scott Carey (Grant Williams) is exposed to a radioactive fallout cloud. To cut a long story 'short', Scott begins to shrink. Much to the dismay of his wife (Randy Stuart) the doctors and scientists can find no cure. Now small enough to live in a doll's house, Scott becomes prey to mundane creatures – most notably a spider. Fighting to stay alive, Scott leaves the comparative safety of the doll's house (big mistake) and faces the perils of the cellar. Finally he manages to leave the basement through an air vent, presumably to the garden outside... Shrinking films are problematic from a SF rationale perspective. Does the food you eat suddenly shrink too so that you can digest the atoms? How does miniaturised haemoglobin cope with proper-sized oxygen molecules in the air? Consequently one needs effort to suspend disbelief. However the attraction of such films—of which *The Incredible Shrinking Man* is the definitive early classic—is that the protagonist invariably has to battle to simply survive encounters which are usually so trivial that they are ignored by the normal-sized. And so seemingly harmless day-to-day environments become nightmarish. *The Incredible Shrinking Man* was awarded the Hugo in 1958 for the most Outstanding Movie.

Indiana Jones and the Last Crusade – film, US (1989) *dir.* Steven (see also **Brian Aldiss**, ***Close Encounters of the Third Kind***, ***The Twilight Zone***, ***Jurassic Park***, and ***Raiders of the Lost Ark***) Spielberg. In 1984 the prequel, *Indiana Jones and the Temple of Doom*, had failed to live up to the promise of the predecessor film, ***Raiders of the Lost Ark*** (1981). This sequel, however, was a return to the excellent form of that first offering, and re-united Harrison Ford, Denholm Elliott and John Rhys-Davies in a quest for the Holy Grail, once again racing against the Nazis. The film opens with a long sequence in which the young Indiana (River Phoenix) finds his adventuring vocation, while suffering the indifference of his father (Sean (***Outland***, ***Time Bandits***, ***Zardoz***) Connery). This, incidentally, gave rise to a spin-off TV series, a children's' cartoon, and a short-lived comics title. Much later, the adult Indiana is set on the trail of his missing father by the villainous Julian Glover, and teams up with his father's assistant, Alison Doody. The professor had gone missing when close to recovering the Holy Grail, which had been his life's quest. After various nail-biting set pieces, Indiana is forced to confront his own faith to save his dying father, while simultaneously defeating the bad guys. Jeffrey Boam's screenplay (from a George (***Star Wars***) Lucas story) contains a great deal of humour, and Ford and Connery make the most of every line. Like the original, this film also won a Best Dramatic Presentation Hugo in 1990, proving once again that SF is a broad church.

Integral Trees, The – novel (1984) by **Larry Niven**. Another fantastical setting rivalling ***Ringworld***, this time a life-supporting gas torus (doughnut shape) around a dense neutron star. The humans that live here are descendants of a ship's crew that got stranded here 500 years ago (or perhaps they chose to colonize here on purpose, the novel is deliberately ambiguous). The story explores the 'world' through some of its inhabitants' struggle for survival.

Interzone – magazine, UK (*crtd* 1982).   Very much of a literary persuasion, *Interzone* provides a short-story forum for authors. Here it is the writing that counts, as long as it is intelligent. It need not be restricted to any particular sub-genre. Consequently regular readers are not large in number as few find many stories to their taste. Having said this most readers find something in each edition so that, and that the quality of writing is high, has meant that the magazine has survived to today. Furthermore, its stories are occasionally anthologised in book form.   As such it has helped nurture a number of writers including **Stephen Baxter**, **Greg Egan**, Ian MacDonald, Paul J McAuley and Geoff Ryman.   Originally *Interzone* was edited by a collective (**John Clute**, **Colin (Foundation SF) Greenland**, Roz Kaveny, Simon Ounsley and David Pringle), though by 1988 David Pringle was the only one left with any real hands-on involvement. In the 1990s he was joined by Paul Brazier who principally took over the typesetting and layout responsibilities, though was occasionally a guest editor for the odd edition. In 2004 Andy Cox took over the editorial reins.

Invasion of the Body Snatchers – film, US (1956), *dir*. Don Siegel. Principal cast: Kevin McCarthy, Dana Wynter, Larry Gates, King Donovan, Carolyn Jones, Virginia Christine, and Sam Peckinpah. Based on the novel *The Body Snatchers* by Jack Finney. A small Californian town is insidiously taken over by aliens. They arrive as pods from which, while the victim sleeps and then dies, a carbon copy of the human emerges complete with memories. A young doctor, Miles, and his girlfriend, Becky, find the truth. Desperately they try to stay awake and escape the town.   The penultimate scene sees Miles attempt to stop passing cars on a duel carriageway to warn people that 'they [the aliens] are here'. The film was remade with better effects in 1978 (*dir*. Philip Kaufman) with San Francisco as the city being invaded and Donald Sutherland as the last survivor.   Memorably Kevin McCarthy reprises his role for a brief scene early on when he tries to warn passing motorists that 'they are here', while Don Siegal plays a cab driver. The 1978 version also stars: Leonard (***Star Trek***) Nimoy, Veronica (***Alien***) Cartwright and Jeff (***The Fly***) Goldblum. (Neither film is to be confused with *Body Snatchers* (1993) *dir*. Abel Ferrara, which is essentially the same story set on an army base but there is debate as to whether it is told nearly so well. (*NB*. A contrary view to one of this guide's compilers).)

However, *Invasion of the Body Snatchers* (1956) is a Festival of Fantastic Films favourite.

Invisible Man, The – novel (1897) by **H G Wells**, subtitled '*A Grotesque Romance*'. A common concept (since *Frankenstein*) is that of the scientist over-stepping the mark in the quest for discovery and/or power. But in SF, the discovery itself can often have consequences for the discoverer... In *The Invisible Man*, a scientist discovers the means of making himself invisible, but in the process becomes a megalomaniac. Under the threat of him as an invisible terror, the population unites and attempts to capture the man... In 1933 Universal released the first film version of the novel. Directed by James Whale, and with Claude Rains making his debut star appearance, it was the closest to the novel out of a number of subsequent remakes and quasi-sequels (such as *The Invisible Man Returns* (1940) and *Invisible Agent* (1942)). Yet Whale's offering was nonetheless disliked by Wells himself. More recently the film *The Hollow Man* (2000) is a return closer to Wells' original vision. Though the novel was published decades before either first Hugo Awards or the *Locus* annual readers poll *The Invisible Man* was one of Wells' most famous and respected works. [A derivative TV series, *The Invisible Man*, was made by ATV in 1958 (the star was nameless being invisible) and another by Universal in 1975 starred David McCallum (which later was re-named as the *Gemini Man* (1976) starring Ben Murphey). Conversely, an alternative spin on Wells' idea—whereby society in the form of the US secret service sought to exploit an innocent (a stock market analyst) who became invisible as a result of a laboratory accident—was used by H F Saint in a novel (1987) which became the light weight, but entertaining, film *Memoirs of An Invisible Man* (1992) starring Chevy Chase, Daryl (*Blade Runner*) Hannah and Sam(*Jurassic Park*) Neill. *dir.* John (*The Thing, Dark Star*) Carpenter.] Wells was the ninth most cited author in the *Concatenation* poll (see also **War of the Worlds** and **The Time Machine**).

It Came From Outer Space – film, US (1953), *dir.* Jack (*The Incredible Shrinking Man*, *Creature from the Black Lagoon*) Arnold. Principal cast: Richard Carlson, Barbara Rush, Charles Drake, and Kathleen Hughes. The screenplay for *It Came From Outer Space* was nominally written by Harry Essex but this was in turn based on an original version by **Ray Bradbury** who worked closely with the film. Plot: Alien space ship lands in the US desert but is spotted on the way down by an astronomer. On arriving in the landing area some of the locals seem to be acting strangely... Is it an invasion...? This is reputedly the first film to portray the alien influence or 'control' of individual humans. A 3-D version adds much to this minor classic. *It Came From Outer Space* is one of the most all-time viewed films of those screened at the Festival of Fantastic Films.

Jeff Hawke – comic character and strip, UK (*crtd* 1954). Conceived by Eric Souster and artist Sydney Jordan, Jeff Hawke was an adult version of, and contemporary with, **Dan Dare** (*crtd* 1950). It ran for 21 years. Set in the near future (a portrayal, which we can now see for the mid-twentieth century perspective, was not that bad), Jeff Hawke was a British astronaut. Earth's space programme relied on conventional rockets. Humanity has basic outposts on the Moon and Mars, while manned craft had reached the gas giants. This in itself did not make the series special. The other backdrop was that the Galaxy was teeming with life and so the Solar system, indeed Earth, was prone to the occasional visitor, and indeed had been for thousands of years. (Hence Hawke's adventures sometimes contained elements that later became commonly associated with the non-SF, other-worldly claims of Eric Von Daniken.) Inevitably these aliens encountered Hawke. Though **hard SF**, the strip was written with a dry wit, and humour vaguely reminiscent of writers such as **Stanislaw Lem** and Douglas (*Hitch-Hikers' Guide*) Adams. The artwork, mainly line drawn inks, was realistic as opposed to impressionistic. Perhaps the most amazing thing about the Jeff Hawke strip was its format, typically of three picture frames in a row. This was because the series appeared in a daily newspaper (principally the *Daily Express*). Despite this constraint, each strip successfully conveyed the story and the individual daily strips work well when combined into a single volume. Two such volumes exist, published in the 1980s by Titan Books, and, as with all good SF, they can be as enjoyed today as when the strips were first published well before other SF epics such as *Star Wars* and *2001*. (See also **Harry Harrison**.)

Job: A Comedy of Justice – novel (1984) by **Robert Heinlein**. Alexander Hergenscheimer is being tested. Bounced from reality to reality, all he can count on is the love of his life, Margrethe, an old safety razor and the fact that his job will be as a dishwasher. This comedy of multiple continua topped the *Locus* readers poll in the 'fantasy novel' category, though added little to Heinlein's already considerable reputation in the latter part of his career.

Journey to the Centre of the Earth – novel (1863) by **Jules Verne**. *Voyage au Centre de la Terre* concerns a Victorian-age exploration through a dormant volcanic crater deep into the Earth. There, in the footsteps of an earlier explorer, a small party discover a route supposedly to the very centre of the Earth. The group battles monsters, pit themselves against the subterranean geology and even discover, and cross, an underground sea. The first film version appeared in 1909 as *Voyage au Centre de la Terre* by Segundo de Chomon, a 9 minute short. In 1959 it served as the basis for a full-length family film (*dir.* Henry Levin) starring James Mason, Arlene Dahl, Pat Boone (the '50s pop star), Peter Ronson, Diane Baker, and Thayer David. Not to be confused with an unrelated, and dire, 1993 TV pilot movie of the same name (*dir.* William Dear).

Judge Dredd – comic character. (*crtd*1977) Judge Dredd first appeared in the British, multi Eagle Award winning ***2000AD*** in its second edition on the 5th March 1977. Created by *2000AD's* then editor, Pat Mills, and *2000AD* writer, John Wagner, with original visualisation by artist Carlos Ezquerra, Judge Dredd is the law enforcer of the future. In the 22nd century the Earth had been ravished by atomic war. There are survivors out in the bad lands, including mutants, while the rest of humanity is crowded into giant mega cities. Mega City 1 smothers North America's east coast, its huge, unemployed masses pampered with 22nd century technology. But crime is rife, and the only way to combat it was to have law enforcers who were both police as well as judge and jury. These enforcers are the Judges. They are fair, for the social good, but firm: ruthlessly firm, passing sentence on the spot. Judge Dredd himself is the clone of an early Judge, and the most respected (by his peers) and feared (by 'perps' (perpetrators of crime)) of all the Judges. He patrols the streets on his lawmaster motor bike sending perps to the isocubes, that is if they have not been gunned down and sent to resyk. Unlike many 'super heroes', Judge Dredd has no super powers but the 22nd century Earth provides the science fiction setting with the occasional odd alien, inter-dimensional encounter and telepaths (the Judges have their own Psi Division, *cf.* the Psi-cops in ***Babylon 5***) supplying additional SF tropes. Some of Dredd's most successful incarnations were drawn by Carlos (***Stainless Steel Rat***) Ezquerra and Brian Bolland. There were also spin-off characters such as Judge Anderson (of the Psi Division), Judge Death (from another dimension) and Mean Machine Angel (from the Cursed Earth). The passable film *Judge Dredd* (1995) was released with Sylvester Stallone in the title role (though a *2000AD* readers' poll a decade and a half earlier nominated Clint Eastwood for the title part (and *2000AD* readers are always right)). Others in the cast included: Armand Assante (as Rico, Dredd's clone brother); Max (***Dune***) Von Sydow (Chief Justice Fargo), Diane Lane (Judge Hershey); and Chris Adamson (as the cyborg Mean Machine Angel). *Judge Dredd* the movie successfully caught the overall image of the Mega City and the 'Cursed Earth' landscapes as well as the impartial ruthlessness of the law but not *2000AD's* full black humour or the juxtaposition of law and order with crime and civil rights that the comic conveyed. Furthermore in the comic the reader never sees Dredd's face as it is always covered (mainly by his Judge's helmet) which is symbolic of the way Mega City law is impersonal, but the film reveals Stallone's features. Judge Dredd can still be read today in *2000AD*, but those not wishing to collect all 1,000 plus editions might be better served in investing in the graphic novel volumes of collected Dredd tales. Judge Dredd and *2000AD* have won numerous Eagle Awards and subsequently the UK National Comics Award (the principal SF and fantasy comic award). There are also three Judge Dredd and **Batman**, as well as a Judge Dredd and **Aliens**, graphic novels. "Give me your perps, your muties, your psychos... and I'll give 'em hell."

Jurassic Park – film, US (1993), *dir.* Steven (see also **Brian Aldiss**, *Close Encounters of the Third Kind*, *The Twilight Zone*, *Raiders of the Lost Ark*, and *Indiana Jones and the Last Crusade*) Spielberg. Based on **Michael Crichton's** 1990 novel of the same name—he co-wrote the screenplay (with David Koepp)—this enjoyable romp won the Hugo for Best Dramatic Presentation in 1994. As in the book, the plot follows the endeavours of a businessman (Richard Attenborough) to bring on-line a theme park populated with dinosaurs, genetically engineered from DNA preserved in amber fossils, using PCR techniques. To satisfy the backers, independent advisors are brought to the park to give a seal of approval. These include a mathematician (Jeff Goldblum), an archaeologist (Sam Neill), and a palaeo-botanist (Laura Dern). However, a plan is afoot to steal the genetic samples stored on site, and the park's systems are disabled by the programmer (Wayne Knight) who is the agent of the rival company. Chaos then ensues as the Saurians escape their enclosures, while the humans try to escape the island on which the park is based. In 1997, a sequel (also based on Crichton's sequel), *The Lost World*, was directed by Janusz Kaminski, starring Jeff Goldblum and Julianne Moore. On the whole this was considerably less satisfying than its predecessor, with a T. Rex ending up in America causing havoc on the streets. *Jurassic Park* has, needless to say, wonderful special effects, some excellent set pieces (such as the first appearance by the T. Rex), and a not inconsiderable underpinning of humour, all of which combine to provide a thoroughly entertaining couple of screen hours. (*The Lost World* 1997 film is not to be confused with the 1912 novel ***The Lost World*** by Sir Arthur Conan Doyle – see also **Gregory Benford**.) *Jurassic Park III*, *dir*. Joe Johnston (2001), was more satisfying as an action movie, though light on SF, and sees Dr Alan Grant (Sam Neill) unwittingly end up on a rescue party searching for a kid who accidentally parachuted onto the dinosaur island of Isla Sorna.

King Kong – film, US (1933), *dir*. Merian Cooper and Ernest B. Schoedsack. This classic still enthrals audiences today, and is one of the most screened movies at the annual British Festival of Fantastic Films. An expedition to Skull Island, led by Carl Denham and Bruce Cabot, and strangely including Fay Wray, sets out to capture a fifty foot tall ape and return it to civilisation as an attraction. Willis O'Brien (mentor of effects genius Ray Harryhausen) brings various monster clashes to life through stop-motion animation effects. These still hold one's attention today, right up to the climax atop the Empire State Building. Initially the film suffered various cuts due to the censors (such as Kong biting the head off a native), but is usually seen restored to full length these days. British mystery writer Edgar Wallace began the script, but it was completed by Schoedsack's wife, Ruth Rose, and James A. Creelman. Nowadays *King Kong* is a cinematic legend, and has spawned innumerable sequels, spin-offs, pastiches, and the forgettable 1976 re-make by Dino de Laurentiis. But there was an earlier run of "ape" movies, such as

Mighty Joe Young (1949) – on which a young Ray (***The Beast from 20,000 Fathoms***) Harryhausen got to work with his inspiration – itself recently re-made as a passable family film (1998) *dir.* Ron Underwood. As for sequels, Toho Studios made *King Kong vs. Godzilla* in 1963 from an idea by Willis O'Brien, pitting the ape against their 1954 creation ***Gojira***, and also *King Kong Escapes* (1968) in which Kong gets to fight a mechanical version of himself, but quite honestly nothing has ever managed to capture the magic of the original.

Kolchak: The Night Stalker – TV series, US (*fb*1973). A spin off series from two TV movies concerning a reporter who happens to stumble across vampires, aliens, werewolves, zombies, cryptozoological species *etc*. Naturally he saves the day despite a sceptical editor, though his stories rarely saw print for fear of causing a panic or bringing the news agency into disrepute. The series is of particular note because of its connections with, and influence on, other media SF (see ***X Files*** and **Matheson, R.**), Principal cast: Darren McGavin (Carl Kolchak), Simon Oakland (Tony Vincenzo), Jack Grinnage (Ron Updyke) and Ruth McDevitt (Edith Cowles).

Kornbluth, Cyril M. – author, US (1923–1958). See **Pohl, Frederik**.

Kubrick, Stanley – Director, see ***2001 A Space Odyssey, Dr Strangelove,*** and ***A Clockwork Orange (A)***

Kuttner, Henry – author, US (1914-1958). Though both Kuttner and his wife, CL Moore (1911-1987, US), had established reputations prior to their marriage in 1940, it is their collaborative work – often published pseudonymously, including Lewis Padgett and Lawrence O'Donnell – for which they are best remembered. These include works such as *The Twonky* (1942) about an alien-possessed robotic TV (badly filmed in 1952), and *Mimsy Were the Borogroves* (1943) where educational toys from the future find their way to the present. Kuttner and Moore were part of the bedrock of the **Golden Age** of SF, and frequently contributed to *Astounding Science Fiction* (see ***Analog***), *Thrilling Wonder Stories* and *Startling Stories*. Kuttner writing alone, as Padgett, wrote a number of linked stories between 1943-48, variously collected as *Robots Have No Tails* (1952) and *The*

Proud Robot (1983), in which (among other things) robots from the future visit the present. Kuttner and Moore's *Vintage Season* (1946), a novella released under the O'Donnell name, was another time-travel tale and was filmed as ***Timescape*** (1991). (See also **Superman**.)

Last Castle, The – novelette (1966) by Jack Vance. Originally published by *Galaxy* and then appearing as part of an ACE double, the 'Last Castle' of the title is the last castle belonging to Man. The humans, who had returned to 'Old Earth' from the stars had 'Meks' ('simple minded' aliens) to help them as well as (bio-engineered?) birds. As time passed many of the humans lost their technological skills and came to rely heavily on the Meks right up to the day that they revolted. The humans struggled to survive as one by one their stronghold castles were overcome, until only the last one remained. Vance wrote *The Last Castle* in the mid-1960s, yet his portrayal of many of the SF tropes, described economically (such as faster than light drive), are still convincing today. Due to the use of castles, the birds (similar to mythical creatures), clans, non-technological nomads, and such, gives *The Last Castle* the feel of a sword-and -sorcery story, and so may be classified as science fantasy. It won the Hugo in 1967 for 'Best Novelette'. It also won the Nebula that year for Best Short Novel.

Lathe of Heaven, The – novel (1971) by **Ursula K Le Guin**. In a greenhouse future, with seven billion undernourished people on an overcrowded planet, Dr Haber makes room by creating an electronic dream world. George Or, as Haber's patient, enters this dream world. Meanwhile back in the real world there were the aliens, the Aldebaranians; they found the whole thing fascinating. Yet the population needed reducing. That was where the pollution generated plague of cancer came in. Billions died... Though not winning it *The Lathe of Heaven* was nominated for a Hugo, and it did come top of the annual *Locus* poll.

Lawrence, Don – graphic artist (1928-2003). Early in his career Don Lawrence drew the English version of the American superhero Captain Marvel. However he is best known for his work *The Rise and Fall of the Trigan Empire* (1965–76). The world Elekton was home to a number of races, some primitive, some technological. The dominant of these were the Trigans.

Despite being a civilisation with hovercraft and jet planes, it had a look similar to the Roman Empire. Like the Roman Empire it was founded by a family, forged from the wilderness and surrounded by enemies, the most treacherous of which were the Lokans. When not preserving its borders, Trigans explored their world to encounter far flung societies and monsters. Rare for its time, the Trigan Empire was drawn completely in full colour. Subsequently, with Martin Lodewijk and scriptwriter Philip Dun, Lawrence created the *Storm* series. The *Storm* adventures concerned an astronaut who returns to the Earth in the far future to encounter aliens and monsters. In the 1960s Don Lawrence drew 28 strips of 'Thunderbirds Are Go', based on the **Gerry Anderson** series, for the UK Daily Mail newspaper. This led him to drawing *Fireball XL5* for *TV 21* (*TV Century 21*) comic.

Left Hand of Darkness, The – novel (1969) by **Ursula K Le Guin**. One potential for SF is to hold a mirror up to our world, to explore subjects rarely discussed in 'normal' circumstances. *The Left Hand of Darkness* is one such exploration. The inhabitants of the planet Winter originated from Earth sufficiently long ago that they have effectively evolved into a new species. The hermaphrodite natives can take on either male or female characteristics. A 'normal' human diplomat visiting Winter learns more of the socio-biology involved, and in doing so has to come to terms with his own sexuality and assumptions of gender role. *The Left Hand of Darkness* won the Hugo in 1970 for Best Novel, and also made it into the *Concatenation* top 20 all-time book poll.

Le Guin, Ursula – author, US (*b*1929). Perhaps it is because she is the daughter of a renowned anthropologist, Ursula K Le Guin's stories are particularly strong when portraying other worlds and societies. Not untypical are her best known SF works ***The Left Hand of Darkness*** in which a Galactic diplomat discovers that 'the humans' of a world have in fact become hermaphrodite and so begins an exploration of gender, and ***The Dispossessed***, concerning a utopian world where there is no personal ownership of material goods. Her fantasy too contains fantastic societies and worlds; such as the *Earthsea* series set on a largely ocean-covered planet. Like other major SF authors (**Niven** with his 'Known Space' or **Asimov** with his 'Trantor' series) Le Guin has written a collection of novels to chart her own future history. Her

'Hainish' universe is based upon the initial premise that there was a precursor civilization that seeded many worlds in the Galaxy (including Earth). Indeed Le Guin started her novel writing career with two Hainish books: *Rocannon's World* (1966) and *Planet of Exile* (1966). In addition, her Hainish novel ***The Telling*** (2000) came top of the 2001 *Locus* poll for best SF novel. She is one of 20th century SF's stalwarts and has won numerous awards. In terms of those determined by readers, ***The Left Hand of Darkness*** won the Hugo in 1970 for Best Novel and she won again in 1975 for ***The Dispossessed***. Both are in the Hainish series. Other than novels, *The Ones Who Walk Away* received the Hugo in 1974 for Best Short Story, while *The Word for World is Forest* won the Hugo for Best Novella in 1973, and *Buffalo Gals, Won't You Come Out Tonight?* for Best Novelette in 1988. The novel ***The Lathe of Heaven*** (1971) concerns the ability of a man to 'dream' different realities into existence. It came top of the 1972 *Locus* readers annual poll for best SF novel and was made into a TV movie in 1980, while Le Guin herself was the 3rd most mentioned author in the *Concatenation* all-time book poll, with *The Dispossessed* and *The Left Hand of Darkness* placing 6th and 7th respectively in the favourite book section

Leiber, Fritz – author, US (1910-1992). Born of two Shakespearean actors, and with Leiber himself having a brief acting career, much of his work is informed by the rigours of the theatre and film, and features personal obsessions (such as cats and chess), and crusades against the hypocrisy of sexual repression. He majored in Psychology and Physiology at the University of Chicago, and spent a year at a theological seminary, before pursuing careers as an editor, and a drama teacher. His first published (short) story, *Two Sought Adventure* (1939), introduced Leiber's most enduring creations, Fafhrd and the Gray Mouser, who continued to appear in stories until 1988. Leiber is often credited with coining the term 'Sword and Sorcery' which aptly describes the tales featuring the two heroes. Arguably Leiber made his strongest impact with his tales of urban fantasy, but this ignores his not inconsiderable contributions to the SF field, his first important work being cited as *Gather, Darkness!* (1943), which concerns the overthrow of a religious dictatorship by super science disguised as witchcraft (and is in some ways reminiscent of **Heinlein**'s *Sixth Column* (1941)). After a bout of alcoholism between 1954-8, Leiber created his Change War stories, beginning with ***The Big Time*** (1958), for which he won a Hugo that same year, which document the conflicts in a war between the 'Spiders' and the 'Snakes' across time and space. The majority of the stories set in the same universe are collected in *The Change War* (1978) which features stories from 1958-1965. ***The Wanderer*** (1964) is a disaster novel detailing the effects of an incursion into the solar system by a planet-sized spaceship, and this won a Best Novel Hugo in 1965. Leiber's story for **Harlan Ellison**'s first *Dangerous Visions* anthology, ***Gonna Roll The Bones*** (1967), won a Hugo for Best Novelette in 1968. In 1970 he won a Best Novella Hugo for *Ship of Shadows* (1969), then won the same award the following year for *Ill Met in Lankhmar* (1970), part of the Fafhrd and Gray Mouser series, and was then honoured with a sixth Hugo in 1976 for his short story *Catch That Zeppelin!* (1975). Leiber has also won two 'Grand Master' awards, a Gandalf (1975) and a Nebula (1981), as well as the 1976 Lovecraft award for Lifetime Achievement.

Lem, Stanislaw – author, Poland (*b*1921). SF is primarily an Anglophone genre, but not solely one. SF has been written in virtually every developed nation, but rarely are non-Anglophone authors translated into English, and it is even more rare for such authors to receive considerable critical acclaim. Stanislaw Lem is one such author. He challenges much of western SF which, arguably due to commerciability, sets out to entertain. SF for Lem is a tool by which to explore the nature of the universe and humanity. As such his works are invariably thought-provoking, and sometimes patience is required reading his work: he is not always quick to come to the point. If one had to categorise Lem, he would be a sort of a cross between a hard and a **new wave** SF writer. His **hard SF** stems from his interest in science: he originally studied medicine and was co-founder of the Polish Astronomical Society. Poignant, occasionally very humorous, Lem for many years was a thorn in the side of Poland's communist regime, but because of his reputation, as well as because his comments were disguised under the veil of SF, he was largely left alone. His most famous work in the West is undoubtedly the novel ***Solaris*** (1961) but a number of his works have been translated into English. Lem's *The Star Diaries* (1971) chronicles the travels through space and time of the explorer Ijon Tichy, while *The Cyberiad* (1965) reveals Lem's fun side, a little reminiscent of Douglas (***Hitch-Hiker's Guide to the***

Galaxy) Adams, but decades earlier. This last is a rare treat for Anglophone SF readers as *The Cyberiad's* English translation is particularly good and includes word play. *The Invincible* (1964) is a fairly representative, cross-section of his early short stories and again is available in English.

Lensmen – book series by **E.E. "Doc" Smith**. The Lensmen series of stories originally appeared in magazine form, in both *Amazing Stories* and *Astounding Science Fiction* (see *Analog*), between 1934 and 1948. It is almost certainly the first true example of what has become known as **space opera**, not only because of the sheer scale of the series – both in the sense of word count, and in the internal story scales of space and time – but also in terms of the intricate structure of the Lensmen universe. The stories span aeons of time and all of galactic space, and the spaceships are huge, on a scale that would not be recalled until the "Culture" stories of **Iain Banks**. The basic conflict is between two super powerful races, the unremittingly evil Eddorians who are behind the Boskone Empire, and the peaceful Arisians who have engineered the creation of races, including humans, to fight the threat. In addition the Arisians have created the Lens, a device (usually seen as a gemstone in a bracelet) which enhances the strength and mental abilities of the wearer, and have guided the development of the Galactic Patrol (an inter-species police/military force). Humans are, of course, at the heart of the Galactic Patrol, though many aliens are also members and bearers of the Lens. Each of the conflicts are resolved in each volume, but the subsequent books reveal that every defeated threat is but a stepping stone to an even larger conflict, until the Eddorians themselves are confronted and beaten. The stories were collected into book form as follows: *Triplanetary* (1948), *First Lensman* (1950), *Galactic Patrol* (1950), *Grey Lensman* (1951), *Second-Stage Lensmen* (1953), *Children of the Lens* (1954), and *Masters of the Vortex* (1960) — though in terms of the internal chronology, this last volume probably takes place somewhere before *Children of the Lens*. The first two books set the scene and introduce the Lens, but it is volumes three to six that tell the main story. *Galactic Patrol* introduces the human hero, Kim Kinnison, who stars also in the next two books, but it is his offspring that confront the Eddorians in *Children of the Lens*. The books are certainly works of their time and, as such, the politics and sexual attitudes (women may not wear the lens, among other things) are somewhat dated, but if this is borne in mind while reading, then the stories are joyfully contrived **space opera**s that are thoroughly entertaining. It was not until after his death in 1965 that Smith became an SF 'best-seller', but the Lensmen have continued to endure. In 1976 William Ellern added *New Lensman*, and David Kyle contributed *The Dragon Lensman* (1980), *Lensman from Rigel* (1982), and *Z-Lensman* (1983); through the eighties and into the nineties there was a Japanese Manga cartoon series called *Lensman*, and this in turn gave rise to a short-lived comic title of the same name from Aircel Comics.

Little Shop of Horrors, The – film, US (1986), *dir.* Frank Oz. One of the most requested movies at the British Festival of Fantastic Films, this started life as a Roger Corman film in 1960 featuring, among others, a young Jack (*The Shining*) Nicholson. It was first adapted as an off-Broadway musical, and this remake is more faithful to that than the original. Seymour Krelborn (Rick (***Ghostbusters***) Moranis) is secretly in love with Audrey (Ellen Greene) in the florists where they both work under the watchful eye of Mr. Mushnik (Vincent Gardenia). However, business on Skid Row is bad and the business may go under unless it can be saved by an unusual plant, christened Audrey II (voice supplied by Levi Stubbs of the Four Tops). But the plant has a taste for human flesh and Seymour must feed it to obtain his heart's desire... This comedy of alien invasion has some wonderful songs by Howard Ashman and Alan Menken, and the animatronic Audrey II (created by Lyle Conway) is visually arresting. The film is full of guest stars, used sparingly but effectively, and includes Steve Martin and Bill Murray in a truly hilarious sequence as dentist and patient, as well as James Belushi, John Candy and Christopher Guest.

Locus – semi-prozine (semi-professional fan/magazine) founded by Charles Brown. *Locus* provides a monthly US-centric view of SF news for the SF community (though does regularly include overview reports from other countries). It is produced to an exceptionally high standard and today pays its contributors, so some might say that it really is a professional publication. However the editor is an SF fan and the news it publishes includes that of the fans within the SF community as well as conventions and such. It is also an invaluable source of (mainly US and UK) SF book publishing news. One of the excellent services it provides is the annual *Locus* readers poll. (Because the poll is a solid indication as to what SF buffs, like we have used the *Locus* poll – which has various categories of winners – as one of the several criteria for deciding which entries to include in this guide.) It won the Hugo for Best Fanzine in 1971, 1972 1976, 1978, 1980, 1981, 1982, 1983, and 1984 before winning the Hugo for Best Semi-Prozine in 1985, 1986, 1987, 1988, 1989, 1990, 1991, 1992, 1996, 1997, 1998, 1999, 2000 2001, 2002, 2003 and 2004. Web page *www.locusmag.com*

Longest Voyage, The – short story (1960) by **Poul Anderson**. Captain Rovic is attempting to circumnavigate his world in the ship *Golden Leaper*, but supplies are running perilously low when they finally spy land. Docked in a barbarous port, Rovic hears tales of a flying ship, said to have come from the stars where, legend has it, the race of men walk in Paradise. Far from the spacelanes of Paradise, Rovic's world lost contact with them so long ago they scarcely know if their own origins are true. Rovic determines to see this ship and its occupant, who is worshipped by the locals, but not all is as it seems... Anderson won the 1961 Hugo for Best Short Story, an award he has won seven times, yet he has never won a Hugo for a novel.

Lord of Light, The – novel (1967) by **Roger Zelazny**. **Arthur Clarke's** Third Law states that 'any sufficiently advanced technology is indistinguishable from magic'. So Zelazny pictures this: long after the death of Earth, a band of people on a colony planet have the technology to give themselves immortality and godlike powers. Indeed they rule their world as the gods of the Hindu pantheon: Kali, Goddess of Destruction; Krishna, God of Lust but all are opposed by: "he who was Mahasamatman, the Binder of Demons, the Lord of Light. Of course he preferred to drop the 'Maha' and the 'atman' and be called Sam..." Many writers have had a go at this Clarke game, and many have failed largely because they have ended up writing fantasy with the SF tucked out of sight in the authors' minds well away from the reader. However *The Lord of Light* works because the SF is always in view even if never centre stage, and the dash of humour helps. *The Lord of Light* won the Hugo for Best Novel in 1968.

Lord of the Rings, The: The Fellowship of the Ring – film, US (2001) *dir*. Peter Jackson. A doomsday weapon – an all-powerful magic ring – is hidden by an innocent soul but the decision is taken to destroy it. To do so a small band carrying the ring must travel far to the volcanic cauldron in which it was originally forged. And so our heroes set off, but the forces of evil are gathering. This production, the second big screen version of J.R.R. Tolkien's fantasy classic, was not only a huge box-office success it also took the 2002 Hugo Award for 'Best Dramatic Presentation'. Though not science fiction this guide uses the Hugo as part of its criteria for entry inclusion and Jackson's *LOTR* films won Hugos. Hugo Awards, though defined as the 'SF achievement award', allow works of fantasy presumably so as not to preclude works of science-fantasy (such as ***Superman***), but loose wording in the World SF Society's constitution means that works of pure fantasy can be nominated as happened in this case. Of course *Lord of the Rings* should come to the attention of the World Fantasy Award, but such are life's little complications... The sequel *The Two Towers* (2002) also won a Hugo in 2003, while the final film in the trilogy, *The Return of the King* (2003), was nominated for, and won, 11 Oscars in 2004 so to hold the Oscar record along with *Ben Hur* and *Titanic*. *The Return of the King* also won the Hugo in 2004 for 'best dramatic presentation (long form)', while that year's 'dramatic presentation (short form)' went to 'Gollum's Acceptance Speech at the 2003 MTV Movie Awards'. Principal cast: Elijah Wood, Ian McKellan, Liv Tyler, Sean Astin, Cate Blanchett, John Rhys (***The Lost World***) Davies, Billy Boyd, Dominic Monaghan, Orlando Bloom, and Christopher Lee.

Lost World, The – novel (1912) by Sir Arthur Conan Doyle. Primarily Conan Doyle is today remembered for Sherlock Holmes. However, Doyle himself often preferred his Professor George Edward Challenger character, and even used to impersonate him from time to time, including in public. Of the Challenger stories, *The Lost World* is perhaps the most famous. Challenger, 'a cave-man in a lounge suit', was an eccentric scientist, explorer and hunter all rolled into one. In *The Lost World* Professor Challenger goes to South America where, on a mountain top plateau, he finds an ecologically isolated land far above the Amazon rain forest. There dinosaurs still roam and the expedition soon discovers that survival is more important than bringing home a trophy. In 1925 Harry O Hoyt's film version of Doyle's book was released (with Doyle's blessing). It was a huge hit despite poor acting: the effects then were considered highly realistic, though very far from today's standards. In fact, Doyle used a pre-production cutting a couple of years before to tease the press that he really knew of a lost world! This film has the distinction of being the first ever shown as an in-flight movie (by the German Air Service Company in 1926). In 1960 Irwin Allen made the second film version starring Claude (*The Invisible Man*) Rains and Michael (*The Day the Earth Stood Still*) Rennie, but this was a lacklustre affair with photo-enlarged lizards, rather than stop-motion. The 2001 TV movie from the BBC was far better. (Principal cast: Bob (*Who Framed Roger Rabbit*) Hoskins (Prof. Challenger), Peter (*Forbidden Planet* and *The Princess Bride*) Falk, Matthew Rhys, James Fox, Tom Ward and Elaine Cassidy.) There were also two made-for-TV movies starring John Rhys (*Lord of the Rings*) Davies as a convincing Challenger (1992). These productions are not to be confused with the 1997 film *The Lost World* based on **Michael Crichton's** sequel to *Jurassic Park*. (Undoubtedly Crichton was paying homage to Doyle.) In 1998 **Greg Bear's** sequel to *The Lost World*, called *Dinosaur Summer* (set just after World War II), sees the circus dinosaurs returned to the plateau above the Brazilian rain forest. Nor should Doyle's novel be confused with the not particularly inspiring US/Australian 1999 TV series of the same title but which did attract a certain following.

Lundwall, Sam – author, Sweden (*b*1941). A prolific writer, editor, SF academic and translator of about 400 books. Most noted in SF circles for championing non-Anglophone SF and in charting European (including British) SF history arguing that it had an earlier, and probably greater, significance to the genre's development than is commonly thought compared to its transatlantic counterparts. This argument was promulgated in his *Science Fiction: An Illustrated History* (1979).

Maison d'Ailieurs, La (**House of Elsewhere, The**) – academic resource (Swiss). An SF museum and academic resource of French language SF based in Yverdon, Switzerland. Founded in 1975 by Pierre Versins, and currently curated by Patrick J. Gyger, this is both a book and magazine collection as well as an exhibition of toys, stamps, posters *etc*. Further details on *www.ailleurs.ch*. (See also: **Foundation**, **SF; SF Museum and Hall of Fame;** and **SF Research Collection**.)

Maitz, Don – artist, US (*b*1953). Firmly rooted in SF, fantasy and historical artwork, Don Maitz has drawn covers for numerous publishing houses that operate on both sides of the Atlantic. In the US his claim to popular 'fame' is that he is the artist behind the 1990s 'Captain Morgan Spiced Rum Pirate' promotional character. His work can be found compiled in *First Maitz* (1988) and *Dreamquests: The Art of Don Maitz* (1993). He won the Hugo Award for best 'Professional Artist' in 1990 and 1993.

Make Room! Make Room! – novel (1966) by **Harry Harrison**. It is the year 1999 and an over-crowded world sees the masses thrown together in cities. Outside, the countryside is heavily protected and geared to food production, but even with the technology of the future there is not enough to go around. It is a world of starving billions, where the most many can hope for is a diet of lentils and soya with the occasional rat if lucky. But in the city of New York, population 35 million, there is a cop who will not simply walk away from what is just another routine unsolved murder. It is worth remembering that earlier in the 20th century, the world's population really was growing at a super-exponential rate (not at the lower rate as it was in the real 1999). Harry Harrison properly researched this book's background and it even contains an academic bibliography at the end; a rarity for SF novels. It is the proverbial Malthusian SF novel and Harrison's wake up call for mankind. *Make Room! Make Room!* was also the basis for a film, ***Soylent Green*** (1973, coincidentally the year of the oil crisis) which though different still captures the gritty, if not grubby, existence this book's citizens endure.

Man in the High Castle, The – novel (1962) by **Philip K Dick**. This is an alternate history novel where the Axis powers won World War II. Robert Childan lives in an America run by the Japanese, a conquering race with whom he has to share his life. He is a jeweller whose values and personal philosophy are challenged by having to go into business with one of the Japanese conquerors. But this *is* Philip K Dick, and this altered perception is not the only one you get: there are worlds within worlds. In this other present there is a book called *The Grasshopper Lies Heavy* which is itself an alternate history about what it would be like if the allies had won the war, and from time to time Dick refers in his alternate universe to another, a reality closer to our own but not of it... *The Man in the High Castle* won the Hugo for Best Novel.

Man in a White Suit, The – film, GB (1951), *dir.* Alexander Mackendrick. A classic comedy in its own right, this film is better known among mundane (non-SF) film buffs for its social comment. Plot: scientist (Alec (***Star Wars***) Guinness) develops a new artificial fabric that is incredibly strong, repels dirt and 'never' wears out. At first the fibre seems like a godsend, but then the workers realise that it will mean fewer jobs and the factory owners fewer factories. Former social adversaries join forces and the disillusioned inventor finds out just how few friends he has. Principal cast: Alec Guinness, Joan Greenwood, Cecil Parker, Vida Hope, Ernest Thesiger, Michael Gough, Howard Marion Crawford, Miles Malleson, George Benson and Edie Martin.

Man Who Could Work Miracles, The – film, UK (1936) *dir.* Lothar Mendes. Based on **H. G. Wells'** *The Man Who Had to Sing* (1898), this concerns a draper's clerk who is given miraculous powers by gods debating the future of humanity. However, he is so inept at using them that he cannot get a woman to love him, and in exasperation nearly destroys the world. Made the same year as ***Things to Come***, also based on Wells' work. Principal cast: Roland Young, Ernest Thesiger, Edward Chapman, Joan Gardner, Sophie Stewart, Robert Cochrane, George Zucco, Lawrence Hanray and George Sanders. The film also featured a young Ralph (***Time Bandits***) Richardson.

Many-Coloured Land, The – novel (1981) by Julian May. When a one-way time tunnel to Earth's distant past, specifically six million B.C., was discovered by those on the Galactic Milieu, every misfit for light-years around hurried to pass through it. Each sought his own brand of happiness. But none could have guessed what awaited them. Not even in a million years... This was the first in 'the Saga of the Pliocene Exile' and came top of the 1982 annual *Locus* poll for best SF novel as well as being nominated for a Hugo.

Martian Chronicles, The – novel (1950) by **Ray Bradbury**. *The Martian Chronicles* is in fact a collection of short stories chronologically portraying the attempts to colonise Mars with some characters Bradbury has previously written. Physically Mars comes across as a cross between a desert-like, thinly atmosphered world complete with the famous canals, and at times the American mid-west with coke bottles littering the Martian surface. The whole colonization effort seems to be largely uncoordinated which leaves the author free to present wildly differing stories and a surreal element to the encounters with Mars and its natives. In one, the mission lands in what turns out to be a Martian lunatic asylum. In another, the third expedition, the colonists are hypnotised into believing that they are once more on Earth, but the Earth of their childhood. The overall premise seems to be that wherever Man will go he will recreate cultural elements of his society. The tragedy is that the Martians seem to suffer, retreating in the face of the colonists' advance, but with an insight into their home world that continually eludes the newcomers from Earth. *The Martian Chronicles* has had some mainstream appeal and, despite being written in the mid-twentieth century, does stand up well to an early 21st century reading which is surely the test of good SF. *The Martian Chronicles* was adapted for TV in 1980 by **Richard Matheson** but, despite an excellent script and a strong cast (including Rock Hudson, Roddy (***Planet of the Apes***) McDowell, Darren (***Kolchak***) McGavin, Gayle Hunnicut, and Nyree Dawn Porter), the tele-series failed to gel and was an expensive failure.

Matheson, Richard – author, US (*b*1926). From the first Matheson, like Robert Bloch and **Ray Bradbury** (whose *Martian Chronicles* Matheson adapted for TV in 1979), mixed elements of both horror and SF in his work. His first published story, *Born of Man and Woman* (1950) for the *Magazine of Fantasy and Science Fiction,* sets this trend and tells a terrifying tale of a mutant kept in a cellar by its parents. His first novel, the excellent *I am Legend* (1954), is set in a future world where a disease has created a race of vampires that have come to dominate the planet. Here Matheson gave vampires a decidedly science fiction (as opposed to fantasy) treatment. It was filmed badly twice. First as *The Last Man on Earth* (1964) starring Vincent Price, and then as *The Omega Man* (1971) with Charlton Heston – as of this writing, there is a third attempt being made, but as yet is only in pre-production limbo. His second SF novel, *The Shrinking Man* (1956), was filmed in 1957 as ***The Incredible Shrinking Man*** and scripted by Matheson. In it the protagonist begins to shrink so that from his diminished perspective the world presents new dangers. (The problem of how he could still breath normal-size air molecules, though, was never addressed.) It won a Hugo in 1958 for Best Dramatic Presentation. He has worked extensively in television, scripting some of the finer moments of ***The Twilight Zone*** (original series), Rod Serling's *Night Gallery*, ***Star Trek***, and ***The Outer Limits*** (modern version). He also created ***Kolchak***, writing the first two feature length episodes, *The Night Stalker* (the eventual series name) and *The Night Strangler* which inspired ***The X-Files***. He supplied many script adaptations for Roger Corman movies, and also wrote *The Master of the World* (1961) adapting **Jules Verne's** story (1904) of the same name simultaneously with Verne's *Robur the Conqueror* (1886). There were also SF elements in his novel *Hell House* (1971), filmed as *The Legend of Hell House* (1973), in which a scientist tries to use technology to rid a house of its ghostly infestation. The romantic time travel fantasy film ***Somewhere in Time*** (1980) was based on his novel *Bid Time Return* (1975), but most of his other film work is, perhaps, more correctly seen as horror. Many of Matheson's SF short stories are available in collections such as *Third From the Sun* (1955) and *The Shores of Space* (1957), and in four volumes sharing the title *Shock!* (1961, 1964, 1966, and 1970). His son, Richard Christian Matheson (*b*1953), has been following in his father's footsteps, working also in TV and film, but his SF leanings are, as yet, only apparent in his scripts for the two time travel comedies *Bill and Ted's Excellent Adventure* (1989) and its sequel *Bill and Ted's Bogus Journey* (1991).

Matrix, The – film, US (1999), *dir*. The Wachowski Brothers. Thomas 'Neo' Anderson is a software programmer and model citizen by day, by night he provides illegal computer services which enable him to pursue his obsession to find out about something called 'The Matrix'. Then one day 'the authorities' come for him at work; he escapes and meets members of the underground who show him what the Matrix really is – an artificial reality programme, a virtual world which contains himself and everything he knows. He then gets to learn about reality... Fast paced with stunning effects, and filmed in such a way that it looks like a Japanese animé cartoon come to life, *The Matrix* was (not entirely unjustly) publicised as being the ***Blade Runner*** for the end of the century. *The Matrix* was nominated for a Best Dramatic Presentation Hugo for 2000; it would have won but that year the voting was under Australian rules which allowed for second and third choice counts which enabled ***Galaxy Quest***

of WSFS members of top ten SF films, hence its eligibility in this guide. There were two follow-up movies made back-to-back in 2003. The first explored some of the science fiction concepts behind the Matrix, while the second was a grand special effects extravaganza of the final battle between the humans and the machines, but unfortunately it failed to reconcile the concepts explored in its predecessor (so possibly setting up a fourth film?). Principal cast: Keanu Reeves, Laurence Fishburne, Carrie-Anne Moss and Joe Pantoliano. A short animated TV series of 9 episodes, *Animatrix*, was broadcast in 2003, provided background to the films explaining how the Matrix came into existence. Given that the imagery in the films owed much to the medium of animé, it was appropriate that this was the vehicle chosen to provide the back-story.

Max Headroom – TV film, UK (1985) based on a concept by George Stone, Rocky Morton and Annabel Jankel. It is 25 minutes into the future and the world relies on media coverage for politics, to run a consumer society, social control, and even entertainment. Having an 'off' button is illegal, not that anyone cares. Then Network 23's star, roving TV reporter, Edison Carter (Matt Frewer), complete with radio link to base and his computer-aided researcher Theora Jones (Amanda Pays), discovers a cover-up that the new subliminal adverts, 'blipverts', cause an explosive neurological reaction amongst overweight viewers. Those behind the 'blipverts' wish to see Carter removed, but he is in the public eye. The solution is to download Carter's personality and create a (not exactly perfect looking) computerised duplicate called Max Headroom as an on-screen stand-in. Only Carter with the aid of his 'blank' (who is not on any computer record) street friend Blank Reg (Morgan Shepard) can save the day. *Max Headroom* was not only successful but, for SF buffs, most welcome in that it dealt with many 1970s SF tropes, such as information war and organ-legging, in a routine way (*the future* is not special in the future). Indeed, though a little dated today, the issues being dealt with were ahead of their time (at least as far as TV SF was concerned and one has to remember that *Max Headroom* was made before digital TV, before the InterNet, and even before satellite TV.) As TV films go, this paved the way for a fair US series (1987) which fortunately retained some of the principal actors, namely those playing Edison/Max, Theora and Reg. Additional principal cast (TV film): Nicholas Grace, Hillary Tindall, Paul Spurrier, and Roger Sloman. Additional principal cast (TV series): George Coe, Jeffrey Tambor, and Chris Young. However it should be remembered that *Max Headroom* has a real impact on the actual TV of the day in 1986 as Max himself headed up a weekly rock music *cum* interview show, it was for a while very popular with a wide-ranging audience.

Merril Collection – academic resource (Ca). Established in 1970 at the Toronto Public Library, College St, The Merril Collection is Canada's equivalent to the **SF Foundation** in the UK and the **SF Research Collection** in the US. Originally known (to 1st Jan 1991) as the Spaced Out Library, it was founded by writer and anthologist Judith Merril with some 5,000 SF, fantasy and related non-fiction books and now has over 54,000 items.

Metal Hurlant – adult comic (1975-87). Co-founded by Philippe Druillet and Jean Giraud, *Metal Hurlant* was the leading French SF comic magazine of the late 1970s. It is survived by its US spin-off publication *Heavy Metal* which featured many of *Hurlant's* strips translated into English and brought a number of non-Anglophone European artists' and writers' work to the attention of an English speaking readership.

Metropolis – film, German (1926), *dir.* Fritz Lang. Everything about this film is big: it took 16 months to make when most films took a few weeks; it had a cast of over 37 thousand people; and it cost a staggering 7 million (1926) marks, bankrupting the studio (UFA) when it flopped. The full length version is just over 3 hours long, though it is usually seen in 75, 83 or 128 minute versions. It is also an enduring masterpiece of SF film. John Fredersen (Alfred Abel) runs a mammoth city in the year 2000 but, fearing a revolution to come, decides to bring it about himself in order to have an excuse to crush the workers. They are being kept in check by the angelic Maria (Brigitte Helm), who is loved by John's son, Freder (Gustav Fröhlich). John has Maria kidnapped in order for mad scientist Rothwang (Rudolf Klein-Rogge) to make a robotic copy of her, so that he can use the automaton to incite the workers to riot, but Freder starts to suspect... The script, by Lang's wife Thea von Harbou, is appallingly sentimental, causing **HG Wells** to comment that it was "quite the silliest film", and even Lang himself in 1959 stated, "I don't like *Metropolis*. The ending is false. I didn't like it even when I made the film." However, the effects, cinematography, imagery, choreography and sheer visual intensity of the film would, taken together, remain unequalled in SF cinema until *2001* was made. The 1970's BBC version is noted for its sympathetic soundtrack, as is the Georgio Moroder produced 1984 tinted version. *Metropolis* was voted into the *Concatenation* top 30 all-time film poll.

Mirror Dance – novel (1994) by **Lois McMaster Bujold**. *Mirror Dance* is a 'Vorkosigan Adventure' (see ***Barrayar*** and ***Vor Game***). Miles Vorkosigan is in danger from his own clone called Mark. His clone, having passed himself off as Miles, has stolen a Dendarii Free Mercenary vessel and intends to go to the outlaw planet of Jackson's Whole where he plans to liberate the clones destined as brain transplant hosts. With Miles down to take the blame, things start to go wrong with the 'rescue'. *Mirror Dance* won the 1995 Hugo for Best Novel as well as coming top of the annual *Locus* readers poll.

Mission of Gravity – novel (1953) by **Hal Clement**. Low gravity planets and high 'g' ones have been used numerous times within SF, but what about a planet whose gravity varied? Hal Clement solved this one with his vision of the world Mesklin. A high gravity world rotating so fast that its equatorial diameter was more than twice its polar diameter. It therefore had a very short day of just eighteen minutes. Someone weighing 180 lb. on Earth would weigh 540 lb. at the equator and an incredible 60 tons at its poles. And so the scene is set for an Earth astronaut at his equatorial base to send the native high-gravity adapted alien sea merchant, Barlennan, across the methane seas to the poles on a salvage operation. Unfortunately for Clement, the Hugos had only just started when they had a year break in 1954, otherwise he surely would have at least been nominated. However such is its reputation that *Mission of Gravity* has been in print every decade since its publication, and Mesklin a world-concept that rivals ***Ringworld***.

Moon is a Harsh Mistress, The – novel (1966) by **Robert A. Heinlein**. On the Moon, in an open penal colony, a revolution is being plotted. With a steady supply of solar power, the Moon's tunnel farms have begun to be a steady source of food for Earth down in its gravity well. However with each shipment valuable water is transported one way. In just a few years the colonists (whose lunar adjusted bodies can never withstand Earth's gravity) will be doomed. An odd assortment of a jack-of-all-trades, his blonde girlfriend and a computer (that only the revolutionaries know is an artificial intelligence) plan the take-over of the century. But not only do they have to confront the authorities, they have to live with the lunar conditions, and the Moon is, as they find out, an uncompromisingly harsh mistress. This is classic authoritarian, meritocratic Heinlein; the politics is laid on with little subtlety. The novel is noted for turning 'TANSTAFL' (there aint no such thing as a free lunch) into a slogan, and for the concept that water ice might be found on the Moon sheltered beneath rock (lunar water ice was, in fact, only first remote-sensed in the late 1990s). *The Moon is a Harsh Mistress* won the Hugo for 'Best Novel' in 1967 as well as being voted into the *Concatenation* top 20 all-time favourite SF poll.

Moorcock, Michael – author, UK (*b*1939). Though not a winner of any Hugo, nor did any of his novels get voted into the *Concatenation* top 20 all-time book poll, he was the 10th most cited author in that poll, albeit spread over a number of titles. This citation, and that he only just missed out on a number of this guide's core-criteria for entry warrants his inclusion. (All other top-ten cited authors met one or more core criteria.) A writer of fantasy (especially noted for his 'Elric' sword and sorcery series) as well as science fiction, he is a versatile and talented author. His most irreverent work (some say) is *Behold the Man* (1969). A tale of an atheist, Karl Glogouer, who, in attempting to further his relationship with the religious Eva, travels back in time to meet Jesus. Circumstances then conspire to include him in the gospels. Alternate worlds and time lines feature in many of Moorcock's works. In *The Rituals of Infinity* (1965) (re-titled *The Wrecks of Time* in the US), alternate Earths are systematically being destroyed by D-squads. Travelling between alternates, it is up to Professor Faustaff to find out what is going on and why, and if possible to stop the destruction. While the 'Jerry Cornelius Chronicles' (*The Final Programme* (1969); *A Cure for Cancer* (1971); *The English Assassin* (1972); and *The Condition of Muzak* (1977)) consist of four novels each portraying, in essence at least, the same story of sibling rivalry. Jerry Cornelius, one of two sons of a brilliant scientist fends off his brother Frank's attempts to take over his father's work. Each of the stories sees recurring characters, such as his ally and lover Miss Brunner, and enemy the Bishop Beesley. Cornelius himself is a colourful and stylish young man fond of a good time, good food, music and company. The Cornelius character was the inspiration for *The Air Tight Garage of Jerry Cornelius* comic strip in **Heavy Metal** while *The Final Programme* itself was made into a film (1974) *dir.* Robert (***The Abominable Dr Phibes***) Fuest. Reportedly Moorcock himself did not like the film, but it did succeed in conveying a (typically slightly camp 1970s) world on the point of self-destruction, peopled with larger-than-life characters. However, in its own terms the film worked. Principal cast: Jon Finch (Jerry Cornelius), Derrick O'Connor (Frank Cornelius), Jenny Runacre (Miss Brunner), Sterling Hayden, Harry Andrews, Hugh Griffith, Julie Ege, Patrick Magee and Graham Crowden. (See also **Michael Whelan**.)

More Than Human – novel (1953) by **Theodore Sturgeon**. Six child 'freaks' are drawn together by circumstance at the home of Alicia Kew. There is Lone, an empathic idiot who can feel the thoughts of children; Janie, with telekinetic powers; Beanie and Bonnie, twin black children with the ability to teleport; Gerry, a morally corrupt genius; and Baby, deformed but possessing a computer-like analytical ability. Together they can "blesh" (blend/mesh) into a gestalt entity that may represent a further stage in Man's evolution, but first they must overcome the collective prejudice and fear of adults... This novel is constructed around a novella called *Baby is Three* (1952), which comprises the centre section of the book. *More Than Human* won the 1954 International Fantasy Award, and has since become a classic of the genre, being reprinted and translated many times. There is also a graphic adaptation, presented by ***Heavy Metal*** and, in its collected form, by Byron Preiss Visual Publications, illustrated by Alex Nino and adapted by Doug Moench in 1979.

NASFiC – see **North American Science Fiction Convention**.

Nebula Award – The annual SF award determined by the members of SF Writers of America since 1966. (Because of its specialised voting base the Nebula is not a prime determinant for entries to be included in this guide, though reference is occasionally made to it.)

Neuromancer – novel (1984) by **William Gibson**. Movements are notoriously easier to spot in retrospect than they are at the time, though **'cyberpunk'** was a little more obvious than some. The 1980s love affair with information technology, and the emerging World Wide Web (internet), was bound to be reflected in the SF of the time and, willingly or not, Gibson was certainly seen as a figurehead of the cyberpunk movement. The world of *Neuromancer* can be said to fairly represent all the elements that are common to cyberpunk works – the near-future time-frame, the Chandler-esque urban environment, the subversion of technology by criminal elements, and the heavy emphasis on IT – but it is also a pretty basic antihero-driven story. Case, an 'interface cowboy' who steals data from cyberspace, has had his connections burned out, having been caught for a previous crime. Then someone wants to employ him for a specific job, and is willing to pay the large sums required to have his interfaces restored. Throughout the action (which involves Case's acquisition of a minder, and travel from Earth to orbiting arcologies) he is unaware that the data he has been hired to steal is an emerging artificial intelligence, Wintermute, and it is only towards the end that Case discovers who has hired him and why. *Neuromancer* was one of the first novels to be published by Ace as part of their then 'new' Ace SF Specials series, edited by the late Terry Carr. They must have been very pleased when Gibson's first novel won the Hugo, Nebula and Philip K. Dick awards for Best Novel in 1985. *Count Zero* (1986), *Mona Lisa Overdrive* (1988), and the collection *Burning Chrome* (1986), all expand upon the *Neuromancer* universe, though are only loosely connected with each other. *Neuromancer* also came joint 9th in the *Concatenation* all-time Best SF Novel poll, and has been adapted into comics form, though sales of this were low and the title was cancelled before the story was completed.

Neutron Star – short story (1966) by **Larry Niven**. Set in Niven's 'Known Space' universe, this story introduces the Puppeteers, a two-headed, three-legged species, whose mercantile empire dominates half the galaxy. Like a lot of short fiction this is a puzzle story. During a close approach to a neutron star, some force reached through the Puppeteers invulnerable hull technology and killed the crew. The Puppeteers would like to repeat this mission since anything that can get past their hull technology would be bad for sales. And so they blackmail a human pilot into re-running the journey and solving the mystery. *Neutron Star* won the Hugo Award in 1967 for the Best Short Story. It was also the title story of a collection of Niven shorts (1968).

New Wave. The term given to the type of SF that focuses on the soft sciences: the psychological, social and economic dimensions. New Wave SF concentrates on the human responses to the hard SF event, rather than the event itself, be it alien invasion, development of an invention or whatever.

Nicholls, Peter – encyclopædist, Australian (*b*1939), Nicholls was the first administrator of the UK SF Foundation (see **Foundation, SF**) and was the editor of its journal *Foundation* between 1971 and '77. He was the author of the *SF Encyclopaedia* (1979), editions of which have won the Hugo for Best Non-Fiction Book in 1980 and later with **John Clute** when revised in 1994 and which was voted 3rd non-fiction book favourite in the *Concatenation* all-time poll, jointly with **Sagan's** *Intelligent Life in the Universe*. Note: the *SF Encyclopaedia* was published in Europe as *The Encyclopedia of Science Fiction*. To date it remains the most complete printed guide to science fiction, produced as it was in a large format with over 1,400 pages.

Nineteen Eighty-Four – novel (1949) by George Orwell. An alternate future story. In 1984 the world is divided into three great powers: Oceana, Eurasia and Eastasia. These are perpetually at war with each other. Throughout Oceania 'The Party' rules with an iron hand. Everything is rationed, there are few luxuries, and the poverty-stricken people are subject to propaganda from the Ministry of Truth. The authorities keep a track of everyone through informers and individual household surveillance. The story concerns one Winston Smith, from the Ministry of Truth who begins an illicit affair and begins to rebel... George Orwell's dystopian future has become a literary classic: something rare for SF, but then Orwell was regarded as a mainstream writer. Two film versions have been made. The first, *1984* (1956) *dir*. Michael Anderson, starring Edmund O'Brien, is not recommended. The second *1984* (1984) *dir*. Michael Radford and starring John Hurt, is much better. Notably in 1954 the BBC broadcast a live play (adapted by Nigel (***Quatermass***) Kneale) that attracted much criticism and even questions in Parliament.

A short time later its second showing, again live, attracted the biggest TV audience since the Coronation.

Niven, Larry – author, US (*b*1938). From the late 1960s to the end of the '70s, of the fictional universes being written, 'Known Space' was the one that arguably best explored scientific and technological ideas. Be it the social impact of teleportation devices, replacement organ surgery, or suspended animation, Niven not only had something to say, but he could neatly package it into a story. The Known Space series stemmed in time from the present day through to a future in which humanity had spread throughout a goodly proportion of our spiral arm. In terms of scope it ranged from the almost mundane solving of a murder (albeit one on an early lunar colony) through to our galaxy's core exploding. His books and short stories tackled first contact (both an extraterrestrial visitation to Earth and Earth explorers discovering alien worlds), biotechnology impacts, neutron stars, telepathy and artificial intelligence. He looked at a variety of ways to reach the stars and the nature of numerous alien species. Though his characters were generally simply designed, as was his writing style, there were more than enough concepts being played with, and juggled so well, that his Known Space books endeared him to a generation of fans. Indeed while his straight-forward writing style and lack of characterization prevented him from being noted as being particularly literary, it did enable him to attract a large readership. His novel ***Ringworld*** (1970) exemplifies all Niven's plus points: characters from a number of species acting their drama out within the constraints of a solid SF concept. In this case the Ringworld is a huge spinning artificial ring encircling a star so that the ring's air, held to its inner surface by centrifugal force, is kept warm. That the ring's edge is roughly one Earth diameter across, and that it encircles a star roughly 100 million miles away at the ring's centre, means that its habitable surface area is many hundred times that of the Earth's. In addition to his Known Space novels, the developing history of Known Space was fleshed out in a number of collections of short stories. These include *Tales of Known Space* (1975) and ***Neutron Star*** (1968), while his short stories, *Inconstant Moon* (the title story of a collection (1973)) and *The Hole Man,* won the Hugo for Best Short in 1972 and '75 respectively. Unfortunately each new idea introduced to the Known Space stories defined a horizon that often impinged on the settings of other stories. And so, as with all series set in an artificial universe, the writer was writing himself into a corner. The portrayal of new concepts had to mesh with what was already written if consistency was to be maintained. Fortunately Niven had other outlets. *The Mote in God's Eye* (1974), and its sequel *The Moat Around Murcheson's Eye* (1993) with Jerry Pournelle concerns a boom-bust civilization stuck in a system where the most accessible wormhole is, by a quirk of nature, hidden. This prevents the high tech, fast-breeding aliens from reaching the stars and plaguing the Galaxy. (Indeed the latter book foresaw a new type of contraceptive that was, in reality, later in the mid 1990s discovered by Prof Chris Arme (UK).) Again with Pournelle, *Lucifer's Hammer* (1977) concerns the effects on the Earth of an impacting asteroid – this was written before the Alveraz *et al* paper in *Science* presenting evidence for a possible asteroid wiping out the dinosaurs. In more recent years Niven's work has been more in the style of fantasy. Indeed while *The Ringworld Engineers* (1980) is a worthy sequel to *Ringworld*, *Ringworld Throne* (1996) reads like a fantasy odyssey of yore. This has attracted a new generation, and slightly different type of reader to Niven whose popularity remains. 2004 saw the publication of *Ringworld's Children*. He came 5th in the *Concatenation* all-time favourite authors poll.

North American Science Fiction Convention – The NASFiC is the convention, enshrined in the **World SF Society** constitution, that is held in the US those years that the **World SF Convention** (**Worldcon**) is not held in North America.

O'Donnell, Lawrence – see **Henry Kuttner** (for whom this was a pseudonym).

Orbital Decay – novel (1989) by Allen Steele. A powerful debut novel set in the near future in Earth orbit. The construction of the Olympus space station attracts a high-tech type of frontier person, the beanjacks, who are constructing the structures that will open up humanity's future in space. Unfortunately there is a secret behind Olympus, which when found out, threatens democracy and freedom, and does not go down well with the beanjacks. *Orbital Decay* came top of the annual *Locus* readers poll in the 'first novel' category.

Orbitsville – novel (1975) by **Bob Shaw**. Mankind had been in space for centuries but had only found one other habitable world. Then Vance Garamond discovers a vast alien space habitat, a sphere centred on a sun. Inside there is the habitable surface area equivalent to thousands of worlds. Which was to be more difficult, the sphere's exploration or reconciling its discoveries' socio-political implications? *Orbitsville* is the definitive Dyson sphere story which won the British Science Fiction Award and spawned a sequel in *Orbitsville Departure* (1983).

Outer Limits, The – TV series (*fb*1963) Created by Leslie Stevens and produced by Joseph Stephano *The Outer Limits* regularly took over TV sets in the US in the early 1960s with a voice saying: "There is nothing wrong with your television set. Do not attempt to adjust the picture... You are about to experience the awe and mystery that leads you from the inner mind to – *the Outer Limits*." This show of unrelated half hour SF shorts was the younger brother to ***The Twilight Zone***, though struggled to obtain its own identity. Episodes included the Hugo-winning *Soldier* (screenplay by **Harlan Ellison**) when a soldier from the future is catapulted back to our time, can events in the present affect the war's outcome in the future? And another Hugo-winning Ellison, *Demon with a Glass Hand*, in which a man from the future, trapped in a present day office block, struggles to find out why he is the last survivor from a future alien attack.

Outland – film, UK (1981), *dir.* Peter (***2010***) Hyams. *Outland* is effectively *High Noon* in outer space. A new Marshal (Sean Connery) begins his stint at a mining station on Io, Jupiter's third moon. With either corrupt, or those who will turn their backs, deputies the Marshal discovers that an illegal drug is being used that helps boosts the miners' output. This is something that the company is happy to quietly tolerate, if not encourage. Unfortunately, a side-effect of prolonged use is manic delusional violence. With only one shuttle per week, and apart from the station's female doctor, the Marshal is on his own. But he has to survive those being sent to get him out of the way. Though in essence a western plot in space, the screenplay, the sets, the effects and photography (which were then state of the art) make *Outland* a solid contribution to the genre. *Outland* was nominated for one Oscar (for Sound), but failed to win. A Festival of Fantastic Films favourite. Principal cast: Sean (***Indiana Jones***

and the Last Crusade, *Time Bandits*, *Zardoz*) Connery, Peter (*Young Frankenstein*) Boyle, Frances Sternhagen, James B Sikking, Kika Markham, Clarke Peters, and Steven Berkoff.

Out of the Unknown – TV series, UK (*fb*1961). A series of individual TV plays that ran for 4 series (the first two in black and white), many of which were based on stories by some of the best SF writers of the time including: **Isaac Asimov**, **J. G. Ballard**, **John Brunner**, **Ray Bradbury**, **Henry Kuttner**, Nigel (*Quatermass*) Kneale, **Frederik Pohl**, **Robert Sheckley**, **Clifford Simak**, **John Wyndham** and Kate Wilhelm. Much credit must go to the producer Irene Shubik who recognised that the works of established SF writers would still appeal to a viewing audience. Sadly this lesson was not learnt by other producers. Unfortunately the third and fourth series were produced by Alan Bromley who gradually took it away from SF towards psychological suspense.

Paladin of Souls – novel (2003) by Lois (*Barrayar*, *Mirror Dance* and *The Vor Game*) McMaster Bujold. A princess' mother dies and she is free to indulge herself by going off on a pilgrimage. Her party soon hits trouble – a demon possessed bear and hostile soldiers – on top of which she is having nightmares. Clearly there is something driving her on this pilgrimage other than whim… This is a fantasy but that did not preclude it from winning the Hugo Science Fiction Achievement Award (which allows fantasy works) for 'Best Novel' in 2004.

Palmer, Raymond – See *Amazing Stories*, **Fandom** and **Fanzines**.

Passage – novel (2001) by Connie (*To Say Nothing of the Dog*) Willis. *Passage* is a humorous, compelling, occasionally disturbing reflection on death and mortality. Dr Joanna Lander is studying Near Death Experiences (NDEs) when she is approached by Dr Richard Wright who has found a way to induce NDEs using dithetamine. Due to a lack of suitable subjects Joanna takes part in the study herself but, instead of seeing the usual tunnel and light most commonly reported in NDEs, she finds herself aboard a ship. As the study progresses the visions become more detailed, subjectively longer and filled with a sense of import. Joanna knows she must unravel the mystery of the NDE's meaning and is led to seek out her old English teacher, only to find him suffering from Alzheimer's. Can she discover something significant before the study's funding is cut? Or does the vision she experiences carry a more personal meaning? *Passage* came top of the 2002 *Locus* poll for 'best SF novel'.

Patterns – *col.* (1989) by **Pat Cadigan**. Winner of the 1990 *Locus* readers poll for Best Collection, *Patterns* contains stories from 1982-1989, including the double award winning *Angel* (1987) first published in *Isaac Asimov's Science Fiction Magazine*. *Angel* concerns the relationship of an empathic alien, exiled to Earth for refusing to mate, with a homeless human who forms a symbiotic relationship with the creature. Like many of the tales in the collection, *Angel* defies easy categorisation, and Cadigan's work over all, though primarily seen (and marketed) as science fiction, contains overt aspects of both fantasy and horror. Many of the stories are perhaps best described as *urban noir*, and contain a warped but recognisable future, often including elements of IT and media technology, along with modern tropes such as cosmetic surgery and drug taking.

Phase IV – film, US (1973), *dir.* Saul Bass. If *Phase IV* were just an 'insects-rebel-against-mankind' movie it would be unremarkable. However the combination of a good SF concept, the undertones of an ecological message (before the eco-boom of the late '70s and '80s), excellent acting and superb photography has made this a favourite with fantastic film buffs. A discorporate alien intelligence lands on Earth. In order to do whatever it is going to do (and the film never reveals whether this will ultimately be anything malicious or not) it merges with a colony of ants. With the intelligence to guide them the ants begin to thrive, create tall structures to live in and, to the annoyance of the local farmers, start marking off sections of cropland. At this point a Governmental agricultural department send in two high-tech ecologists who, from the safety of a hermetically sealed control centre, proceed to study the colony within the 'infected' area. The ants outwit the ecologists at every turn, even adapting to the insecticide they use. Finally the younger ecologist realises that he must go out and confront the ant queen. Ken Middleham was responsible for many of the high quality ant shots. Principal cast: Nigel Davenport, Michael Murphey and Lynne Frederick.

Planet of the Apes, The – film, US (1968), *dir.* Franklin Schaffner. Based on the novel *La Planète des Singes* (*Monkey Planet*) by Pierre Boule (1963), the film's screenplay was by Michael Wilson and Rod (***The Twilight Zone***) Serling. Astronauts, led by Charlton (***Soylent Green***) Heston, crash land on a planet which, they quickly discover, is populated by talking apes and dumb, animal-like humans. Initially unable to speak due to a throat wound, Heston nonetheless demonstrates his intelligence to two scientist chimps, Zira (Kim Hunter) and Cornelius (Roddy ***The Martian Chronicles*** McDowell). After regaining his speech, Heston is condemned as an abomination and sentenced to death, causing him to escape to the forbidden zone, where he learns a devastating truth... *The Planet of the Apes* was the other (to ***2001: A Space Odyssey***) SF hit of '68, and it spawned four sequels, in addition to a sci-fi TV series as well as a cartoon series and comics. All five films were adapted for Marvel comics, beautifully drawn by Alfredo Alcala. *The Planet of the Apes* received an Oscar for the ape make-up; an Oscar which should have gone to *2001* but the voting Academy members, it is believed, thought that Kubrick used real apes! Of the sequels *Escape from the Planet of the Apes* (1970) is the only other 'Ape' film of note and sees the ape scientists return to the present in another space craft, and the roles reversed as ultimately they become hunted by the human authorities. It transpires that the ape scientists were the progenitors of the future's speaking apes. Though the other sequels were weak, together they do convey a time-loop *cum* parallel time-line tale. *Planet of the Apes* came sixth in the Blackwood/Flynn poll of WSFS members for the top SF films. Principal cast: Charlton Heston, Roddy McDowell, Maurice Evans, James Whitmore, James Daly and Linda Harrison.

Pohl, Frederik – author, US (*b*1919). Pohl, in addition to writing, has been an editor and a literary agent, as well as holding a number of 'straight' jobs, including advertising copywriter. Born in New York, his first stints as an editor were at the age of nineteen with *Astonishing Stories* and *Super Science Stories*; and through most of the sixties Pohl was at the helm of *Galaxy* (working with Horace Gold) and *If*, which won three Hugos for Best Magazine during Pohl's tenure as editor. Pohl was a member of the Futurians, an SF society who boasted such luminaries as **Isaac Asimov**, Damon Knight, and Cyril M. Kornbluth, and he collaborated with these and others, including Jack Williamson. *The Space Merchants* (1953), with Kornbluth, is typical of Pohl's habit of writing telling and critical social commentary in the context of an SF satire, in this case on consumerism and advertising, Another telling collaboration with Kornbluth is *Wolfbane* (1959), a surrealistic tale of invasion by alien robots in which the Earth is kidnapped! Though he released little work during his editorships in the sixties, Pohl began to work exclusively on fiction from the seventies onwards. Pohl shared a Hugo for his 1972 short story (with Kornbluth) *The Meeting*, a posthumous collaboration, tying with *Eurema's Dam* by R.A. Lafferty (1914-2002). The publication of **Gateway** in 1977 won him the Hugo, Nebula, *Locus* and John W. Campbell Memorial awards for Best Novel: though both *Man Plus* (1976) and *JEM: The Making of a Utopia* (1979) were contenders in their time, with the former winning a Nebula. The seventies also saw Pohl release a book of memoirs, *The Way the Future Was* (1978), which contains fascinating insights about the Futurians. The eighties were very productive indeed, seeing: three more novels in the Heechee sequence, of which *Gateway* had been the first; a sequel to *The Space Merchants* called *The Merchants' War* (1984); and fourteen other titles including *Black Star Rising* (1985), in which aliens demand to speak to the President of a Chinese-conquered America; *The Coming of the Quantum Cats* (1986), where the barriers between alternate universes fall and chaotic battles are fought across realities; and *The Day the Martians Came* (1988) collecting stories written over two decades with new material. Pohl won a short story Hugo in 1986 for *Fermi and Frost* (1985), and a John W. Campbell for *The Years of the City* (1984). Pohl has continued publishing into the nineties with novels and with a collection of Heechee universe related tales, *The Gateway Trip* (1990).

Post-apocalyptic. The term given to stories set in a world following a catastrophic disaster, such as global war, planetary pandemic, cosmic event *etc*.

Postman, The – novel (1985) by **David Brin**. In the aftermath of a near-future nuclear war one man copes by taking over the uniform and mail bag of a dead postman. He becomes a symbol of hope. This *Locus* poll-winning book was turned into a somewhat mediocre film starring Kevin Costner.

Predator – film, US (1987), *dir.* John McTiernan. A covert US military rescue team stumbles across a high tech alien in the South American jungle. The alien has a pretty neat near-invisibility camouflage force field (which wowed cinema audiences at the time) and nifty laser gun. It transpires that the alien is a hunter out for some sport and so sees if the military team is up to a match. *Predator* did extremely well at the box office and began a small cult following. A sequel was made, this time set in a US city, but it added little to the story other than the 'Predators' had been apparently having their sport on Earth for at least a couple of centuries. Dark Horse comics produced several *Predator* series, pitting them against the ***Aliens*** and also ***Batman***. In 2004 there was an Alien/Predator cross-over film. The *Predator* was created by Stan Winston, and the special effects (including the alien's camouflage) were by R. Greenberg. The original film was nominated for, but did not win, a Hugo in 1988. Principal cast: Arnold (***Terminator***) Schwarzenegger, Carl Weathers, Elpiladia Carrillo, Bill Duke, Jesse Ventura, Sonny Landham, Richard Chaves, R G Armstrong and Kevin Peter Hall.

Premio Italia – The principal SF award in Italy. It is broadly run along the lines of the Hugo Award and all those who attend the annual Italcon (Italy's national convention) are eligible to vote. The list of past winners can be found on *www.fantascienza.com/italcon/premi/index.html*

Princess Bride, The – film, US/UK (1987), *dir.* Rob Reiner. Every now and then the SF community throws in a wild card, and *The Princess Bride* is one such. At best it is speculative fiction, but it is hardly SF since it is firmly rooted in sword and sorcery fantasy. A comedy adventure, *The Princess Bride* concerns two lovers, Buttercup and Westley who are separated when Westley goes off to make his fortune. Years pass and Buttercup believes him dead. The land's Prince takes Buttercup for his bride, but she is kidnapped for political reasons. However on the kidnappers' trail is a mysterious swordsman... Though a hugely entertaining film in its own right, readers can be forgiven for asking why it is in this SF guide? The answer is that it won the Hugo for 'Best Dramatic Presentation' in 1988 proving once again that SF is a broad church. (It was the first fantasy film to win a Hugo; the similar feat for books took place in 2001 with ***Harry Potter and The Goblet of Fire***. Other Hugo nominations for Best Dramatic Presentation that year were ***Robo Cop*** and ***Predator***.). Principal cast: Cary Elwes (Westley), Robin Wright (Buttercup), Mandy Patinkin, Chris Sarandon, Christopher (***Little Shop of Horrors***) Guest, Wallace Shawn, Andre the Giant, Peter (***The Lost World*** and ***Forbidden Planet***) Falk, Peter Cook, Mel Smith and Billy Crystal.

Prisoner, The – TV series, UK (*fb*1968).   Patrick (***Scanners***) McGoohan plays a secret agent (possibly the UN agent John Drake from McGoohan's previous series, *Danger Man*) who wants to retire. Having given in his resignation, he is followed driving home. As he packs his bags, gas enters the room and he falls unconscious.   He awakes, to find himself in a duplicate room in a 'village' (actually Portmeirion in Wales). Everyone in the Village wears a badge with a number; the agent's is number '6'. Many are other agents who have gone missing and who are kept by those running the Village. These 'captors', in the main, are equally anonymous: so who are the prisoners and who are the warders? Only number '2', who is clearly the head warden, and his butler (Angelo Muscat), are obviously on one side and not the other. There is frequently a new number '2' (though Leo McKern played him for three episodes) but each number '2' is always after information from number '6' as to why he resigned? Escape from the closed circuit TV monitored Village is almost impossible, as is discovering who has built the Village in the first place. With this the scene was set for one of the most enigmatic yet intelligently scripted SF series of the '60s.   It seemed to have something to say about many aspects of life and politics of that time. It was popular with a mass audience (it had extremely high viewing figures for a show of its type back then) and remains a most intriguing and challenging series, even if some of the imagery is now clearly dated.   McGoohan himself, and perhaps a few colleagues, created the concept.   He also produced the series and even wrote some of the episodes. The series attracted a dedicated fan following and, some three decades since originally aired, the annual gathering of *Prisoner* fans is still a regular feature of the UK convention calendar.   It has been repeatedly shown in both the UK and the US, and all episodes are available on video. In the UK in 2001, nearly three and a half decades later, a national TV station, Channel 4, held a poll for the top 100 TV personalities of all time – McGoohan's character in *The Prisoner* came 27th. A four-issue comics mini-series (also available in graphic novel format) did not quite live up to the TV programmes, though was a brave attempt.

Prix Aurora. The principal Canadian SF Award (known up to 1991 as 'The Casper'). Given in a variety of categories both English and French for long and short written SF, 'Other' SF (such as radio or TV), art and fan awards. Given since 1980.

Prix Apollo. The French SF Award for best SF novel published in France regardless of whether the work was originally in French. Given since 1972.

Quantum Leap – TV series, US (first broadcast 1989). Starting with a fair feature-length pilot, *Quantum Leap* concerned the adventures of physicist Sam Beckett who journeys through time entering the bodies of others somewhere back in the past but only as far back as the date of Beckett's own birth; he is, it transpires, part of an uncontrollable process operating within this restricted window on time. He is aided by Al, a colleague from his own present (but our – the viewer's – future). Al appears, (only to him) as a hologram, helping Sam put right things that have gone wrong in the lives of those into which he has 'leaped'. It soon becomes apparent that there is some sort of purpose behind Sam's plight and it is hinted that this is down to God. Many of Quantum Leap's episodes are unrelated, but some touched upon time travel paradoxes (in a couple of episodes Sam and Al even encounter alternate reality versions of themselves) while others relate to the supernatural but rarely explicitly (so leaving room for some rational explanation). Though a decidedly above-average series, this in itself would not warrant its inclusion in this guide. However, of note is that early on *Quantum Leap* was due to be axed but, due to the cast cultivating a level of fan interest that could not be ignored, it survived for 95 episodes over five years. While all the programme's devotees ('leapers') were not fully fledged SF fans, some undoubtedly were and, all said and done, the programme is a testimony to viewer power. Principal cast: Scott Bakula (Sam) and Dean Stockwell (Al). Series created and produced by Donald Bellisario.

Quarantine – novel (1992). **Greg Egan's** debut novel is an ultra-**hard SF** exploration of the very nature of reality (and the universe). It is the late twenty-first century, a time when bio-engineering means that people can technologically modify their minds in many ways. Mankind's global society is shaped such that information systems are breached as fast as they are improved. Then one night the stars went out. 'The Bubble' quarantines the Earth and its solar system from the rest of the universe. Meanwhile Laura, in the care of a psychiatric hospital with severe congenital brain damage, somehow defies monitoring and repeatedly escapes. How and why is what private investigator Nick Stavrianos has been hired to find out, but may uncover more than he bargained for...

Quatermass – TV and films, UK (*fb*1953). Created by Nigel (***1984***) Kneale, Professor Bernard Quatermass thrilled audiences with his alien encounters as head of the British Experimental Rocket Group. In *The Quatermass Experiment* (July-Aug 1953), astronaut Victor Carroon (Duncan Lamont), one of a three man team, returns to Earth without his companions. He then begins changing into some creature. Quatermass (Reginald Tate) must determine what has happened. Hammer adapted the six half-hour episodes of live TV as *The Quatermass Xperiment* (a.k.a. *The Creeping Unknown*) in 1955, starring Brian Donlevy as Quatermass and Richard Wordsworth as Carroon. (This film revived the flagging fortunes of Hammer and began its forays into SF and horror.) The second TV series, *Quatermass II* (Oct-Nov 1955) saw the Professor (John Robinson) uncover an alien invasion plot. Hammer filmed this in 1957 with Donlevy as *Quatermass II* (a.k.a. *Enemy from Space*). The third series, *Quatermass and the Pit* (Dec '58-Jan '59), had André Morell in the role, and concerned the discovery of what appears to be an unexploded bomb. It turns out to be something quite different that triggers people's ancient racial memories. Hammer waited until 1967 to adapt this to film (see below). Of the three original TV adventures, only the last two are still available, the film stock of the first having rotted in storage. A final adventure, *Quatermass the Conclusion*, was aired in 1978 and starred John Mills. Concerning the 'harvesting' of humans by aliens, it was very disappointing, but was nonetheless adapted to film. However even edited down to film length it was unsatisfactory (if anything this made it worse still!). The scripts of the original 3 series are available in book form, as is a novelization of the last, all by Nigel Kneale.

Quatermass and the Pit – film, GB (1967) is also known as *Five Million Years to Earth* in the US. *dir.* Roy Ward Baker, written by – and faithfully based on his third (1958) *Quatermass* TV series – Nigel Kneale. *Quatermass and the Pit* is one of the rare above average SF offerings from the Hammer film studios. The remains of a five million year old primitive apeman is found by workmen digging for the London underground rail, then a metallic object appears. At first it is thought to be the remains of a German V2 rocket and Professor Quatermass is called in. Surprisingly a primitive apeman's skull is found inside the craft. The site turns out to have a history of hauntings while further in the rocket there are insect-type aliens. More discoveries and Quatermass begins to piece together what must be happening while half of London turns violently against the other half. Can Quatermass save the day...? This slightly limp re-make is nonetheless a favourite at the Festival of Fantastic Films and probably the best of the Hammer adaptations from the BBC TV series. Principal cast: Andrew Kier (Quatermass), James Donald, Barbara Shelley, Julian (***Indiana Jones and the Last Crusade***) Glover, Duncan Lamont (Victor Carroon from the first TV series), Edwin Richfield and Peter Copley.

Raiders of the Lost Ark – film, US (1981), *dir.* Steven (see also **Brian Aldiss**, ***Close Encounters of the Third Kind***, ***The Twilight Zone***, ***Jurassic Park*** and ***Indiana Jones and the Last Crusade***) Spielberg. This Lucasfilm production was an homage to the cliff-hanger serials frequently shown, in both the US and England, as part of kids' Saturday morning pictures, and to the adventure pulp magazines that complemented the early SF pulps. Archaeologist Indiana Jones (Harrison (***Blade Runner***) Ford), when not teaching, recovers ancient artefacts for his college, run by Denholm Elliott. Put on the trail of the lost Ark of the Covenant by the US government, Jones finds himself in a race to find the Ark before the Nazis do. Running into an old girlfriend (Karen Allen) along the way who provides a vital clue, Jones uses his contacts (including John Rhys-Davies) to track down the resting place of the Ark, but only to lose it to the villains, played by Ronald Lacey and Paul Freeman. The fast-paced and perilous adventures along the way build to a special effects climax where God has the last word. This roller-coaster romp, scripted by Lawrence Kasdan from a story by George (***Star Wars***) Lucas and Philip (***Invasion of the Body Snatchers*** (1978) re-make)

Kaufman, beautifully revived all the cliff-hanger clichés of the serials, and won the 1982 Hugo for Best Dramatic Presentation. It spawned a lack-lustre prequel, *Indiana Jones and the Temple of Doom* (1984), but a much better sequel, **Indiana Jones and the Last Crusade** (1989).

Red Dwarf – TV series, UK (*fb*1988).   Written by Rob Grant and Doug Naylor, this low budget BBC comedy concerns David Lister: a lowly, unkempt technician on the interstellar cargo ship Red Dwarf who is sentenced to stasis for illegally keeping a cat. While in stasis the ship's crew is killed due to an error made by one Arnold Rimmer (Lister's immediate superior) the 2nd Technician in charge of the 'Z' shift. Three million years later the radiation from the accident has died down and Holly (the ship's computer who is now a little frayed around the edges) releases Lister from stasis. To keep him company he brings back Rimmer as a hologram.   Meanwhile over the millennia Lister's cat's descendants evolved into an intelligent species (surviving, due to Red Dwarf's size, in unaffected areas), the last of which (imaginatively called 'Cat') bumps into Lister and Rimmer. And so the scene is set for one of the Galaxy's greatest, if least known, epic sagas since ***The Hitch-Hiker's Guide to the Galaxy***. Though superbly making takes on many SF tropes (aliens, shape shifting, mind transference, cyberspace entertainment, time travel, entropy reversal *etc*) the series has not won any major SF awards, such as the Hugos, but has attracted favour among fans at UK conventions in addition, when on air, to having been one of BBC 2's top ten most viewed programmes.   (It has also won mainstream awards such as the Emmy.) In series II they find the service mechanoid Kryten 2X4B 523P who added considerably to the banter as well as providing a counter to the somewhat dim-witted Holly. In series III Holly became female (played by Hattie Hayridge, as the actor Norman Lovett had moved away from the London studios to Edinburgh). The change, though fair, was not entirely successful as the original actor was so dead-pan in his delivery. Also in series VI Red Dwarf was left behind with the action instead centred on a 'Starbug' shuttle.   Nonetheless throughout this evolution the scripts largely remained excellent up to series VII when the show's success encouraged the BBC to add canned laughter. (Why? Who knows?) That, and that one of the writers (Rob Grant) and principal actors (Chris Barrie (Rimmer)) left, meant that series VII was for some fans disappointing. Series VII did though end with the return to Red Dwarf and, in the final minutes, the original Holly reappeared. Series VIII saw the return of Rimmer who was resurrected, along with Red Dwarf's original crew of hundreds by nanobots. (Note: following season 7, many of the earlier seasons were re-edited, with new effects added, though the original episodes are favoured by fans). Principal cast: Chris Barrie (Rimmer), Craig Charles (Lister), Danny John-Jules (Cat), Norman Lovett and Hattie Hayridge (Holly), Robert Llewellyn (Kryten), Claire Grogan and Chloe Annett (Kolchanski). Finally, following the successful 1991 airing of early (UK) episodes in the Los Angeles area, Universal thought it necessary to re-make the series for a US audience with a different cast (apparently following the Los Angeles' audience reception – the least said about this the better), save for Robert Llewellyn.

Rendezvous With Rama – novel (1973) by **Arthur C. Clarke**. This was Clarke's first novel in five years, since the publication of ***2001: A Space Odyssey*** (1968), though four collections of his short works had appeared in the interim. In truth, not much happens in this book: a gigantic alien spaceship makes an incursion into the solar system and is investigated by humans. Asteroid-sized, it is hollow, containing cities and a small sea (large lake) but otherwise seems totally impervious to human enquiry. Then the ship leaves the solar system and the human explorers return to Earth. Clarke delights in tweaking our Sense of Wonder, emphasising the scale of the artefact and maintaining its mystery, but gives us little by way of character and plot. Nonetheless, *Rendezvous With Rama* swept the awards in 1974, winning a Hugo, Nebula, John W. Campbell, and British Science Fiction Association Award for Best Novel, as well as topping the annual *Locus* readers poll for best novel. Whether the novel directly inspired *Eon* by **Greg Bear** is a moot point, *Rama* did however give rise to three sequels. Written with Gentry Lee during the late-eighties and early-nineties, they were uniformly dull excursions into the enigma of Rama and did little to enhance Clarke's reputation. They were *Rama II* (1989), *The Garden of Rama* (1991), and *Rama Revealed* (1993), but all are best forgotten. Sci-fi Channel released a made-for-TV production in 2005.

"Repent, Harlequin!" Said the Ticktockman – short story (1965) by **Harlan Ellison**. This short opens with a long quote from

Henry David Thoreau's *Civil Disobedience*, which is more or less what the tale is all about. In 2389 it becomes a crime to be late, and howsoever long you have delayed the Master Schedule will be deducted from your life. But the Harlequin will not keep to society's timetable, in fact deliberately disrupts it. Indeed, he calls for revolution. So the Master Timekeeper, the Ticktockman, is set to apprehend the tardy terrorist... Ellison is, self-reportedly, always late, and this satirical sideswipe at society's obsession with time-keeping, and what it implies about their way of thinking, will find many sympathetic readers. *Repent...* won the 1966 Hugo and Nebula for Best Short Story, and has been adapted twice into comic form, most notably by Jim Steranko, but also by Alex Nino. It can be found in the collections *Paingod and Other Delusions* (1965), *Alone Against Tomorrow* (1971), and *All the Sounds of Fear* (1973).

Research Collection, SF – see **SF Research Collection**.

Return of the Jedi – film, US/GB (1983), *dir.* Richard Marquand. This was the final part of the second trilogy, but since the second trilogy was filmed first this was the third *Star Wars* film... if you follow the drift. Rescuing Han Solo, Luke Skywalker – now a Jedi knight – reunites the team. Off they go to lead the rebels to destroy the evil Empire's new Death Star. Despite really being a soft re-make of *Star Wars* (there are cuddly teddy bear aliens (the Ewoks) and in the end a number of the principal cast turns out to be related) the film romps along lubricated with great special effects. But do special effects make a movie? *Return of the Jedi* may well have been riding on *Star Wars* coat tails when the fans voted it for the Best Dramatic Presentation Hugo in 1984, but it was also later voted into the *Concatenation* poll at number 20, not to mention was nominated for (but did not win) 4 Oscars. Principal cast: Mark Hamill, Harrison Ford, Carrie Fisher, Alec Guiness, Anthony Daniels (C3PO), Kenny (*Time Bandits*) Baker (R2D2), and Dave Prowse (Darth Vader), James Earl Jones (Voice of Vader). Sebastian Shaw (Vader unmasked) and the voice of Frank (*Little Shop of Horrors*) Oz (Yoda).

Riders of the Purple Wage – novella (1967) by **Philip José Farmer**. First published in **Harlan Ellison's** *Dangerous Visions* (1967) anthology, this story shared the 1968 Hugo for Best Novella (with *Weyr Search* (1968) by Anne McCaffrey). It is the pun-laden tale of Chibiabos Winnegan, an artist, and his grandfather, who faked his death 25 years before to escape taxes. Chib has problems of his own, with a show coming up and an influential critic making unwanted advances, not to mention his vaguely rebellious artistic friends, so the last thing he needs is to be stalked by the taxman searching for grandpa. Farmer riotously enjoys playing with the words right up to the last outrageous gag, lampooning subjects all the way.

Ringworld – novel (1970) by **Larry Niven**. Set in Niven's 'Known Space' universe, a mixed-species band sets off to explore a strange artefact discovered by the Puppeteers – a two headed, three footed species. As most of the Puppeteers have left Known Space for the outer Galaxy, and because they do not relish danger, they need our explorers to scout the artefact for them. The artefact in question is a huge ring, so large that it encircles a sun. It has atmosphere on its inner surface, held in place by the centrifugal force from the ring's spinning. With the ring's surface width roughly an Earth diameter wide and with a diameter of the ring itself some hundreds of millions of miles, its habitable area is the equivalent of several thousand Earths. Our explorers have to find out if anyone is living there, who built the Ringworld and why? The Ringworld is a grand concept whose fundamentals are largely based on solid scientific principles, as such it is the very stuff of hard science fiction. *Ringworld* won the Hugo in 1971 for Best Novel, came top of the annual *Locus* readers poll, and was voted into the all-time top 20 best books in the *Concatenation* poll. He wrote three direct sequels: the **hard SF** *Ringworld Engineers* (1979); the highly disappointing science fantasy *The Ringworld Throne* (1996); and a mix of space opera and hard SF *Ringworld's Children* (2004).

Rise of Endymion, The – novel (1997) by **Dan Simmons**. This novel furthers the ***Hyperion*** saga. *Endymion* introduced us to Raul Endymion, a Hyperion native who is inextricably linked to Aenea, a young girl who, it would seem, is the new messiah, destined to overthrow the Pax. *The Rise of Endymion* continues that story as it follows Aenea as she comes of age. *The Rise of Endymion* came top of the 1998 *Locus* poll for best SF novel.

Robinson, Kim Stanley – author, US (*b*1952). Robinson's first short stories were published in 1975, though he was in fact a student at the time, ultimately gaining a PhD in English in 1982 from the University of California. His thesis on the novels of **Philip K. Dick** was later published (1984), the same year as his first SF novel, *The Wild Shore*, which was published as one of Terry Carr's New Ace Science Fiction Specials. It was the first of a trilogy of novels set in alternate versions of the same area of Orange County, California. Together with *The Gold Coast* (1988) and *Pacific Edge* (1990), the three present a *status quo*, a dystopian and a utopian version of the future. *The Wild Shore* topped the *Locus* readers poll in the 'first novel' category, and *Pacific Edge* won a John W. Campbell Award, while *The Years of Rice and Salt* topped the *Locus* poll for 'best SF novel' in 2003. However, it is Robinson's Mars trilogy that has gained him the most acclaim. At the time (1992-96), publishers seemed determined to put out as many books with Mars in the title as they could, though few were as memorable as Robinson's trio. Comprised of *Red Mars* (1992), **Green Mars** (1993), and **Blue Mars** (1996), the story covers the first 200 years of humans' terraforming and colonisation of the red planet, and the building of a utopia. Thoroughly researched, these books are a hard-SF fan's dream. However, so concerned is Robinson to be as soundly-based as possible in presenting his arguments, he occasionally digresses from the plot so slowing the action. However, such is the SF public's fascination with our planetary neighbour that *Red Mars* won a Nebula in 1993, and both *Green Mars* and *Blue Mars* each won both the Hugo Award for best SF novel and topped the *Locus* poll in 1994 and 1997 respectively. A companion collection to the *Mars* trilogy of short stories and novellas called *The Martians* was published in 1999.

Robo Cop – film, US (1987), *dir.* Paul (***Starship Troopers*** and ***Total Recall***) Verhoeven. In the future one of the most crime-ridden precincts in the US is Metro West of down-town old Detroit. When during a bust a veteran cop, called Murphy (Peter Weller (see also **Philip K Dick**)), gets fatally wounded the megacorporation OCP seize the opportunity to turn him into a law enforcing cyborg – Robocop. Prompted by flashes of memory from his previous life, Robocop discovers that OCP has its links with Detroit's criminal world and is using it to further its development plans. The film is a bit like *Hill Street Blues* meets ***Judge Dredd*** (the ***2000AD*** version) and is as engaging as you might expect such a combination to be. Unfortunately, the video versions and many of *Robocop's* TV screenings were substantially censored. Finally, the film spawned two sequels (1990 and 1993 the latter starring Robert Burke) as well as a watered-down TV series. None lived up to the promise that the original held out. There was also a comic series from DC and Dark Horse (including *RoboCop vs. **Terminator***). RoboCop was designed by Rob (***The Thing***) Bottin, and also featured Nancy Allen, Dan O'Herlihy and Miguel Ferrer.

Rocky Horror (Picture) Show, The – musical (theatre)/film (1973/5). Film *dir.* Jim Sharman. *The Rocky Horror Picture Show* (1975) is the film of Richard O'Brien's comedy musical play *The Rocky Horror Show* (1973). *Rocky* is a cult, ultra-camp production that has attracted such a following that the play has been on stage somewhere in the world virtually continually since its premiere and attracts an audience which regularly includes devotees who dress up and who even have added to the script, shouting set rejoinders from the aisles. The 'plot', which is punctuated by a narrator, centres around Frank 'n Furter and his 'party' from the planet Transylvania. Frank's quest for lovers has led him to build himself a man "in just seven days". However this Adonis does not prevent Frank from 'propositioning' Brad and Janet, the two newly engaged who sought shelter from a storm in the Transylvanians' mansion. Nor does it stop others from uncovering the aliens' presence... Rocky Horror's following includes a hefty contingent of SF fans. In the 1980s virtually every national UK convention (the **Eastercon**) screened the film, which itself was the 7th most viewed of all films shown at the Festival of Fantastic Films in the 1990s. It also came 11th in the *Concatenation* all-time film poll. Principal cast: Tim Curry, Susan Sarandon; Barry Bostwick, Richard O'Brien, Charles Gray, Patricia Quinn, Little Nell, Meatloaf, Jonathan Adams and Peter Hinwood.

Roddenberry, Gene – TV producer, US (1921–1991). Gene Roddenberry created the TV series he considered to be a 'wagon train to the stars' – ***Star Trek***. However his interest in SF dated from his school days and ***Astounding Stories*** magazine. He went on to become a writer both of short stories and TV scripts, but began by doing this under an assumed name as by day he was a police sergeant. In 1952 he wrote his first SF script called *The Secret Defense of 117* which was aired on *Chevron Theater*. In

1954 he left the police to write full time, working on series such as *West Point* and *Have Gun, Will Travel*. By 1963 he created, and was producing, the series *The Lieutenant* for MGM. ***Star Trek*** (*fb*1966) followed and the rest, as they say, is history. *Star Trek* was not at first deemed a success and so the series was axed after three seasons. He eventually married Majel Barratt, who played nurse Christine Chapel. Roddenberry went on to write pilots for other series but these never came close to the standard he had set with *Star Trek*. As such the most successful of his other offerings was *Genesis II* (1973). It concerned a scientist waking up in the far future after a suspended animation experiment goes wrong (rather, it works too well). He finds a post-nuclear holocaust future where a small surviving community of civilization is threatened by mutants. However *Star Trek's* syndicated success gave Roddenberry a second chance and so in 1987 a sequel series ***Star Trek: The Next Generation*** was first aired. In 1968 Roddenberry won a Special Award Hugo for *Star Trek*. The individual episodes that won Hugos were *The Menagerie* and *City on the Edge of Forever* (the latter written by **Harlan Ellison**). The episode *The Inner Light* won a Hugo for *ST: Next Generation*. Unfortunately Roddenberry died before seeing the subsequent Trek series *Deep Space Nine* and *Voyager* broadcast, but did manage to take his creation to the big screen and must have been assured of *Star Trek's* continued success.

Rollerball – film, US (1975) *dir.* Norman Jewison and scripted by William Harrison, based on his short story *Roller Ball Murders* (1973). In the future the world is run by big business corporations and the masses are entertained by the tough sport of rollerball. However when one rollerball player, Jonathan E, becomes too successful the authorities fear him becoming a symbol for the masses and so too powerful. Jonathan is offered retirement, but he will not quit the sport. The authorities then decide to change rollerball's rules so making it a tougher game... Watch out for Ralph (***Time Bandits***, ***The Man Who Could Work Miracles*** and ***Things to Come***) Richardson's cameo as the caretaker of the run down artificial intelligence computer that holds the world's historical records. Though a US production, the filming was done in West Germany and the UK. Principal cast: James Caan (Jonathan E.), John Houseman, Maud Adams, John Beck, Moses Gunn, Pamela (***Buck Rogers***) Hensley, Barbara Trentham, and Ralph Richardson. [The 2002 version (*dir*. John

McTiernan and starring Chris Klein) does not have the broader SF trappings of a world-dominating political elite controlling the population on one hand by providing rollerball as an opiate for the masses and on the other by editing historical records. It instead simply takes the game's higher ratings arising out of violence and accidents as the motivator. Harrison did not write the screenplay.]

Russell, Eric Frank – author, English (1905-1978)   Though a contemporary of the ever so British **John Wyndham**, Eric Frank Russell wrote mainly for the US market and principally for **John W Campbell's** *Unknown* and *Astounding Science Fiction* (see *Analog*) magazines.   Campbell did not entertain invasions by vastly superior aliens or **hard SF** with technology at its centre – Russell's writing certainly does not come from such cliché-ridden quarters – he had ecology in his SF long before the post-1960s boom in environmental concerns   Yes, Russell had aliens, but they were quirky and had their own strengths and weaknesses.   Yes, Russell had space ships, but it was how their crews interacted with their hardware and circumstances that intrigued the man.   His *Allagamogossa*, which won him the Hugo for Best Short Story in 1955, illustrates this well.   The crew of a war ship have been ordered to undergo an equipment audit of all things.   Unfortunately they do not seem to have their 'offog'.   Worse, they cannot remember ever having an offog or even knowing what one is!   So the ship's engineer makes up some passable, but nonsensical device, and the crew get through their administrative scrutiny.   However circumstances conspire that their ruse will be discovered on their return to Earth, so they take remedial action, but this itself has the unforeseen result of grounding the entire Earth space fleet...!   His novels notably include *Sinister Barrier* (1943).   It concerns invisible (in the normal vision spectral range) aliens who manipulate humans causing wars and suffering, an emotion on which the aliens feed (no ray gun toting alien invasion here, in fact the aliens view humans as property).   Rare for SF of its time it is told as a detective-styled story.   However Russell was not a profligate novel writer, though he did write many short stories, eight volumes of which have been published, writing mainly in the 1940s to mid 1960s.   *The Best of Eric Frank Russell* is a representative collection published the year of his death in 1978. His last ten years before his death, in terms of his writing, were quiet (giving some cause to speculate why). Nonetheless much of his work is considered an essential part of '**Golden Age** SF'.

Sacred and the Profane, The – comic, US (*fp*1977). First published as a five-part black and white strip in Mike Friedrich's independent comic ***Star Reach*** between 1977-78, *The Sacred and the Profane* was substantially expanded by writer Dean Motter and artist Ken Steacy for Marvel's mid-eighties 'adult' comic magazine *Epic Illustrated*, which version was subsequently collected in a single edition by Eclipse in 1987. Sister Marianna is aboard the starship *St. Catherine's* on the Catholic Interstellar Crusade, along with Arch-Bishop Franklin and Purifier Joshua. The ship comes across an alien presence in the void, but the fanatic Joshua starts a Holy War, plunging the ship into devastating conflict. As tensions mount, the people on the ship bring their darkest feelings to the fore and every relationship becomes a morality play. Meanwhile Joshua's mind snaps as he conceives his mission to exterminate the aliens, seeing them as servants of Satan. The original *Star Reach* episodes are rare and expensive, but the Eclipse collected version is still available. Ken Steacy also drew for *Epic* adaptations of **Harlan Ellison**'s Earth-Kyben war stories, and these were collected as *Night and the Enemy* (1987) by Comico.

Sagan, Carl – planetary scientist/SF author/TV presenter, US (1934–1996). Having studied under the astronomer Gerard Kuiper, Sagan chose to specialise in planetary science and exobiology. He spent much of his life literally turning science fiction into science fact. He was actively involved in the Mariner, Viking, Voyager and Galileo space missions and has over 600 academic papers and other publications to his name. He was also never afraid to speak out over political issues with science at their heart, such as the greenhouse effect and the nuclear winter (Sagan was the 'S' in the initial nuclear winter TTAPS (Turco, Toon, Ackerman, Pollack and Sagan) paper). This heady cocktail of scientific interests demonstrates Sagan's own well developed 'sense of wonder' and that, and his love to share his enthusiasm in discovering the nature of the Universe, made him an ideal front man in public understanding of science exercises. The most famous of these was his TV series *Cosmos*, which itself captivated SF fans who voted the book of the series the best non fiction Hugo in 1981, while his popular science book

Intelligent Life in the Universe was voted joint 3rd non-fiction favourite in the *Concatenation* all-time poll. His last popular science book of note was *Demon-Haunted World* (1997). He did not spend much time writing SF but of note did write ***Contact*** (1985), the film of which he never saw completed (but which was dedicated to him) due to his untimely death from pneumonia in 1996 after a two year battle against a bone-marrow disease. The film won the Hugo in 1998 for Best Dramatic Production. (See also **Sternbach, Rick**.)

Scanners – film, US (1980), dir. David (***The Fly***) Cronenberg. Scanners are telepaths created by the effects of a drug, ephemerol, and it is also the drug they need to block out the thoughts of others. Everything appears to be controlled by the large corporation ConSec. However a super-scanner decides to take over the whole scanning world and only our hero can stop him. Yet despite this simple plot, and the fact that Cronenberg finished writing the screenplay while actually directing it, this is an engaging film, albeit a rather black portrayal of telepathy. Much of the script is intelligent except that the apparent intermittent ability of the protagonist to telepathically detect non-scanner adversaries is not explained (even when drug free) which requires the viewer's equally intermittent effort in suspending disbelief. Two sequels and a TV movie, followed but neither added anything to the original and several exploitation movies were made using 'scanner' in their titles (for example *Scanner Cop* (1993)), but none were of the quality of the original *tour de force*. Principal cast: Stephen Lack, Jennifer O'Neill, Patrick (***The Prisoner***) McGoohan, Lawrence Dane, Michael (***Total Recall***) Ironside, and Robert Silverman.

Schismatrix – novel (1985) by **Bruce Sterling**. One year after **William Gibson's** *Neuromancer* (1984), Sterling published one of the definitive **cyberpunk** novels. Set in his Shaper/Mechanist universe (short stories of which can be found in Sterling's collection *Crystal Express* (1989)), *Schismatrix* portrays a future of autonomous orbiting and space habitats in which the Shapers, champions of biotechnology, and the Mechanists, prosthetic cyborgs, carry out their conflicts. Abelard Lindsey, a renegade Shaper with a Mechanist right arm, has a serious death wish, but also an uncanny luck. He's hoping it will run out among the microbe-ridden habitats, each a republic unto itself, that comprise the Schismatrix. Full of corporate self-interests, criminals, and politicians, not to mention aliens, surely Lindsey can run afoul of someone. And if that doesn't work, he can always visit the trashed and melted planet Earth... Blackly witty, frantic and driven, this novel is typical of the best that came out of cyberpunk and was easily the most mature of Sterling's early works. (Science note: Schismatrix features the concept of a space station's habitability being undermined by fungi. This actually began to take place on the Russian Mir space station in the late 1990s.)

Science Fantasy – a sub-genre of SF whose stories are fundamentally fantasy (for instance a man flying unaided by technology) but rationalised with science or pseudo-science (for instance the man is an alien who gets his powers from the Sun. *cf*. **Superman**).

Science Fiction – currently the earliest known use of the term was 1851 in William Wilson's *A Little Earnest Book Upon A Great Old Subject* (1851, coincidentally the year Mary (*Frankenstein*) Shelley died). Wilson wrote: [the poet Thomas] "'Campbell says that fiction in Poetry is not the reverse of the truth, but her soft and enchanting resemblance'. Now this applies especially to Science-Fiction, in which the revealed truths of science may be given, interwoven with a pleasing story which itself may be poetical and true." (Source: **Aldiss** and Wingove's ***Trillion Year Spree***.)

'Sci-Fi' – is a cant term (used especially by non-SF media folk) that has generated controversy in some circles. On one hand its coining is attributed late in the first half of the 20th century to the American SF collector **Forrest J Ackerman** as an abbreviation of Science Fiction (inspired by the then new term 'Hi-fi'). More recently, following redefinition (including reportedly by Terry Carr and Damon Knight), it has become the shibboleth term some SF critics and fans use for science fiction made purely for financial gain with no artistic or literary merit of its own. For example, while both the book *Monkey Planet* and its film ***The Planet of the Apes*** are science fiction, the spin-off TV series and indeed the cartoon series, were made purely for commercial reasons that brought nothing new to the overall plot or concept. Surprisingly SF fans do also use their own abbreviation for 'popular' SF, **'skiffy'**, but not without a sense of irony. The writer (and SF critic) Kingsley Amis referred to mainstream commentators and publishers, ignorant of the genre, who use the term 'sci-fi' as an SF abbreviation as "trendy triflers". **Brian Aldiss** is similarly critical. Whatever your view, any term that has increased either the profile or analysis of the genre (take your pick) is surely to be welcomed but it should perhaps be used with greater care especially by those with an interest in the genre.

Seedling Stars – collection of short stories (1957) by **James Blish.** The idea of altering the environment to benefit humans has been around since the invention of farming some 12,000 years ago. In *Seedling Stars*, James Blish turns this idea on its head, to alter humans to fit the environment. As humans move outwards across the galaxy, they encounter a variety of alien worlds—some Earth-like, but most not. After all, with the right technology it is much easier to alter human DNA than it is to alter an entire planet. We encounter humans altered to survive freezing wastes, an arboreal existence and life within a puddle of water. With the latter scenario humans have been genetically engineered to be only a few millimetres in size. Living in a puddle on an alien planet they join forces with amoebae in a war against other microscopic life forms. Despite the vast changes that have taken place to the human genome on these various worlds, the people still remain human. They still have their human spirit and their curiosity. It is, Blish argues, this that make a human Human, however alien they may appear.

SEFF – See **Fan Funds**.

Seiun, The. The principal Japanese SF Award which has a number of categories including best SF translated to Japanese.

Semiprozine – see **fanzine**.

Sense of Wonder – The wonderment, or awe, felt when the full scope of the SF concepts underpinning a story become manifest.

SF Chronicle – magazine (US). Originally edited by Andrew Porter, contents include articles concerning SF news, convention reports and book reviews. Also short SF stories. *SF Chronicle* has won the Hugo for Best Semi-Prozine in 1993 and 1994. (See also **Fandom**)

SF Foundation – academic resource (UK). (See **Foundation, SF**.)

SF Museum and Hall of Fame – infotainment (US). Founded in 2004 and based in Seattle, this is a museum of predominantly US book and Hollywood cinematic SF. Further details on *www.sciencefictionexperience.com*. (See also **Maison d'Ailleurs**.)

SF Research Collection – academic resource (US). The US equivalent of the UK SF Foundation (see **Foundation, SF**), based at the University of Maryland.

Shatter – comic, US (*crtd* 1984). In one sense this is a 'gimmick' comic, the gimmick being that all the artwork was created on an Apple Mac computer, by artist Michael Saenz. However the scripts, mostly by Peter Gillis, are literate, witty and, above all, good SF. The lead character, Sadr al-din Morales a.k.a. Shatter, like 50% of the global population is a temp. He often takes police work and, needing money to buy an original canister of Coke syrup, he accepts a contract to track down a mass murderer. Before he knows it he is embroiled in multi-party intrigues for the control and distribution of RNA-transfer technology, the effects of which are temporary when used on most subjects but, in Shatter's case, transferred skills 'stick' and further treatments are not necessary. *Shatter* started life as a one-off special and then continued as a back-up strip in *Jon Sable, Freelance* issues 25-30, before gaining its own title which ran for 14 issues. The story, including all previous appearances up to issue 4 of the actual title, was collected as a trade paperback and is still available today.

Shaw, Bob – author, UK (1931–1997). Though writing SF from 1954, alongside careers in engineering and journalism, Shaw did not become a full time writer until 1975. Though rarely excellent, he was an author who regularly, and invariably, turned out above-average, if not good, SF. Shaw produced over a score of novels and half a dozen collections of shorts in three decades of writing. Yet classics like British SF Award-winning *Orbitsville* (1975) and *Other Days, Other Eyes* (1972) make Shaw required reading. *Orbitsville* was one of the first novels to do justice to the concept of a Dyson's sphere: a hollow sphere with a sun at its centre and a habitable inner surface. Here, in addition to the obvious playing out of the sense of wonder at the structure, Shaw adds the socio-political dimension of the sphere's colonists potentially providing those disaffected with the State a place to go. Less grand, but nonetheless as stimulating, *Other Days, Other Eyes* explores the implications of 'slow glass': a glass through which light travels so slowly that images may be 'stored' for viewing later; such as 12 hour glass that allows the sun to shine out of it, so providing illumination, at night. But Shaw also had a sense of humour as revealed by *Who Goes Here?* (1977) featuring the space legionnaire 'Warren Peace' (geddit?) soldiering across the galaxy. This humour spilled over into Shaw's fan activity, for Shaw was a regular at many UK conventions. Indeed, for many years (1970s to early 1990s) one of the UK **Eastercon's** highlights was the Bob Shaw speech which themselves have been collected into fan volumes (*The Eastercon Speeches* (1977) and *A Load of Old BoSH* (1995)). Shaw never won a Hugo for his professional SF (though he won numerous other awards) but did pick up two Hugos for Best Fan Writer in 1979 and 1980. His book *The Ragged Astronauts* (1986), about a balloon journey between a twin planetary system with a common atmosphere, was nominated for a Hugo.

Sheckley, Robert – author, US (*b*1926). Sheckley is a writer from the **Golden Age** of SF, but one arguably ahead of his time. It is not that he particularly explored those SF tropes more commonly used today (such as that of cyberspace), his stamping ground was very much that of futures and alien worlds, but that his tales frequently had an element of humour or were written with his tongue firmly in his cheek. Back in the 1960s this was rarely done with success. As such, much of his work, with only minor alteration, could as easily pass for material written today. Sheckley prefers the short story to the novel, though he has written over a dozen of those. *Mindswap* (1966) concerns one Marvin Flynn who books a mindswap holiday on Mars – exchanging bodies with a Martian. However the Martian does not return Flynn's body so precipitating a hectic chase in a series of temporary bodies on different worlds. Mind control also appears in *The Status Civilization* (1960) which sees a mind-wiped convict arrive on a penal world where the entire society is based on rewarding crime (providing you can get away with it). *Immortality Inc* (1958), his first novel originally published as *Immortality Delivered*, was not only nominated for a Hugo but turned into the film ***Freejack*** (1992). While his short story *The Seventh Victim* was turned into the film *La Decima*

Vittima (1965) (or *The Tenth Victim*). Set in a future world murder has been legalised for public entertainment (*dir*. Elio Petri's Principal cast: Marcello Mastroianni and Ursula Andress). He has also successfully used material prepared by others. He co-wrote with **Harry Harrison** *Bill The Galactic Hero On The Planet of Bottled Brains* (1990), and even a ***Babylon 5*** novelization, *A Call to Arms* (1998).

Shockwave Rider, The – novel (1975) by **John Brunner**. Though only a runner up in the annual *Locus* readers poll, *The Shockwave Rider* is very much an SF readers' book in that, of all types of people, SF readers are most likely to be immune to the Alvin Toffler-type 'future shock' it describes. Set in a future where information technology has spawned a society easily manipulated, Nickie Haflinger escapes from a high-powered Government think tank and evades the authorities using a succession of identities that he can electronically validate. Before long he joins up with a threatened community that lives a simpler life and together they fight for the right to live their own lives the way they want. *The Shockwave Rider* is noted for being one of the first SF novels to use concepts which are, in all but name, the World Wide Web and the computer virus.

Silent Running – film, US (1971), *dir*. Douglas (***Blade Runner***) Trumbull. In the future eco-catastrophe has destroyed wildlife. In space a series of arks preserves what is left. However the operation is costly and so is cancelled. One crewman rebels and hijacks the last surviving ark taking it off on an orbit through Saturn's rings. With only three robots to help him, it is a fight for survival. Though a straight-forward plot, *Silent Running* has a quiet charm and bags of poignancy. The robots (actually controlled by amputees who could just squeeze inside the compact casings) almost steal the show. Trumbull also worked on the special effects of ***2001: A Space Odyssey*** and ***Close Encounters of the Third Kind***. *Silent Running* came 8th in the *Concatenation* all-time poll. Principal cast: Bruce Dern.

Silverberg, Robert – author, US (*b*1935). One of science fiction's most prolific authors, Silverberg won a Hugo for Most Promising New Author in 1956, which promise has been fulfilled many times over. Though there are gaps in his publishing career, his most sustained period of excellence is probably that between

1967 and 1976 and yielded some 25 novels, of which at least a dozen are widely regarded as being among the best SF ever written. These include: *Thorns* (1967), a novel of alienation, one of Silverberg's recurrent themes; *The Anvil of Time* (1969), about political prisoners in a pre-historic prison/death camp; *Up the Line* (1969), a satirical time travel story; *Tower of Glass* (1970), in which android builders seek an end to slavery through the intercession of their not-so-divine maker; *The World Inside* (1971), about overpopulation; *The Book of Skulls* (1971), about immortality; and the excellent *Dying Inside* (1972), in which a telepath comes to terms with his fading power, is complemented by *The Stochastic Man* (1975), in which a man develops the ability to see into the future. After a four year gap in production, Silverberg's publishing resumed, though much of his output is best described as high fantasy, rather than SF. Notwithstanding this, his first Majipoor book, *Lord Valentine's Castle* (1980), topped the annual *Locus* readers poll in 1981 in the 'fantasy novel' category. Awards, oddly, seem to have consistently passed Silverberg by, at least for his novels; however, he has won the 1969 Hugo for Best Novella with *Nightwings* (1968; not to be confused with the 1969 novel of the same name), and the same award in 1987 for *Gilgamesh in the Outback* (1986), a sequel to his 1984 novel *Gilgamesh the King*; in addition, he has also won a Hugo for Best Novelette in 1990 for *Enter a Soldier. Later, Enter Another* (1989). Recently there has been an attempt to reprint much of Silverberg's short fiction, starting with *The Collected Stories of Robert Silverberg, vol. 1* (1991), and this topped the *Locus* poll in 1992 for best collection. He has also worked extensively as an editor, topping the *Locus* poll in 1971 for the anthology *The Science Fiction Hall of Fame* (1970), compiling the *New Dimensions* series (1971-79), and taking over the *Universe* (1990-92) series of anthologies from Terry Carr.

Simak, Clifford D – author, US (1904-1988). Simak is the Hugo Best Novel Award-winning author of **Way Station** (1964), ***The Big Front Yard*** (Best Novelette 1958), and *Grotto of the Dancing Deer* (1981). Though not winning a Hugo he was nominated for one in 1982 for *Project Pope* (1981) about an AI created to be the ultimate pontiff. The typical Simak novel has its principal protagonist set in the US countryside either together with, or to encounter, exotic circumstances. In *All Flesh is Grass* (1965), which was nominated for a Nebula, an invisible barrier encloses a small out-of-the-way American township. While in *Ring Around the Sun* (1952) it is the effects on a small town of a combination of new inventions (like the everlasting light bulb) and the locals beginning to disappear that form the puzzle. Not for Simak tales of huge space craft and the adventures of astronauts, his characters tended to travel to the stars by teleportation (***Way Station***), or inter-spatial doorways (***The Big Front Yard***), and even psychic projection, be they human sensitives as in the Hugo-nominated *Project Pope* (1981), or telepaths in the Hugo-nominated *Time is the Simplest Thing* (1961). While in *The Werewolf Principle* (1968) initially the plot is turned on its head when the protagonist thinks that two aliens lurk within him. Simak's work has also touched upon light humour with the Hugo-nominated *The Goblin Reservation* (1968) in which a kidnapped Professor is taken to an ancient world which stores information on Earth. There he meets goblins, dinosaurs and even William Shakespeare. Though ***Way Station*** remains his masterpiece, Simak is noted by critics for *City* (1952) in which mankind leaves for a planet that becomes an expanded Wisconsin; the Wisconsin of many of his rural settings. As our world and its literature becomes increasingly urbanised, Clifford D Simak provides refreshing perspectives out in fields of corn and away from the streets. In 1976, Simak was awarded a Grand Master Nebula, reflecting the immense respect he had built up over the decades.

Simmons, Dan – author, US (*b*1948). Simmons is one of very few recent authors who seem to be both happy and extremely competent in writing across genre boundaries and, since his debut in 1982, one of the most honoured. He was a full-time public school teacher, and director of programmes for gifted children, until 1987; by which time he had already won the World Fantasy Award for his 1985 debut novel, *Song of Kali*. Indeed, his first published story, *The River Styx Runs Upstream* (1982), published in *Twilight Zone Magazine* (and later collected in *Prayers to Broken Stones* (1991)) won the Rod Serling Memorial Award. However, from an SF perspective, it was in 1989 that Dan Simmons made his greatest impact. He published three novels that year; *Carrion Comfort*, which topped the *Locus* readers poll in 1990 in the 'horror novel' category, about three mutant humans who can control normal people and feed from their psychic experiences; *Phases of Gravity*, a largely mainstream novel about the epiphanies of a retired astronaut; and ***Hyperion***, winner of the 1990 Hugo for Best Novel which also topped the *Locus* readers poll the same year. Both *Hyperion* and its sequel, ***The Fall of Hyperion*** (1990), were published later in 1990 as one novel, *Hyperion Cantos*, though the sequel on its own topped the *Locus* poll in 1991. Two more novels set in this universe were published, *Endymion* (1996) and ***The Rise of Endymion*** (1997), and the latter was sufficiently popular to win the *Locus* Award. *Summer of Night* (1991) came top of the *Locus* poll in 1992 in the 'horror/dark fantasy' category, and was followed by the not-quite-sequel *Children of the Night* (1992), both referring to the lineage of a certain Transylvanian 'Family'. Also in 1992, Simmons gave us *The Hollow Man*, about a mathematician who is also an unwitting telepath coming to terms with the death of his wife. The dark fantasy, *Fires of Eden* (1994), also topped the *Locus* poll in 1995 for best fantasy as did ***Ilium*** in 2004 for best SF novel.

Skiffy – a term SF fans occasionally use as an abbreviation of 'popular' SF. It originated out of disdain for the mis-use of '**sci-fi**'.

Slaughterhouse 5 – film, US (1972), *dir.* George Roy Hill based on **Vonnegut's** 1969 novel of the same name. A reasonable, albeit far from perfect, adaptation of the book, *Slaughter House 5* (1969) concerns the life of one Billy Pilgrim. Like all of us Pilgrim has one life, but uniquely his is not experienced linearly from birth to death. Instead he jumps about: one moment he is at home with his family in a modern (1970s) American town, the next he is in Dresden during the allied fire bombing, the next in a glass dome on planet Tralfamadore living with a Hollywood starlet while the Tralfamadorians look on, and the next he is in the future, expounding on the nature of time and the consequences of our actions to a lecture hall of humans. The film won the Best Dramatic Presentation Hugo in 1973. Principal cast: Michael Sacks and Valerie (***Superman***) Perrine

Sleeper, The – film, US (1973) *dir.* Woody Allen. A satirical comedy. Miles Munroe (Woody Allen), a health food nut, wakes up a couple of centuries after being given an anaesthetic for a minor ulcer operation. He finds himself in what he at first takes to be a utopia, but soon discovers he is in a totalitarian state. Aside from the protagonist awaking in the future after prolonged sleep, there is little resemblance to the plot of **H G Wells'** *When*

The Sleeper Wakes – a.k.a *The Sleeper Awakes* – (1899). However the plot is a superb vehicle for Allen's self-deprecating, and life-observing humour. *The Sleeper* won the Best Dramatic Presentation Hugo in 1974. Principal cast: Woody Allen, Diane Keaton, John Beck, Mary Gregory, Bartlett Robinson, John McLiam, Mary Small, Peter Hobbs, Susan Miller, Brian Avery and Spencer Milligan.

Smith, E.E. "Doc" – author, US (1890-1965). A food chemist by training, Smith was hugely influential in the early pulp magazines and published the first of his *Skylark* stories in ***Amazing Stories*** in 1928 (in the same issue of which was the very first appearance of **Buck Rogers**, *Armageddon—2419AD* by Philip Nowlan). The *Skylark* stories were collected into book form starting with *The Skylark of Space* (1946) and starred the scientist-adventurer-hero Richard Seaton who, in this and subsequent volumes, battled against the evil 'Blackie' DuQuesne. In each meeting the bad guy contrived an ingeniously villainous plot, using devices of unimaginable scale and power, only to be thwarted by the even more inventive hero. But it was with Smith's next series, ***Lensmen***, that he is most associated and with which, to a great extent, he is credited with the invention of **space opera**. These stories, beginning with *Triplanetary* (first published in magazine form in 1934), tell the tale of the conflict between the aeons-old races of the dastardly Eddorians, and the good and noble Arisians, and of a weapon, the Lens, which increases the physical and mental powers of its wearers, which include humans who, with their alien allies, make up the Galactic Patrol. Not counting posthumous book releases, Smith's last work of note was *The Galaxy Primes* (1965), published in the year of his death, in which four outstanding members of humanity, two men and two women, each a psionic 'Prime', travel in Earth's first starship, the *Pleiades*, to confront evil in the universe. Though all Smith's work is a simplistic rendering of the battle between good and evil, as a whole it demonstrated a triumph of imagination and introduced the vast scales of space and time with which we have become familiar in the present. While some might find the overtly militaristic politics and archaic sexual attitudes a little off-putting (if not downright offensive), it is as well to remember that these are works of their time, being the 1920s to 1940s, and that with a little forgiveness one can find Smith's output hugely enjoyable, and a great evocation of the SF Sense of Wonder.

Snow Queen, The – novel (1980) by **Joan D Vinge.** The Hegemony is all that remains of a once powerful interstellar empire. The planet Tiamat, orbiting twin suns, is on the very edge of the Hegemony and is only accessible *via* a nearby rotating black-hole – the black-hole represents the entrance to a wormhole through which ships can travel. However when the black-hole's orbit takes it close to the twin suns they flare up. On these occasions Tiamat not only becomes cut off from the Hegemony (and its technology), but its climatic belts shift and the technophobic 'summers' move north to the lands of the 'winters'. Cut off from technology imports, and with a migrant population, the 'winters' civilization declines. Matters return to normal when the black hole moves away from the suns. The Hegemony, while providing technology goods, does not allow the 'winters' to have the scientific knowledge that would allow them to develop their own industries. The Hegemony, it transpires, needs to maintain an economic advantage so as to secure an antiathagenic (anti-ageing) virus found only in a species on Tiamat. (The virus does not live long away from its natural host despite the best efforts of the Hegemony's scientists, and so Tiamat's importance continues.) On one cycle the 'Snow Queen' attempts to break the boom-bust cycle. Now this description may lead you to think that *The Snow Queen* is **hard SF**. Not a bit of it, the hard SF is explained in just a few pages scattered throughout the book, the rest of the story is revealed through the eyes of the non-scientific locals. Consequently, the book reads much like a fantasy novel and is concerned with the complex politics and people of Tiamat. This is not surprising as Joan Vinge not only acknowledges that the book is inspired by Hans Cristian Andersen's fairy tale *The Snow Queen* but because she herself is an anthropologist: so what science there is is mainly restricted to that specialism and this serves to underpin, as opposed to lead, the story. *The Snow Queen* is the first volume of a trilogy. A way of travelling faster-than-light is uncovered in *World's End* (1984). This enables the Hegemony to return to Tiamat in *The Summer Queen* (1992). *The Snow Queen* won the Hugo in 1981 for Best Novel and came top of the annual *Locus* readers top ten poll.

Solaris – film, Russia (1972), *dir*. Andrei (*Stalker*) Tarkovsky. Based on the 1961 **Stanislaw Lem** story, *Solaris* was billed as Russia's answer to *2001: A Space Odyssey* (even though it was an answer that took four years in the coming and lacking that film's spectacle). A research station is placed in orbit about the unknown planet 'Solaris' and its huge ocean. The ocean is thought to be intelligent but no one has found a way to communicate with it. Psychologist Kris (Donatas Banionis) Kelvin is sent to help, but soon discovers that all is not well and that the station is haunted by 'projections' of people. Shortly, Kris having encountered his former wife (who in reality had committed suicide) it becomes apparent that these projections come from the scientists' own minds. After a while it becomes obvious that the planet's 'ocean' is using such projections to determine frames of reference as a basis for communication. Kris Kelvin then spies an island – that we presume is artificial. On it there is his former home and it is clear, as the film comes to an end, that this is the venue for future dialogue. The film is very much for those into **new wave** SF. However it has to be said it is very drawn out running as it does to 165 minutes (though the first US release was 132 minutes) and that opinion is greatly divided as to its merits. Nonetheless, it was voted 15th favourite film in the *Concatenation* poll. A Hollywood version was released in 2003.

Somewhere in Time – film, US (1980), *dir*. Jeannot Szwarc. A sentimental love story, based on **Richard Matheson's** *Bid Time Return* (1975), about a couple separated by time, until our hero literally wills himself back through the decades... and that really is all there is to the plot. *Somewhere in Time* is on the list of all-time best attended movies screened at the Festival of Fantastic Films, which is odd for a convention whose regulars usually like their science fiction mixed with horror. *Somewhere in Time* is decidedly gushy and sentimental, but it does give an unusual spin on time travel, and the photography and acting are superb. Principal cast: Christopher (***Superman***) Reeve and Jane Seymour.

Son of Frankenstein – film, US (1939), *dir*. Roland V Lee. In this the all-star cast second follow-up to Whale's 1930 ***Frankenstein***, the old baron's son returns to take over where dad left off. Need more be said? The photography is atmospheric and the sets are splendid even if not very pragmatic. It was considered a 'slick' production for its time, and in retrospect is especially worth watching alongside ***Young Frankenstein***. A favourite among Festival of Fantastic Film attendees, *Son of Frankenstein* is generally agreed to contain Lugosi's finest performance.

Principal cast: Basil Rathbone, Boris Karloff, Bela Lugosi, Lionel Atwill, Josephine Hutchinson, Donnie Dunagan, Emma Dunn, Edgar Norton, and Lawrence Grant.

Soylent Green – film, US (1973), *dir.* Richard (***20,000 Leagues Under The Sea***, ***Fantastic Voyage***) Fleischer, and based on **Harry Harrison's** ***Make Room! Make Room!*** (1966). Set in 2022 (not 1999 as in (*Make Room! Make Room!*) some 40 million (not 35 as in the book) people are crammed into the city of New York. In a world barely, despite extreme measures, able to support its huge population a rich executive of the Soylent (food) Corporation is murdered. Detective Frank Thorne (Charlton Heston) finds himself unable to walk away from the case and discovers that the killing was instigated by the powerful Soylent Corporation itself. Sol (Edward G Robinson), Thorne's elderly researcher (or 'book') side kick, uncovers the motive, but its up to Thorne to reveal the truth to the world... *Soylent Green* was voted into the top 30 *Concatenation* all-time film poll. However while both the film *Soylent Green* and the book *Make Room! Make Room!* are excellent in their own ways, their respective stories are markedly different. In *Soylent Green* the murder victim is a senior director of the Soylent Company who, shocked at what the world has come to and his company's role, has to be silenced by the other members of the Soylent board. Finding this out is integral to the film's climax. (In the book the murder was not pre-motivated as the reader learns early on.) Principal cast: Charlton (***Planet of the Apes***) Heston, Edward G Robinson (his last film), Leigh Taylor-Young, Chuck Connors, Joseph Cotton, and Brock Peters

Space opera – SF set in space with many, typically battling, space craft and usually involving one or more interstellar empires.

Speaker for the Dead – novel (1986) by **Orson Scott Card**. The second in the (original) Ender trilogy after ***Ender's Game*** (Card subsequently wrote a novel concerning a spin-off character from the original trilogy.) Due to light speed time dilation, a thousand years have passed since Ender wiped out Earth's former alien enemy, the Buggers. Hero turned scorned war criminal, now presumed dead, Ender and his sister Valentine roam the stars. Meanwhile another intelligent race has been found on a far flung world. Mankind, having wiped out the first intelligent species it encountered, is concerned that relations with this new species will fare well. Unfortunately on the new species' planet two exobiologists die, murdered by the seemingly peaceful aliens. Ender, now a quasi-religious 'speaker for the dead', goes to the planet to give testimony on behalf of the murder victims. Arriving Ender finds an exotic ecology, and an intelligent species with a very alien life cycle. Meanwhile powers on Earth vie for interstellar political control, a struggle countered by Ender's sister Valentine using the faster-than-light communications web to lobby her cause. *Speaker for the Dead* won the Hugo Award for Best Novel in 1987 and came top of the *Locus* annual readers poll. The final title in the trilogy, ***Xenocide***, sees the might of Earth turn against the new intelligent species' home world out of fear of its biology. Mankind seems poised once again to wipe out an entire civilisation.

Spinrad, Norman – author, US (*b*1940). Spinrad began his SF career with *The Last of the Romany* (1963) in *Astounding Science Fiction* (see ***Analog***). An influential voice in both the American and British **new wave** SF of the sixties, he was a contributor to *New Worlds* magazine, notably with the serialisation of ***Bug Jack Barron*** (1969). In *The Iron Dream* (1972) Adolf Hitler, unable to become a politician in Germany, moves to the US and becomes an SF writer. His novel "Lord of the Swastika" forms the major part of *The Iron Dream*, which won the French Prix Apollo in 1974. Spinrad's *The Void Captain's Tale* (1983), in which Eros drives a spaceship, is popular among fans but, from the mid-eighties on, his work has tended more toward the mainstream, though is still informed by SF. In *Little Heroes* (1987), America's social and economic divisions are taken to their logical extreme, while *Russian Spring* (1991) features a post-*perestroika* USSR. *Pictures at 11* (1994) confronts the very real possibility of nuclear terrorism when TV station personnel are held hostage by a group who have built a 'dirty' nuclear weapon.

Stainless Steel Rat, The – novel (1961) by **Harry Harrison**. This comedy-thriller began as a short story in 1957 for *Astounding Science Fiction* (see ***Analog***) and introduced one of Harrison's most enduring creations, the arch-criminal turned law-enforcer, 'Slippery' Jim di Griz. Coerced by the authorities, Jim is set to catch a mass-murderess, Angelina, who has her own battleship. After several comic adventures, he succeeds, and eventually

Angelina becomes his wife and fellow agent. Over the following series of books, they have many adventures, and two sons, James and Bolivar, who in their turn help mum and dad to fight evil; Harrison then provides retrospective tales of the Rat's early days. The first 'Stainless Steel' book came joint 9th in the *Concatenation* all-time Best SF poll, and has been adapted into comics form by Carlos Ezquerra for *2000 AD*. There are at least nine Stainless Steel Rat novels, the most recent being *The Stainless Steel Rat Goes to Hell* (1997), but one should be wary of the collection entitled *Stainless Steel Visions* (1992) which contains only one Jim di Griz tale, *The Golden Years of the Stainless Steel Rat*. A CD of songs was released with *The Stainless Steel Rat Sings the Blues* (1994) but, as a marketing gimmick, was largely unsuccessful.

Stalker – film, Russia (1979), *dir.* Andrei (***Solaris***) Tarkovsky. *Stalker* is loosely based upon the brothers **Boris and Arkadi Strugatski's** excellent novel *The Roadside Picnic*. In *The Roadside Picnic*, alien ships temporarily land in various countries and depart. They leave behind zones of danger into which explorers are sent who risk their lives for the possibility of great rewards. In *Stalker* the zone that appears (in some nameless place) is some sort of essence of human imagination with a Wishing Room at its centre. The film takes us with the stalker (Alexander Kaidanovsky) and a scientist and a writer through the dangerous zone to find the wishing room. However, to enter the room all three have to blindly place their trust in the zone. Tarkovsky successfully portrays the alienness of the zone and has some scenes effectively convey tension: these are among the best of its kind to emerge from film (to rival Hitchcock!). However Tarkovsky's message is truly contentious: let go of reason and your instincts will tell you what is right. *Stalker* not only came in the top 30 of the *Concatenation* all time poll, but a follow-up mini-survey of fans in eastern Europe saw it cited in nearly every ballot! Principal cast: Alexander Kaidanovsky, Nikolai Grinko, and Anatoly Solonitsyn.

Stand on Zanzibar – novel (1968) by **John Brunner**. Though published a couple of years after **Harry Harrison's** ***Make Room! Make Room!*** (1966), *Stand on Zanzibar* is acknowledged as being one of the early serious attempts, using the demographic projections of the day, to base a story in the more crowded 21st century. At the beginning of the 20th century it was possible to stand the nearly 2 billion people of the world on the Isle of Wight (by the year 2000 the world population had in fact topped 6 billion!). By 2010, in Brunner's future, the world population was well over 10 billion (an accurate projection in the late 1960s though today it is thought that that level of population would be reached closer to the middle of the 21st century). However, with a world population of 10 billion you would need something the size of Zanzibar on which to stand it. In Brunner's future the gap between the rich and the poor nations had not been eliminated (as it had in so many futuristic novels of the 1960s), recreational drug usage was commonplace, genetically modified pets were available, and artificial intelligence was about to be created. It was a time of eugenic laws, genetic screening, economic domination by multinationals, and international tension. Brunner himself refers to *Stand on Zanzibar* as a 'non-novel'. Unlike a novel which commonly has a single story frequently told from a single perspective, *Stand on Zanzibar* portrays a future world through the different, but intertwining stories of half a dozen lead characters, in addition to short snippets: newscasts, television programmes, and extracts of the future writer *cum* philosopher Chad C Mulligan. Though an uncommon format, it is one that is very effective in presenting the complexity of the world of the early twenty-first century. There is now no doubt that in the real world, before the middle of the century, we will have to address many of the questions the book raises. *Stand on Zanzibar* is often cited as one of Brunner's four classics. It won the Hugo Award for Best Novel in 1969 and appeared in the top twenty of the *Concatenation* all time poll. A sequel, *The Sheep Look Up* was published in 1972.

Star, The – short story (1955) by **Arthur C. Clarke**. A Jesuit priest is returning to Earth from an investigation of the Phoenix planetary nebula, the remains of a gigantic supernova. At the outer fringes of the system, the investigating team discovered the last artefacts of the civilisation that had once lived here, locked in a vault. But, having accurately dated the supernova, it is the calculation of when the supernova's light shone on Earth that causes the Jesuit's crisis of faith... Science fiction writers, somewhat like doctors, are among the most secular of people and, in the early days of SF, religion was hardly acknowledged at all, though by the sixties this was to change. This story, which won the Best Short Story Hugo in 1956, asks a powerful question in what is little more than a vignette, but which still has resonance today. *The Star* formed the basis for a (1980–90s)s ***Twilight Zone*** episode. It can be found in various collections, including *The Best of Arthur C. Clarke: 1937–1971* (1973).

Star Reach – comic, US (*crtd* April 1974). Due to the restrictions of the Comics Code Authority (a self-regulatory body set up by the industry in the wake of Frederick Wertham's *Seduction of the Innocent*, which attacked comics for their supposed influence on children), and the fact that the two major comics publishers, Marvel and DC, rigidly adhered to this code, Star Reach Publishing was set up to produce non-code approved comics. This was one of the first attempts by writers and artists to retain their creative rights (the industry standard was then "work for hire", where art and script were owned by the company, along with any rights associated with further use of the character). Star Reach published 18 issues of *Star Reach* between April 1974 and October 1979; it was an 'anthology' title which attracted the work of Jim Starlin, Neal Adams, Frank Brunner, and other industry favourites, not to mention **Ray Bradbury** and **Roger Zelazny**. Among the best remembered tales are Howard Chaykin's *Cody Starbuck* (which character had a one-shot spin-off title of his own), and *Gideon Faust* (written by Len Wein); P. Craig Russell's *Parsifal*; ***The Sacred and the Profane*** by Dean Motter and Ken Steacy; Gray Lyda's *Tempus Fugit*; and Lee Marrs' *Stark's Quest*. Star Reach also published a sister title, *Imagine*, which had six issues between April 1978 and July 1979. The originals command quite high prices today, however Eclipse published *Star Reach Classics* (six issues) between March and August 1984, and a collected version of *The Sacred and the Profane* in 1987, which are available at reasonable prices. For those who believed that comics only 'grew up' in the mid-eighties, *Star Reach* will provide a startling insight into what was going on a decade before.

Starship Troopers – novel (1959) by **Robert A Heinlein.** In the future a person has to earn the right for citizenship and so have the right to vote *etc*. One way to be granted the privileges of Citizenship is through having earned the right by fighting to protect society. It is also a future in which mankind no longer fights war among his own species but against aliens. This is the story of Johnny Rico who enrols in the toughest and most efficient fighting force the world has ever seen. One enemy species in particular, a species of insect like hive/colony creatures, is in effect the ultimate communist race; an allusion the author himself refers to. Indeed, *Starship Troopers* does have a number of nationalistic traits typically associated with the political Right. This does not mean that Heinlein set out to write an *overtly* political book—rather it is an attempt to portray, in true SF style, a better society than ours, albeit one under adversity. Having said that Heinlein did have an interest in politics and did serve in the US navy. In 1998 Paul (***Robo Cop*** and ***Total Recall***) Verhoven directed the film of the same name. Unfortunately it did not feature Heinlein's *Starship Troopers'* powered amour suits which turned troops into the supermen needed to combat the equally super aliens. *Starship Troopers* won the Hugo Award for Best Novel in 1960 despite all the fuss.

Stars My Destination, The – novel, US (1955) by **Alfred Bester**. See ***Tiger! Tiger!***

Startide Rising – novel (1983) by **David Brin**. In a time when humans have raised (uplifted) other species to sentience, a starship crewed by dolphins and humans stumbles on a collection of derelict spacecraft millions of years old. These craft can only belong to the fabled Progenitors – the first intelligent race in the galaxy. Before they can report their discovery to Earth the crew of the starship find themselves embroiled in galactic intrigue. The dolphin's starship hides on an abandoned world, while in space above them, the hostile species of the galaxy begin a war over who should have the right to the humans' and dolphins' information. This is the second of Brin's 'Uplift' novels. The conflict continues in Brin's ***The Uplift War*** (1987), and the adventures of the starship's crew continue in some of the later Uplift stories. *Startide Rising* won the Hugo for Best Novel and came top of the annual *Locus* poll in 1984.

Starstream – comic, US (*crtd* 1976). This forgotten comic of the seventies had only four unnumbered issues, but credibly adapted the work of **Theodore Sturgeon, A.E. van Vogt, Larry Niven, Robert Silverberg,** Barrington J. Bayley, **John W. Campbell jnr, Poul Anderson** and **Isaac Asimov** among others. Incredibly all four issues are available at reasonable prices at most comic marts and conventions. Artist Jack Abel does particularly nice work on Campbell's *Who Goes There?* and Asimov's *Does a Bee Care?*, but after these four issues the Western Publishing Company seemed to disappear.

Star Trek – TV series, US (*fb*1966). Conceived by **Gene Roddenberry**, who was also the show's producer, *Star Trek* was sold to NBC as 'a wagon train to the stars'. It portrayed the adventures of one starship *Enterprise* of an Earth led 'Federation' of planets on a five year mission "to boldly go where no man has been before". The ship had a crew of 430, some of whom were alien: notably the ever so logical (emotionless) Vulcan called Spock, who had basic telepathic powers and a classy line in nerve pinches. For its time the show broke new ground. Its crew was multi-ethnic and some women held officers' posts. Reputedly the show screened the first inter-ethnic kiss. Of SF appeal was the show's technology. There were set devices: phaser (ray gun), photon torpedoes, teleporter, tricorder (detector) and so forth, each of which had predetermined functions and recognised limits. While of popular appeal were the characters, all be they somewhat two-dimensional. Nonetheless, each had a distinct relationship with each of the others and this added solidity to the picture of the future. A Russian ensign, Pavel Chekov, proved the Cold War would not exist in the future; Japanese helmsman Lt. Sulu showed that WWII was forgiven; chief engineer Montgomery Scott demonstrated that Europeans could play too and that Scotland still built ships; and communications officer Lt. Uhura had the dual distinction of being both female and black, so charting the death of sexism and racism in a role praised by Martin Luther King. *Star Trek* writers included **Richard Matheson**, Jerome Bixby, **Norman Spinrad**, Robert Bloch, **Theodore Sturgeon**, and **Harlan Ellison** among others. Of the series' three seasons, episodes of note include 'The Menagerie' which won the 1967 Hugo for Best Dramatic presentation. Written by Gene Roddenberry, 'The Menagerie' was a two-parter cobbled together from the series pilot. Spock mutinies and kidnaps his former commanding officer Commander Pike who is ill having been badly injured. He then sets the Enterprise on a course for Talos IV, a forbidden planet. The ship locked on course, Spock is tried *en route* to Talos IV. It turns out that once Commander Pike was held captive there in a zoo, held prisoner in a make-believe world by alien telepathic illusions. The aliens could give Pike the illusion of being a whole man again and so a better quality of life. 'The City on the Edge of Forever' also won a Best Dramatic Presentation Hugo in 1968. The Enterprise finds a planet on which an artificial intelligence looks after an ancient time portal. The ship's Dr McCoy, deranged having accidentally been injected with some pharmaceutical, stumbles through the portal to 1920s New York. There he changes the past so that the Federation never came into being. With the Enterprise gone, and Kirk and Spock protected by the portal's temporal field, the two have to follow McCoy back and put right what went wrong. This episode was written by **Harlan Ellison**. *Star Trek* was axed due to its low (Neilson) viewer ratings. However the studios and networks were not prepared for the dogged devotion of the viewers it did attract, let alone the international appeal or that its audience grew with repeat showings, which years later amounted to a substantial following. A decade after the TV series, the launch of the spin-off film *Star Trek: The Motion Picture* was to break the then record for first-day box office takings. More recently there have been spin-off TV series. ***Star Trek: The Next Generation*** admirably brought *Star Trek* into the 1990s with a new Enterprise and new crew (numbering 1,125), while *Star Trek: Deep Space Nine* (1993-1999) set on a space station was a sanitised reflection of ***Babylon 5***. *Star Trek Voyager* (1995-2002) attempted to rekindle the original flavour of *Trek* with the latest Federation starship (crew 148) that has to make its way home on a voyage lasting many decades having been flung by an alien force across the Galaxy. The series *Enterprise* (*fb*2001) told the story of the very first Enterprise starship as Earth was beginning to form interstellar relations and exploration. Finally a word about *Star Trek* and SF fan terminology. Many SF fans enjoy *Star Trek*. Anyone who regularly watches the series is known as a 'Trekker', while anyone who goes to *Star Trek* conventions, hence who has the dedication for a weekend diet solely of S*tar Trek*, is known as a 'Trekkie'. Quality novelizations of *Star Trek* episodes were provided by **James Blish**. *Star Trek* first appeared in the UK in comic form a year before its TV broadcast in *TV21* (see **Gerry Anderson**). Principal cast: William Shatner (Capt Kirk), Leonard (***Brave New World***, ***Invasion of the Body Snatchers***) Nimoy (Mr Spock), DeForest Kelly (Dr Leonard McCoy), James Doohan (Lt Cmndr Montgomery Scott), Nichelle Nichols (Lt Cmndr Uhura), Walter (***Babylon 5***) Koenig (Ensign Pavel Chekov) and George Takei

(Chief Helmsman Sulu). (See also **Joe Haldeman** (who also wrote the Star Trek novel *Planet of Judgement* (1977), **Greg Bear** and *The Twilight Zone*.)

Star Trek: The Next Generation – TV series, US (*fb*1987). The follow-up series set 80 years on to *Star Trek*. *Next Gen* saw a new, larger more powerful, Enterprise and a new crew. Continuity with the original series and spin-off films, better effects, the inclusion of story line elements that ran through the series and more rounded characters meant that the series was in many ways an improvement on the original 'Classic' (as it is known) *Star Trek*. Captain Jean-Luc Picard continues the mission of exploration. First officer William Riker is the Kirk-like character while an android, Data, substitutes for Spock, and the chief medical officer is now a woman, Dr. Beverly Crusher. There is: a blind, black engineer, Geordi La Forge, proving that disability is no barrier to a career; an empathic ship's counsellor, Deanna Troi; a Klingon security officer, Lt. Worf following the death of the original officer, Tasha Yar, and the bridge crew is completed by Dr. Crusher's young son, Wesley. Transporter chief O'Brien eventually left to go to *Deep Space Nine*, where he was later joined by Worf. There was, briefly, another doctor played by Diana Muldaur, veteran of the original series' episode 'Is there in truth no beauty?' Regular guest characters included: a bartending alien, Guinan; a god-like pan dimensional being, 'Q'; Troi's mother, Lwaxana, was played by Majel Barratt, wife of **Gene Roddenberry** and the original series' nurse Christine Chapel. The episode 'The Inner Light' won the Hugo Award for Best. Dramatic Presentation in 1993. In it, the Enterprise stumbles across an ancient unmanned craft deep in space. A beam from the craft hits Captain Picard who falls unconscious. Picard finds himself reliving a life on an alien world, growing old and dying. The world itself is slowly drying up and it transpires that the probe was an attempt to preserve the planet's culture. The final two-parter, 1994 episode 'All Good Things' won the 1995 Hugo for Best Dramatic Presentation. Though *Next Gen* ended its TV run in 1994, since then there have been spin-off feature films of which *Star Trek: First Contact* (1996), *dir*. Jonathan Frakes, has been cited in the *Concatenation* follow-up mini poll to all-time film favourites. Spin-offs have included comics and books, as well as a 'Technical Manual' by **Rick Sternbach**. Principal cast: Patrick (***Dune***) Stewart (Capt. Jean-Luc Picard), Jonathan

Frakes (Cmndr. William Riker), Levar Burton (Lt. Cmndr. Geordi La Forge), Michael Dorn (Lt. Worf), Gates McFadden (Dr Beverly Crusher), Marina Sirtis (Counsellor Deanna Troi), Brent Spiner (Lt. Cmndr. Data), Wil Wheaton (Wesley Crusher), Whoopi Goldberg (Guinan), Colm Meany (Transporter Chief O'Brien) and Denise Crosby (Tasha Yar).

Star Trek II: The Wrath of Khan – film, US (1982), *dir*. Nicholas (***Star Trek VI – The Undiscovered Country***, ***Time After Time***) Meyer. This second *Star Trek* film was a sequel to a 1966/7 season episode called 'Space Seed'. Khan (Ricardo Montalban reprised his role from the TV series) and his comrades, previously left marooned by Kirk, manage to escape when a Starfleet survey team visits their world. Bent on revenge against Kirk, Khan sets out to destroy the Enterprise using a captured Star Fleet craft. This solid **space opera**, like much of *Star Trek*, is best enjoyed with one's brain in neutral (the science has holes in it through which one can drive a starship). The great effects make for a spectacular space battle, and the regulars deliver the ham just the way Trekkers like it. It was voted 14th in the *Concat* poll.

Star Trek IV – The Voyage Home – film, US (1986), *dir.* Leonard Nimoy. With its environmental theme and a sub-text of hope (science can solve the big problems), *The Voyage Home* went down well with both the fans and a wider audience. An alien craft broadcasts whale song at Earth and Kirk *et al* go back to the mid-1980s to bring back two whales from the past. Frolics and japes lubricate the plot, but the crew are definitely ageing. Though not winning, it was nominated for a Hugo. (See also **Ian Watson**.)

Star Trek VI – The Undiscovered Country – film, US (1991), *dir.* Nicholas (***Star Trek II: The Wrath of Khan***, ***Time After Time***) Meyer. The Klingon Empire and The Federation are on the verge of peace when Kirk and McCoy are accused of assassination. Tried by the Klingons, Kirk and McCoy can count on their friends to help them out. This is the last time the original crew showed off their best features. The story helped bridge the original *Star Trek* with that of *Star Trek: The Next Generation* with the Klingons coming to an uneasy peace with the Federation. This made *The Undiscovered Country* a favourite with Trekkers (and the box office takings were good too). Though not winning, it was nominated for a Hugo.

Star Wars – film US/UK (1977), *dir*. George Lucas. A little confusingly, this first *Star Wars* movie was billed as part IV, and was supposedly meant to be part of a series of three trilogies – this movie being part one of the second trilogy, with sequel films ***The Empire Strikes Back*** and ***Return of the Jedi*** to follow. Set "a long time ago, in a galaxy far, far away," the Rebels are fighting a desperate battle against the mighty Empire. Even now the Empire plans to crush the resistance with a moon-sized battle station, the Death Star. The only hope for the rebels lies in the plans of the Death Star stored in a small robot called R2D2 (Kenny Baker) by Princess Leia (Carrie Fisher). This robot has fallen into the hands of the young Luke Skywalker (Mark Hamill). Luke, a farmer on a desert planet, finds himself caught up in the battle and rushes off to save Princess Leia from the clutches of the evil Darth Vader (David Prowse). Aiding him is the (supposedly) last of the Jedi knights (Alec Guiness) and a small time smuggler Han Solo (Harrison Ford). With superb special effects the film was ground breaking. It was one of the first of the really big budget science fiction movies to be made, and came out the same year as ***Close Encounters of the Third Kind***. It was also one of the first movies to develop a spin-off industry with comics, toys and novels based around the movie (though this had been done many times before with TV series (*cf.* **Gerry Anderson's** puppet series of the 1960s and 70s). Although the plot was not the most inspiring (some critics say based on the *Wizard of Oz*) the sheer speed and action, as well as the model work and photography carries one through. It was the first film to truly bring the scale and imagery of **space opera** to the big screen, something that buffs had been waiting for for a long time. Not surprisingly, the film won the Hugo for Best Dramatic Presentation in 1978 and was also voted 6th favourite desert asteroid film in the all time *Concatenation* poll. Equally not surprisingly the movie spawned a host of imitations, though most of them did not amount to anything more than a pale rip-off. But it, and ***Close Encounters***, did suggest to movie makers that SF films could make BIG money. So it could be argued that this movie was the production impetus for better high-budget films like ***Dune*** and ***Alien***. It also confirmed John (***Close Encounters, Raiders of the Lost Ark***) Williams as a major genre composer of feature film music. *Star Wars* was nominated for 11 Oscars (including Best Picture, Best Director, Best Supporting Actor (Guinness), and Best Screenplay), winning 7 (art direction, film editing, visual effects, costume design, sound, original score, and sound effects). In 1998 the first three *Star Wars* films were re-released with the latest digital special effects enhancements, with fair box office success prior to the 1999 release of the first part of the first trilogy *The Phantom Menace* which was followed by the second part of the first trilogy, *Attack of the Clones*, in 2002. Despite better effects and box-office success, neither of these two won a Hugo. Principal cast: Mark Hamill, Harrison (***Blade Runner***) Ford, Carrie Fisher, Peter Cushing, Alec Guinness, Anthony Daniels, Kenny (***Time Bandits***) Baker, and David Prowse.

Stella – magazine, Sweden (*crtd* 1886). Pre-dating **Analog** by getting on for half a century this short-lived magazine promulgated European authors such as Kurd Lasswitz and **Jules Verne**. It was followed by another Swedish magazine *Hugin* (*crtd*1916) which ran to 1920 and was edited by Otto Witt. *Der Orchideengarten* was an Austrian-German-Swiss magazine which included nearly all the European continental SF writers in its 54 issues between 1919 and 1921, including: Capek, Guy de Maupassant, Kipling and **Wells**, and even included American genre writers such as Edgar Allan Poe.

Sterling, (Michael) Bruce – author, US (*b*1954). He was born in Brownsville, Texas, but during his youth spent two and a half years in India, due to his father's work. On his return to the US, Sterling obtained a degree in journalism from the University of Texas, Austin. That same year he sold his first SF short story, *Man-Made Self* (1976), to the anthology of Texan SF, *Lone Star Universe*, though reportedly he had already sold *Living Inside* (1974) to **Harlan Ellison's** *The Last Dangerous Visions*. Sterling's early novels to some extent prefigured the dawning **cyberpunk** movement. However, it was in 1985 (one year after **William Gibson's** *Neuromancer*) that Sterling published one of the definitive cyberpunk novels, the Nebula-nominated ***Schismatrix***. Set in his Shaper/Mechanist universe (short stories of which can be found in Sterling's collection *Crystal Express* (1989)), *Schismatrix* portrays a future of autonomous orbiting and space habitats in which the Shapers, champions of biotechnology, and the Mechanists, lovers of prostheses in the cyborg sense, carry out their conflicts. *Mirrorshades* (1986), edited by Sterling, was the quintessential cyberpunk anthology, and for many years he was cyberpunk's most vocal advocate. Though still recognisably cyberpunk, Sterling's next novel, the Hugo-nominated *Islands in the Net* (1988), displayed a greater maturity, especially in the politicisation of the action. In fact this is almost a political thriller in its depiction of the governmental and corporate interests that fight for control of information, communication and the systems that make them possible. While collaborative novels were rare in the eighties, it seemed inevitable that one day Sterling and Gibson should write together. In that sense, then, it wasn't especially surprising when *The Difference Engine* (1990) was released. This is a so-called steampunk novel, set in an alternate past where Charles Babbage perfects his mechanical computer, and Lord Byron leads an English technocracy in changing the world. His second collection, *Globalhead* (1992), was a runner-up in the annual *Locus* readers poll. Though computers still play a large part in Sterling's fiction, the *Locus* runner-up *Heavy Weather* (1994), was in fact about a group of 'storm chasers' attempting to chart the progress of global warming and changing weather patterns. His Hugo-nominated *Holy Fire* (1996) seems to show Sterling emerging completely from his cyberpunk phase, portraying a near-future European creative renaissance through the eyes of Mia Ziemann, a 93-year-old who has many decades of life left thanks to medical technology. Sterling's work is often surprising and unfailingly thought-provoking and, for some at least, his work continually outranks that of Gibson, Lewis Shiner, Harold Waldrop and other contemporaries. It seems reasonable to hope, therefore, that there is much more to come from Sterling's fertile imagination.

Sternbach, Rick – artist, US (*b*1951). He has worked for both SF and science magazines, contributing to *Galaxy, The Magazine of Fantasy and Science Fiction,* **Analog**, and *Astronomy Magazine*, and has also worked on the TV series *Cosmos* (see **Carl Sagan**) and ***Star Trek: The Next Generation*** (as technical consultant and illustrator, producing *The ST: TNG Technical Manual* in 1991), and for film companies Paramount and Disney. In 1976 he was a founder member of the Association of Science Fiction/Fantasy Artists (ASFA), and won Hugos in 1977 and '78 for Best Professional Artist.

Strange Case of Dr Jekyll and Mr Hyde, **(*The*)** – novel (1886) by Robert Louis Stevenson; the 'The' was usually added to the title in reprints from 1896 onwards. An Edinburgh doctor (Jekyll) formulates an elixir that releases his baser nature (Hyde). Hyde then indulges his passions which include murder. Unfortunately, the Hyde part slowly takes over and he is finally hunted down. Written in great haste while recovering from a haemorrhage, the idea came to him during a cocaine-induced nightmare. (*NB*. The cocaine was medically prescribed.) Written in just three days, the 30,000 word story did not meet the approval of his wife who dismissed the manuscript, burning it, as "utter nonsense". Fortunately for us, Stevenson spent the next three days rewriting the work: fortunately for him, it was an instant success and helped get him out of debt. Many film versions were made from 1908 onwards, but the Paramount US (1931) version, *dir.* Rouben Mamoulian, perhaps has received the greatest critical acclaim. The Hammer re-worked version *Dr Jekyll and Sister Hyde* (1971), in which Hyde is female, is a favourite at the Festival of Fantastic films.

Stranger in a Strange Land – novel (1961) by **Robert A Heinlein**. Valentine Smith, the first human raised by Martians, returns to Earth, complete with psi powers, but finds society incomprehensible. After indoctrination by Jubal Harshaw, a character many associate with Heinlein himself, Smith is cast as a messiah. The book, perhaps because of its anti-religious stance and espousal of 'free love', gained a cult following in the late sixties, and introduced the word 'grok' (meaning to comprehensively understand) to the English language. Winner of the 1962 Hugo for Best Novel, *Stranger* was, in its time, the longest SF novel yet written, but has since had text restored and been released in an even lengthier version (1990).

Strugatski, Arkady and Boris – authors, Russian, Arkady (1925-1991), Boris (*b*1931). Considering SF is supposed to be a genre that explores the alien and different, it is to westerners' discredit that they publish so little non-Anglophone SF. The Strugatski brothers are, like **Stanislaw Lem**, a welcome exception to this rule. Probably their best known works, not least because they are often published together, are (*Skazka o troike*) *The Tale of Troika* (1968) and (*Piknik na obochine*) *Roadside Picnic* (1972), both being nominated for the **John W Campbell** Memorial Award (though not winning). The first is a sequel to (*Ponedel'nik nachinaetsia v subbotu*) *Monday Begins on Saturday* (1965), which uses folk tale and magic motifs to explore the division between science and society; the sequel continues this theme, lampooning the administrative bureaucracy of their country. While *Roadside Picnic* combines **new wave** with **hard SF** when aliens, briefly stopping off on Earth, leave behind the detritus of their interstellar roadside picnic. Unfortunately the 'rubbish' contains items that: fascinate humans, are potentially useful, as well as the downright dangerous. This was adapted by the brothers as Tarkovsky's film ***Stalker*** (1979), though with major changes. Despite severe censorship the Strugatskis managed to slip many subversive meanings into their works and, before *perestroika*, even managed to visit the UK-hosted 1987 **World SF Convention** (**Worldcon**), where they were warmly welcomed (with their KGB minders separated in the bar).

Stuart, Don A. – see **Campbell, John W. jnr**.

Sturgeon, Theodore – author, US (1918–1985). Sturgeon was born Edward Hamilton Waldo in New York, and published much of his early short stories under the pseudonyms E. Hunter Waldo and E. Waldo Hunter. His first published SF story was *Ether Breather* (1939) in *Astounding Science Fiction* (see ***Analog***), and he contributed regularly to other magazines such as *Galaxy* and *Unknown*. While he is considered a vital contributor to science fiction's **Golden Age**, he is also remembered as instrumental in the creation of modern SF, influencing such diverse writers as **Harlan Ellison** and Samuel Delaney, with his tales of love and transcendence which often confronted the taboos of the time (the forties and fifties), especially sexual mores. So, while traditional (short) stories such as *Microcosmic God* (1941), about a scientist who creates a miniature life form, easily found a home, more challenging and confrontational work, such as *Bianca's Hands* (1947), was refused by the more puritanical US markets before finally being published in the UK. Like **Robert Silverberg**, Sturgeon had many productive periods, interspersed with long periods of inactivity; and, also like Silverberg, awards seemed to pass Sturgeon by. Many of his short stories can be found in various collections such as *Caviar* (1955), and *The Worlds of Theodore Sturgeon* (1972), but he only wrote five novels. One of Sturgeon's strongest themes is of the triumph of the alienated and outcast over circumstance and persecution. His first two novels explore this theme through their protagonists; in *The Dreaming* explore this theme through their protagonists; in *The Dreaming Jewels* (1950) an odd young boy, Horty, runs away from home to join a circus where he learns he has strange powers and a connection to jewel-like aliens, eventually defeating the evil of the adults around him; and in his best-remembered work, ***More Than Human*** (1953), based on the novella *Baby is Three* (1952), six 'freaks' find that together they can form a gestalt with psi-powers which they can use against the cruelty of the normal world. Sturgeon's utopian (and Hugo-nominated) *Venus Plus X* (1960) concerns the awakening of Charlie Johns by the inhabitants of a future world of sexual androgyny. Sturgeon did win one Hugo in 1971 for Best Short Story, *Slow Sculpture* (1970), and *More Than Human* won the International Fantasy Award in 1954 as well as being placed joint 10th in the *Concatenation* all-time Best SF poll.

Superman – comic and character, US (*crtd* 1938). Launched into space by his parents from the doomed planet Krypton, baby Kal El crashes on Earth where he is brought up by Jonathan and Martha Kent, a farming couple, in the mid-west US town of Smallville. Under Earth's yellow sun, the boy gains incredible powers of flight, strength and invulnerability. His senses also become acute especially his (x-ray) vision which can see through most objects (but not lead). And so Superman was born, sworn to uphold justice and the American way. The only thing that could stop Superman was radiation from the mineral kryptonite, meteoric fragments of his home world, and magic. When not flying around doing super deeds, Kal El lived an alter ego life as mild mannered reporter Clark Kent for the *Daily Planet* newspaper in the city of Metropolis. Superman was created by Jerry Siegel and Joe Schuster and was launched in DC's *Action Comics* whose strip writers included luminaries such as **Alfred Bester** and **Henry Kuttner**. Superman has also appeared in many different media, including: the Fleischer brothers' cartoons (1940-43); a radio series (1940-52); a film serial starring Kirk Alyn (1948); a six season US TV series starring George Reeves (1953-57); a Broadway musical (1966); and a TV movie starring David Wilson (1975). However in 1978 the US/UK feature film revived interest in the character. *dir.* Richard Donner. Principal cast: Christopher (***Somewhere in Time***, ***Village of the Damned***) Reeve, Margot Kidder, Jackie Cooper, Gene Hackman, Ned Beatty, Sussanah York, Valerie Perrine, Glen Ford and Marlon fellow reporter on the planet) in the TV series and Kirk Alyn. *Superman* the film won the Best Dramatic Presentation Hugo in 1979. Three sequels followed, of which of note was *Superman 2* US (1980) *dir.* Richard Lester, which featured criminal Kryptonians (played by Terence Stamp, Sarah Douglas and Jack O'Halloran) arriving on Earth having escaped their Phantom Zone (another dimension) prison. *Superman 3* UK (1983) *dir.* Richard Lester, guest starring comedian Richard Pryor and Robert Vaughn, marked the start of a downhill slide but had one redeeming feature, a battle between Superman's good and evil selves. The screenplay for *Superman 4: The Quest for Peace*, UK (1987) *dir.* Sidney Furie, was by Christopher Reeve himself. It is notable only because he battles another super hero created from DNA taken from a strand of Superman's hair by Lex Luthor. That hair itself contains no DNA seems to have escaped Reeve. The special effects in this last offering are a little ragged. Finally on the film front there was the unexceptional *Supergirl*, UK (1984) *dir.* Jeannot (***Somewhere in Time***) Szwarc which is only watchable by fantastic film buffs due to the camp performances by Faye Dunaway (the evil sorceress) and her ally Peter Cook. In the nineties there was a new TV series, *The New Adventures of Superman*, later re-titled *Lois and Clark* to tie in with the characters' marriage in the comic version. The series contained little of note save for a couple of one-off adventures with a time travelling **H.G. Wells**. The nineties also saw a new animated series. Finally, the early 2000s saw another TV series, *Smallville*, which dealt with Clark Kent's early years discovering his powers. Notwithstanding the media offerings, some of which were bland, and the contortions of the on-going story in the comics of the late 1980s and 1990s (especially those relating to Superman's death and re-birth), Superman was undeniably one of America's twentieth century icons and looks fit to survive well into the 21st.

Superman – film UK/US (1978). Winner of the 1979 Hugo for Best Dramatic Presentation. (See **Superman** – comic and character.)

TAFF – See **Fan Funds**.

Telepathist – novel (1964) by **John Brunner**. Gerald Howson was a cripple and a bit of a social outcast; even his mother resented having to look after him. At twenty Howson was convinced that the world was uncaring. Then he began to suspect that something unusual was going on. At first, putting it down to remarkably good hearing, he seemed to be able to understand people at a distance. Before long he realised that he had certain abilities... and so did others. He was telepathic. As he began to harness his powers, he was set to work chasing out other people's nightmares. Now he had social status. His popularity increased, and seemingly with it his telepathy. He could even create telepathic art, or project his thoughts out into space. But the genes that gave him his abilities were the very same that made him deformed. Would he ever become a whole man? *The Telepathist* grew out of three short stories (*City of the Tiger* (1958); *The Whole Man* (1959); and *Curative Telepath* (1959)) published in US pulp magazines.

Telling, The – novel (2000) by **Ursula K Le Guin**. A tale from her Hainish universe in which an observer from the Ekumen is repeatedly requested to visit the hinterlands of the planet Aka to study the natives. The 81st request is granted so off goes Observer Sutty. Aka is a world where everything written in the old scripts has been banned. However in the wilderness there are the remnants of a cult practising the banned religion. Will the old aural tradition return to replace the modern scripts that have been written to Corporation specifications or will the Corporation's version prevail and the old traditions finally be wiped out? The novel came top of the 2001 *Locus* poll for best SF novel (and also won the local (Pacific NW US) 2001 Endeavour Award)..

Terminator, The – film, US (1984), *dir.* James (***Aliens***) Cameron. Sarah Connor (Linda Hamilton) has no idea that she is being stalked by a cyborg from 2029 AD. It has been sent back in time by a self-aware computer, Skynet, that is waging war against the human population; a war that it is losing thanks to Sarah's as yet unborn son, John. The Terminator (Arnold (***Total Recall*** and ***Predator***) Schwarzenegger) is a single-minded killing machine, but John Connor has sent back a champion, Kyle Reese (Michael (***Aliens***) Biehn), to protect his mother. A deadly cat and mouse game is played out against a Los Angeles backdrop, with a hopelessly ill-prepared police force (represented by Paul (***Star Trek II***) Winfield and Lance (***Aliens***) Henriksen) providing cannon-fodder... This is an action-packed film from James Cameron, that actually represents one end of a time loop (although that is not completely apparent until the sequel, ***T2:***

Judgement Day), with only brief glimpses of the future war. The relentlessly paced script was written by Cameron and Gale Anne Hurd (the film's producer), and the effects were provided by Stan (***Predator***) Winston. *The Terminator* came 12th in the *Concatenation* all-time best SF film poll, and also came 7th in the Blackwood/Flynn poll of WSFS members for the top ten SF films. It gave rise to a comics series from Dark Horse Publishing (who also produce comics set in the ***Alien*** and the ***Predator*** universes). A third *Terminator* film was released in 2003 that actually took us up to Judgement Day as opposed to the second movie which only portrayed it in dream sequences.

Terminator 2: Judgement Day – film, US (1991), *dir.* James (***Aliens***) Cameron. Following the tremendous success of the first film, the budget for this sequel was substantially increased (depending on how the money is counted, the figure is anywhere between $65 million and $95 million). Linda Hamilton returns as Sarah Connor, institutionalised because of her 'delusion' that there will be a nuclear war in 1997. She has become expert in survivalist techniques, and has been training her son, John (excellently played by relative newcomer Edward Furlong), for the role he will play in the future war. He is the son also of Kyle Reese (Michael Biehn briefly reprising his role in a cameo appearance—at least, in the extended version), but there is more to the time loop than this. An increasingly desperate Skynet has sent back another Terminator (Robert Patrick), the T-1000, able to shapeshift somewhat due to its composition of liquid metal, to fulfil the first Terminator's mission. The future's John Connor has also, again, sent back a protector—a reprogrammed old-style Terminator (Arnold (***Predator*** and ***Total Recall***) Schwarzenegger). While playing much the same cat and mouse game as in the forerunner movie, the heroes this time also have the goal of stopping the creation of Skynet, and so averting the war. And the reason Skynet is possible at all...? You will have to see the film! James (***Aliens***) Cameron shares the screenplay credits with William Wisher. The shape-shifting effects were created using the, then, relatively new computer generated image 'morphing' techniques. *T2: Judgement Day* won the Best Dramatic Presentation Hugo in 1992, and (like its predecessor) gave rise to two linked spin-off comics series from Boxtree, *Cybernetic Dawn* and *Nuclear Twilight*. There was also a trilogy of three spin-off novelizations, by S. M. Stirling of which the first, *T2: Infiltrator*, would have made for an excellent follow-up to this second film. It depicts Sarah and John Connor accidentally meeting the human secret agent, on which Skynet was to base its Terminator ('Arnold') human form, and together they have to outwit an advanced female terminator who brought with her the ability to construct several Arnolds. However what we got in 2003 was a third action movie with little new on the SF front.

That Hell-Bound Train – short story (1958) by Robert Bloch. Originally published in *The Magazine of Fantasy and Science Fiction* (Sept. '58), no Bloch collection is complete without this winner of the 1959 Hugo for Best Short Story. Martin makes a deal with the Devil: Satan can have his soul if he will grant Martin the ability to stop time. Old Nick agrees and gives Martin a watch which, when wound to a stop, will halt the passage of Time; Martin, for his part, intends to use it when he is at his happiest. But as life goes on, and Martin samples the delights that existence has to offer, he never quite gets round to using the watch, until one day he dies and the Devil reappears to take Martin on that Hell-bound train to the Depot Way Down Yonder. It is only when the train is underway that Martin decides to exercise his option... As deal-with-the-Devil stories go, this is one of the best, with its concentration on the pleasures and pitfalls of life, and the portrayal of the dissatisfaction we all sometimes feel, all seen through the eyes of the simple protagonist.

They'd Rather Be Right – novel (1954) by Mark Clifton and Frank Riley, also published as *The Forever Machine*. In the future someone invents 'Bossy', an artificial intelligence originally designed to guide aeroplanes. Given sufficient facts Bossy could also solve other problems. Bossy was something else, an artificial intelligence that had a direct effect on those connected with it. The story is set in a future largely of peace due to 'opinion control'. Yet 'opinion control' had caused mankind to stagnate as it impeded original thought. Bossy counteracted this effect and so became a threat to society. Nonetheless there seemed no limit to the problems Bossy could solve – perhaps even immortality? Of the two authors, credit for *They'd Rather Be Right* largely goes to Mark Clifton (1906–1963). Clifton began his Bossy stories with Alex Apostolides in 1953 with two shorts, published in *Astounding Science Fiction* (see **Analog**), *Crazy Joey* and *Hide! Hide! Witch!*, before teaming up with Frank

Riley for this novel, which won the 1955 Hugo. In 1958 sections of the first two stories were added, and other text restored, the whole being re-issued as *The Forever Machine*.

Them! – film, US (1954), *dir.* Gorden Douglas. Screenplay by George Worthing (*It Came From Beneath the Sea* and *Earth vs the Flying Saucers*) Yates. This was the largest grossing Warner film of 1954, a good year for SF films—that included ***The Creature from the Black Lagoon, Gojira*** and ***20,000 Leagues Under the Sea***. Near atomic testing grounds in Nevada, two cops (James Whitmore and Chris Drake) find a terrified little girl, a destroyed trailer-home, and a small pile of sugar. Dr. Medford (Edmund Gwenn) and his beautiful daughter Patricia (Joan Weldon) must soon join forces with an FBI agent, James (***The Thing***) Arness, to battle mutated giant ants. They win one victory in the desert, but a queen escapes to Los Angeles... Special effects man Ralph Ayers purportedly only built two principal ants, worked by levers for the close-ups, but was still nominated for an Oscar, though it lost to *20,000 Leagues*. Several giant insect/arachnid movies followed in subsequent years, including *Tarantula* (1955), *The Deadly Mantis* (1957), and *The Black Scorpion* (1959), but only the first of these was any good.

Thing, The – film, US (1951), *dir*. Christian Nyby (and reportedly Howard Hawkes) GB Title *The Thing From Another World,* based on the **John W** (*Astounding Stories*) **Campbell jr** short story *Who Goes There* (1938), originally written under the pseudonym of Don A Stuart, which was later re-titled *The Thing From Another World*. "How did it get here?" proclaims the film's promotional poster; 'it' being the 'Thing', an extraterrestrial. The answer is self-evident early on when a polar-based air force team find a spaceship buried in the ice. Nearby they also find a frozen alien. Taking the creature back to their polar base it thaws, waking to cause havoc and destruction as it feeds on the blood of its victims... Other than its polar base setting and the discovery of an extraterrestrial, Nyby's film has little to do with Campbell's story and it offended some SF fans of the time who (rightly) believed it would kick-start a 'monster movie' cycle. Despite this the film was ground-breaking cinematic SF for its time in that it was a serious attempt to portray an alien biology. Though dated it is still hugely enjoyable and is on the list of all time best attended of movies screened at the Festival of Fantastic Films. It is particularly noted for its closing dialogue: "I bring you warning–to every one of you listening to the sound of my voice. Tell the world, tell this to everyone wherever they are: watch the skies, keep looking–watch the skies." Principal cast: Robert Cornthwaite, Kenneth Toby, Margaret Sheriden , Bill Self, Dewey Martin, James (***Them!***) Arness (as The Thing), and Douglas Spencer,

Thing, The – film, US (1982), (*dir*. John (***Dark Star, Village of the Damned***) Carpenter. The 1982 *The Thing* is a far closer portrayal of John W Campbell's story *Who Goes There?* (see previous entry). Set in Antarctica, the US meteorological station is visited by two Norwegians from the next sector chasing a sleigh dog. The Norwegians accidentally die when explosive goes off but the surviving dog turns out to be something else... Here, as in *Who Goes There?* the alien is a shape-changer and soon the base's personnel do not know whom to trust... The special effects for its time were ground-breaking and Carpenter slowly increases the film's tempo through to its fiery conclusion. A nod is made towards the 1951 version in that the video playback of the Norwegians discovering the alien spacecraft might have been a representation of that in the Nyby version showing the researchers encircling the buried object. The then state of the art effects are also worthy of note, created by Rob (***Total Recall***) Bottin, Roy Arbogast, and Albert Whitlock. Principal cast: Kurt Russell, Wilford Brimley, TK Carter, David Clennon, Keith David, Richard Dystart, Charles Hallahan, Peter Maloney, Richard Masur, Donald Moffat, Joel Polis and Thomas Waites.

Things to Come – film, UK (1936), *dir*. William Cameron Menzies. Co-scripted by **HG Wells**, and filmed under his close supervision, it is based on his novel *The Shape of Things to Come* (1933) and charts the future history of a town from the (then 1936) present day. It accurately predicted World War II, the use in subsequent wars of biochemical agents (not just chemical warfare), and ultimately (at least in essence) space exploration. Though obviously incredibly dated by today's standards, the effects for its time were ground-breaking and Vincent Korda's art direction was praised in countless reviews following its release. However it was not a box office success. Principal cast: Raymond Massey, Edward Chapman, Ralph (***Rollerball, Time Bandits***) Richardson, Margaretta Scott, Cedric Hardwicke, Sophie Stewart, Derrick de Marney and John Clements.

This Immortal – novel (1966) by **Roger Zelazny**, also published in a shorter version in *The Magazine of Fantasy and Science Fiction* as *And Call Me Conrad*. It is the future and there has been a terrible war with the Vegans. Earth is scarred, but through it all comes a colourful man about whom rumours abound. But the records, which should reveal all about the man they call Conrad Nimikos, are mysteriously incomplete. Some say that he once had a different name — that he was the hero who fought the Vegan empire to a standoff. Some even say that he has other names. Who is Conrad Nimikos, Commissioner of the Earth Office Department of Arts, Monuments and Archives, and incidentally the one man who may have a chance to spare the now-hapless Earth another bout with the aliens? You and I know him as *This Immortal*. *This Immortal* jointly won the 1966 Hugo Award for Best Novel.

This Island Earth – film, US (1955), *dir*. Joseph Newman. (*NB*. The Metaluna sequences were directed by Jack Arnold (Newman recognised his own limitations as a director).) Based on a novel (1952) by Raymond F. Jones, from an original series of shorts (1949-50) in *Thrilling Wonder Stories*. A famous scientist becomes part of a mysterious project to develop new technologies. Only later he discovers that this is a front for aliens. Locked in a genocidal war, the inhabitants of the war-torn, resource-depleted Metaluna have secretly recruited human scientists to produce weapons to fight the Zahgons who are bombarding Metaluna. When their plan is discovered, the scientists are kidnapped and taken on a trip to the dying planet. With some fantastic visual effects for its time (due to Clifford Steine), colourful photography and a story that is still interesting today (and notwithstanding some dodgy schoolboy science), *This Island Earth* is representative of the better of mid-1950s US film SF complete with a nifty alien monster. The film is on the list of all time best attended of movies screened at the Festival of Fantastic Films. Principal cast: Jeff Morrow, Rex Reason, Faith Domergue, and Eddie Parker.

Three Laws of Robotics, The – See **Asimov**.

Thunderbirds – TV series, UK (*fb*1965). **Gerry Anderson's** *Thunderbirds* was the most famous, and successful, of Anderson's puppet series. 22 episodes were made and 2 feature films.   Plot base: Multi billionaire Jeff Tracy and his family operate an independent high tech 'International Rescue' service *incognito* from their island home. The Thunderbirds themselves were giant rescue craft.   Thunderbird 1 was a rocket scout, Thunderbird 2 a heavy duty transporter, Thunderbird 3 a space ship, Thunderbird 4 a submarine, and Thunderbird 5 a space station which acted as the operation's communications centre. The Tracys were aided by their London agent, Lady Penelope and her butler (an erstwhile safe-cracker) Parker travelling in a heavily armoured pink Rolls Royce. A children's science fiction programme yes, but one that could be enjoyed by parents too. Thunderbirds won Anderson a Silver Medal for Outstanding Artistic Achievement from the Royal Television Society in 1966. While Anderson himself was one of four Guests of Honour at the 1995 combined **Euro** and **World SF Convention** (**Worldcon**) in Glasgow and the 1998 Festival of Fantastic Films.

Tiger! Tiger! – novel, US (1955) by **Alfred Bester**. Better known in the US as *The Stars My Destination* (and serialised in *Galaxy* magazine), the revenge-laden plot is based slightly on *The Count of Monte Cristo*. Left to die in a space wreck, Gully Foyle has few options, but miraculously survives by 'jaunting' (teleporting) away from the wreck. On Earth, jaunting happens all the time, but only on a planetary scale—Foyle, however, has jaunted 25 light years! This makes Gully the most sought after man of his time, but he is pursuing vengeance against those who left him to die... Although not as honoured as Bester's ***The Demolished Man*** ((1953) as winner of the first ever Hugo Award for Best Novel), *Tiger! Tiger!* is probably his best work. In 1979, before graphic novels became common, Byron Preiss and Howard Chaykin published the first volume of their graphic adaptation of this novel through Baronet, who unfortunately went out of business before publishing the second volume. In 1992 Epic (an imprint of Marvel Comics) did publish *The Complete The Stars My Destination*. Bester made two false starts on writing this novel, the first in Surrey and the second in London, before managing to complete the book in Rome (the full story can be found in Bester's essay *My Affair With Science Fiction* (1975), partially reprinted in the Epic volume). *Tiger! Tiger!* was placed fifth in the *Concatenation* All-Time Best SF Novel poll.

Time After Time – film, US (1979), *dir.* Nicholas (***Star Trek II***, ***Star Trek VI***) Meyer, and based on Karl Alexander's 1976 story. **H G Wells** invents a time machine which one of his 'friends' then steals. The thief turns out to be Jack the Ripper and though the time machine returns on automatic, the Ripper has been let loose somewhere in time. Wells finds out that the Ripper has travelled from Victorian England to modern day (late 70s) San Francisco. (Strangely the journey was in space as well as time due to the dubious premise that the period time travelling took several hours during which the Earth rotated: this was not Wells' own portrayal of time travel (see ***The Time Machine***).) Having to overcome culture shock, Wells befriends a banking clerk and sets out to track down his adversary while on the way dealing with a couple of time paradoxes. An amusing film portraying a fictional historic aspect of the genre as fact: one would like to think that Wells himself would have approved. Principal cast: Malcolm (***A Clockwork Orange***) McDowell, Mary Steenburgen, David Warner.

Time Bandits – film, UK (1980), *dir.* Terry (***Brazil***) Gilliam. When God created the universe it was a bit of a rush job – it was undertaken in under a week. Not surprisingly there were a few holes and these connect different places in time and space. All of which was of fundamental importance to one of God's repair crews, a gang of dwarves. Fed up with maintenance, and with God's map to guide them, they used the holes to gather riches throughout history. Then, one day a hole appears in the bedroom of one Kevin, a boy living in present-day British suburbia and Kevin gets caught up in the dwarves' adventure. A spectacular science fantasy comedy in true Gilliam style with a great support cast. *Time Bandits* was voted one of the *Concatenation* top 20 all-time films. Principal cast: Craig Warnock, David Rappaport, Sean (***Indiana Jones and the Last Crusade***, ***Outland***, and ***Zardoz***) Connery, John Cleese, Ian (***Alien***) Holm, Ralph (***Rollerball***, ***The Man Who Could Work Miracles*** and ***Things to Come***) Richardson, Michael Palin and Kenny (***Star Wars***) Baker.

Timelike Infinity – novel (1992) by **Stephen Baxter**. Set near the beginning of Baxter's Xeelee sequence of novels and short stories, this was his second novel. Michael Poole launches a wormhole on a relativistic journey which brings it back to Earth 1500 years later, allowing the occupying Qax to send an invasion back through time, bypassing an era when Earth was under the domination of another alien race, the Squeem. Meanwhile, human rebels from the future, the Friends of Wigner, capture Poole's colleague Miriam Berg in order to coerce him to help in the fight against the Qax. Baxter's Xeelee universe was richly detailed over the course of 4 novels and some 22 short stories, and contained weirdly conceived aliens against a hard-SF backdrop where his skill in entertaining with maths and engineering detail shine.

Time Machine, The – novella (1895) by **HG Wells.** An Edwardian inventor builds a time machine and travels to the year 802,701 where he finds that divergent evolution has produced two races of mutually dependent (indeed, symbiotic) humans; the peaceful, surface-dwelling Eloi and the 'evil', subterranean Morlocks. Published 36 years after Darwin's *Origin of Species*, and just six years after Alfred Wallace's popularisation of it, the concept of evolution was becoming more accepted, at least in intellectual circles. In this light *The Time Machine* can be seen as an attempt to take 'natural' selection to its limits by looking at the effect of social trends on the genetic make-up of thousands of generations. A century later, **Stephen Baxter** wrote an authorised sequel, *The Time Ships* (1995). (See also ***Time After Time*** and **Superman**.) There is little doubt that if there had to be just one time travel story to define the trope for SF then *The Time Machine* would be it. Subsequently (and indeed a few times before) there have been numerous time travel tales. Many from the 20th century onwards have added twists and explored the concept further. (See also ***Back to the Future***, ***The Big Time***, ***Fall of Hyperion***, **Harry Harrison**, **Robert Heinlein**, **Richard Matheson**, ***Quantum Leap***, **Robert Silverberg**, ***Somewhere in Time***, **Superman** and **Ian Watson**.)

Time Machine, The – film, US (1960), *dir*. George (***War of the Worlds***) Pal. Rod Taylor stars as the time traveller, George (or is it **H. George Wells**?), in the trimmed but reasonably faithful film adaptation of Wells' book ***The Time Machine***. Travelling to the far future, Darwinian processes have caused the upper classes to evolve into a surface-living enfeebled play time society (the Eloi), while the workers have become subterranean cannibalistic brutes (the Morlocks)... The speeded up decay of a deceased Morlock was the Oscar-winning special effect highlight of its day. The film is largely carried by Wells' strong plot. Unfortunately the film left out many of Wells' images of the future. Principal cast: Rod Taylor, Alan Young, Yvette Mimieux, Sebastian Cabot, Tom Helmore, Whit Bissell and Doris Lloyd. (Not to be confused with the 2002 version, *dir*. Simon Wells (H. G. Wells' grandson) starring Guy Pearce (as Alexander Hartdegen the Time Traveller), Samantha Mumba and Jeremy Irons. There is time travel and the Morlock/Eloi human speciation into predator/prey, but there the similarities largely end. However this version includes an interesting, but not an original, take on the nature of time travel.)

Timescape – novel (1980) by **Gregory Benford**. It is 1998 and artificial chemicals are mutating life. Ecosystems are stressed and the world's food supply begins to fail. Two Cambridge research physicists realise that they can use sub-atomic physics to send a message back in time to warn a generation. Meanwhile back in 1962, a Californian physicist keeps finding something spoiling his experiments. As he begins to realise what is happening, he comes to understand he has to change world events, for in the future he sees global collapse... Benford's *Timescape* is one of the hardest SF portrayals of time travel. Tightly written, the story weaves between the present and the future (or is it present and past?) with just enough factual physics to suspend disbelief. Though *Timescape* was only a runner up in the annual *Locus* readers poll (coming fifth in the 'SF novel' category), it did win a Nebula and the John W Campbell Memorial Award.

Timescape – film, US (1991), *dir*. David N. Twohy. Recently widowed Ben Wilson and his daughter start a hotel but, before it opens, a tourist coach arrives with a party that will pay well above the usual rates to stay for three nights in the unfinished building. That the tourists are from the future is soon established, but why are they there? Based on the novella *Vintage Season* by husband, Lawrence O'Donnell (real name **Henry Kuttner**), and wife, C.L. Moore, *Timescape* is representative of the time travel themes Kuttner explored between the 1930s and 50s in a number of novels (such as *Tomorrow and Tomorrow* (1951)) and comics (for instance *The Time Trap* published by *Marvel Science Stories* (1938)). *Timescape* is the only recent adaptation of his work and, as a film in its own right, in both the UK and US, it was one of the top ten most hired SF videos out of all of 1991. Principal cast: Jeff Daniels, Ariana Richards, Emila Crow, Jim Hanie, David Wells, Nicholas Guest, Robert Colbert, Time Winters, and George Murdock.

Titan – novel (1979) by John Varley. Astronauts find to their astonishment something very strange around the orbit of Jupiter: Themis, just 1300 kilometers in diameter, apparently an artificial construct, a ringworld. It catches them, and their whole world turns upside-down. Furthermore it is not what it seems… *Titan* came top of the *Locus* poll for best novel in 1980.

To Say Nothing of the Dog – novel (1998) by **Connie (*Passage*) Willis** is a time travel story set in the same universe as her *Doomsday Book* . 'Time-lagged' Ned Henry is in dire need of a rest. He has been shuttling back and forth between the 21st century and the 1940s searching for a Victorian artefact called the 'bishop's bird stump'. The exercise is part of a project to restore Coventry Cathedral that was bombed in World War II. But then another time traveller, Verity Kindle, accidentally changes something so she and Ned must go back to the Victorian era (1888) to put things right. Written with humour, *To Say Nothing of the Dog* contains numerous literary references bound up in a mystery. It is hard to take a nap when in the middle of saving the world and its space-time flow. It won the 1999 Hugo for 'Best Novel'.

Total Recall – film, US (1990), *dir.* Paul (***Robo Cop*** and ***Starship Troopers***) Verhoeven. Loosely based on **Philip K Dick's** story *We Can Remember It For You Wholesale*. Quaid is happy with his wife and life as a manual worker but then – having tried to take a 'virtual' holiday, using a memory implant machine – starts to recall strange memories about another existence on Mars. When he becomes the target for an assassination team it is clear that his new memories are not figments of his imagination and he must go to Mars. It soon transpires that the fate of the whole Martian colony is at stake... Purportedly Ronald Shusett and Dan O'Bannon (see ***Alien***) spent ten years, on and off, working on the script, and the budget for the movie was a then record breaking $60 million (one year later ***Terminator 2*** cost at least $65 million). However the investment paid off and Rob (***The Thing***) Bottin, among others, enabled the film to win an Oscar for its special effects. Though primarily an action movie, *Total Recall* is stuffed with SF tropes and contains some scenes that are pure Philip K Dick such as the discussion as to whether the characters are still hooked up to a memory implant machine or in reality? This film was popular both with fans and with the public.

Principal cast: Arnold (*The Terminator*) Schwarzenegger, Rachel Ticotin, Sharon Stone, Rony Cox, Michael (*Scanners*) Ironside, Marshall Bell, Mel Johnson jr. and Michael Champion.

To Your Scattered Bodies Go – novel (1971) by **Philip José Farmer**. The first of the 'Riverworld' series. The planet called Riverworld itself is home to the resurrected billions of old Earth. All their hatreds, prejudices and predilections are intact. Only one thing has changed; they know that they cannot die, but are fated to an apparently endless resurrection, a form of reincarnation—those who come back, come back as young adults. One man called Richard Burton, the womaniser and adventurer, arrives and sets out to unravel the meaning of it all. *To Your Scattered Bodies Go* won the Hugo for 'Best Novel' in 1972 and was followed by seven further novels in the series.

Trillion Year Spree – non-fiction book (1986) by **Brian Aldiss** with David Wingrove. There are a number of non-fiction books about the genre of SF, but this one is a decided cut above many of the rest. *Trillion Year Spree* is an update of Aldiss' earlier work *Billion Year Spree* and is a history of SF, albeit one with a slightly personalised perspective. Though light on the cinematic, TV and comics dimensions, it is a superb tour of much of SF, especially its literary dimension, and it won the Hugo in 1987 for Best Non-Fiction and was voted the 2nd most favourite non-fiction title in the *Concatenation* poll.

Truman Show, The – film, US (1998), *dir*. Peter Weir. Truman Burbank is your average middle class American who has a lovely wife, works in an office, *etc*. However, he is completely unaware that his entire world is one gigantic biosphere dome that is, in fact, a television studio. For Burbank, born and raised in this artificial world, is the unwitting star of the 'real-life', and top viewing, soap opera 'The Truman Show'. 'How will it end?' One day he begins to notice a few cracks in the logic of his world. Still unsuspecting of the truth, he seeks to escape from his home town... *The Truman Show* won the 1999 Hugo Award for Best Dramatic Presentation. Principal cast: Jim Carrey, Laura Linney, Noah Emmerich, Natascha McElhone, Holland Taylor and Ed Harris.

20 Million Miles to Earth – film, US (1957), *dir.* Nathan (***First Men in the Moon***) Juran. Famous largely because this was a first outing for stop-motion effects wizard Ray Harryhausen, the film is among the best attended during screenings at the Festival of Fantastic Films. The fairly standard plot has it that the first expedition to Venus, on returning to Earth crashes into the sea off Italy. The sole survivor, Calder (William Hopper), is concerned at the escape of a specimen. Not recognising what he has, a local zoologist (Frank Puglia) has been keeping the creature, but it has a phenomenal growth rate and escapes. Christened an Ymir, it goes on a rampage, beating a poor elephant to death, before being cornered by the military at the Coliseum and bazooka'd to oblivion. Purely a showcase for Harryhausen's talents, with then cutting-edge special effects, the script was poor (by Bob Williams and Christopher Knopf) and the direction lacklustre. The value of the film almost solely lies in it representing the best of the effects of its time and, today, in seeing the now very dated portrayal of SF tropes.

Twilight Zone, The – TV series, US (*fb*1959), created by Rod Serling. Winning the Best Dramatic Presentation Hugo three years in a row (1960-62), this anthology series (and ***The Outer Limits***, *fb*1963) is fondly remembered for a few classic episodes by the likes of Serling, **Richard Matheson**, and **Ray Bradbury**. Its original incarnation lasted 5 seasons, spawning some 156 episodes, 18 of them double-length, and span off into a magazine incarnation, several Serling collections and some Serling-edited anthologies. There was a film in the mid-80s, *Twilight Zone: The Movie* (1983), featuring remakes of four episodes directed by Joe Dante, John Landis, George Miller, and Stephen (see also **Brian Aldiss**, ***Close Encounters of the Third Kind***, ***Jurassic Park***, ***Raiders of the Lost Ark***, and ***Indiana Jones and the Last Crusade***) Spielberg. It included Richard Matheson's *Nightmare at 20,000 Feet* (1963) which had originally starred ***Star Trek***'s William (Capt. Kirk) Shatner, his role being reprised in the film by John (*3rd Rock from the Sun*) Lithgow. (This film should not be confused with the incredibly lame *Twilight Zone: Rod Serling's Lost Classics* (1993) *dir.* Robert Markowitz based on two scripts – *The Theatre* and *Where the Dead Are* – originally (and wisely) rejected from the 1960s series.) The *Twilight Zone* TV series' second incarnation (*fb*1985) had creative consultant **Harlan Ellison** and writers such as Alan Brennert and George

R.R. Martin, with stories adapted from **Arthur C. Clarke**, **Theodore Sturgeon**, and **Robert Silverberg**, and the directorial contributions of Wes Craven and Joe Dante. It tried to re-create the magic of the original, but failed as often as not. It was a similar story when *The Outer Limits* was revived in the 1990s; both fell prey to budget cuts and the demands of syndication. There was an extremely short-lived comic title (from Now Publishing, 1990) which featured work by Ellison, but it folded soon after its conception along with the publisher.

2000AD – comic (*crtd*1977). The winner, as well as its characters being winners, of numerous Eagle and National Comics Awards (premiere British comics awards), *2000AD* has had several highly successful comic strips including that of **Judge Dredd**. However the publication really came into its own after just a couple of years with its merger with another comic, *Star Lord*. *Star Lord* brought with it characters such as the *Strontium Dogs* (post-nuclear mutant bounty hunters with an alien medic, The Gronk), and *Ro-Busters* (a robotic rescue service (*à la* ***Thunderbirds***)) which were later to evolve into the *ABC Warriors*. For a while *2000AD* even carried **Dan Dare** who survived suspended animation, emerging as a hero tough enough for the 1980s, to once again battle the Mekon. As *2000AD* continued attempts were made to reconcile the time lines of some of the strips so as to bring them into the same universe. However, while such alignments were frequently ill-fitting, they did generate some of *2000AD*'s best work: for instance *Necropolis* with *Judge Dredd* and *Strontium Dog*. Though containing fantasy strips (such as the sword and sorcery series *Slaine*), *2000AD* really scores with its SF. Not only has it created its own classic stories, such as *Skizz* (an alien stranded on contemporary Earth), but it has also recognised SF's literary dimension with occasional story references to authors and novels. Two *Skizz* stories were published, in 1983 and 1991, the latter in full colour. That *Skizz* had its roots firmly embedded in the genre shone through some of the artwork, if not outrightly displayed in some of the editorial banter. Meanwhile *The Ballad of Halo Jones* (young lady works her ticket off Earth and ultimately into a high-gravity war zone) inspired a hit song. Of the other strips *2000AD* ran some stories based on **Harry Harrison's *Stainless Steel Rat***. Then there are the short one off stories such as the 'Future Shock' series, a number of which were quite good. Though, alas one one-off was poorly transferred to the big screen (with no formal involvement with *2000AD*), *Hardware* (*dir*. Richard Stanley, 1990) which concerned a war robot that seals and takes over the dwelling trapping an occupant. *2000AD's* slow conversion over the decades from a largely black and white format to full colour throughout, and better paper quality, in the late 1990s did facilitate more detailed artwork (though sometimes, it must be said, at the expense of the story), but drove the comic's price up in real terms. (It also has to be said that *2000AD* is not afraid of occasionally trying out experimental art styles that really ought to be reserved for the Tate.) Consequently *2000AD* in the 1990s did not have quite as large a reader base as it did in the early 1980s. In 2001 IPC sold *2000AD* to Rebellion who (so far) appear to be sympathetic to *2000AD's* history, writers and artists. With a new lease of life, it still has an almost cult following. Of the too-many-to-list-in-full writers and artists that have shaped *2000AD*, key personnel (droids) include: David Bishop, Brian Bolland, Brett Ewins, Carlos Ezquerra, Tom Frame, Kevin Gosnell, Dave (***Watchmen*** and ***V for Vendetta***) Gibbons, Alan Grant, Peter Knight, Steve MacManus, Mike McMahon, Alan (***Watchmen***) Moore, Pat Mills, Kevin O'Neill, Robin Smith, Tom Tully and John Wagner. Note their names; some have done good work outside of *2000AD* including for North America. It is worth noting that there is a worthy monthly spin-off comic for a slightly older readership called the *Judge Dredd Megazine* which also includes other *2000AD* material and reprints. Borag Thungg Earthlets!

2001: A Space Odyssey – film, UK (1968), *dir.* Stanley (see also **Brian Aldiss**, ***A Clockwork Orange*** and ***Dr. Strangelove***) Kubrick. **Arthur C. Clarke's** short story *The Sentinel* was the humble beginning for this, probably the greatest science fiction film yet made. It won the 1969 Hugo for Best Dramatic Presentation; in 1979 it was voted Best SF Film Ever by the readers of *Starburst* magazine; it came second by ranking (first by weighting) in the *Concatenation* all-time Best SF Film poll, but first in the Blackwood/Flynn poll of WSFS members for the top ten SF films of all time. It was nominated for four Oscars (Best Director, Story and Screenplay, Art Direction/Set Decoration, and Special Visual Effects), winning in the Best Visual Effects category. (The Honorary Oscar for Make-up went to ***Planet of the Apes*** as, apocryphally, the Academy thought Kubrick used real ones!) The so-called 'Dawn of Man' sequence, with proto-hominids gaining intelligence due to their encounter with a black monolith, segues into the balletic docking sequence at an orbiting space station. Dr Hayward Floyd (William Sylvester) travels to the moon where another, buried, monolith has been found which, when uncovered, sends a signal towards Jupiter. The spaceship *Discovery* is sent to investigate, with astronauts Frank Poole (Gary Lockwood) and David Bowman (Keir Dullea), a trio of frozen scientists, and the in-board computer HAL 9000 (using the voice of Douglas Rain). However, due to conflicting instructions, HAL becomes homicidal during the trip, and Bowman must fight for his life when he becomes the last human survivor of the mission. Eventually he discovers a gigantic monolith in the Jupiter system and is whisked, *via* a 'star-gate', to an enigmatic environment where his development is accelerated until he dies, only to be reborn as a Star Child, returning to Earth to contemplate its future. *2001* has been stimulating discussion ever since it first opened, and continues to do so today, over three decades later. The fact of its continued popularity is a mark of the respect engendered by this 'ultimate trip', and no one seriously doubts the enormous impact the film has had, both across the SF genre and in film-making generally. Though words like 'classic' are over used, it would not be inappropriate in this case; nor would 'masterpiece'. Also starring: Leonard Rossiter, Robert Beatty, Daniel Richter, and Ed (*UFO*) Bishop. (See also ***Colossus: The Forbin Project***.)

2010 – film, US (1984), *dir.* Peter (*Outland*) Hyams. Peter Hyams screenplay of **Arthur C Clarke's** novel sequel to *2001: A Space Odyssey*: Clarke actively worked with Hyams on the film. A few years after the events of 2001 astronomers on Earth notice that the abandoned *Discovery* space ship's orbit, between Jupiter and its moon Io, is changing. The Russians have a ship ready to leave Earth for Jupiter but do not have the computer expertise to download *Discovery's* HAL 9000 computer. So, despite growing political tensions with the US, the Russians take some Americans with them. Arriving at the Jupiter system they sense life on another of Jupiter's moons, Europa. It then becomes apparent that the alien monolith is still active. Despite the military tensions back home, the American and Russian crew work together in a race against time before the monolith executes a programme of action. Though not the cinematic classic that Kubrick's *2001* clearly is, *2010* is nonetheless a solid SF offering. Hyams includes some nice touches such as Arthur Clarke feeding the birds in front of the White House (far left on the wide screen version only) and the space scenes are excellent, courtesy of Richard Edlund, but in the end *2001* was too tough an act to follow. Nonetheless, *2010* won the Hugo for Best Dramatic Presentation in 1985. Principal cast: Roy Scheider (Hayward Floyd), John Lithgow, Helen Mirren, Bob (*Close Encounters*) Balaban, Keir Dullea, Douglas Rain, Madolyn Smith and Dana Elcar.

20,000 Leagues Under the Sea novel (1870). **Jules Verne's** powerful story of one Captain Nemo and his super submarine which, mistaken by those sailors who saw it as a monster, roams the seas attacking war ships and vessels containing munitions. Verne clearly views the ocean depths as a frontier capable of being colonised with the use of technology. Indeed the book is most predictive and describes the ship's mysterious power source in sufficient detail that in today's terms it could easily be taken for nuclear power! In 1954 *dir*. Richard (***Soylent Green***, ***Fantastic Voyage***) Fleischer brought the book to the big screen in Walt Disney's first live-action picture. A colourful production with excellent special effects for its time, Fleischer's imagery successfully captures a period SF setting (quite close to the engravings that illustrated the book's first edition). Kirk Douglas plays the sailor who finds himself aboard the Nautilus, while James Mason embraces the part of the idealistic and somewhat tortured Captain Nemo. The film was nominated for 3 Oscars, winning 2 (for special effects and art direction). In 1996 a lack-lustre TV movie (*dir*. Rod Hardy) was released starring Richard Crenna and Ben (Nemo) Cross.

UFO – TV series, UK (*fb*1970), a **Gerry Anderson** series. Aliens have been visiting Earth and harvesting organs (as their race is dying out). To prevent panic a secret organization is set up to defend Earth, SHADO (Supreme Headquarters Alien Defence Organization). With Moon-based rocket fighters, a submarine fleet and ground forces, the fight is on to protect Earth. Unlike his other series, UFO's plot develops over several episodes across two series, and his characters, though somewhat wooden are far less two-dimensional compared to the characters in his previous puppet series such as ***Thunderbirds***. (For instance the Commander loses his wife due to the pressures of his job, and then in another episode fails to save his son.) Principal cast: Ed (*2001*) Bishop, George Sewell, Peter Gordeno, Wanda Ventham, and Gabrielle Drake.

UK (see also **Conventions, Clubs** and **fandom**). The UK SF community meets both in clubs and societies (mainly centred in pubs) and at conventions. There is usually a convention somewhere in the UK most weekends. Most conventions are specialised, be they focusing on a TV series, or a specialised aspect of the genre (such as role-playing-games). The principal film convention is the **Festival of Fantastic Films** (a small, almost international, event held in Manchester in the autumn since 1990). However the Fest's future is currently (2005) not assured though Bradford does have SF film events and London has had four annual film fests since 2002. Also since 2002 *SFX* magazine has run an annual TV dominated SF convention. The principal book orientated convention is the Novacon (run by the Birmingham SF Society in November). While the main 'bringing together of all the UK SF clans' event is the long-running, annual **Eastercon** held since 1948 over the long Easter Bank Holiday weekend: though these days it is no longer the largest convention and sometimes fails to encourage film and TV SF. Attendance which consequently has dwindled since the mid-1990s especially as there are these other events. The vagaries of the different organising committees means that most conventions are very variable in quality and so no one should be considered typical even within a series. The main SF organization is the British SF Association which produces both news and reviews magazines (*www.bsfa.co.uk*).

Ultraviolet – TV series, UK (*fb*1999). Joe Aherne's complex screenplay unfolds over just 6 episodes as a modern scientific take on the concept of vampires (though the word is never used, instead they refer to 'code Vs'). Apparently 'code Vs' have co-evolved with humanity. Yes they are immortal. Yes, they drink human blood. Yes they cannot stand sunlight. No, they are not affected by crucifixes, unless the 'code V' has religious beliefs. No, they cannot be seen in mirrors or on TV (this is the weakest element in the entire premise). The 'code Vs' have been living quietly through the centuries, but in modern times their food source (us) has become contaminated with pollutants and so they act. "Believe me, our free range days are over." Detective sergeant Michael Coldfield discovers a secret organization, the CIB (funded by the Vatican, it is alluded), while trying to find out why his best friend has disappeared. He gets recruited into it. Other members of the CIB team also have their own reasons: a husband of one became a code V, another has to choose between becoming a code V or dying of a form of leukaemia. Intelligently written, the series contains numerous twists and it is best never to make assumptions. Principal cast: Jack Davenport, Susannah Harker, Idris Elba and Philip Quast.

Unknown Worlds of Science Fiction – comic/magazine, US (*crtd*1975). Not to be confused with the 1939 pulp magazine, *Unknown Worlds*, this short-lived comic mag had six issues in 1975 and one 'special' in January 1976, presenting a mixture of original work and SF adaptations within a framing device based on **Bob Shaw**'s "slow glass", as featured in his classic *Light of Other Days* (1966), itself adapted in the first issue (along with ***The Day of the Triffids***). Other adaptations include: **Alfred Bester**'s *Adam and no Eve* (1941), **Harlan Ellison**'s *"Repent, Harlequin!" Said the Ticktockman* (1965), Neal Adams' adaptation of **Larry Niven**'s *All the Myriad Ways* (1970), **Michael Moorcock**'s *Behold the Man* (1966), and Frederic Brown's *Arena* (1944) among others. Probably the best of the original tales was *War Toy* in issue 2, by Tony Isabella and George Perez. The magazine section contained news and reviews, reader's letters, and interviews with notables such as **Ray Bradbury, Frank Kelly Freas, Frank Herbert** and **Theodore Sturgeon**, among others. Though not published under the Marvel imprint, the names on the masthead, such as Stan Lee and Roy Thomas, are well known from there (the actual imprint, Curtis, was used for some Marvel magazines, such as *Marvel Preview* which also adapted SF stories). Though this title is much sought after, all issues can still be found with a judicious search at comic marts and conventions, and are not (yet) overpriced. This is a good starting point for SF readers who are wary of comics, partly due to the familiarity of the subject matter, and the gorgeous artwork throughout is sure to seduce the reader further.

Uplift War, The – novel (1987) by **David Brin**. This is the climax of the original 'Uplift' trilogy begun in *Sundiver* (1980) which introduces the complex 'Uplift' universe, in which most intelligent life has been uplifted to sentience by one of five Patron races, themselves being the product of a now-vanished race known as the Progenitors. Humans, however, seem to have arisen solely through evolution, and have themselves uplifted Terran dolphins and chimpanzees. The second novel, ***Startide Rising*** (1983) which, like *The Uplift War* won both the Hugo and topped the annual *Locus* readers poll for best novel, also won the Nebula. In this a human and dolphin led ship has discovered a Progenitor artefact which may prove that Humanity is also a Progenitor-created race. This 'heresy' leads to the events in *The Uplift War* in which the colony of Garth, mainly composed of humans and uplifted chimps, is invaded and occupied by hostile aliens in the service of openly corrupt Patron races. But this is just one small conflict in a struggle that embraces Earth and all the Five Galaxies... The conflict spills over into three further Uplift books: the Hugo-nominated *Brightness Reef* (1995), *Infinity's Shore* (1996) and *Heaven's Reach* (1998).

US (see also **Conventions, Clubs** and **fandom**). The US SF community is the largest of any nation. SF fans meet both in clubs and societies (mainly centred in cafes) and at conventions. There is usually a convention somewhere in the US most weekends. One of the more organised western US clubs is the San Francisco Bay Area SF Association and its web page is as good a place as any to start surfing for further information *www.basfa.org*. On the east coast there is the New England SF Association *www.nesfa.org*. The US has one advantage over the rest of the world in that, having the largest SF community and with many hotels large enough for conventions a few thousand strong, the US happens to host the **World SF Convention** (**Worldcon**) more than two years out of three. Even when the Worldcon is held outside the US, US fans hold their own event, the North American Science Fiction Convention (the **NASFiC**). Other annual conventions of note include: Westercon which is usually held in July west of the 104th meridian and in odd numbered years north of the 37th parallel, Boskone (held in Boston); Corflu (the SF fanzine convention); Baycon (San José); LosCon (Los Angeles), and Minicon (Minneapolis). See *Locus* magazine for a more complete US listing (*www.locusmag.com*).

van Vogt, A.E. – author, Canada (1912-2000). Alfred Elton van Vogt was born in Winnipeg, but moved to the US in 1944, nearly five years after publishing his first SF story, *Black Destroyer*

(1939), in *Astounding Science Fiction* (see **Analog**). Along with other writers such as **Robert Heinlein** and **Isaac Asimov**, van Vogt was an integral part of the **"Golden Age"** of SF. He is known for writing in 800 word blocks so as to keep each page fresh and the pace fast. Much of his work is thematically linked **space opera**, incorporating ideas about mutants, evolution and supermen; galactic empires; mental disciplines, extrasensory perception and psi powers. His first novel, *Slan* (1946), originally published in 1940, is the story of Jommy Cross, a mutant with mental and physical powers superior to humans. However, Slans are hated by humans and are hunted down unmercifully. Where **Sturgeon's** mutants are often unfairly persecuted, and usually triumph due to love and understanding, van Vogt's seem to bring their persecution upon themselves, often through arrogance. *The Weapon Shops of Isher* (1951) and its sequel, *The Weapon Makers* also known as *One Against Eternity* (1947), is quite different. In this far future, the House of Isher has governed the solar system for nearly five thousand years, and its dictatorial ambitions are held in check by the Weapon Shops, who will sell anyone a 'defensive' weapon that is immensely superior to those of the Empire. The irony is that both institutions were founded by the same immortal man. Shortly after his move to the US, van Vogt began the series of stories that eventually gave rise to three novels set in the Null-A universe. *The World of Null-A* (1948) and its sequels, *The Pawns of Null-A* (1956 – also known as *The Players of Null-A*) and *Null-A Three* (1984), are grand **space opera** with a quasi-immortal protagonist with special mental abilities, galactic-scale space battles, empires and aliens. But the tales turn around the concepts of General Semantics (a linguistic/philosophical movement founded by Alfred Korzybski in 1938 based on ideas contained in his *Science and Sanity* (1933)). *The Voyage of the Space Beagle* (1950) is a fairly typical collection of van Vogt's short stories, though he won a legal claim that Ridley Scott's ***Alien*** (1979) was at least partially based on its first story. During most of the fifties and the early part of the sixties, van Vogt continued to publish "fix-ups" (his term) of magazine stories rewritten with the addition of new material. From the mid-sixties on, van Vogt resumed publishing original material, but with the so-called **new wave**, SF had changed so that offerings like *The Silkie* (1969) came across as, at best, juvenile. This is not to say that van Vogt did not continue to produce some good material, such as *Tyranopolis* (1973) and

Computerworld (1983), but that these stories often seemed more nostalgic than contemporary.

Verne, Jules – author, France (1828-1905). Born and raised in Nantes, Verne is usually cited as one of the two 'founding fathers' of SF (the other being **H.G. Wells**), though groundwork had certainly already been laid by such as Mary Shelley and Edgar Allan Poe. Verne's tales are usually travel romances and, to some extent, their popularity in English-speaking countries is based on poor translations and movie adaptations. He certainly had a belief in the concept of Progress, and of the utility of science and technology in that endeavour and, in that sense, some of his work can rightly be seen as SF. Of particular interest are: ***Journey to the Centre of the Earth*** (1863), in which explorers enter the Earth's crust through an extinct volcano; *From the Earth to the Moon* (1865) and its sequel, *Around the Moon* (1869), the former being filmed as long ago as 1902 by Georges Méliès as *Le Voyage dans la Lune*; ***20,000 Leagues Under the Sea*** (1870) (filmed in 1916 and by Disney in 1954) and its sequel, *The Mysterious Island* (1874) (a dire film version of which appeared in 1928 as well as a passable one in 1961), about Captain Nemo and his submarine the *Nautilus*; and *Robur the Conqueror* (1886) and its sequel, *The Master of the World* (1904), about Robur and his fabulous airship (filmed in 1961 as *Master of the World*, starring Vincent Price and adapted by **Richard Matheson**). Verne's work was, in the main, quite optimistic, but towards the end of his career his visions had become much darker and dealt often with the corrupting influence of power. He died in 1905 (by which time Wells had produced his most famous works) fortuitously missing the First World War, which would certainly have confirmed his darkest speculations.

V for Vendetta – comic, UK/US (*crtd*1981). Created originally for the comic magazine *Warrior* in 1981, by *2000AD* alumni Alan Moore and David Lloyd, *V* suffered a five year gap of publication following *Warrior*'s demise, but was completed for DC comics in 1987-88. In the near future (then 1997) Britain is a fascist state recovering from (an implied) nuclear winter, and the government experiments on people in concentration camps. One such victim becomes "V", an anarchist-terrorist or perhaps freedom fighter, challenging the authority of the state. This wide-ranging tale of hypocrisy and obsession has no easy, linear, storyline and neither does it have any clear ending. In its original form, the artwork was printed in black and white, which influenced Lloyd's style very positively, but colour was added when DC took over the reigns. Luckily Lloyd himself oversaw the wonderful, contrasting pastel colouring which complemented the chiaroscuro style of the original art. *V for Vendetta* is still available today in a collected volume. Alan Moore went on to revolutionise the industry, with others, in the mid-eighties with his work on DC's *Swamp Thing* and the seminal title **Watchmen**.

Village of the Damned – film, UK (1960). *di*r. Wolf Rilla. Based on **John Wyndham's** *The Midwich Cuckoos* (1957), a village is mysteriously cut off by some sort of field. Inside the villagers fall asleep. When the field disappears and everyone wakes up, all the women discover that they are pregnant. Their subsequent children all have blonde hair and are amazingly bright. As time goes on it turns out that they have paranormal powers and plan to take over the world. Who will stop them and how? This is one of the few UK SF fantastic films to be made compared to Hollywood's output at the time. Nonetheless its quality (again for its time) surpasses that of many of its US counterparts. Unfortunately at the time the **World SF Convention** (**Worldcon**) was being staged in the US for a number of years in a row and the Hugos for Best Dramatic Presentation went regularly to episodes of the *Twilight Zone*, nonetheless this work remains a favourite at the Festival of Fantastic Films. Principal cast: George Sanders, Barbara Shelley, Michael Gwyn, Laurence Naismith, John Phillips, Richard Vernon, Jenny Laird, Richard Warner, Thomas Heathcote and Martin Stephens.. (There was a sequel, *Children of the Damned*, in 1964, *dir*. Anton M Leader starring Ian Hendry. Here the children are born around the world, but are brought together in London by Ian Hendry and Alan Badel. Though the children pose no threat, it is decided to destroy them anyway, and only Hendry and Barbara Ferris even try to defend them.) Another re-make, *Village of the Damned* (1995) transferred the plot to modern America. *dir*. John (*The Thing*, *Dark Star*) Carpenter. Principal cast: Christopher (*Superman*) Reeve, Linda Kozlowski, Kirstie (*Star Trek II*) Alley and Mark (*Star Wars*) Hamill.)

Vinge, Joan D – author, US (*b*1948). Joan Vinge graduated from San Diego State University with a degree in anthropology and married author and editor **Vernor Vinge** in 1972. A year after her divorce from Vernor (and subsequent marriage to SF editor, Jim Frenkle), Joan published *The Snow Queen* (1980) which won the 1981 Hugo for Best Novel. In fact her 1977 novelette, *Eyes of Amber* (1977), had already won her a Hugo in 1978 for Best Novelette. It concerns a virtually destitute woman who takes command of her life and, in the process, rediscovers how her home world relates to the greater community of humanity beyond. However the promise of these two Hugos remained unfulfilled when Joan turned her attention to juvenile books and film tie-ins. Most of her original work is probably best seen as science fantasy, taking an anthropological slant on fairy tales translated to an SF setting.

Vinge, Vernor – author, US (*b*1947). A professor of Mathematics at San Diego University, Vinge began publishing SF in 1965 with *Apartness* for *New Worlds* magazine, and was a frequent contributor to *Astounding Science Fiction* (see ***Analog***). Though he published his first novel, *Grimm's World*, as long ago as 1969, it was not until the mid-1980s (after his marriage to Joan D. Vinge, 1972-79) that he came to prominence. *The Peace War* (1984) and its sequel, *Marooned in Realtime* (1986), were both nominated for Hugos and tell the tale of the development of impenetrable spheres inside which time stands still, to be used as a defensive weapon, though they are soon used offensively; and, in the sequel, are woven into a time-travel tale that explores the near extinction of Humankind. These two novels were released in a collected edition as *Across Realtime* (1993) following the success of Vinge's 1993 Hugo Award winning novel, *A Fire Upon the Deep* (1992). This **space opera** is set in a galaxy where humans are a minor player in the fight against 'The Blight', a civilisation-destroying intelligence that threatens to overwhelm the other races, by exploiting their galaxy-spanning 'internet'. Set in the same universe, but 300,000 years before these events, *A Deepness in the Sky* (1999) is the story of Pham Nuwen of the Qeng Ho trading fleet and their trials against the Emergents above the world of Arachna. Vinge is not the most prolific of authors, but he does produce considered 'hard' SF that can be quite telling. His short stories are available in two collections, *True Names and Other Dangers* (1987) – not to be confused with his 1981 novel, *True Names* – and *Threats and Other Promises* (1988).

Vonnegut, Kurt – author, US (*b*1922). As sophisticated as **Philip K Dick**, and occasionally as humorous as Douglas (*Hitch-Hiker's Guide to the Galaxy*) Adams, Kurt Vonnegut is one of those few authors as recognised by mainstream readers as he is by SF. Yet clearly one of his best known novels, *The Sirens of Titan* (1962), must be SF. It sees the stranding of an alien ship on Titan for over 20,000 years. This extraterrestrial machine causes the 'uplift' (see **Brin**) of humanity from primitive apes merely so that someone can carry out repairs so it can continue its mission. It also introduces the alien Tralfamadorians, who return in later works (including *Slaughter House 5*). Nonetheless, despite the material he worked on Vonnegut himself claimed no particular allegiance to SF. Perhaps this was because much of his writing was inspired by observations on life and society. His novel *Slaughter House 5* (1965) – also known as *The Children's Crusade: A Duty-Dance with Death* – was itself more than a little autobiographical, with one major plot strand relating the experiences of an American prisoner of war during the bombing of Dresden, just as Vonnegut himself had been. It was nominated both for a Hugo and a Nebula, but the film of that book won the Best Dramatic Presentation Hugo in 1973. He also won other awards for *Cat's Cradle*, and *The Sirens of Titan*. In *Cat's Cradle* (1963), the race is on to find the children of Dr. Felix Hoenikker, inventor of 'ice-nine' which could conceivably destroy the world. In a number of Vonnegut's stories a hack SF writer appears called Kilgore Trout, including his most recent *Timequake* (1997). Allegedly loosely based on the SF writer **Theodore Sturgeon**, though a hack Kilgore Trout speaks the truth out of the side of his mouth. In *Timequake*, Trout appears as the only human aware that time has looped back on itself, and that everyone is being forced to re-experience events again, though they cannot change them. On the film front, of interest is *Harrison Bergeron* (1995). It was based on a Vonnegut story concerning a 21st century government that exerts its control by (mechanically) discouraging individual thought, creativity and talent. However the mother of one bright student realises that his intelligence may get him into trouble and (unwittingly) puts him into the hands of those who really run things and cherish his abilities, providing, that is, he plays ball. Is society really going this way...? *dir*. Bruce Pittman. Principal cast: Sean Astin, Linda Goranson, Christopher Plummer, Miranda dePencier, Buck Henry, Eugene Levy, Howie Mandel and Andrea Martin.

Vor Game, The – novel (1990) by **Lois McMaster Bujold**. Banished from his home world, ***Barrayar***, the somewhat disadvantaged, but brilliant diplomat-strategist, Miles Vorkosigan seeks out his old friends the Free Dendarii Mercenaries. Unfortunately Emperor Gregor, also an old friend, has been the victim of foul play and may die. If Gregor dies Miles may become the new Emperor, which is something that Miles definitely does not want to be! *The Vor Game* continued to reveal Bujold as an intelligent writer who spices her novels with a dash of wit. It won the Hugo for Best Novel in 1991.

Wanderer, The – novel (1964) by **Fritz Leiber**. This book is about the catastrophic incursion into our solar system of two planet-sized spaceships, or rather planets that have been converted into spaceships, and the conflicts engendered by them. It is also something of a melancholic love story between an inhabitant of one of the planets and an Earthman. The story is told from numerous viewpoints in a complexly fragmented narrative that has since been copied many times but, arguably, never bettered. By the time the Wanderers leave the system, a minor but destructive war has taken place, with many dead on all sides, Earth has lost its moon, and the romance has blossomed. *The Wanderer* won the 1965 Hugo for Best Novel, and it remains one of Leiber's most enervating and imaginative SF tales.

War of the Worlds, The – novel (1898) by **H.G. Wells**. Set at the end of the nineteenth century, *The War of the Worlds* charts one man's struggle to survive a Martian invasion of England. From the Martian's first arrival, in Woking, through to their advance on London (and other capital cities from other landing sites), mankind can do little but run from the Martian heat-ray mechanical tripods. Wells depicts the invasion of England with great attention to local detail; the idea being to give the novel as realistic a feel as possible despite the outlandish concept. Apparently the idea came from a discussion Wells had with his brother, in which his brother was welcoming the news of real-life British troops on a particularly vicious victory (some might say massacre). Wells, sensitive to human rights, asked how his brother would feel if Britain was treated this way. His brother laughed saying that nothing could beat the British army. Wells then wrote *The War of the Worlds* in which British troops were ineffective. The novel was famously adapted to radio by Orson

Wells in 1938, just before Halloween, and is famous as the broadcast that panicked America. *The War of the Worlds* has also been a film (*dir.* George Pal, 1953), starring Gene Barry, which won an Oscar for Special Effects, courtesy of Gordon Jennings. The film is on the list of all time best attended of movies screened at the Festival of Fantastic Films, and it won a retro-Hugo (an unofficial Hugo voted on at the 2004 Worldcon 50 years on from the 1954 Worldcon which did present Hugos for SF in 2003). It also inspired a short-lived but fondly remembered comics series (*Killraven the Hunter*, Marvel Comics by Don McGregor), a 'concept' album of songs and spoken-word featuring Richard Burton (Jeff Wayne, 1978), as well as a lacklustre sequel US TV series (1988-90) starring Jared Martin. Notwithstanding the afore, the mechanical tripods in John Christopher's juvenile-SF tetralogy *The Tripods*, especially as portrayed in the 1984 BBC series, could be said to have been inspired by Wells' three-legged Martian machines. A true classic of the genre, *The War of the Worlds* is still in print today.

Watchmen – graphic novel (1986) by writer Alan Moore and artist Dave Gibbons (both **2000AD**). Originally published in 12 monthly issues, *Watchmen* is truly deserving of the title of graphic novel. Set in an alternate world of 1985, which has had 'superheroes' since the thirties, an ex-hero (now covert government operative) called the Comedian is killed. Colleagues Rorschach and Nite Owl begin an investigation that gradually draws in all the heroes, while the USA and USSR creep closer to nuclear armageddon... As the narrative moves back and forth in time, we discover some disturbing things about the heroes' world, the police's attitude toward the vigilantes, and the fears of the general population. Gibbons work is detailed with subtlety, and Moore's writing was even more sophisticated than his work on *V for Vendetta* (1981). *Watchmen* was awarded a Hugo in 1988 in the special Other Forms category.

Watson, Ian – author, UK (*b*1943). Though not quite meeting the restricted criteria this guide has set itself to define 'core', or 'best', for 'essential' SF (see the section 'About this guide and its use'), Watson comes close on a number of criteria for a more substantial inclusion. Indeed, he has been involved in projects with those who are elsewhere in this guide – hence justification for this mention. He wrote the screenplay for the Stanley (***2001:***

A Space Odyssey, *Dr Strangelove* and *A Clockwork Orange*) Kubrick project that Steven (see **Brian Aldiss**, *Close Encounters of the Third Kind*, *The Twilight Zone*, *Jurassic Park*, *Raiders of the Lost Ark*, and ***Indiana Jones and the Last Crusade***)) Spielberg took forward as the film *AI*: the treatment was loosely developed from a treatment Kubrick had considered of the **Aldiss** short story *Super-Toys Last All Summer Long*. Of note is Watson's the 1978 award-winning short story *The Very Slow Time Machine* which itself was the title story in a 1979 anthology of his shorts. This was a very inventive treatment of the time machine concept and begins with the time traveller and his machine appearing, and though the traveller himself appears to be moving backwards he has a message for those in the narrator's present. . His novel *The Jonah Kit* (1975) won the fan-voted British SF Association Award for 1978. It describes how a Russian astronaut mind-melds with a whale long before Spock did in the film ***Star Trek IV: The Voyage Home***. Only this time it was not just the species that was saved but a universe.

Way Station – (1963) by **Clifford D Simak**. Enoch Wallace puzzled the authorities. There appeared to be few records of him, and the picture they had pieced together – if it was to be believed – was that he was well over 100 years old, although he only looked 30. He lived alone in a farm in a secluded part of the countryside. His only source of income seemed to be gems which his postman sold for him. At the back of his home was a small grave-yard which contained the remains of his parents and, Government agents discover, those of a 'monster'. The authorities did not know it, but Enoch manned a 'Way Station' for the interstellar community. As such, he was the nearest thing Earth had to an ambassador. But disturbing the graves of another intelligent species is considered a major offence and Earth comes under the close scrutiny of off-world powers. *Way Station* is a typical Simak book, with its rural setting and the juxtaposition between the mundane and the exotic. At its heart is, these days, a fairly standard concept – teleportation. But with *Way Station* Simak produced the quintessential, tightly written treatment. All told, *Way Station* is one of those rare books one can recommend a non-SF reader as an introduction to genre literature. Not only did *Way Station* win the Hugo Award in 1964 for 'Best Novel' but Simak's fellow American SF writers must have enjoyed it too as it also won the Nebula. *Way Station* made it to the top 20 in the *Concatenation* all-time poll.

Weapon Shops of Isher, The – novel (1951) by **A E van Vogt**. 7,000 years into the future the Earth is dominated by the Empress Innelda Isher. Farra Clarke is the owner of an ordinary atomic engine repair shop in an ordinary village far from the capital city. But one day the life of the village is turned upside down by the sudden appearance of a weapon shop. Totally invulnerable to every known weapon, the weapon shops offer to sell certain individuals arms that are unequalled even by the Empire's own military. But these weapons can not be used against other people except in self defence. Farra enters the weapon shop to remonstrate with the owner and finds that he is a marked man. The news in the village is that Farra is in league with the weapon shop people. Then things start to get really bad. His son, Cayle, seeking a commission in the army, steals money from Farra's bank account. The bank forecloses on Farra's loan and sells his business to his competitor who promptly shuts it down. Seeking to kill himself, Farra returns to the weapon shop. There he begins to learn the truth about the weapon shops. They are a mysterious organisation that acts as a counter balance to the power of the Empire. He also uncovers the corruption at the heart of the Empire. Only Robert Hedrock, one of the weapon shops' Council, has the perspective to resolve the situation. *The Weapon Shops of Isher* (1951) plot was followed by the sequel *The Weapon Makers* (1947). Do not get confused by the publication dates of the novels; they are fix-ups of magazine stories from 1941-43, but the second half was published in book form first. In *The Weapon Makers*, humans are on the verge of developing interstellar travel: a development that Empress Innelda wishes to control, and which will trigger a crisis in the *status quo*. At the same time an alien race notices humans for the first time and, again, only Hedrock (himself hunted by the Weapon Shops) can find a way to a satisfactory outcome. Both these books pre-dated the Hugo Awards but, such is its critical acclaim, it would be nice to think that at least the first would have won one, had they existed at the time.

Weird Science – comic, US (*crtd* 1950). In May-June of 1950, Bill Gaines' EC Comics began publishing sister SF titles *Weird Science* and *Weird Fantasy*. Due to name changes from previous titles the first issues of each are numbered 12 and 13 respectively. *Weird Science* began re-numbering with issue 5 (though the cover did not bear this number), and *Weird Fantasy* with issue 6 (ditto).

Consequently there are two different nos.12-15 of the former, and nos.13-17 of the latter. Some SF writers' work was freely adapted, such as that of **Ray Bradbury** and **Richard Matheson** (Bradbury's name became associated with the comics once he'd noticed what was going on and had come to an arrangement with Gaines), and some SF authors wrote directly for the comics, notably Otto Binder and **Harry Harrison.** (Harrison even drew for *Weird Science* with Wally Wood.) Gaines effectively invented the modern comic and, as well as attracting good writers, he was blessed with a brilliant stable of artists, including Wally Wood and Frank Frazetta. Though fairly innocuous by today's standards, comics in the mid-fifties attracted harsh criticism from those who believed they had a corrupting influence on children (Frederick Wertham, author of *Seduction of the Innocent*, an attack on the comics industry, also worked with Senator McCarthy and Richard Nixon on the 'House Un-American Affairs Committee'). Though the industry was already self-regulating through the Association of Comics Magazine Publishers, changes occurred in 1953 which led to the formation of the much more strict Comics Code Authority. *Weird Science* combined with *Weird Fantasy* with their respective issue(s) 23 (Spring 1954) as *Weird Science-Fantasy* and, following another name change, to *Incredible Science Fiction* with issue 30 (July-August 1955), the now familiar 'stamp' of the CCA started to appear on the covers. Due to poor sales the comic died with issue 33 (Jan-Feb 1956). However, all issues of all EC titles are still available today, either as single comics published by Gladstone, or in the hardbound volumes of Russ Cochran's Complete EC Library.

Wells, Herbert George – author, UK (1866-1946). Along with **Jules Verne**, Wells is surely the co-founder of modern science fiction, though being before that term was coined Wells' work was known as scientific romance. Science was one of Wells' earliest influences, indeed his lecturers included the Darwinist Thomas Henry Huxley. However, his imagination was as much informed by socialism, and the twin themes of socialism and science run throughout his work. There is usually only one 'impossible' hypothesis in each of his tales (invisibility, hibernation, antigravity *etc*), which are then portrayed in a recognisable, contemporary setting (unless deliberately set in an alien landscape or, possibly, the future but with a protagonist contemporary to the reader). A science journalist and essayist from 1891, Wells began writing short SF in 1894, and the following year wrote the novel ***The Time Machine: An Invention***. His speculations about the future evolution of humankind are somewhat tragic and tragedy runs through much of his work. Certainly it was central to *The Island of Dr. Moreau* (1896) in which a castaway lands on an island where a scientist is creating genetically modified animals. This was first filmed in 1932 as *Island of Lost Souls*, dir. Erle C Kenton, starring Charles Laughton, Richard Arlen and Bela (***Son of Frankenstein***) Lugosi. Co-scripted by SF author Philip Wylie; it was next filmed in 1977 under the original title, dir. Don Taylor, with poor performances by Burt Lancaster, playing Moreau the mad scientist, and Michael York; a further version appeared in 1996, dir. John Frankenheimer, in a modern setting. (Principal cast: Marlon (***Superman***) Brando, Val Kilmer, David Thewlis, Fairuza Balk and Ron Perlman). Wells' brother once remarked that, 'to Verne invisibility would have been an adventure into the unknown', but in ***The Invisible Man: A Grotesque Romance*** (1897) it is a tragedy with dire consequences for the protagonist. In 1898 Wells published both ***The Man Who Could Work Miracles*** and his classic tale of alien invasion, ***The War of the Worlds***. *When the Sleeper Wakes* (1899, a.k.a. *The Sleeper Awakes* 1910) was the inspiration for Woody Allen's film ***Sleeper*** (1973), though they share little in common, other than a protagonist 'sleeping' through to the future. Wells has always provided inspiration for film makers, and his novel ***The First Men in the Moon*** (1901) was no exception, being filmed as *First Men in the Moon* (1964), dir. Nathan (***20 Million Miles to Earth***) Juran, co-scripted by Nigel (***Quatermass***) Kneale with special effects by Ray (***The Beast from 20,000 Fathoms***) Harryhausen, starring Lionel Jeffries. Wells joined the intellectual, socialist Fabian Society in 1903, and his work became slightly more pessimistic, while at the same time concentrating on future societies and social inequality, though there were also many utopian elements. His most utopian work (though still containing a pessimistic thread) was probably *The Shape of Things to Come* (1933), which Wells adapted for the screen and was filmed under his close supervision as ***Things to Come*** (1936). Wells, though always popular in Britain, also influenced the development of SF in America as much of his work was published by **Hugo Gernsback**, serialised in ***Amazing Stories***. Wells, the most British and influential of SF authors, was the 9th most cited author in the *Concatenation* poll, and has appeared as a character himself in many SF works, notably ***Time After Time*** (story 1976, filmed 1979).

Westercon – see **US**.

Westworld – film, US (1973), *dir.* **Michael Crichton**. In the holiday resort of Delos, you can relax in one of three fantasy worlds peopled with robots: Roman World, Medieval World, or West World. Two businessmen (James Brolin and Richard Benjamin) on holiday in West World run across a single-minded gunslinger (Yul Brynner) and Benjamin kills him. But things are going wrong at the resort, such as a pleasure-robot refusing a seduction, and the next day Brynner returns to kill Brolin, the safeguards having failed. Benjamin finds himself hunted through a robot revolt, and even the staff are overwhelmed as their former slaves turn. This Festival of Fantastic Films favourite was followed by an extremely poor sequel, *Futureworld* (1976), featuring Brynner with Peter Fonda in a plot where robots are being substituted for world leaders, but is best missed. An MGMTV series, *Beyond Westworld* (1980), aired 3 of only 5 episodes made before dying, which tells you all you need to know. Crichton returned to the idea of a theme park getting out of control for ***Jurassic Park*** (1990).

Weyr Search – novella (1967) by Anne McCaffrey. Introducing the world of Pern, this Hugo-winning novella and its Nebula-winning novella counterpart *Dragon Rider* (1968), formed the basis of the first Pern novel, *Dragonflight* (1968). On Pern, a 'lost' human colony, biogenetically engineered dragons are pair-bonded with their human riders at birth. Their fiery breath was needed in times past to scorch out the threat of an interplanetary fungus, known as Threads. But, centuries after the last Thread outbreak has been seen, the Dragon Riders have become decadent and a new threat can only be met if they first find a Weyr Woman to lead them back to glory. While probably best seen as fantasy, the various dragon/Pern novels do have a fairly solid grounding in SF, as far as the biotechnology used in the creation of the dragons goes, and they remain popular with both SF and Fantasy fans alike (at least four of the series have been nominated for Hugos). *Weyr Search* shared the 1968 Hugo for Best Novella with **Philip José Farmer's *Riders of the Purple Wage*** (1967).

Where Late the Sweet Birds Sang – novel (1976) by Kate Wilhelm. Wife of Damon Knight, Wilhelm started writing SF in 1956. *Where Late...* is itself comprised of three novella-length sequences. In a post-holocaust world, high in the Appalachians, a small colony of clones are trying to survive until civilisation can spread again. But, in their isolation, they have become inward-looking, and the community begins to find itself trapped and its development stunted... *Where Late the Sweet Birds Sang* won the 1977 Hugo (and Jupiter) Award for Best Novel, and also topped the annual *Locus* readers poll.

Whelan, Michael – illustrator, US (*b*1950). Whelan's SF career started in 1975 with book covers for DAW, following a stint at the Los Angeles Art Centre College of Design, prior to which he had studied Art and Biology at San José State University. He is noted for his covers on the re-issues of Edgar Rice Burroughs' 'John Carter/Barsoom' books and **Michael Moorcock's** 'Elric' titles. In addition to pictures, Whelan has produced sculptures some of which have been mass-produced and are commercially available. He has won 12 Hugos for Best Professional Artist (most of them in the 1980s with the exception of 1987), which is one more than **Frank Kelly Freas**, and one Hugo in 1988 for Best Non-Fiction Book, *Michael Whelan's Works of Wonder* (1987). His most recent Hugo was in 2000. Also, he has topped the annual *Locus* readers poll for Best Artist on many occasions, usually by substantial margins. His 1992 Hugo was awarded in the category of Best Original Artwork (only the second time this category has been awarded) for his piece *Summer Queen*. His earlier, non-Hugo, work has been collected as *Wonderworks* (1979).

Who Framed Roger Rabbit – film, US (1988), *dir.* Robert (***Back to the Future***, ***Contact***) Zemeckis. Based on Gary K Wolf's story, *Who Censored Roger Rabbit?*, this fantasy supposes that movie cartoons actually co-exist with us in the real world. Most of them live in Toon Town near Hollywood (where else?). Roger Rabbit is one such cartoon character and, yes, he gets framed for murder. There is someone out to control Toon Town. Someone who hates Toons. However, a human private detective comes to Roger's rescue and together they track down the bad guy... Fantasy borders science fiction, and there is no doubt that the mix of real-life cinematography and cartoons is ingenious. It captured a huge audience on release, including many within the SF community.

Not surprisingly it won the Hugo for Best Dramatic Presentation in 1989. Principal cast: Bob (***The Lost World***) Hoskins, Christopher (***Back to the Future***) Lloyd, Charles Fleischer (voice of Roger R.), Stubby Kaye and Joanna Cassidy.

Wild Shore, The – novel (1984) by **Kim Stanley Robinson.** Published the same year as **William Gibson's** *Neuromancer* and also as part of the New Ace Science Fiction Specials series, *The Wild Shore* missed most of the awards, but did top the annual *Locus* readers' poll. It is a dystopian look at an alternate future in Orange County, California where a small community of post-war survivors develop their own culture, and dream about what might have been. In fact, two more 'Orange County' books followed, *The Gold Coast* (1988), which presents a more business-as-usual future, and *Pacific Edge* (1990) a decidedly utopian view. Robinson re-visits a lot of the same ground in his more successful *Mars* trilogy, but for many the earlier series is qualitatively better.

Willis, Connie – author, US (*b*1945). Having had a number of short stories published in the 1970s, she began to move towards novels in the 1980s. If there are themes to her writing then they may include humour and juxtaposing characters with settings as in her Hugo-winning ***Passage*** and ***To Say Nothing of the Dog*** novels. Here time travel is one of the tropes she enjoys exploring. Her ***Doomsday Book*** (1992) sees a time traveller visit England in the grips of the Black Death, our protagonist survives but not without experiencing the anguish. Even a knowledge of modern medicine cannot help the plague's victims.

Wingrove, David – author, UK (*b*1954), see ***Trillion Year Spree***.

Wolfe, Gene – author, US (*b*1931). Wolfe graduated in mechanical engineering from the University of Houston and was for a while senior editor for *Plant Engineering Magazine*. He began writing SF at the beginning of the 1970s and won his first major award, a Nebula, for *The Death of Doctor Island* (1973) in which a boy from an artificial environment is treated for psychological disturbance. Perhaps best known for the multi-award winning tetralogy ***The Book of the New Sun*** (1980-1983) of which *The Claw of the Conciliator* (1981) and *The Sword of the Lictor* (1982) topped the annual *Locus* readers poll in the 'fantasy novel' category. A collection of his short stories can be found in *The*

Island of Doctor Death and Other Stories (1980). *Soldier of the Mist* (1986) topped the *Locus* readers poll that year about a man, Latro, who is condemned to having a memory that only lasts for 24 hours. Wolfe was also voted 7th most popular author in the *Concatenation* readers' poll.

World of Null-A, The – novel (1948) by **A.E. van Vogt**. The author based the (not inconsiderable) action of the Null-A books around the concepts of General Semantics, as developed by Count Alfred Korzybski in his 1933 work *Science and Sanity*. It is largely concerned with the rejection of two-value, either/or 'Aristotelian' logic in favour of non-Aristotelian (Null-A) thinking, which is perception-based. It is Null-A thinking that is the protagonist Gilbert Gosseyn's 'secret weapon', more than his 'extra' brain which can control enormous energies and allows instantaneous teleportation. In *The World of Null-A*, Gosseyn quickly finds that he is not who he appears to be and, having accepted that, comes into conflict with a conspiracy to take over the Earth and Venus, while having to adjust to the fact that he is killed and resurrected in a new body! While trying to avert an interstellar invasion, Gosseyn must also unravel the mystery of himself. In the second novel, *The Pawns of Null-A* (1956 – also known as *The Players of Null-A*) we find out that Gosseyn's origins have a bearing on those of the human race as a whole, while at the same time being plunged into a galactic war sparked off by the attack on Venus in the first book. It is intimated that the Milky Way was colonised by a race fleeing a doomed galaxy, and that Gosseyn is intimately linked with these progenitors. This was confirmed in *Null-A Three* (1984) when a third Gosseyn body wakes up in interstellar space and accidentally teleports two warring factions from the origin galaxy into the still tense, post-war atmosphere of our own. The first two books, originally published as serials between 1945 and 1948-9, certainly represented something new in SF at that time, and US critics (such as a young Damon Knight) found themselves confused, though Europeans (especially the French and English) welcomed them both unreservedly. Indeed, the first book is thought to have single-handedly founded French SF publishing and was the first post-war SF novel to be published there.

World SF Convention (Worldcon) The 'World Science Fiction Convention', 'Worldcon', and 'Hugo Award' are service marks of the **World Science Fiction Society** which is the unincorporated literary society that underpins the world's annual gathering of the SF clans; though in reality each Worldcon owes its successes and failures to the hosting country's convention organising committee. However despite the Worldcon's venue being democratically voted for by the delegates attending the Worldcon two years previously, the Worldcon is mainly held in the US (hence the need for the **Eurocon**) and its Americanphile constitution still divides the world into 4 parts: Western North America, Central America (including Mexico and the Caribbean), Eastern North America, and 'site(s) outside of North America' (from article III, sections 3.6 - 3.8). Worldcons are massive affairs with attending memberships typically over 6,000 (such as Glasgow 1995) to over 10,000 (a number of the US conventions), though typically those actually attending is 5-15% lower than this, as a number register purely to collect the convention literature or to vote for the Hugos (the **Hugo Awards** being voted on by the Worldcon memberships). Typically Worldcons consist of three or four programme streams in halls capable of holding an audience several hundred strong, as well as a film programme, about half a dozen specialist programme streams for one or two hundred each, and a plethora of smaller workshops and informal activities. A large dealers' room (primarily selling books, but also software and videos), and an art (and model) exhibition are also fundamental to Worldcons. Past Worldcons have been held in, and had the following Guests of Honour:-

1939 New York, US; Frank Paul
1940 Chicago, US; **E.E, 'Doc 'Smith**
1941 Denver, US; **Robert Heinlein**
1946 Los Angles, US; **A.E van Vogt**, E. Mayne Hull
1947 Philadelphia, US; **John W. Campbell jr**, L Jerome Stanton
1948 Toronto, Canada Robert Bloch, Bob Tucker
1949 Cincinnati, US; Lloyd Esbach, Ted Carnell
1950 Portland, US; Anthony Boucher, **Theodore Sturgeon**
1951 New Orleans, US; **Fritz Leiber**,
1952 Chicago, US; **Hugo Gernsback**
1953 Philadelphia, US; Willy Ley, **Isaac Asimov**
1954 San Francisco, US; **John W. Campbell jr**, Robert Bloch
1955 Cleveland, US; **Isaac Asimov,** Sam Moskowitz, Anthony Boucher
1956 New York, US; **Arthur C. Clarke**, Robert Bloch
1957 London, Britain; **John W. Campbell jr**

Year	Details
1958	Los Angeles, US; **Richard Matheson**, Anthony Boucher
1959	Detroit, US; **Poul Anderson,** John Berry, **Isaac Asimov** and Robert Bloch
1960	Pittsburgh, US; **James Blish**, **Isaac Asimov**
1961	Seattle, US; **Robert A. Heinlein**, **Harlan Ellison**
1962	Chicago, US; **Theodore Sturgeon**, Wilson Tucker
1963	Washington DC, US; Murray Leinster, **Isaac Asimov**
1964	Oakland, US; Leigh Brackett, Edmund Hamilton, **Forrest J. Ackerman**, Anthony Boucher
1965	London, Britain; **Brian Aldiss**, Tom Boardman
1966	Cleveland, US; L. Sprague de Camp, **Isaac Asimov**
1967	New York, US; Lester del Ray, Bob Tucker, **Harlan Ellison**
1968	Oakland, US; **Philip José Farmer**, W. Daughterty, **Robert Silverberg**
1969	St. Louis, US; Jack Gaughan, **Harlan Ellison**, Eddie Jones
1970	Heildberg, Germany; E.C. Tubb, **Robert Silverberg**, H. Franke, E. Shorter
1971	Boston, US; **Clifford D. Simak,** H. Warner, **Robert Silverberg**
1972	Los Angles, US; **Frederick Pohl**, B. & J. Coulson, Robert Bloch
1973	Toronto, US; Robert Bloch, W. Rotsler, Lester del Ray
1974	Washington DC, US; **Roger Zelazny**, J. Klein, A. Offutt
1975	Melbourne, Australia; **Ursula K. Le Guin,** S. Wood, M. Glickson, D. Tuck, John Bangsund
1976	Kansas City, US; **Robert Heinlein**, G. Barr, Wilson Tucker
1977	Miami Beach, US; Jack Williamson, R. Madle, **Robert Silverberg**
1978	Phoenix, US; **Harlan Ellison,** B. Bowers, F. Busby
1979	Brighton, Britain; **Brian Aldiss**, **Fritz Leiber**, **Bob Shaw**, H. Bell
1980	Boston, US; Damon Knight, Kate Wilheim, B. Pelz, **Robert Silverberg**
1981	Denver, US; **Clifford D. Simak; C.L. Moore,** R. Hevelin, E. Bryant
1982	Chicago, US; A. Bertram Chandler, **Frank Kelly Freas**, L. Hoffman, M. Randall
1983	Baltimore, US; **John Brunner**, D. Kyle, Jack Chalker
1984	Los Angles, US; Gordon Dickson, D. Eney, Jerry Pournelle, Robert Bloch
1985	Melbourne, Australia; **Gene Wolfe**, Ted White
1986	Atlanta, US; **Ray Bradbury**, Terry Carr, **Bob Shaw**

Year	Details
1987	Brighton, Britain; Doris Lessing, **Alfred Bester**, **Arkady & Boris Strugatsky**, **Jim Burns,** Ray Harryhausen, Joyce & Ken Slater, David Langford, **Brian Aldiss**
1988	New Orleans, US; Donald Wollheim, R. Sims, M. Resnick
1989	Boston, US; Andre Norton, Ian & Betty Ballantine, The Stranger Club
1990	The Hague, Netherlands; **Harry Harrison**, Wolfgang Jeschke, **Joe Haldeman**, Andrew Porter, C. Q. Yarbro.
1991	Chicago, US; **Hal Clement**, Martin Greenberg, Richard Powers, J. & J. Stopa, Marta Randall
1992	Orlando, US; Jack Vance, Vincent DiFate, W. Willis, Spider Robinson & Mike Resnick
1993	San Francisco, US; **Larry Niven**, Alica Austin, Tom Digby, J. Finder, Guy Gavriel Kay, Mark Twain
1994	Winnipeg, Canada; Anne McCaffrey, George Bar, R. Runte, B. Longyear
1995	Glasgow, Britain (also a **Eurocon**); Samuel R. Delany, **Gerry Anderson,** Les Edwards, Vin¢ Clarke, Dianne Duane & Peter Morwood
1996	Los Angeles, US; James White, Roger Corman, Elsie Wolheim, T. & S. Shibano, Connie Willis
1997	San Antonio, US; Algis Budrys, **Michael Moorcock**, Don Maitz, R. Tackett, N. Barrett jr.
1998	Baltimore, US; **C. J. Cherryh**, Stanley Schmidt, **Michael Whelan**, J. Michael Straczynski, Charles Sheffield, Milton Rothman.
1999	Melbourne, Australia; George Turner, **Gregory Benford**, J. Michael Straczynski, Bruce Gillespie
2000	Chicago, US; **Ben Bova**, **Bob Eggleton**, Jim Bean, B & A Passovoy, Harry Turtledove
2001	Philadelphia, US; **Greg Bear**, Stephen Youll, Gardner Dozois, G. Scithers, E, Friesner
2002	San José, US; **Vernor Vinge**, David Cherry, 'Ferdinand Feghoot', Tad Williams, Bjo & John Trimble
2003	Toronto, Canada; George R. R. Martin, **Frank Kelly Freas**, M. Glyer, Spider Robinson, 'Robert Bloch'
2004	Boston, US; Terry Pratchett, William Tenn, Jack Speer, Peter Weston.
2005	Glasgow, Britain (also a Eurocon); **Robert Sheckley**, Christopher Priest, Lars-Olov Strandberg, Jane Yolen, Greg Pickersgill

2006 Los Angles, US; **Connie Willis**, James Gurney, Frankie Thomas, Howard deVore.

2007 Yokohama, Japan. Sakyo Komatsu, **David Brin**, Yoshitaka Amano, **Michael Whelan**, Takumi Shibano.

Worldcons are less variable than national conventions. Having said this, the ones held in the US (which is most years) tend to be the largest with currently over 10,000 attending, whereas in the UK they attract between 5,000 and 7,000, while the Australian Worldcons have around 2,000 attending. Consequently, unlike the more intimate **Eurocons**, Worldcons are usually comparatively gigantic affairs and therefore are impersonal: for instance, unless *rendez-vous* arrangements are specifically made, it is possible to meet someone one day, and not see them again for the rest of the convention! On the other hand, nothing else in the SF world compares to the spectacle of a Worldcon.

World SF – The International association of SF professionals – professionals being defined in its broadest form to include: writers, artists, agents, editors, critics *etc*. Founded in Dublin in 1976, its first President was **Harry Harrison**. Not so active today, it has done much good work over the years, producing books, holding meetings in various countries and presenting awards to those who have helped disseminate and further the appreciation of SF.

World SF Society – The WSFS is the unincorporated literary society that sponsors (in the political sense) the annual **World SF Convention (Worldcon)** and which manages the **Hugo Award**. It should not be confused with **World SF**.

Wyndham, John – author, UK (1903-1969). Born in Birmingham as John Wyndham Parkes Lucas Beynon Harris, Wyndham started publishing SF with *Worlds to Barter* (1931) in *Wonder Stories*, and before WWII was best known as either John Beynon Harris or John Benyon (the best examples of this work can be found in the collection *Wanderers of Time* (1973)). However, it is after WWII in his incarnation as John Wyndham that he is best remembered, for such novels as ***The Day of the Triffids*** (1951), filmed in 1963, and also a UK TV series (1981), ***The Chrysalids*** (1955); and *The Midwich Cuckoos* (1957), filmed variously as a virtual re-make – and a true, albeit Americanised, re-make, *Village of the Damned* (1995) . Wyndham brought a middle-class domesticity to cataclysmic situations that make his books almost surreal, contrasting SF invasions with fond and keen observations on Britishness. He is one of the few SF authors to be included on school syllabuses in England and, though he died in 1969, his work is still in print today.

Xenocide – novel (1991) by Orson Scott Card. Though nominated for a Hugo (but did not win) in 1992, *Xenocide* did get into the annual *Locus* readerstop ten poll. Furthermore its two prequels ***Ender's Game*** and ***Speaker for the Dead*** both won Hugos for Best novel. Having learnt to live with the descolada virus, Ender and the colony on Lusitania learn that Earth is sending a war fleet to sterilise the planet. Ender has his work cut out for him if he is to prevent xenocide as he is also protecting the last of the buggers (Earth's former enemy).

X-Files, The – TV series, US (*fb*1993), created by Chris Carter. Loosely inspired by ***Kolchak: The Night Stalker*** (most clearly seen in the first season episodes *Squeeze* and *Tooms*, which are virtual reworkings of *Kolchak: The Night Strangler*), this is the on-going story of FBI special agents Fox 'Spooky' Mulder (David Duchovny) and Dana Scully (Gillian Anderson) and their fight against an international shadow conspiracy in league with (would-be colonist?) aliens. This was originally a 'cult' TV series which, through deft marketing, has gained a much wider audience. Mulder and Scully work the FBI's collection of X-Files. These are unsolved mysteries that imply paranormal involvement, be it alien or supernatural, and the series reflects the ongoing concerns of (mainly US) paranoia regarding Government conspiracies, especially as they relate to UFO phenomena. It could be argued that, on the whole, the better episodes are those which stand alone and are not connected to the conspiracy story, largely because (due to the multiple writers working on the series) this story has become increasingly confused and unresolvable. However, it is the larger story that has provided both the consistent framework for the individual tales, and the supporting cast of continuing characters. These include FBI Assistant Director Skinner (Mitch Pileggi), the conspirators known as the Cigarette-Smoking Man (William B. Davis) and the Well-Manicured Man (John Neville), mercenary agent-at-large Alex Krycek (Nicholas Lea), and Mulder's allies from The Lone Gunmen – Frohike (Tom Braidwood), Langly (Dean Haglund) and Byers (Bruce Harwood). The fifth season contains episodes co-scripted by Stephen King (*Chinga*) and **William Gibson** (*Kill Switch*), and also contains an appearance by Darren McGavin (the actor who played Kolchak) in the episode *Travellers*, which was a nice (if overdue) touch, as an FBI agent who had encountered the X-Files early in his career. The show then made the transition to film with *X-Files: Fight the Future* (1999), which featured Martin (*Space: 1999* – see **Gerry Anderson**) Landau, extending the conspiracy plot. A sixth season of *The X-Files* began production in 1999, following the break for the making of the film. The series has inspired a number of spin-offs, including comics series (both 'straight' and parody), novels, and the inevitable guides and reference material, not to mention spawning innumerable web-sites on the internet.

Years of Rice and Salt, The – novel (2002) by Kim Stanley Robinson. A 700 years worth of alternate history in which the plague wiped out China as well as the West and Islam rules the world. *The Years of Rice and Salt* came top of the *Locus* poll for best novel in 2003.

Young Frankenstein – film, US (1974), *dir.* Mel Brooks. More homage than parody, *Young Frankenstein* actually used some of the original sets and designs from James Whale's classic ***Frankenstein*** (1931). Co-scripted by Brooks and Gene Wilder (in the same year as *Blazing Saddles*), this opens with the ancestral home bequeathed to Dr. Frankenstein (Wilder) along with servant, Igor (Marty Feldman), an assistant (Terri (***Close Encounters***) Garr), and grandpa's secret recipe for making a monster (Peter Boyle). Soon the creature is on the rampage and the villagers are up in arms, while a blind hermit (Gene Hackman) teaches the monster the art of cigar-smoking. Strangely susceptible to a violin piece, the monster returns to be civilised by Wilder, culminating in an excellent performance of *Puttin' On the Ritz*. Taunted, the creature rampages again, this time kidnapping Frankenstein's fiancée (Madeline Kahn) and ravishing her. With the villagers on the warpath, Frankenstein must make one final bid to calm his creation, even if he should lose his life... Also starring Cloris Leachman as the housekeeper, Frau Blucher, this film is a favourite at the annual Festival of Fantastic Films, and won the 1975 Hugo for Best Dramatic Presentation. Other members of the cast include: Kenneth Mars, Richard Haydn, Liam Dunn and Danny Goldman.

Zardoz – film, UK (1974), *dir*. John Boorman. In the 23rd century the world is divided into two. Near-immortals, 'eternals', are aesthetes who live in a valley (the Vortex) protected by a forcefield, whereas in the outlands people live a hand-to-mouth existence or are forced by exterminators into growing crops for the eternals. The exterminators follow their god Zardoz which appears to them as a giant floating head. One exterminator, Zed, wants to know more about his god and so hides inside the Zardoz head and is carried back to the Vortex. There he is a source of amusement, until he threatens to upset the *status quo*... It has to be said that buffs either hate or love this movie. Some say that it is pompous and fatuous and is a revolt-of-the-masses film. Others that it is a comment on the illusion of materialism while successfully conveying a future that is truly alien to our present. Which ever, it nonetheless remains a fantastic film favourite and does contain a number of incidental throw-away concepts. For instance when Zed enquires as to why the eternals are restricted to the Vortex and not, say, explore space, the wistful reply comes: "Ah, the stars... another dead end." Principal cast: Sean (***Outland***, ***Indiana Jones and the Last Crusade***) Connery, John Alderton, Charlotte Rampling, Sara Kestelman, Sally Anne Newton, Niall Buggy, Besco Hogan, Jessica Swift, Bairbre Dowling, Christopher Carson and Reginald Jarman.

Zelazny, Roger – author, US (1937-1995). Born and raised in Ohio, Zelazny obtained an MA from Columbia University and worked in Social Security from 1962-69. It was in 1962 that he published his first SF short, *Passion Play*, in ***Amazing Stories***. Arguably Zelazny produced his finest work in the first few years of his career; ***This Immortal*** (1966) about Conrad Nomikos, an immortal human who works as Art Commissioner in a post-holocaust Earth dominated by aliens from Vega, won the 1966 Hugo for Best Novel (sharing the honour with ***Dune*** by **Frank Herbert**) and, in the same year, Zelazny picked up two Nebula Awards for Best Novella, *The Dream Master* (1965), and Best Novelette, *The Doors of His Face, the Lamps of His Mouth* (1965). He won the Best Novel Hugo again in 1968 for ***Lord of Light*** (1967), in which advanced humans use technology to set themselves up as gods from the Hindu pantheon, but would not be honoured again until 1976, some years after beginning his *Amber* fantasy series. The first of the Merlin *Amber* novels was *Trumps of Doom* (1985), which topped the annual *Locus* readers poll in the 'fantasy novel' category. Zelazny has won four other Hugos; two for Best Novella with *Home is the Hangman* (1975), which also won a Nebula and was incorporated into the novel *My Name is Legion* (1976), and *Twenty-four Views of Mount Fuji, by Hokusai* (1985), which was featured in the collection *Frost and Fire* (1989); and two Hugos for Best Novelette with *Unicorn Variation* (1981), contained in the 1984 *Locus* poll-topping collection *Unicorn Variations* (1983), and *Permafrost* (1986), also contained in *Frost and Fire*. His other novel of note is the Hugo (and Nebula) nominated *Doorways in the Sand* (1976) concerning innocent Fred Cassidy who is accused of stealing an alien artefact (exchanged by humanity for the Mona Lisa and other works of art). He finds himself chased by the authorities, telepaths, alien hoodlums and, if they were not enough, the Galactic police.

APPENDIX - THE COLLECTOR'S CORE CHECKLIST

These check lists should help newcomers to the genre establish their collections. Titles in a bold font relate to entries in the main body of the guide and so should be considered as core requirements for any collection. Titles in normal font might be considered by more dedicated SF enthusiasts. The titles of collections of shorts are included (but not the titles of short stories themselves unless they happen to be the titles of collections).

Because these days most people have video recorders, we have similarly, and separately, listed the film titles below. TV series present a few problems, as frequently their inclusion in the guide was due to particularly good episodes that won awards and most series, no matter how good, have bad episodes too. We therefore leave it to readers to decide what they want in their collection but have provided a list of those series covered in the guide.

BOOKS (NOVELS NOVELLAS, AND COLLECTIONS OF SHORTS)

Key ! = warning see either title or author entry
(entries in brackets) = not recommended

Adams, Douglas – **Hitch-hiker's Guide to the Galaxy, The** (1978)	☐
Aldiss, Brian – *Billion Year Spree* (1973)	☐
Aldiss, Brian – *Frankenstein Unbound* (1973)	☐
Aldiss, Brian – *Helliconia Spring* (1982)	☐
Aldiss, Brian – *Helliconia Summer* (1983)	☐
Aldiss, Brian – *Helliconia Winter* (1985)	☐
Aldiss, Brian – **Hothouse** series (available in collected form as a novel)	☐
Aldiss, Brian – *Non-Stop* (1958, revised 2000)	☐
Aldiss, Brian with Wingrove, David – **Trillion Year Spree** (1986)	☐
Aldiss, Brian in collaboration with Sir Roger Penrose – *White Mars* (1999)	☐
Anderson, Poul – *The Boat of a Million Years* (1989)	☐
Anderson, Poul – *Saturn Game, The* (1989)	☐
Anderson, Poul – *There Will Be Time* (1972)	☐
Anderson, Poul – *Queen of Air and Darkness, The* (1973)	☐
Asimov, Isaac – *Caves of Steel*, *The* (1953)	☐
Asimov, Isaac – *End of Eternity*, *The* (1955)	☐
Asimov, Isaac – **Foundation** series:-	
Forward the Foundation (1992)	☐
Foundation (1951)	☐
Foundation and Earth (1986)	☐

- ***Foundation and Empire*** (1952) ☐
- ***Foundation's Edge*** (1982) ☐
- *Prelude to Foundation* (1988) ☐
- ***Second Foundation*** (1953) ☐
- Asimov, Isaac – ***Gods Themselves, The*** (1972) ☐
- Asimov, Isaac – *Gold* (1991) ☐
- Asimov, Isaac (ed) – *Hugo Winners, The* (1962) ☐
- Asimov, Isaac – *I, Robot* (1950 ☐
- Asimov, Isaac – *Naked Sun, The* (1956) ☐
- Asimov, Isaac – *Nightfall and Other Stories* (1969) ☐
- Asimov, Isaac – *Pebble in the Sky* (1950) ☐
- ! Asimov, Isaac – *Rest of the Robots* (1964) hardback version ☐
- Asimov, Isaac – *Robots and Empire, The* (1985) ☐
- Asimov, Isaac – *Robots of Dawn, The* (1983) ☐
- Ballard, J G – ***Crystal World, The*** (1966) ☐
- Ballard, J G – ***Hello America*** (1981) ☐
- Banks, Iain – *Consider Phlebas* (1987) ☐
- Banks, Iain – *Player of Games, The* (1988) ☐
- Banks, Iain – *Use of Weapons, The* (1990) ☐
- Banks, Iain – *Excession* (1996) ☐
- Banks, Iain – *Feersum Endjinn* (1994) ☐
- Banks, Iain – *Inversions* (1998) ☐
- Baxter, Stephen – ***Timelike Infinity*** (1992) ☐
- Baxter, Stephen – *Time Ships* (1995) ☐
- Baxter, Stephen – *Vacuum Diagrams* (1998) ☐
- Bear, Greg – ***Blood Music*** (1983) ☐
- Bear, Greg – *Anvil of Stars* (1992) ☐
- Bear, Greg – *Dinosaur Summer* (1998) ☐
- Bear, Greg – *The Forge of God* (1987) ☐
- Bear, Greg – *Moving Mars* (1993) ☐
- Bear, Greg (Ed) – *New Legends* (1995) ☐
- Bear, Greg – *Queen of Angels* (1990) ☐
- Bear, Greg – *Slant* (1997) ☐
- Benford, Gregory – *Beyond Infinity* (2004) ☐
- Benford, Gregory – *Eater* (2000) ☐
- Benford, Gregory – *Foundation's Fear* (1997) ☐
- Benford, Gregory – *In the Ocean of Night* (1977) ☐
- Benford, Gregory – *Matter's End* (1994) ☐
- Benford, Gregory – *Sailing Bright Eternity* (1995) ☐
- Benford, Gregory – ***Timescape*** (1980) ☐
- Bester, Alfred – ***Demolished Man, The*** (1953) ☐
- Bester, Alfred – *Golem 100* (1980) ☐

Bester, Alfred – ***Tiger! Tiger!*** (1955)	☐
Blish, James – *After Such Knowledge* trilogy:-	
Doctor Mirabilis (1964)	☐
Black Easter (1968)	☐
The Day After Judgement (1971)	☐
Blish, James – ***A Case of Conscience*** (1959)	☐
Blish, James – 'Cities in Flight Series'	
They Shall Have Stars (1956)	☐
Clash of Cymbals, A (1959)	☐
Earthman, Come Home (1956)	☐
Life For The Stars, A (1962)	☐
Blish, James – ***Star Trek*** series (1967 – 77):-	
Vol 1	☐
Vol 2	☐
Vol 3	☐
Vol 4	☐
Vol 5	☐
Vol 6	☐
Vol 7	☐
Vol 8	☐
Vol 9	☐
Vol 10	☐
Vol 11	☐
Vol 12 (with J A Lawrence)	☐
Blish, James – ***Seedling Stars*** (1957)	☐
Blish, James – *Spock Must Die* (1970)	☐
Boule, Pierre – *Monkey Planet* (*Planète des Singes*)	☐
Bova, Ben – *Colony* (1978)	☐
Bova, Ben – *Mars* (1992)	☐
Bova, Ben – *Millennium* (1976)	☐
Bova, Ben – *Voyagers* (1981)	☐
Bradbury, Ray – ***The Martian Chronicles*** (1946-50)	☐
Bradbury, Ray – ***Fahrenheit 451*** (1953)	☐
Bradbury, Ray – *The Stories of Ray Bradbury* (1981) Vol I	☐
Bradbury, Ray – *The Stories of Ray Bradbury* (1981) Vol II	☐
Brin, David – *Brightness Reef* (1995)	☐
Brin, David – *Heaven's Reach* (1998)	☐
Brin, David – *Infinity's Shore* (1996)	☐
Brin, David – *Kil'n People* (2002	☐
Brin, David – *Otherness* (1994)	☐
Brin, David – ***Postman, The*** (1985)	☐
Brin, David – *River of Time, The* (1987)	☐

Brin, David – ***Startide Rising*** (1983) ☐
Brin, David – *Sundiver* (1980 ☐
Brin, David – ***Uplift War, The*** (1987) ☐
Brunner, John – *Sheep Look Up, The* (1972) ☐
Brunner, John – ***Shockwave Rider, The*** (1974) ☐
Brunner, John – ***Stand on Zanzibar*** (1968) ☐
Brunner, John – *Squares of the City* (1965) ☐
Brunner, John – *Stone That Never Came Down* (1973) ☐
Brunner, John – ***Telepathist*** (1964) ☐
Bujold, Lois McMaster – ***Barrayar*** (1991) ☐
Bujold, Lois McMaster – *Borders of Infinity, The* (1989) ☐
Bujold, Lois McMaster – *A Civil Campaign* (2000) ☐
Bujold, Lois McMaster – *Falling Free* (1988) ☐
Bujold, Lois McMaster – ***Mirror Dance*** (1994) ☐
Bujold, Lois McMaster – ***Paladin of Souls*** (2003) ☐
Bujold, Lois McMaster – ***The Vor Game*** (1990) ☐
Burgess, Anthony – ***Clockwork Orange, A*** (1962) ☐
Cadigan, Pat – *Fools* (1992) ☐
Cadigan, Pat – ***Patterns*** (1989) ☐
Cadigan, Pat – *Synners* (1991) ☐
Campbell, John W. jnr. – *Black Star Passes, The* (1953) ☐
Campbell, John W. jnr. – *Invaders from the Infinite* (1961) ☐
Campbell, John W. jnr. – *Islands of Space* (1957) ☐
Card, Orson Scott – ***Ender's Game*** (1985) ☐
Card, Orson Scott – *Ender's Shadow* (1999 ☐
Card, Orson Scott – *Eye for Eye* (1987) ☐
Card, Orson Scott – ***Last of the Winnebagos, The*** (1988) ☐
Card, Orson Scott – *Songmaster* (1980) ☐
Card, Orson Scott – ***Speaker for the Dead*** (1986) ☐
Card, Orson Scott – *Xenocide* (1991) ☐
Card, Orson Scott – *Wyrms* (1987) ☐
Cherryh C J – ***Cyteen*** (1980) ☐
Cherryh C J – ***Downbelow Station*** (1981) ☐
Cherryh C J – *Rimrunners* (1989) ☐
Cherryh C J – *Serpent's Reach* (1980) ☐
Clarke, Arthur C. – *Against the Fall of Night* (1991 edition published with the Benford novella *Beyond the Fall of Night*) ☐
Clarke, Arthur C. – *Best of Arthur C. Clarke: 1937–1971, The* (1973) ☐
Clarke, Arthur C. – *Childhood's End* (1953) ☐
Clarke, Arthur C. – *City and the Stars* (1956) ☐
Clarke, Arthur C. – ***Fountains of Paradise, The*** (1979) ☐
! (Clarke, Arthur C. (with G. Lee) – *Garden of Rama, The* (1991))

! (Clarke, Arthur C. (with G. Lee) – *Rama II* (1989))
! (Clarke, Arthur C. (with G. Lee) – *Rama Revealed* (1993))
Clarke, Arthur C. – ***Rendezvous with Rama*** (1973) ☐
Clarke, Arthur C. – *Tales From the White Hart* (1957 ☐
Clarke, Arthur C. – *2001: A Space Odyssey* (1968) ☐
Clarke, Arthur C. – *2010: Odyssey 2* (1982) ☐
Clarke, Arthur C. – *2061* (1988) ☐
Clarke, Arthur C. – *3001* (1997) ☐
Clement, Hal – *Close to Critical* (1964) ☐
Clement, Hal – *Iceworld* (1953) ☐
Clement, Hal – ***Mission of Gravity*** (1954) ☐
Clement, Hal – *Needle* (1950) ☐
Clement, Hal – *Ocean on Top* (1973) ☐
Clement, Hal – *Star Light* (1971) ☐
Clement, Hal – *Through the Eye of a Needle* (1978) ☐
Clifton M. & Riley F. – ***They'd Rather Be Right*** (1954) ☐
    retitled and expanded as *The Forever Machine*
Clute, John & Nicholls, Peter –
    Encyclopedia of Science Fiction, The (1979 & 1993) ☐
Crichton, Michael –*Andromeda Strain*, ***The***(1969) ☐
Crichton, Michael – *Congo* (1980) ☐
Crichton, Michael – *Jurassic Park* (1990) ☐
Crichton, Michael – *Lost World, The* (1985) ☐
Crichton, Michael – *Sphere* (1987) ☐
Crichton, Michael – *Terminal Man, The* (1971) ☐
Dick, Philip K. – ***Do Androids Dream of Electric Sheep?*** (1968 ☐
Dick, Philip K. – *Flow My Tears the Policeman Said* (1974) ☐
Dick, Philip K. – *Little Black Box, The* (1987) ☐
    retitled as *We Can Remember It For You Wholesale*
Dick, Philip K. – ***Man in the High Castle, The*** (1962) ☐
Dick, Philip K. – *Man Who Japed, The* (1956) ☐
Dick, Philip K. – *Second Variety* (1987) ☐
    retitled *We Can Remember It For You Wholesale*
Dick, Philip K. – *Time Out of Joint* (1959) ☐
Dick, Philip K. – *Vulcan's Hammer* (1960) ☐
Doyle, Sir Arthur Conan – ***The Lost World*** (1912) ☐
Egan, Greg – *Axiomatic* (1995) ☐
Egan, Greg – ***Diaspora*** (1997) ☐
Egan, Greg – *Oceanic* (1998) ☐
Egan, Greg – *Permutation City* (1994) ☐
Egan, Greg – ***Quarantine*** (1992) ☐
Ellison, Harlan (Ed) – *Again Dangerous Visions* (1972) ☐

Ellison, Harlan – *Alone Against Tomorrow* (1971) US ☐
Ellison, Harlan – *All the Sounds of Fear* (1973) UK ☐
Ellison, Harlan – *Angry Candy* (1988) ☐
Ellison, Harlan – *Beast That Shouted Love at the Heart of the World, The* (1969) ☐
Ellison, Harlan (Ed) – *Dangerous Visions* (1967 ☐
Ellison, Harlan – *Deathbird Stories* (1975) ☐
Ellison, Harlan – *From the Land of Fear* (1967) ☐
Ellison, Harlan – *I Have No Mouth, and I Must Scream* (1967) ☐
Ellison, Harlan – *Paingod and Other Delusions* (1965) ☐
Ellison, Harlan – *Shatterday* (1980) ☐
Ellison, Harlan – *Time of the Eye, The* (1974) UK ☐
Farmer, Philip José – *Dare* (1965) ☐
Farmer, Philip José – *Doc Savage: His Apocalyptic Life* (1973) ☐
Farmer, Philip José – *A Feast Unknown* (1969) ☐
Farmer, Philip José – *Flesh* (1960 ☐
Farmer, Philip José – *The Lovers* (1961) ☐
Farmer, Philip José – *The Other Log of Phileas Fogg* (1973) ☐
Farmer, Philip José – **Riders of the Purple Wage** (1967) ☐
Farmer, Philip José – *Strange Relations* (1960) ☐
Farmer, Philip José – *Tarzan Alive* (1972) ☐
Farmer, Philip José – **To Your Scattered Bodies Go** (1972) ☐
Forward, Robert L. – **Dragon's Egg** (1980) ☐
Gaiman, Neil – *American Gods* (2001) ☐
Gibson, William – *Burning Chrome* (1986) ☐
Gibson, William – *Count Zero* (1986) ☐
Gibson, William – *Mona Lisa Overdrive* (1988) ☐
Gibson, William – **Neuromancer** (1984) ☐
Gibson, William & Sterling, Bruce – *The Difference Engine* (1990) ☐
Greenland, Colin – *Take Back Plenty* (1990) ☐
Greenland, Colin – *Harm's Way* (1993) ☐
Haldeman, Joe – *Forever Free* (1999) ☐
Haldeman, Joe – **Forever Peace** (1997) ☐
Haldeman, Joe – **Forever War** (1974) ☐
Haldeman, Joe – **Hemmingway Hoax, The** (1990) ☐
Haldeman, Joe – *Planet of Judgement* (1977) ☐
Haldeman, Joe – *Worlds* (1981) ☐
Haldeman, Joe – *Worlds Apart* (1983) ☐
Haldeman, Joe – *Worlds Enough and Time* (1992) ☐
Haldeman, Joe – *World Without End* (1979) ☐
Harrison, Harry – *Bill, the Galactic Hero* (1965) ☐
Harrison, Harry – **Make Room! Make Room!** (1966) ☐
Harrison, Harry – **Stainless Steel Rat, The** (1961) ☐

!Harrison, Harry – *Stainless Steel Visions* (1992)! ☐
Harrison, Harry – *Technicolor Time Machine* (1967) ☐
Harrison, H. & Sheckley, R. –
    Bill, The Galactic Hero on the Planet of Bottle Brains (1990) ☐
Heinlein, Robert – *Day After Tomorrow, The* (1951) ☐
    a.k.a *Sixth Column* by Anson MacDonald
Heinlein, Robert – *Door Into Summer, The* (1957) ☐
Heinlein, Robert – **Double Star** (1956) ☐
Heinlein, Robert – *Glory Road* (1963) ☐
Heinlein, Robert – **Job: A Comedy of Justice** (1984) ☐
Heinlein, Robert – *Methuselah's Children* (1941) ☐
Heinlein, Robert – **Moon is a Harsh Mistress, The** (1966) ☐
Heinlein, Robert – *Stranger* (1990) ☐
Heinlein, Robert – **Stranger in a Strange Land** (1961) ☐
Heinlein, Robert – *Time Enough For Love* (1973) ☐
Herbert, Frank – *Chapter House Dune* (1985) ☐
Herbert, Frank – *Children of Dune* (1976) ☐
Herbert, Frank – *Destination: Void* (1966) ☐
Herbert, Frank – *Dosadi Experiment, The* (1977) ☐
Herbert, Frank – **Dune** (1965) ☐
Herbert, Frank – *Dune Messiah* (1969) ☐
Herbert, Frank – *Green Brain, The* (1966) ☐
Herbert, Frank – *God Emperor of Dune* (1981) ☐
Herbert, Frank – *Hellstrom's Hive* (1973) ☐
Herbert, Frank – *Heretics of Dune* (1984 ☐
Herbert, Frank – *Whipping Star* (1970) ☐
Herbert, Frank & Anderson, Kevin – *House Atreides: Prelude to Dune* (1999) ☐
Herbert, Frank & Herbert, Brian – *Man of Two Worlds* (1986) ☐
Huxley, Aldous – **Brave New World** (1932) ☐
Jones, D.F. – *Colossus* (1966) (See **Colossus: The Forbin Project**) ☐
(Jones, D.F. – *Colossus and the Crab* (1977))
(Jones, D.F. – *Fall of Colossus, The* (1974))
Keyes, Daniel – **Flowers for Algernon** ☐
Kress, Nancy – *Beggars and Choosers* (1994) ☐
Kress, Nancy – **Beggars in Spain** (1993) ☐
Kuttner, Henry – *Mimsey Were the Borogroves* (1943) ☐
Kuttner, Henry – *Proud Robot, The* (1983ed) ☐
Kuttner, Henry – *Tomorrow and Tomorrow* (1951) ☐
Kuttner, Henry – *Twonky, The* (1942 ☐
Kyle, David – *Dragon Lensman* (1980) ☐
Kyle, David – *Lensman from Rigel* (1982) ☐
Kyle, David – *Z-Lensman* (1983) ☐

Le Guin, Ursula K. – *Buffalo Gals, Won't You Come Out Tonight?* (1987)	☐
Le Guin, Ursula K. – ***Dispossessed, The*** (1974)	☐
Le Guin, Ursula K. – ***Lathe of Heaven, The*** (1971)	☐
Le Guin, Ursula K. – ***Left Hand of Darkness, The*** (1969)	☐
Le Guin, Ursula K. – *Planet of Exile* (1966)	☐
Le Guin, Ursula K. – *Rocannon's World* (1966)	☐
Le Guin, Ursula K. – ***Telling, The*** (2000)	☐
Le Guin, Ursula K. – *Word for World is Forest, The* (1972)	☐
Leiber, Fritz – ***Big Time, The*** (1958)	☐
Leiber, Fritz – *Change War, The* (1978)	☐
Leiber, Fritz – *Gather, Darkness!* (1943)	☐
Leiber, Fritz – *Ill Met in Lankhmar* (1970)	☐
Leiber, Fritz – *Ship of Shadows* (1969)	☐
Leiber, Fritz – ***Wanderer, The*** (1964)	☐
Lem, Stanislaw – *Cyberiad, The* (1965)	☐
Lem, Stanislaw – *Invincible, The* (1964)	☐
Lem, Stanislaw – ***Solaris*** (1961)	☐
Lem, Stanislaw – *Star Diaries, The* (1971)	☐
Longyear, Barry B. – ***Enemy Mine*** (1979)	☐
Lundwall, Sam – *Science Fiction: An Illustrated History* (1979)	☐
Matheson, Richard – *Bid Time Return* (1975)	☐
Matheson, Richard – *I am Legend* (1954)	☐
Matheson, Richard – *Hell House* (1971)	☐
Matheson, Richard – *Master of the World* (1961)	☐
Matheson, Richard – *Shock!* (different volumes 1961,	☐
1964,	☐
1966	☐
and 1970)	☐
Matheson, Richard – *Shores of Space, The* (1957)	☐
Matheson, Richard – *Shrinking Man, The* (1956)	☐
Matheson, Richard – *Third From the Sun* (1955)	☐
May, Julian – ***Many-Coloured Land, The*** (1981)	☐
McAuley, Paul – ***Fairyland*** (1995)	☐
McCaffrey, Anne – *Dragonflight* (1968)	☐
! McCaffrey, Anne – *Dragon Rider* (1968)	☐
! McCaffrey, Anne – ***Weyr Search*** (1967)	☐
McDevitt, Jack – ***Hercules Text, The*** (1986)	☐
McDonald, Ian – ***Desolation Road*** (1988)	☐
McIntyre, Vonda N. – ***Dreamsnake*** (1978)	☐
Miller, Walter M. jnr – ***Canticle for Leibowitz*** (1959)	☐
Miller, Walter M. jnr – *Conditionally Human* (1962)	☐
Miller, Walter M. jnr – *Saint Leibowitz and the Wild Horse Woman* (1997)	☐

Miller, Walter M. jnr – *View From the Stars, A* (1965) ☐
Moorcock, Michael – *Behold the Man* (1969) ☐
Moorcock, Michael – *Cure for Cancer, A* (1971) ☐
Moorcock, Michael – *Condition of Muzak, The* (1977) ☐
Moorcock, Michael – *English Assassin, The* (1972) ☐
Moorcock, Michael – *Final Programme, The* (1969) ☐
Moorcock, Michael – *Rituals of Infinity* a.k.a. *Wrecks of Time, The* (1965) ☐
Niven, Larry – **Convergent Series** (1979) ☐
Niven, Larry – *Inconstant Moon* (1973) ☐
Niven, Larry – **Integral Trees, The** (1984) ☐
Niven, Larry – **Neutron Star** (1968) ☐
Niven, Larry – **Ringworld** (1970) ☐
Niven, Larry – *Ringworld Engineers, The* (1980) ☐
Niven, Larry – *Ringworld's Children* (2004) ☐
(Niven, Larry – *Ringworld Throne* (1996))
Niven, Larry – *Tales of Known Space* (1975) ☐
Niven, Larry & Pournelle, Jerry – *Lucifer's Hammer* (1977) ☐
Niven, Larry & Pournelle, Jerry – *Moat Around Murcheson's Eye, The* (1993) ☐
Niven, Larry & Pournelle, Jerry – *Mote in God's Eye, The* (1974) ☐
Orwell, George – **Nineteen Eighty-Four** (1949) ☐
Pohl, Frederik – *Annals of the Hechee, The* (1987) ☐
Pohl, Frederik – *Beyond the Blue Event Horizon* (1980) ☐
Pohl, Frederik – *Black Star Rising* (1985) ☐
Pohl, Frederik – *Coming of the Quantum Cats, The* (1986) ☐
Pohl, Frederik – *Day the Martians Came, The* (1988) ☐
Pohl, Frederik – **Gateway** (1977) ☐
Pohl, Frederik – **Gateway Trip, The** (1990) ☐
Pohl, Frederik – *Heechee Rendezvous* (1984) ☐
Pohl, Frederik – *JEM: The Making of a Utopia* (1979) ☐
Pohl, Frederik – *Man Plus* (1976) ☐
Pohl, Frederik – *Merchants' War, The* (1984) ☐
Pohl, Frederik – *Years of the City, The* (1984) ☐
Pohl, Frederik – *Way The Future Was, The* (1978 ☐
Pohl, Frederik & Kornbluth, Cyril M. – *Space Merchants, The* (1953) ☐
Pohl, Frederik & Kornbluth, Cyril M. – *Wolfbane* (1959) ☐
Robinson, Kim Stanley – **Blue Mars** (1996) ☐
Robinson, Kim Stanley – *Gold Coast, The* (1988) ☐
Robinson, Kim Stanley – **Green Mars** (1993) ☐
Robinson, Kim Stanley – *The Martians* (1999) ☐
Robinson, Kim Stanley – *Pacific Edge* (1990) ☐
Robinson, Kim Stanley – *Red Mars* (1992) ☐
Robinson, Kim Stanley – **The Wild Shore** (1984) ☐

Robinson, Kim Stanley – ***The Years of Rice and Salt*** (2003) ☐
! Rowling, J. K., – ***Harry Potter and the Goblet of Fire*** (1999) ☐
Russell, Eric Frank – *The Best of Eric Frank Russell* (1978) ☐
Russell, Eric Frank – *Sinister Barrier* (1943) ☐
Sagan, Carl – ***Contact*** (1985) ☐
Saint, H.F – *Memoirs of an Invisible Man* (1987) ☐
Sawyer, Robert J., – ***Calculating God*** (2000) ☐
Sawyer, Robert J., – ***Hominids*** (2002) ☐
Shaw, Bob – *Eastercon Speeches, The* (1977) ☐
Shaw, Bob – *Load of Old BoSH, A* (1995) ☐
Shaw, Bob – ***Orbitsville*** (1975) ☐
Shaw, Bob – *Other Days, Other Eyes* (1972) ☐
Shaw, Bob – *Ragged Astronauts, The* (1986) ☐
Shaw, Bob – *Who Goes Here?* (1977) ☐
Sheckley, Robert – *Babylon 5: A Call to Arms* (1998) ☐
Sheckley, Robert – *Immortality Inc* a.k.a. *Immortality Delivered* (1958) ☐
Sheckley, Robert – *Mindswap* (1966) ☐
Sheckley, Robert – *Status Civilization, The* (1960) ☐
Sheckley, Robert – see Harrison, H. & Sheckley, R. –
    Bill, The Galactic Hero on the Planet of Bottle Brains (1990)
Sheffield, Charles – *Web Between the Worlds*, *The* ☐
Shelley, Mary – ***Frankenstein*** (1818) ☐
Silverberg, Robert – *Anvil of Time, The* (1969) ☐
Silverberg, Robert – *Collected Stories of Robert Silverberg Vol 1* (1991) ☐
Silverberg, Robert – *Enter Soldier. Later Enter Another* (1989) ☐
Silverberg, Robert – *Gilgamesh the King* (1984) ☐
Silverberg, Robert – *Gilgamesh in the Outback* (1986) ☐
(Silverberg, Robert – *Lord Valentine's Castle* (1980))
(Silverberg, Robert – *Nightfall* (1990))
Silverberg, Robert – *Nightwings* (1968) ☐
Silverberg, Robert – *Stochastic Man, The* (1975) ☐
Silverberg, Robert – *Thorns* (1967) ☐
Silverberg, Robert – *Tower of Glass* (1970) ☐
Silverberg, Robert – *Up the Line* (1969) ☐
Silverberg, Robert – *World Inside, The* (1971) ☐
Simak, Clifford D – *All Flesh is Grass* (1965) ☐
Simak, Clifford D – ***Big Front Yard, The*** (1958) ☐
Simak, Clifford D – *City* (1952) ☐
Simak, Clifford D – *Goblin Reservation, The* (1968) ☐
Simak, Clifford D – *Project Pope* (1981) ☐
Simak, Clifford D – *Ring Around the Sun* (1952) ☐
Simak, Clifford D – *Time is the Simplest Thing* (1961) ☐

Simak, Clifford D – **Way Station** (1964) ☐
Simak, Clifford D – *Werewolf Principle, The* (1968) ☐
Simak, Clifford D – *The Worlds of Clifford Simak* (1960) ☐
Simmons, Dan – *Carrion Comfort* (1989) ☐
Simmons, Dan – *Children of the Night* (1992) ☐
Simmons, Dan – *Endymion* (1996) ☐
Simmons, Dan – **Fall of Hyperion, The** (1990) ☐
! Simmons, Dan – *Fires of Eden* (1994) ☐
Simmons, Dan – *Hollow Man, The* (1992) ☐
Simmons, Dan – **Hyperion** (1989) ☐
Simmons, Dan – **Ilium** (2003) ☐
Simmons, Dan – *Lovedeath* (1993) ☐
Simmons, Dan – *Phases of Gravity* (1989) ☐
Simmons, Dan – *Prayers to Broken Stones* (1991) ☐
Simmons, Dan – **Rise of Endymion, The** (1997) ☐
Simmons, Dan – *Summer of Night* (1991) ☐
! Simmons, Dan – *Song of Kali* (1985) ☐
Smith, E.E. 'Doc' – *Children of the Lens* (1954) ☐
Smith, E.E. 'Doc' – *First Lensmen* (1950) ☐
Smith, E.E. 'Doc' – *Galactic Patrol* (1950) ☐
Smith, E.E. 'Doc' – *Galaxy Primes* (1965) ☐
Smith, E.E. 'Doc' – *Grey Lensman* (1951) ☐
Smith, E.E. 'Doc' – *Masters of the Vortex* (1960) ☐
Smith, E.E. 'Doc' – *Second-Stage Lensmen* (1953) ☐
Smith, E.E. 'Doc' – *Skylark of Space, The* (1946) ☐
Smith, E.E. 'Doc' – *Triplanetary* (1948) ☐
Spinrad, Norman – **Bug Jack Baron** (1969) ☐
Spinrad, Norman – *Iron Dream, The* (1972) ☐
Spinrad, Norman – *Little Heroes* (1987) ☐
Spinrad, Norman – *Pictures at 11* (1994) ☐
Spinrad, Norman – *Russian Spring* (1991) ☐
Spinrad, Norman – *Void Captain's Tale, The* (1983) ☐
Steele, Allen – **Orbital Decay** (1989) ☐
Stephenson, Neal – **Cryptonomicon** (1999) ☐
Stephenson, Neal – **Diamond Age, The** (1995) ☐
Sterling, Bruce – see Gibson & Sterling
        – *The Difference Engine* (1990)
Sterling, Bruce – *Crystal Express* (1989) ☐
Sterling, Bruce – *Globalhead* (1992) ☐
Sterling, Bruce – *Heavy Weather* (1994) ☐
Sterling, Bruce – *Holy Fire* (1996) ☐
Sterling, Bruce (ed) – *Mirror Shades* (1986) ☐

Sterling, Bruce – ***Schismatrix*** (1985) ☐
Stevenson, Robert Louis – ***Strange Case of Dr Jekyll and Mr Hyde, The*** (1886) ☐
Stirling S. M. – *T2: Infiltrator* (2001) ☐
Strugatski & Strugatski – *Monday Begins on Saturday* (1965) ☐
Strugatski & Strugatski – *Roadside Picnic* (1977) ☐
Strugatski & Strugatski – *Tale of Troika, The* (1972) ☐
Sturgeon, Theodore – *Baby is Three* (1952) ☐
Sturgeon, Theodore – *Caviar* (1955) ☐
Sturgeon, Theodore – *Dreaming Jewels, The* (1950) ☐
Sturgeon, Theodore – ***More Than Human*** (1953) ☐
Sturgeon, Theodore – *Venus Plus X* (1960) ☐
Sturgeon, Theodore – *The Worlds of Theodore Sturgeon* (1972) ☐
Vance, Jack – ***Last Castle, The*** (1966) ☐
van Vogt, A.E. – *Computerworld* ☐
van Vogt, A.E. – *Pawns of Null-A* a.k.a. ☐
    – *Players of Null-A* (1956)
! (van Vogt, A.E. – *Silkie, The* (1969))
van Vogt, A.E. – *Slan* (1946) ☐
van Vogt, A.E. – *Tyranopolis* (1973) ☐
van Vogt, A.E. – *Voyage of the Space Beagle, The* (1950) ☐
van Vogt, A.E. – *Weapon Makers, The* a.k.a. ☐
    One Against Eternity (1947)
van Vogt, A.E. – ***Weapon Shops of Isher, The*** (1951) ☐
van Vogt, A.E. – ***World of Null-A***, **The** (1948) ☐
Varley, John – ***Titan*** (1979) ☐
Verne, Jules – *Around the Moon* (1869) ☐
Verne, Jules – *From the Earth to the Moon* (1865) ☐
Verne, Jules – ***Journey to the Centre of the Earth*** (1864) ☐
Verne, Jules – *Master of the World, The* (1904) ☐
Verne, Jules – *Robur the Conqueror* (1886) ☐
Vinge, Joan D. – *Eyes of Amber* (1977) ☐
Vinge, Joan D. – ***Snow Queen, The*** (1980) ☐
Vinge, Joan D. – *Summer Queen, The* (1992) ☐
Vinge, Joan D. – *World's End* (1984) ☐
! Vinge, Vernor – *Across Realtime* (1993) ☐
Vinge, Vernor – ***Deepness in the Sky, A*** (1999) ☐
Vinge, Vernor – ***Fire Upon the Deep, A*** (1992) ☐
Vinge, Vernor – *Grimm's World* (1969) ☐
! Vinge, Vernor – *Marooned in Realtime* (1986) ☐
! Vinge, Vernor – *Peace War* (1984) ☐
! Vinge, Vernor – *Threats and Other Promises* (1988) ☐
! Vinge, Vernor – *True Names* (1981) ☐

Vinge, Vernor – *True Names and Other Dangers* (1987) ☐
Vonnegut, Kurt – *Cat's Cradle* (1963) ☐
Vonnegut, Kurt – *Sirens of Titan, The* (1962) ☐
Vonnegut, Kurt – **Slaughter House 5** (1969) ☐
  a.k.a. *The Children's Crusade: A Duty-Dance with Death*
Vonnegut, Kurt – *Timequake* (1997) ☐
Watson, Ian – *Jonah Kit, The* (1975) ☐
Watson, Ian – *The Very Slow Time Machine* (1979) ☐
Wells, H.G. – **Invisible Man, The** (1897) ☐
Wells, H.G. – *The Shape of Things to Come* (1933) ☐
Wells, H.G. – **Time Machine, The** (1895) ☐
Wells, H.G. – **War of the Worlds, The** (1898) ☐
Wells, H.G. – *When the Sleeper Wakes* a.k.a ☐
  The Sleeper Wakes (1899)
Willis, Connie – **Doomsday Book** (1992) ☐
Willis, Connie – **Passage** (2001) ☐
Willis, Connie – **To Say Nothing of the Dog** (1998) ☐
Wilhelm, Kate – **Where Late the Sweet Birds Sang** (1976) ☐
Wood, Lee – *Faraday's Orphans* (1996) ☐
Wolfe, Gene – **Book of the New Sun, The** (1980-83) or:-
  The Citadel of the Autarch (1983) ☐
  The Claw of the Conciliator (1981) ☐
  The Shadow of the Torturer (1980) ☐
  The Sword of the Lictor (1982) ☐
Wolfe, Gene – *Island of Dr Death and Other Stories The* (1980) ☐
Wyndham, John – **Chrysalids, The** (1955) ☐
Wyndham, John – **Day of the Triffids, The** (1951) ☐
Wyndham, John – *Midwich Cuckoos* (1957) ☐
Zelazny, Roger – **And Call Me Conrad** (a.k.a. **This Immortal** (1966)) ☐
Zelazny, Roger – *Doorways in the Sand* (1976) ☐
Zelazny, Roger – *Dream Master, The* (1965) ☐
Zelazny, Roger – *Frost and Fire* (1989) ☐
Zelazny, Roger – **Lord of Light** (1967) ☐
Zelazny, Roger – **This Immortal** (1966) ☐
Zelazny, Roger – *My Name is Legion* (1976) ☐
Zelazny, Roger – *Permafrost* (1986) ☐
Zelazny, Roger – *Trumps of Doom* (1985) ☐
Zelazny, Roger – *Unicorn Variations* (1983) ☐

FILMS

Abominable Dr Phibes, The ☐
Abbott and Costello Meet Frankenstein (see *Frankenstein* – films) ☐
A.I. (see **Aldiss, Brian**) ☐
Alien ☐
Aliens ☐
Alien^3 ☐
Alien Resurrection ☐
Android ☐
Andromeda Strain, The (see **Crichton, Michael**) ☐
Attack of the Clones: Star Wars ☐
Back to the Future ☐
Back to the Future II ☐
Back to the Future III ☐
Barbarella ☐
Batman (1989) ☐
Batman of the Future: Return of the Joker (2000) ☐
Beast from 20,000 Fathoms, The ☐
(Ben Hur – see *Lord of the Rings,The*)
Bill and Ted's Bogus Journey (see **Matheson, Richard**) ☐
Bill and Ted's Excellent Adventure (see **Matheson, Richard**) ☐
(Black Scorpion, The)
Blade Runner ☐
(Body Snatchers (1993)) (see *Invasion of the Body Snatchers*)
Boy and His Dog, A ☐
Boys From Brazil, The ☐
Brave New World (1980) ☐
(*Brave New World* (1998)) ☐
Brazil ☐
Bride of Frankenstein, The ☐
Carrie ☐
Charly ☐
Children of the Damned (see **Wyndham, John**) ☐
Clockwork Orange, A ☐
Close Encounters of the Third Kind ☐
Colossus: The Forbin Project ☐
Contact ☐
Congo (see **Crichton**) ☐
Creature from the Black Lagoon ☐
! *Crouching Tiger, Hidden Dragon* ☐
Curse of Frankenstein, The ☐

Creeping Unknown, The	☐
(a.k.a. *The Quatermas Experiment*)	
Darkman (see **Edward Scissorhands**)	☐
Dark Star	☐
(*Day of the Triffids (1963)*)	
Day the Earth Stood Still	☐
(*Deadly Mantis, The*)	
Destination Moon	☐
Dr Jekyll and Mr Hyde (1931)	☐
Dr Jekyll and Sister Hyde	☐
Dr Phibes Rises Again (see **Abominable Dr Phibes, The**)	
Dr Strangelove	☐
Earth vs *the Flying Saucers* (see **Them**!)	☐
Escape from the Planet of the Apes	☐
Evil of Frankenstein, The	☐
!(***Edward Sissorhands***)	☐
Empire Strikes Back, The: Star Wars	☐
Fantastic Voyage	☐
Fahrenheit 451	☐
Final Programme, The (see **Moorcock, Michael**)	☐
Forbidden Planet	☐
Forbin Project, The (See ***Colossus: The Forbin Project***)	☐
First Contact (See *Star Trek: First Contact* below)	
First Men in the Moon, The (see **Wells, Herbert George**)	☐
Five Million Years to Earth (see ***Quatermass and the Pit*** below)	
Flash Gordon (1980)	☐
Flesh Gordon	☐
Fly, The (1958)	☐
Fly, The (1986)	☐
Fly II, The (1989)	☐
Frankenstein (1930)	☐
Frankenstein Created Woman	☐
Frankenstein Meets the Wolf Man	☐
Frankenstein and the Monster From Hell	☐
Frankenstein Must Be Destroyed	☐
Frankenstein Unbound	☐
Freejack	☐
! (*Futureworld*) (see **Westworld**)	
Galaxy Quest	☐
Ghost of Frankenstein	☐
Ghostbusters	☐
Godzilla: King of the Monsters (a.k.a. *Gojira*)	☐

Godzilla (1998)	☐
Gojira (a.k.a. ***Godzilla: King of the Monsters***)	☐
Golem: And How He Came Into The World	☐
Gothic (see ***Frankenstein***)	☐
(*Hardware* (see ***2000AD***))	
Harrison Bergeron (see **Vonnegut, Kurt**)	☐
Hollow Man, The (see ***Invisible Man, The***)	☐
Horror of Frankenstein	☐
House of Dracula	☐
House of Frankenstein	☐
I Married a Monster From Outer Space	☐
I Married a Monster (1998)	☐
Impostor (see **Dick, Philip K.,**)	☐
Incredible Shrinking Man, The	☐
Indiana Jones and the Last Crusade	☐
(*Indiana Jones and the Temple of Doom*)	
Invasion of the Body Snatchers (1956)	☐
Invasion of the Body Snatchers (1978)	☐
(*Invisible Agent*)	
Invisible Man, The (1933)	☐
(*Invisible Man Returns, The*)	
Island of Lost Souls (1932) (see **Wells, Herbert George**)	☐
Island of Dr Moreau, The (1977) (see **Wells, Herbert George**)	☐
Island of Dr Moreau, The (1996)	☐
It Came From Beneath the Sea (see ***Them!***)	☐
It Came From Outer Space	☐
Johnny Mnemonic (see **Gibson, William**)	☐
Journey to the Centre of the Earth (1959)	☐
(*Journey to the Centre of the Earth* (1993))	
Judge Dredd	☐
Jurassic Park	☐
Jurassic Park III	☐
King Kong (1933)	☐
King Kong Escapes	☐
King Kong vs. Godzilla	☐
Kolchak: The Night Stalker	☐
Kolchak: The Night Strangler	☐
(*Last Man on Earth, The*)	
Legend of Hell House, The (see **Richard Matheson***)*	☐
Little Shop of Horrors, The (1960)	☐
Little Shop of Horrors, The(1986)	☐
! ***Lord of the Rings, The: The Fellowship of the Ring*** (2001)	☐

! ***Lord of the Rings, The: The Two Towers*** (2002)	☐
! ***Lord of the Rings, The: The Return of the King*** (2003)	☐
Lost World, The (1925)	☐
(*Lost World, The* (1960))	
Lost World, The (1992)	☐
Lost World, The (1997)	☐
Lost World, The (2001)	☐
Man in a White Suit, The	☐
Man Who Could Work Miracles, The	☐
Master of the World (see **Verne, Jules**)	☐
Matrix, The	☐
Max Headroom	☐
Memoirs of An Invisible Man (see ***Invisible Man, The***)	☐
Metropolis	☐
Mighty Joe Young (see ***King Kong***)	☐
Minority Report (see **Dick, Philip K.,**)	☐
(*Mysterious Island, The* (1928))	
Mysterious Island, The (1961) (see **Verne, Jules**)	☐
(*Nightfall*) (see **Asimov**)	
Night Stalker, The (see *Kolchak…* above)	
Night Strangler, The (see *Kolchak…* above)	
(*1984* (1952))	☐
(*1984* (1956))	☐
1984 (1984)	☐
Omega Man, The (see **Richard Matheson** entry)	☐
Outland	☐
Paycheck (see **Dick, Philip K.**)	☐
Phantom Menace, The: Star Wars	☐
Phase IV	☐
Planet of the Apes, The	☐
(*Postman, The*) (see **Brin, David**)	
Predator	☐
Princess Bride, The	☐
*Quatermass Experiment, The (*a.k.a. *The Creeping Unknown* above*)*	
Quatermass and the Pit (a.k.a. ***Five Million Years to Earth***)	☐
(*Quatermass The Conclusion*)	
Quiet Earth, The	☐
Raiders of the Lost Ark	☐
Revenge of Frankenstein, The	☐
Return to the Lost World (see ***Lost World, The***)	☐
Return of the Jedi: Star Wars	☐
Robo Cop	☐

Robo Cop II	☐
(*Robo Cop III*)	
Rocky Horror Picture Show, The	☐
Rollerball (1975)	☐
(*Rollerball* (2002))	
Runaway (see **Crichton, Michael**)	☐
Scanners	☐
(*Scanner Cop*)	
Screamers (see **Dick, Philip K.,**)	☐
Silent Running	☐
Slaughterhouse 5	☐
Sleeper, The	☐
Solaris (1972)	☐
! *Solaris* (2003)	
Somewhere in Time	☐
Son of Frankenstein	☐
Soylent Green	☐
Space Truckers (see ***Barbarella***)	☐
Sphere (see **Crichton, Michael**)	☐
Stalker	☐
Starship Troopers	☐
Star Trek: First Contact	☐
Star Trek: The Motion Picture	☐
Star Trek VI – The Undiscovered Country	☐
Star Trek IV: The Voyage Home	☐
Star Trek II: The Wrath of Khan	☐
Star Wars	☐
(*Supergirl*)	
Superman (1978)	☐
Superman II	☐
Superman III	☐
Superman IV – The Quest for Peace	☐
T2 – Judgement Day	☐
Tetsuo (see ***Edward Scissorhands***)	☐
Terminal Man, The (see **Crichton, Michael**)	☐
Terminator, The	☐
Them!	☐
Thing, The (1982)	☐
Thing From Another World, The (1951)	☐
Things to Come	☐
This Island Earth	☐
Time After Time	☐

Time Bandits	☐
Time Machine, The (1960)	☐
Time Machine, The (2002)	☐
Timescape	☐
(*Titanic* – see ***Lord of the Rings, The***)	
Total Recall	☐
Truman Show, The	☐
! ***20 Million Miles to Earth***	☐
20,000 Leagues Under the Sea (1954)	☐
! (*20,000 Leagues Under the Sea* (1996))	
(*Twonky, The* – see **Kuttner H.**)	
Twilight Zone: The Movie (1983)	☐
(*Twilight Zone: Rod Serling's Lost Classics* (1993))	
2001: A Space Odyssey	☐
2010	☐
Village of the Damned (1960)	☐
Village of the Damned (1995)	☐
Voyage au Centre de la Terre (see **Verne, Jules**)	☐
Voyage dans la Lune, Le (see **Verne, Jules**)	☐
War of the Worlds	☐
Wolf Man, The (1940) (see ***Frankenstein Meets The Wolf Man***)	☐
Westworld	☐
Who Framed Roger Rabbit	☐
Young Frankenstein	☐
Zardoz	☐

TV SERIES

Animatrix (see ***Matrix, The***)
Arthur C. Clarke's Mysterious World
Babylon 5
Batman (1960s)
Batman (1990s)
Batman of the Future (2000)
! (*Beyond Westworld* – see ***Westworld***)
Blake's 7
(*Buck Rogers in the 25th Century*)
Captain Scarlet (see **Anderson, Gerry**)
Crusade (see ***Babylon 5***)
Dan Dare
Day of the Triffids (see Wyndham, John)
Doomwatch

Dr Who
Enterprise (see ***Star Trek***)
Fireball XL5 (see **Anderson, Gerry**)
(*Gemini Man*)
Joe 90 (see **Anderson, Gerry**)
Kolchak: The Night Stalker
[(*Lois and Clark* – see *The New Adventures of Superman*)]
! [(*Lost in Space* – see ***Babylon 5*** main entry)]
(*Lost World, The*)
Martian Chronicles, The (1980)
Max Headroom
(*New Adventures of Superman, The*)
[*Night Stalker, The* – see *Kolchak: The Night Stalker* above]
Outer Limits, The
Out of the Unknown
(*Planet of the Apes, The*)
Prisoner, The
Quatermass and the Pit
Quantum Leap
Ray Bradbury Theatre
Red Dwarf (UK)
(*Red Dwarf* (US))
(*Rendezvous with Rama*)
(*Robo Cop*)
Secret Service (see **Anderson, Gerry**)
Smallville (see **Superman**)
(*Space 1999*)
Stingray (see **Anderson, Gerry**)
Star Trek
(*Star Trek: Deep Space Nine*)
Star Trek: The Next Generation
Star Trek Voyager
Supercar (see **Anderson, Gerry**)
Superman (1950s)
Thunderbirds
(*Tripods*)
Twilight Zone, The (1960s)
Twilight Zone, The (1990s)
UFO
Ultraviolet
(*War of the Worlds*)
X Files, The

Jonathan Cowie has been active within the SF community since the late 1970s. In the 1970s and 1980s he was involved in organising a dozen or so SF literary and cinematic conventions, including the 1984 European SF convention and the 1987 UK national SF Easter convention These days he still makes an annual pilgrimage to the European SF Convention (Eurocon) and was one of its special guests in 1994 (Romania), 1997 (Germany) and 2001 (Romania). Additionally, he undertakes public understanding of science projects and recognises that SF can play a part as a vehicle to help promote science. With regards to the latter, almost every year since 1979, he has given talks on an exotic aspect of science fact at either at the UK national, European, or (European venued) World SF Conventions.

Jonathan is a postgraduate environmental biologist. When not enjoying SF he works co-ordinating the science policy views of specialist learned biological societies principally to the UK Government, its Departments and Agencies. In between all of this he is a science writer – in the main for scientific journals and learned society news magazines but also on science for non-academic publications – and has written the university primer textbook *Climate and Human Change: Disaster or Opportunity?*

Tony Chester has also attended numerous SF conventions, and has helped out with running a good many of them on the day. In addition, he has been on the central organising committee of one or two: most notably the *Rocky Horror* convention *Denton*. Tony's SF roots go back to the 1970s when he worked on various genre publications. He has an interest in SF graphic novels and books and has been active in that part of the UK SF community. He has written SF and his SF-horror novel *Best Friend* has sold on continental Europe (but strangely – publishers note – not the UK). He divides his interest in SF with that of music.

Both Jonathan and Tony are associated with the Science Fact and Fiction *Concatenation* and organising its various projects since 1987 – see *www.concatenation.org*. These have accrued two MacIntyre Awards (presented at the UK annual national convention) and three Eurocon Awards (presented at the annual European SF Convention).

Did your breakfast cereal end up containing an alien parasite?

Was your journey to work via the Death Star trench?

How many customers did you have to use your neuralizer on?

Did your lunch date have the table manners of the bugblatter beast of Traal?

Did you fix the photocopier by reversing the neutron flow through the dilithium crystals?

Was your journey home delayed 'cos your tube was derailed by Doc Ock?

If so round off your week with a visit to the...

LEAGUE
OF THE
NON-ALIGNED

The friendly London based TV and Film Science Fiction group

We meet every second and fourth Saturday of the month from 6pm at

THE HORSESHOE INN

Melior Street, London SE1

(5 mins from London Bridge Station)

WWW.LOTNA.ORG.UK

IF YOU NOTICE THIS NOTICE YOU'LL NOTICE THIS NOTICE WAS REALLY WORTH NOTICING!

Porcupine Books

37 Coventry Road, Ilford, Essex IG1 4QR, UK
Tel: +44 (0)20 8554 3799   websales@porcupine.demon.co.uk

Second-Hand Science Fiction/Fantasy/Horror Books

Books for the Reader and for the Collector

www.porcupine.demon.co.uk

The Science Fact and Fiction
CONCATENATION

www.concatenation.org   ●   Established 1987   ●   info@concatenation.org

A quarterly review of science and science fiction including:

- News (both science and SF with national SF event news including some across Europe and beyond) presented as summaries with many hyperlinks for you to follow up detail.
- A forthcoming season's British SF and popular science book release list.
- A diary of national conventions and major film releases.
- An annual SF film top ten.
- SF book reviews.
- Science and non-fiction SF book reviews.
- Author interviews.
- Major convention reviews.
- Articles by scientists, SF authors and others.
- And much, much more including whimsy with Gaia.

Plus:

A series of SF projects and contributions to other ventures from convention press liaison and science & SF international cultural exchange, to international SF events and publications.

All brought together by a loose team of a score and various regular associates.

Check out

www.concatenation.org

Google 'science fiction and science' and *Concatenation* is a top three site out of over 660,000.
Concatenation and the *Concatenation* team have between them won three Eurocon Awards.